ALIEN SECRETS

Hunter pivoted, laser pistol in both hands, as he tracked and killed a running Saurian.

But then something yawned open to Hunter's right. He wasn't sure at first what it was. It *looked* like a pucker in space, a place where light was being sharply bent, distorting the wall and struggling shapes beyond. It flickered, swelled, then stabilized into a hole hanging in the air, a foot above the deck and stretching five feet across. A sharp wind kicked up as the atmosphere inside the dome began streaming into the opening.

"What the hell?"

Several Saurians and their Gray allies were cut down in the mad dash for the portal, but at least a dozen leaped through and vanished. Master Sergeant Coulter looked like he was about to follow them through. "Belay that, Coulter!"

And in the next instant, the hole in space winked out.

ALIEN SECRETS

SOLAR WARDEN, BOOK ONE

IAN DOUGLAS

HARPER
Voyager

Harper*Voyager*
An imprint of HarperCollins*Publishers* Ltd
1 London Bridge Street
London SE1 9GF

www.harpercollins.co.uk

First published by HarperCollins*Publishers* Ltd 2020
This paperback original edition 2020

1

A catalogue record for this book is available from the British Library

ISBN: 978-0-00-828888-4

Printed and bound in the UK by CPI Group (UK) Ltd, Croydon CR0 4YY

MIX
Paper from
responsible sources

FSC
www.fsc.org
FSC™ C007454

This book is produced from independently certified FSC™ paper to ensure
responsible forest management.

For more information visit: www.harpercollins.co.uk/green

For Brea,
who turns chaotic ramblings
into polished prose.

PROLOGUE

Germany may have recovered a flying saucer as early as 1939.

GENERAL JIMMY DOOLITTLE
REPORTING ON SWEDISH "GHOST ROCKETS," 1946

9 May 1945

HE HURRIED DOWN the tunnel, boots clicking on stone, a small mob of aides and adjutants close on his heels. He glanced at his watch. Damn . . . there wasn't much time.

SS Obergruppenführer Hans Kammler had reason to hurry. The Eidechse was waiting for him . . . but more to the point, the damned Soviets were in Silesia and closing in fast. Their patrols had already been reported outside of Ludwidsdorf, and while Kammler doubted those reports were accurate, Czech partisans were definitely in the area.

The war had officially ended yesterday; it had been nine days since Der Führer's death . . . but Kammler was under no illusions as to his fate if he were captured. The partisans were murderous bastards with a serious grudge against the SS. Farther east, the Soviets were rolling into Lower Silesia like swarming locusts.

There were the Americans, of course. Patton and his Third Army were reported to be heading directly toward Lower Silesia. If he could reach them, surrendering was *at least an option. Dornberger and von Braun, he knew, had intended to go that route and avoid the tender mercies of the Communists. But though he did have extensive knowledge of Germany's top secret wonder weapons, Kammler was little more than an engineer and an administrator . . . a very good administrator, but not someone who could offer his services to the enemy and hope to receive a hero's welcome. Kammler's résumé included such pearls as designing gas chambers, crematoriums, and the camp at Auschwitz, as well as using slave labor here to carve out der Riese, the enormous underground complex of tunnels and chambers housing the Reich's most sensitive work. He would, he knew, face war crimes trials . . . and probable execution.*

No . . . there would be no escape in that direction either.

An elevator took him and his entourage up three levels to a small shed with a wooden door opening into the night outside. Ahead, through the trees, a shimmering blue haze could just be seen, against which was silhouetted the towering bulk of the coolant tower.

"Stark, Sporrenberg, with me," he said. "The rest of you stay here."

Stark was carrying two black leather bags, like doctor's satchels, heavy with the secrets they contained. "Thank you, all of you," he told them. "Perhaps we'll meet in happier days."

"Herr General," his driver said. "Those papers . . . they might buy us—buy you—safety with the Americans!"

"No, Prueck. I have too much blood behind me. And I will not be taken alive. I will not face some kangaroo court of so-called justice!"

He turned and strode toward the woods, Stark and Sporrenberg trailing just behind him.

"Herr General," his adjutant said, urgency turning his voice ragged. "They—they're right, sir! There are

rumors, stories, that the Americans are looking for the Reich's scientists. To snatch them before the Russians can reach them."

"But I am not a scientist, Stark," Kammler replied quietly. *"Not like von Braun or those other cowards. No . . . this is the only way."* He stopped and turned. *"You two shouldn't come any closer. It's dangerous, Die Glocke. I'll take those."*

"I had no idea that Projekt Kronos would have such . . . practical applications, General," Gruppenführer Jakob Sporrenberg said.

Stark hefted the two black cases he was holding. *"I can manage, Herr General. And screw the danger."*

"No arguments! Give me the papers, Untersturmführer!"

"Jawohl, Herr General!"

Stark vanished back in the direction of the complex entrance, and Kammler and Sporrenberg proceeded through the eerily lit woods. On their left, the cooling tower blocked out much of the sky. Raised on an immense concrete support structure—a ring positioned on ten enormous pylons—the wooden tank contained thousands of liters of water used to cool the ranks of electrical generators buried in an underground chamber deep below. Nearby, power cables snaked up through heavy pipes and ran along the forest floor. The two generals followed the cables along a well-worn path. The bags were heavy—perhaps forty kilos' worth in all—but, fortunately, there was not much farther to go.

Ahead, Die Glocke hovered half a meter off the ground, a metallic acorn shape four meters high and three wide, bathed in a blue-violet nimbus of its own generation. Six heavy power cables, each as thick as a man's thigh, were connected to the device by means of ports around the swollen base. Several technicians stood off to the side, awaiting their final order. A hatch stood open in the thing's side, spilling red light into the blue-lit night.

The two men hauled the leather bags up and began passing them through the hatch. For Kammler, it felt like swarms of ants were crawling on his skin, the effect of the enormous electrical charge bleeding into the air.

"You know what to do, Jakob," he said. "The last of the slave workers . . . they are to be eliminated."

"Ja. It will be done. Tonight."

"And Damlier, Prueck, Stark, and the rest. They know far too much."

"It's already been arranged, Herr General."

"Good. I knew I could count on you, Jakob." Kammler cracked a rare smile. "And now, our guest is waiting for me!"

He turned again and clambered up and through the hatch.

Inside, strapped into a narrow wire framework, the Eidechse turned its bulbous head, looking at Kammler through those lustrous golden eyes. Kammler suppressed a shudder. The thing, man-shaped but utterly alien, was the ultimate in Untermenschen.

I might say the same of you, General.

Kammler heard the words in his head, but the creature's lipless mouth did not move. How were you supposed to keep secrets from a damned thing that could read thoughts. . . .

Strap in, General. We must leave this place.

"Ja . . . ja."

Outside, the technicians were uncoupling the massive power cables. They, too, would not survive this night . . . even if they survived Die Glocke's power field. Sporrenberg, too. His death had also been arranged.

There would be, there could *be, no loose ends.*

How far? *the voice in his head asked.*

Kammler took a deep breath. "I would say . . . about twenty years. That ought to be enough."

He felt the power field building around him . . .

CHAPTER ONE

I was a Flight Security Supervisor (FSS) for the Minuteman missiles at Grand Forks AFB, North Dakota, from May 1973 until December 1978. We had an incident around 1977, when strange lights took over our missiles. . . . I just wanted to confirm that these incidents were happening.

USAF TECHNICAL SERGEANT
THOMAS E. JOHNSON (RET.), 2017

10 October 2017

A GROUP OF prisoners, clad in ragged black-and-white stripes, were being herded off the truck in the valley below. Guards screamed and shouted, their voices muted by the distance. Half a kilometer away, Navy lieutenant commander Mark Hunter crouched on the barren hillside, his form smothered by the shaggy folds of his ghillie suit.

"Bastards!" he whispered, pressing his high-tech binoculars against his camo-painted face. The binoculars, zoomed in twenty times, were recording 1080 HD video in 3-D stereoscopic mode, recording every detail of the North Korean test site below. A faint rumble, like distant thunder, sounded from the valley, and a dust cloud boiled from the open tunnel mouth. "Uh-oh," Hunter added. "Thar she blows."

Hunter and the other seven men of his squad were spread out along the slope, all of them invisible under their ghillies, all of them armed, but with four of them concentrating at the moment on several items of high-technology equipment. Sanders was monitoring the seismic recorder, Brunelli a radiation counter, Nielson was on the AN/PED-1, while Colby was using headphones to listen to a broadband radio scanner. Taylor, Kline, and Minkowski were on overwatch, alert for the approach of North Korean sentries.

They'd already scouted the area, photographing everything and uploading it all to an orbiting satellite. They'd collected soil samples; these would be tested back in Japan for the presence of certain isotopes, which would prove whether or not the recent bomb test had been of an ordinary atom bomb, or of a much larger and more deadly thermonuclear warhead. Right now the SEALs were just observing the activity in the valley below.

"Whatcha got, Sandy?" Hunter asked. The team members were linked by small, voice-activated radios with earplug receivers.

"A small quake . . . three . . . maybe 3.5. Might be subsidence of the main chamber, or maybe a tunnel collapse."

"Brewski?"

"No new radiation, at least not yet. But the background count is still pretty high."

"Copy that."

Hunter felt exposed up here under a dull, overcast sky, and was still concerned that the NKs might have infrared sensors that could detect them despite the heat-masking effects of the ghillies. They'd been up here for hours already though, silent, unmoving, and there'd been no sign at all that the North Koreans were aware of their presence.

He glanced at the pile of rubble that was Nielson. If things went south, or if direct intervention was called for, they could call in a flight of Tomahawk cruise missiles from off the coast, and the AN/PED-1 LLDR, or light-weight laser designator rangefinder, would guide them in smack on-target.

He sincerely hoped that wouldn't be necessary. He doubted that it would even do anything. That was a huge mountain over there.

The southern flank of Mantapsan—Mantap Mountain—was the site of North Korea's lone nuclear test facility, an isolated and barren wilderness honeycombed with tunnels. The village of Punggye-ri lay twelve kilometers to the southeast, while just two kilometers to the east was the Hwasong concentration camp, the largest in North Korea and the source of the slave laborers who'd been forced to carve tunnels hundreds of meters long into the side of the granite mountain.

Pyongyang had set off six nuclear tests here, beginning in 2006. The last and biggest, estimated at between two hundred and three hundred kilotons—ten times the power of the weapon dropped on Hiroshima—had been detonated just five weeks ago, on September 3. The North Koreans had claimed that this had been their first test of a thermonuclear weapon—a hydrogen bomb—and it was to verify this claim that the squad—eight men out of SEAL DEVGRU—had been deployed, first to Yokosuka, Japan, then to the rugged coast of North Korea. They'd inserted by an MH-60 Blackhawk stealth helicopter, an aircraft identical to the ones used to take down bin Laden two hundred miles inside Pakistan. Flying nap-of-the-earth through the rugged mountain passes of eastern North Korea, they'd touched down in the middle of the night less than ten kilometers from their target. An overland trek through the roughest terrain imaginable had brought them here to this hillside, giving them a vantage point from which they could observe the base directly.

Satellite imaging could do only so much. Sometimes, when it was vitally important to get solid intel, ground truthing was necessary.

And the US Navy SEALs were very, *very* good at this sort of op.

"The background rads are *not* good, Skipper," Brunelli whispered over Hunter's earpiece. "We're at ninety rads. I would suggest it's time to get the hell out of Dodge."

Hunter continued watching the tableau below. The prisoners were being forced into a line. One man struggled then fell, and was mercilessly beaten by two guards with truncheons.

They'd known they were going into a contaminated area. The reports from defectors coming out of North Korea over the past month had told of trees and vegetation dying near the test site, and of personnel from the test site not being allowed into the capital of Pyongyang because of the possibility of contamination. A couple of seismic tremors had jolted the mountain within minutes of the blast, and the Chinese had warned that the entire mountain could collapse, releasing a vast cloud of deadly radioactivity across the region.

The hillside on which the SEALs were hiding was as sere and blasted as the face of the Moon. Dead trees and dead grasses covered the slope, confirming the defectors' reports. Their ghillies, rather than incorporating leaves and the greenery assorted with woods, were festooned with gray and brown knotted strips, making each of them resemble a pile of rock, even from close by. Hunter couldn't see Brunelli even though the other SEAL was just a few meters away . . . and he *knew* where the man was.

Below, the prisoners were being led into the gloom of the open tunnel mouth. Satellite imagery had suggested that the North Koreans were using slave laborers from Hwasong to clear out collapsed tunnels. If the leaked radiation was bad up here, it must be ten times worse down there . . . a death sentence for men forced to work in those depths for more than an hour or two.

How, Hunter wondered, did they deal with the guards?

Rotating them in shifts of perhaps fifteen minutes each? Or maybe they simply hadn't told them that working in those tunnels was to be sentenced to a slow and very nasty death. The Democratic People's Republic of Korea was not known for its concern for *people*.

"Got anything, Colby?" Hunter asked.

"Negative, Skipper. Chitchat between the command post and a forward bunker . . . Hold it. Someone's yelling."

Hunter's spine prickled at that. Had they been discovered?

"Commander!" EN1 Taylor whispered with sharp urgency.

"Whatcha got, Taylor?"

"Sir! What in the everlasting fuck is *that*?"

Hunter rolled on his side, turning to look. *Something* was emerging from behind the crest of their hill. "Oh, my *God* . . ."

A flying saucer—there was no other term for the thing. At least sixty yards across, its surface gleaming silver with such a high polish that it was imperfectly reflecting the rocks and scree over which it soundlessly drifted, it hung in the leaden North Korean sky effortlessly and soundlessly, drifting slowly against the wind.

Hunter had been a Navy SEAL for twelve years, now. He knew intimately the aircraft both of the United States and of other countries, as well—from the new F-35 Lightning II fighters to the hush-hush SR-72 "Son of Blackbird" now being developed by the Skunk Works.

As for the DPRK, their air force still consisted of obsolete hand-me-downs from China and Russia, the Q-5, the Chengdu J-7, and the like. So this—this was something new.

The eerily silent movement of this thing reminded Hunter of a dirigible, like the Navy airships used to track incoming drug smugglers in the waters around Mexico. But this thing, this *monster* . . .

Hunter raised the binoculars and let the autofocus

sharpen the image before pressing the trigger button for the high-def video. It was tough to get the entire craft in frame all at once. He zoomed back so that he was getting more than a vast, curved mirror floating overhead.

Video of a real, live, honest-to-God flying saucer! The boys back in Yokosuka weren't going to *believe* this. . . .

He saw something breaking the polished surface . . . a kind of window or transparency, wider than it was tall. There was white light spilling through . . .

Silhouettes.

They were backlit, and Hunter could see no details at all. No, that wasn't true—one shadow looked distinctly human, though it was nothing more than a shadow. The other shapes were smaller, shorter, with large heads.

The human shape raised a hand . . . *fuck!*

It was *waving* at him!

Distantly, Hunter was aware of the guards in front of the tunnel shouting, followed by the sharp rattle of AKM automatic rifles. The saucer continued moving past the SEAL position and took up a stationary vantage point almost directly over the tunnel mouth. He held the binoculars steady while risking a quick glance away to see what was happening. A dozen DPRK guards stood in front of the tunnel, firing up at the intruder. When nothing happened, several dropped their weapons and ran. Hunter lowered the field of view on his binoculars to capture their reaction, as the remaining guards emptied their magazines into the sky. They then stood there, blank astonishment on their faces. Hunter brought the binoculars back up to the hovering craft.

And then the *real* earthquake began.

Hunter felt the vibration beneath his body, heard the growing rumble from the mountain in front of him. Again, he dropped the angle on his binoculars and zoomed farther back, trying to get the entire panorama into his field of view. An immense cloud of dust exploded from the tunnel mouth as the remaining guards fell flat on the ground.

Mantap Mountain was collapsing; Hunter could see the top of the mountain subsiding slightly, could see an avalanche of rock and soil cascading down the mountain's southern flank. Above it all, the silvery UFO seemed to be silently taking it all in.

The quake subsided, as did the billowing dust.

And the UFO was . . . gone.

Hunter had not seen it go. His attention had been on the dust and the guards on the ground, and he'd missed its departure. It should be on the video he'd shot, though.

"Radiation levels are climbing, Skipper," Brunelli said. It was, Hunter thought, a tribute to the man's nerve that he'd continued monitoring his instruments through-out the encounter. His voice was shaking, though. He'd seen it, too.

Several prisoners stumbled out of the dust swirl filling the tunnel entrance. One staggered and fell, lying next to one of the guards sprawled in the dirt. An Army truck raced up, and more soldiers began piling out.

It was definitely time to leave.

One by one, they left their hides and inched back up the slope. It took another hour, but they managed to get over the top of the ridge without being spotted.

As Hunter crawled, flat on his belly and still shrouded by the tangled mess of his ghillie suit, all he could think about was that spaceship. Hell, that's all it could be! Certainly, nothing like that had ever been constructed by any nation of Earth.

And what the hell had it done to the test site? He'd not seen any beams or missiles, nothing by which it could have attacked Mantap Mountain, but he was certain that it had done *something* to cause the mountain's collapse.

A bigger question than *how* was *why?* Men had just died in those contaminated tunnels, of that much he was certain. Death in a cave-in, he supposed, was preferable to dying from radiation poisoning.

Still, he'd just watched a goddamned flying saucer kill an unknown number of people down there.

Hunter wasn't sure what he thought about the whole topic of UFOs. For the most part, he didn't think about them at all. He was willing to concede that there was other intelligent life elsewhere in the universe, sure, but he was highly skeptical that any of it had made it to Earth. After all, why would they? A civilization that powerful, that advanced—surely there was little they could learn from a planet full of squabbling, arrogant, noisy apes!

They wouldn't be swarming around the planet like the place was Grand Central Station, if even half of the reported sightings were true.

But he'd just seen a flying saucer.

What else could it be?

It wasn't a secret American aircraft. It wasn't Russian or Chinese, and it *sure* as hell wasn't North Korean.

So . . . aliens?

Like most Americans, he was quite familiar with the look of the iconic "Grays" so prevalent on book covers, TV shows, and movies like *Close Encounters of the Third Kind*. The shapes he'd glimpsed had that look.

One of them, though, had looked human. And it had *waved* at him. It had seen him despite his camouflage and *waved* at him!

Mark Hunter's world was trembling now, threatening to shatter and plunge him into an abyss of unreality, of dissociation, of insanity.

It had *waved* at him . . .

THAT THOUGHT followed him fifty-five kilometers overland, winding through deep valleys and along forested ridgetops, took them through the night, through the next day, and well into the following night. The plan originally had called for extraction by means of the stealth

MH-60, but someone up the chain of command had decided that trying to sneak the aircraft into North Korea a second time—and this time with the North Korean military thoroughly aroused—was not the best of ideas. The SEALs would walk out, using GPS and darkness to thread their way along a route calculated to avoid all villages, hamlets, and military bases. Forty hours later, they reached the beach north of Hoemun-ri, an exhausting trek that pushed the eight SEALs to the absolute limits of their endurance and conditioning. As expected, a quartet of SEALs were waiting for them on the beach with a couple of CRRCs—combat rubber raiding craft. One SEAL scanned each of them with a Geiger counter, while another checked their personal dosimeters and logged the numbers. Their equipment, securely packed into backpacks, was stored on the boats.

"How'd it go in there, Commander?" one of them, Master Chief Cagliostro, asked.

"You will never believe it, Master Chief," Hunter replied. He was still shaking, still questioning his own reality. "Hell, *I* don't believe it!"

"We saw a flying saucer, Master Chief!" Taylor said, excited. "A fuckin' flying saucer!"

"Yeah?" TM1 Fullerton asked, grinning. "Don't tell me—little green men from Mars? Were they helping you or the gooks?"

"Fuck you!" Nielson said. "We got video. Didn't we, Skipper?"

"We got *something*."

"Hop in the Zodiacs," Cagliostro said, skepticism all over his face. "We'll sort it all out later."

The CRRCs took them back through the surf and out to a waiting submarine, a *Virginia*-class fast-attack submarine, the USS *Illinois*. The first Hunter saw of it was the gray vertical pipe of the boat's photonics mast—not periscope—rising above the water in the near-darkness a few yards away.

According to the opplan, the sub was supposed to stay submerged, but would move in close when she picked up the approach of the CRRCs on sonar. Aboard each Zodiac were a couple of sets of diving gear—masks, tanks, belts, and flippers—and one of the beach SEALs would accompany each member of the recon team down to the *Illinois*'s airlock, taking them down two by two. That way, the sub did not have to surface and risk detection, and men who might be wounded and who certainly were exhausted could be sure of getting aboard.

Hunter was one of the first two SEALs to make the descent. He stepped out of the diver airlock, dripping, and requested permission to come aboard from the executive officer who greeted him.

"Absolutely, Commander," the man said. "Welcome aboard. How'd it go?"

Hunter drew a deep breath. He wasn't ready to talk about what he'd seen . . . not until the video had been uploaded. "It was . . . interesting, sir," he said. "I don't think the North Korean test site will be a problem anymore."

Commander Rodriguez looked concerned. "Why? You didn't call in a strike."

"No, sir . . . but I think *somebody* did."

Hunter noticed a man standing behind Rodriguez. He was wearing a jumper without rank insignia, so likely he was a civilian contractor of some sort. "Lieutenant Hunter?"

"Yes, sir?"

"I'm Walters." He held up a small wallet, then flipped it shut, but Hunter was able to catch the letters *CIA* before they vanished. A spook.

"You and your men will be sequestered forward. Under no circumstances will you discuss your mission with the officers or men of this crew . . . understand?"

"Yes, sir."

"And I strongly recommend that you not discuss it with each other. I'll want to talk to each of you, though you will be fully debriefed back at Yokosuka." He pronounced the port's name wrong—with four syllables—instead of the way the Navy traditionally pronounced it—Yo-KUS-ka. This clown was definitely a suit, not a sailor.

Brunelli came through the lock behind Hunter, and a sailor led them both forward to what normally was the torpedo room, but which served as quarters for SpecOps personnel like the SEALs during missions.

Hunter looked around the compartment, found a bunk, and sat down. He'd expected the Agency to show up sooner or later. Any op into North Korea would be an extraordinarily risky, extraordinarily *sensitive* move. The debriefing would grill Hunter and his men about everything they'd seen.

They wouldn't have heard about the flying saucer, though, would they? They'd want to hear about the guards and the concentration camp prisoners, about the earthquakes and the radiation readings, but they couldn't know about that huge silvery UFO.

Right?

He decided that it would be best if none of them mentioned what they'd seen in the gray skies over Mantapsan. He would discuss the incident with the others only to warn them to keep quiet about what they'd all seen.

That didn't stop him from thinking about it, though. Because, the thing was, Mr. Walters, though wearing a blue jumpsuit and a ball cap with the *Illinois* logo emblazoned on its front, looked like he *ought* to be in a dark suit and sunglasses, maybe with a receiver earpiece in one ear. One of the quintessential Men in Black.

Hunter had heard the stories. Whispered rumors of conspiracies and secret government groups and agencies, of vast cover-ups concerning UFOs. He'd never believed any of them, of course. After all, this was the *government* they were talking about: How could *anything* concerning UFOs be kept secret by more than two people for more than fifteen minutes before the whole thing was leaked to the *New York Times*? No, all that conspiracy crap was utter bilge, pure and simple.

And yes, he'd read once about some papers from the Truman era purportedly establishing a secret agency or committee called—variously—Magic-12, MJ-12, Majestic-12, or even Majik-12. That had been when? Around 1984? He thought that was it. The story had been widely discredited since, though—a hoax, and, according to what he'd seen, not all that convincing of one.

No. It was all garbage.

An amusing thought occurred to Hunter then. Yeah, he *would* mention the UFO they'd seen—it had been part of their observation of the North Korean test site, after all—and he would see how Mr. Walters responded. If he didn't seem interested, or didn't believe it, or simply dismissed it, then Hunter would know he was right, and there were no secret-agency conspiracies, no MJ-12, none of that garbage. If Walters went all Hollywood on Hunter, however—*don't talk to anyone about this or you're in big trouble*—well, maybe there was something to it.

It would be amusing to find out . . . and even more amusing to yank Walters's chain.

He was smiling as, two at a time, the rest of the team was ushered forward to the torpedo compartment. Then, once the recon team's gear had been stored forward, the *Illinois* slipped beneath the waves and proceeded northeast. She would circle around the northern tip of Hokkaido, then bear southwest for the US naval base at Yokosuka, Japan.

And then, Hunter thought, no matter what happened with Walters, the shit would *really* hit the fan.

"LIEUTENANT COMMANDER? Have a seat."

Hunter had been led aft to a small office—Captain Magruder's office, in fact, which had been set aside for the interview. It was, like the offices of COs since the beginnings of submariner history, painted puke green, cramped, and with just barely enough room for a chair, a fold-down desk, and a bunk. Hunter took the proffered bunk.

They were one day out from Yokosuka, and Walters had interviewed each of Hunter's men in turn. It was . . . disquieting. Each man had been led back to the forward torpedo room, somber, tight-lipped, and unwilling to discuss what had gone on with the Agency spook.

They were equally unwilling to discuss the encounter with the UFO, even Minkowski, who'd seemed positively ebullient about that enigmatic *thing* in the sky. Had they been threatened?

The idea that this might be the case did not sit well with Hunter. That this *civilian* had evidently come down hard on the men, on *his* men—the SEAL was now furious. *No one* did that with Hunter's team members and fucking got away with it.

Walters took up a clipboard with papers on it, then pressed a switch on a small box which he set conspicuously on the desk in front of him. "Lieutenant. We're recording this conversation, all right?" Without waiting for a reply, he looked down at his clipboard. "What is your name, rank, and service number?"

"Mark Francis Hunter," Hunter replied. "Lieutenant commander." The Navy had used Social Security numbers for identification since 1972. He gave it.

"Place of birth?"

"Dayton, Ohio."

"Date you entered the service?"

"Eight March 2006. Look, what the hell—"

"*I* will ask the questions, if you please, Commander. Date of birth?"

"Oh-five, oh-nine, nineteen eighty-six. *Sir.*"

Walters glanced up at the small note of defiance in Hunter's voice, then looked back at his clipboard. "Education?"

"Bachelor of science, Virginia Tech University. And then Annapolis. And I will *not* answer any more questions until you tell me what you said to my men. Sir."

Walters sighed, and leaned back in the chair. "I said nothing to them that I will not be saying to you, Commander. Your full cooperation in this debriefing is very much appreciated. Okay?"

"Sir."

He reached forward and picked up the minirecorder. "Now tell me about the mission. From the beginning, please."

Hunter compressed his lips, then leaned forward and gave a small shrug. "Yes, sir."

And he began talking, starting with the squad being told of the op, flown from SEAL Team One headquarters at the Amphibious Warfare HQ on Coronado, in San Diego, to the Navy base at Yokosuka; he made a point of pronouncing the city's name *right*.

He continued with their nighttime insertion by parachute off of a specially rigged MH-60 Blackhawk, their landing, their brutal overland trek, and their positioning above the Mantap Mountain base.

He talked about what they'd seen: their survey of the base, the dead vegetation, the NK guards and slave laborers, the slight seismic quakes, the high background radioactivity.

"We were about to pack it in, get out of Dodge," Hunter continued, "when EN1 Taylor said—"

Walters switched off the recorder. "We don't need to talk about what happened next."

"Sir?"

"The first man I interviewed, Master Chief . . . ah . . ." He consulted his clipboard. "Minkowski. He told me all about it. That portion of the record has been erased. And you, Commander, will erase everything that you *think* you saw in there from your mind. Do you understand?"

Hunter felt a sharp chill at that. Walters was acting

more and more like the Men in Black, or what Hunter believed those mythical personages were supposed to be like, by the moment.

"I *said*, do you understand?"

"Or what?"

Walters blinked. "I beg your pardon?"

"Or what? What happens if I don't forget?" *Or if I can't forget. . . .*

"Mr. Hunter, may I remind you that when you were inducted into the SEALs, you signed nondisclosure papers and took an oath of secrecy. If you were to divulge any information which has been determined to be classified as confidential or above, you would be subject to the provisions of the Uniform Code of Military Justice, specifically Articles 92, 104, 106a, and 134 . . ."

Hunter suppressed a chuckle. The UCMJ laid out what offenses were subject to court-martial; 92 was about failure to obey a lawful order, 106a had to do with espionage, 104 was aiding the enemy, and 134 was the military's catchall: "conduct prejudicial to good order and discipline." How the hell was his story of a UFO violating any of those articles?

Well, he'd been ordered not to talk about things declared secret, yeah. They could get him on Article 92. And 134 was always there to catch anything not listed in the rest of the UCMJ.

"*However,*" Walters said, after running through those articles as well as several points from the Military Rules of Procedure and the Classified Information Procedures Act, "in all probability the case would not even come to trial. If it did, you would get a dishonorable discharge and at least twenty years in Portsmouth. If you were lucky. But people have also been known to . . . disappear."

Hunter's eyebrows jumped up on his forehead. "You're threatening to *kill* me?"

"Let's just say, Commander, that we know where you live, where your *family* lives, and leave it at that. If you

say *anything* about what you think you saw, we will come
down on you like one hundred tons of concrete blocks,
and I doubt very much if anyone will hear anything you
might wish to say. Some . . . *gentlemen* from DC will be
along to talk to you about this, but you will discuss it with
no one else. Do we understand one another?"

Hunter didn't reply at first. He was still digesting Walters's threat . . .

. . . and what that meant for the whole idea of government UFO conspiracies and cover-ups.

My God, he thought. *It's* real. *All of it.*

*And I saw a man, a human, on board that craft . . .
and it* waved *at me.*

"I *said*, Commander, do we understand one another?"

It was all real. The UFO. The conspiracies.

The threats.

"Sir. *Yes*, sir," Hunter replied.

There was no option but to play along.

CHAPTER TWO

I can assure you the flying saucers, given that they exist, are not constructed by any power on Earth.

PRESIDENT HARRY S. TRUMAN, 1950

22 September 1947

HE RATTLED THE *papers in his hand. "This is horseshit, Roscoe!"*

"Maybe so, Mr. President," Roscoe H. Hillenkoetter replied. "But it's damned critical horseshit. We need to know what's happening here."

"Yes, but . . . flying saucers? Little green men from Mars?" He dropped the report dismissively on his desk. "Show me! I'm from Missouri."

"So am I, Mr. President. And you've seen the reports out of Wright Field."

Roscoe Hillenkoetter had been the director of the Central Intelligence Group since May of this year . . . before that he'd been the director of Central Intelligence, as well. And as of four days ago, with the National Security Act and the creation of the Central Intelligence Agency, he was the director of that, too, the Central Intelligence Agency's very first.

For Hillenkoetter, the world had become a very different place in the last few months, much more uncertain, much stranger, much scarier *ever since something had* crashed in the desert outside of a town called Roswell, New Mexico. He'd only been head of the CIG for two months at that point.

What a hell of a way to kick things off.

But he was one of the few men who'd been in the know almost from the beginning—not to mention one of the men who'd been trying to shut down the rampant rumors and speculation coming out of New Mexico since early July.

"Yes," Truman said. "But I don't like it. Who are these things, these creatures anyway? What are they doing in our airspace? Why the hell are they here? Is it an invasion?"

"Mr. President, I just wish to hell I knew."

The wreckage from the desert crash site had been gathered up and shipped to Wright Field outside of Dayton, Ohio. Wright Field was the location of the Air Force's T-2 Intelligence Department—formerly the Technical Data Laboratory created in 1942—the place where captured German aircraft had been shipped after the war to see what made them tick. Now they were being tasked with the same for whatever this thing was. Whether they would be able to make anything out of the debris remained to be seen.

They also had several bodies from the crash on ice. Hillenkoetter shuddered at the memory. He'd seen them. Those creatures had not been human.

A number of reports had come out of T-2 since July of that year, including the one Truman had just mentioned. The crash wreckage did not incorporate technology known to any nation or group on Earth, and was therefore almost certainly extraterrestrial in origin. Mars was the popularly assumed origin of the craft and its diminutive crew, though the planet Venus was sometimes bandied about as an alternative. In fact, nothing was known about the craft's origins or capability, and that single, simple statement was terrifying in its impli-

cations. Somebody, no one knew who, was able to travel to Earth from God knew where, enter US airspace with impunity, and outrun or outmaneuver the best combat aircraft in the US inventory.

What was even worse was the fact that these extraterrestrials had been here for years before 1947. The US government had even recovered wreckage from one after the so-called Battle of Los Angeles in early 1942, and from Cape Girardeau, Missouri, the year before that.

And there were rumors, originating with the German scientists of Operation Paperclip, that a ship had crashed in Germany back in 1936 or 1939—the stories differed—and that some of the amazing technology coming out of the Third Reich during the war had been due to back-engineering technology from recovered vehicles. Alien *vehicles.*

"Okay, Roscoe," Truman said. "According to this report you've just submitted, you want to create a kind of scientific committee to study these crashed saucers. That right?"

"Yes, Mr. President."

"Who do you suggest we approach?"

"There's a list appended at the end, sir. Vannevar Bush, certainly. And the new secretary of defense."

"James Forrestal? Okay."

"General Vandenberg, of course." Hoyt Vandenberg *had been the second director of central intelligence before Hillenkoetter, and had been the duputy commander in chief for the US Army Air Forces.*

Truman leafed ahead to the list of suggested names. "Okay. I've got it. And the upshot of all this is to create a group to recover crashed saucers?"

"In part, yes, sir. We know that these . . . people *aren't perfect. Sometimes their aircraft crash. One, maybe two in Germany before the war. One in New Mexico. One in Missouri. The one we shot down over Los Angeles in '42. When they crash, we need to be able*

to dispatch teams to cordon off the area, and keep civilians out. We need to recover the wreckage, as we did at Roswell, and move it to a safe location. We need to have engineers and scientists, good engineers and scientists, who can learn all they can from the debris, and see how we can use it."

"You mean build our own flying saucers. . . ."

Hillenkoetter shrugged. *"Maybe. We know the Germans were working on that."* He'd seen the drawings and schematics for the Nazi Haunebu I, II, and III. The Allies had come so damned close to losing, closer than any man on the street was aware.

Some things simply had to be kept secret from the public.

"We also need," he continued, *"to keep a lid on this whole thing. If we fail to maintain control over what the public knows about this, there could be real panic."*

Truman grunted. *"That damned radio show."*

Hillenkoetter nodded. The War of the Worlds *had* panicked a good many people who'd heard it. In fact, the degree of panic had been grossly overstated by the newspapers—they were keen on pointing out the deficiencies of radio, their new competitor, as opposed to print media—but war jitters certainly had contributed to some small degree of panic, at the very least, especially in New Jersey where the Martians were supposed to have landed.

"Yes, sir."

"I don't mind telling you, Roscoe, that I don't like the idea of deliberately deceiving the American public."

"Neither do I, Mr. President. But it'll be necessary, at least for a time. And we don't want the Soviets getting wind of this."

"No, we do not." Truman considered the problem for a moment. *"Okay. I'll draw up an executive order."*

"Thank you, sir."

"Don't thank me. As director of Central Intelligence

and *director of the CIA, you've got yourself a spot on this committee, whether you like it or not. And I'll expect you to keep me in the loop."*

"Absolutely, Mr. President."

"I know the scientists think they got a wrecked spaceship out of the Pacific near LA, but I've always thought that whole incident was just war jitters, okay? That, or some kind of long-range Jap reconnaissance aircraft. We just don't know. We can't know."

"We know the Japanese didn't have anything that could reach us at the time."

"Floatplanes off a submarine?"

He shook his head. "They didn't have anything like that in '42. The I-400 class wasn't in operation until '44."

"Well, this whole thing sounds pretty damned iffy to me. But if we're being invaded from out there, we need to know about it. And we need to be able to fight back if push comes to shove."

"Yes, Mr. President."

"Now get the hell out of here and let me get to some nice, safe, normal world problems. Like what Stalin is doing in Europe, and what we'll do if he gets the bomb!"

The bomb.

Nuclear weapons were nothing compared to this. And as Hillenkoetter walked out of the Oval Office, he wondered how much the President knew about the Nazi Haunebu saucers, their atom bomb experiments, or their other secret, almost magical weapons . . . and how close the Allies had been to total annihilation.

HUNTER WALKED up the sidewalk of the apartment complex on Witherspoon Way, located in the small and quiet Californian community of El Cajon just seventeen miles from downtown San Diego. At the door to the lobby, he stopped and looked up and down the street.

Nothing. *Damn*, he thought. *You're getting way too paranoid.*

Of course, he remembered the old dictum: *just because you're paranoid, it doesn't mean they're not out to get you!*

His debriefing at Yokosuka had been a lot less exciting than the interview with Walters on board the *Illinois*, at least to start with. They'd put him in a room with a bunk, desk and chairs, and its own head. He presumed the other SEALs in the squad had been sequestered this way as well, but he never saw them while he was on the base and so didn't know for sure.

The next day, a couple of suits with badges identifying them as DIA—the Defense Intelligence Agency—had received him in a small and dingy office and questioned him about the mission. They'd asked him about what he and the others had seen, but when he told them truthfully they'd just nodded and jotted down something in their notebooks.

As he'd stood up to leave, however, one of them had stopped him. "I would keep your, ah, sighting quiet, if I were you, Lieutenant," he'd said. "There are folks here who really, *really* don't want you spreading wild stories about spaceships, y'know? Especially if you've been ordered to keep your mouth shut."

"I saw what I saw," Hunter said, his voice almost a growl. "I have video to prove it!"

The other DIA man had given him a tight-lipped grin. "Not anymore, you don't."

Of course. Everything they'd brought back from the mission—video, seismic and radiation readings, isotope sample—it all had been taken off the submarine at Yokosuka. Hunter was positive he wouldn't see or hear of those recordings again.

"So—are you certain of what you saw?" the other agent said.

"Of course I am! Are you calling me a liar?"

"Absolutely not. But . . . well . . . your eyes could have been playing tricks. Or . . . just maybe . . . what you saw was some sort of very secret US aircraft. You know we have massive black projects going. Maybe someone way up the chain of command decided to send one in to have a look around."

Hunter did know about black budgets and black projects. As a Navy SEAL, he operated in and around those shadows himself.

"What I saw," he said, angry and stubborn, "was technology that must have been *centuries* ahead of anything we have now! Okay?"

"But how do you know that, Lieutenant? I understand they have some really spooky things going down back in Nevada. Real Star Wars stuff! Hey, you told us yourself you saw a human through that porthole, right? What would a human be doing on a spaceship if it was from another planet?"

The other agent nodded. "And you know . . . if you're so certain it wasn't an *American* secret aircraft . . . I don't know. Maybe it was Chinese! Beijing was *extremely* concerned about the possibility of radiation leakage from that test site. And they could have some supersecret black-ops assets as well, stuff we don't even know about."

"Then God help us all," Hunter had told them. "That thing we saw would fly rings around the Lightning II or anything else in our inventory!"

"Well . . . so you believe." The agent opened a briefcase and handed Hunter several documents.

"What are these?"

"An oath of secrecy. You'll swear not to tell *anyone* about what you saw."

"But I'm already under oath. When I got my security clearance. I never de-oathed!"

"I know. But if you would, please."

"Wasn't my promise to Walters enough?"

"Who is Walters?"

"The CIA man—"

"There *is* no Walters."

Hunter had looked at the two agents warily. They were serious about this fiction they were making him participate in. Serious enough to go to all this trouble.

The agent seemed to pretend the last part of their conversation hadn't even happened, pulling out more papers. "And these are documents informing you of the national security aspects of this mission, and of the penalties you face if you divulge *any* information to anyone. We need you to read and sign them."

With a sigh, Hunter had glanced through the papers . . . then signed.

"And initial here, please. And here. And here. . . ."

Hunter had done as he'd been told, grumbling to himself a bit ungraciously, but obviously he would get nowhere with these people. They were *nicer* than Walters had been, certainly, but just as determined to enforce his cooperation.

The SEALs were reunited again when they were given orders to return by first-available military transport. Twelve and a half hours later, they'd touched down at Naval Air Station North Island and the complex of naval bases at Coronado, the Silver Strand just across the bay from San Diego.

And once again, he and his men had been separated, given solitary quartering, and interviewed by both military and civilian personnel. No one had even alluded to the UFO this time, and he just played ball to get it all over with. He read and signed more nondisclosure papers, and was reminded again both of the importance of national security interests, and of the severity of the penalties should any service member violate his oaths.

By this time, Hunter *knew*, without a shadow of a doubt, that whatever he and his men had seen out there at Mantapsan, it had been *real*—real as in a genuine spacecraft from some other world. Everyone who questioned him insisted that it might have been something out of some secret American program, something so secret it would be devastating to national security if he revealed it.

"Everyone knows," one guy with FBI credentials had told him, "that the military has cooked up some pretty strange stuff. You know . . . Area 51, and all that."

That secret base in the Nevada desert was notorious as the place where alien spacecraft were reverse engineered and tested, but it was also well-known as the site of flight tests of top secret human aircraft. The SR-71 Blackbird and the F-117 Nighthawk, the so-called Stealth Fighter, had been tested there, and scuttlebutt had it that there were other, newer, even more radically advanced aircraft there now.

"Maybe," said the man who'd flashed a DIA card at him, "you saw a SAD/SOG op."

Hunter scowled at that. The Special Activities Division/ Special Operations Group was a highly secret organization working under CIA direction responsible for covert ops in which the US government wanted to maintain plausible deniability.

His interviewers had done their best to plant seeds of doubt in his mind. Had he *really* seen an alien spaceship? He couldn't know . . . not for *certain*.

But although he said nothing, Hunter was by now certain that what he'd seen had not been built or deployed by any nation on Earth. Why would the government, which had deployed the SEALs in the first place—and deployed numerous high-value assets in support, including a USAF SpecOps transport and a *Virginia*-class submarine— turn around and send in that whatever-it-was to yank the rug out from under the people they already had on the ground? It made no sense!

Of course, Hunter was always more than ready to accept the fact that *the government* was a misnomer. The term implied a monolithic whole that *always* knew what it was doing. Bullshit! Hunter knew well that all too often, not only did the left hand not know what the right was doing, but the head didn't know what *either* was doing, and the hands were wrestling with each other over interservice and interdepartmental turf wars.

Maybe . . .

No. He didn't buy it. With technology like *that*, people very high up the ladder within the government would damn well know what it was doing . . . and who else was on the ground at the time.

So . . . aliens. By the time he left Naval Base Coronado on liberty, he was feeling distinctly paranoid. Renting a car, he drove east to El Cajon, frequently checking the rearview mirror for signs of a tail. Gerri lived in an apartment complex on Witherspoon. He parked on Chatham Street two blocks south from the place and walked, just so he could check and see if he was being followed.

Now he was there, and though he still hadn't seen anyone out of the ordinary, he was almost certain he was being followed. But with no proof, there was nothing to do but go in.

Gerri Galanis lived on the second floor, Apartment 2D, and she was waiting for him when he buzzed from the lobby. "Mark!" she cried, opening the door. She was tall, brunette, and stunning in a microscopic bikini. "I thought you'd *never* get here!"

"Had to work late at the office, hon," he replied, keeping his voice nonchalant. He'd phoned her when he'd arrived at Coronado two days ago, but had not been able to wrangle liberty until this afternoon. He'd called her again a couple of hours ago, and they'd made plans to go to the beach—hence the bikini.

Hunter was just glad they'd seen fit to issue him a pass. He'd seriously questioned whether they would ever allow him off base after the multiple grillings he'd received. His relief was palpable as he looked at the gorgeous woman before him, and he took Gerri in his arms and gave her a deep and thorough kiss.

Hunter had been divorced by his wife a year ago, and he was still wrestling with that. Eve had said it was because he was never home . . . though, damn it, she'd known he was in the Navy when she'd married him, and knew what it meant to be a Navy wife. Privately, he still wondered if she'd found someone else, but he also could admit that the role of Navy spouse was not for everyone. And the deployment schedules for the SEALs were worse than most, and DEVGRU—what used to be called SEAL Team Six—was the worst of all. You never knew when the phone would ring in the middle of the night, and twenty-four hours later you would be squelching through the mud in a swamp somewhere in Venezuela, or freezing your ass off on top of a mountain in Afghanistan.

Or dodging flying saucers in North Korea.

He'd picked Gerri up at a bar just two months ago. She was cute and she was fun and she didn't ask too many questions. She cocktailed at the Kitten Klub downtown, with occasional gigs working the pole onstage. Hunter didn't mind at all the idea of her displaying her body in front of noisy men; she actually liked what she did and she was *good* at it.

Just like Hunter.

"Ready for the beach?" he asked her.

"Well . . ." Her hand wandered on his torso and she kissed him again. "Maybe in a minute . . . or two." Her grin was infectious.

Sex with Gerri was *always* fantastic, but even better was the relaxation, the decompression that Hunter had learned most to appreciate. Though he wouldn't admit it even to himself, he was sore as hell from the brutal hike up and down those North Korean mountain slopes, and still felt washed out and rag-doll limp inside.

She made him feel alive once more.

After a long and pleasant interlude, they lay together in her bed, bare legs entangled, thoroughly wrapped in one another's arms. "So, Mr. SEAL," she said, playfully stroking him. "Can you tell me *anything* about where you've been this past week?"

"Uh-uh," he said. With one finger, he stroked the curve of hair and skin just behind her left ear. She shivered, and cuddled closer.

"Mmmm. Not even where you've been?"

"Sorry, babe. You know I can't."

Especially this time!

He pushed the urgent thought away. He'd been trying not to think about . . . that.

Normally, the secrecy imposed on members of the SEAL teams wasn't that big a deal. You simply didn't talk about what you did at all—just said you were in the Navy. She'd seen him in uniform months before, though, and noticed the huge and clunky "Budweiser" badge that declared him to be a Navy SEAL. So she knew that much, at least.

Even so, that was all she would know. SEALs didn't talk about their missions, even when they weren't classified. The barflies who claimed to be Navy SEALs to any and all who would listen were fucking liars, every damned one of them.

"It's just I worry about you," she said.

"And if you knew where I was and what I was doing, that wouldn't help one little bit, now, would it?"

She sighed. "I guess not."

"So . . ." He gave her butt a stinging slap. "Let's go to the beach!"

"Ummm . . ." She was working her way down his chest with kisses . . . then down his stomach. "In a minute," she told him. "In *just* a minute . . ."

It took considerably longer than a minute, but eventually they worked their way down the steep slope and onto the sand at Black's Beach, a tough-to-reach stretch of coastline just north of the Scripps Oceanographic Institute and Torrey Pines bluffs.

Gerri had brought him here a month ago. Divided

between the city of San Diego and Torrey Pines State Park, the northern part of the beach had long been a secluded gathering place for naturists. Technically, public nudity was illegal in California, and the city of San Diego had banned nude sunbathing on the southern part of the beach in the '70s, but the part of Black's Beach belonging to the park was still clothing optional, unofficially at least. Gerri and Hunter found a good spot, put down a blanket, and peeled out of their shirts and swimsuits.

In the middle of October there weren't many other people in evidence, either clothed or nude. The air was cool for Southern California—sixty-two degrees with a strong, offshore breeze—and the powerful surf pounded on the rocks. An underwater canyon out there funneled the incoming waves, and made the southern part of the beach a mecca for experienced surfers. A couple of surfers were out there now, riding in on a big roller.

Hunter glanced up at the sky . . . then back to the bluffs looming over the beach.

No one.

"Mark?" his companion asked. "What's worrying you?"

"What makes you think anything is worrying me?"

"You asked me to drive in my car. You *never* do that. During the drive here, you kept checking behind us, like you thought we were being followed. In the parking lot you took your time checking out *everything*: the people on the deck over at Scripps, the other cars in the lot, even the sky. When we came down the trail, you kept looking back over your shoulder. And now you're doing it again."

"Sorry. Am I that obvious?"

"Yes! And it's driving me nuts!"

He scanned the deep blue and empty sky overhead. Funny how he kept looking up, just in case. . . .

"I just . . ." Damn. What could he tell her? That he was afraid government spooks were watching them, even out here?

They were getting an eyeful right now if they were.

"I just . . . I'm just having a bit of nerves," he told her. "Where we were, what we did . . . it was really rugged. To get out, we hiked over thirty miles in rough terrain like you wouldn't believe. Took us two days to do it, and that was just because we were really humping it. I'm still . . . I don't know. Still getting my head together, I guess."

She lightly caressed his leg. "If you want to talk about it," she said. "You know I won't tell a soul."

He nodded. "I know, babe."

He believed her. Last month, she'd taken him to meet her parents in La Mesa, and when her father asked them what he did for a living, she'd laughed and said, "*Dad!* He works in San Diego and he has a short haircut! What do you *think* he does?" About 30 percent of the working population in San Diego worked at the Coronado bases.

When her father pressed the issue, she'd told him, "He takes wonderfully good care of me! And that's all that matters, right? Now quit pestering him about it!"

And there the matter dropped. By the end of the evening, her parents were assuming that he was Navy . . . but the SEALs were never even mentioned. She was *good*.

Yeah, Gerri could keep a secret.

But he wasn't going to test it.

Instead, they lay down on the blanket and watched the sky—the blessedly empty sky—for almost an hour, as the sun slowly westered toward the horizon.

"Tell me something, babe."

"Sure."

"What's your take on UFOs? Life on other planets?"

"Flying saucers?"

"I guess."

She shrugged. "I don't know. I believe there's life out there. I mean, the universe is so *big*, right? There *has* to be other life . . . other intelligence. To assume anything else seems pretty damned arrogant."

"Yeah . . ."

"But according to everything I've read, even the nearest stars are so awfully far away. You have to wonder how any of those races could make it all the way here. If you believe the saucer nuts, Earth must be like LAX, with thousands of UFOs zipping in from space every year. That just doesn't sound very likely to me."

"Yeah. That's what I always thought."

The words just slipped out. He'd intended them to mean simply that—that he'd long believed in extraterrestrial life, but not in UFOs. But the way he'd said it sounded more like, "I thought that before . . . but not now."

"So . . . you saw a UFO?" she asked.

Damn. She *was* quick on the uptake. But one of the things Hunter liked about Gerri was how quick she was, how smart, so he wasn't exactly surprised.

"I don't know." He didn't like the idea of lying. Perhaps misdirection was the best way to go. "Remember, all *UFO* means is 'unidentified flying object.' Doesn't necessarily mean spaceships. *Lots* of stuff in the sky could be unidentified, depending on circumstances."

"Yes," she pressed, "but you're a trained observer, right? Disciplined. You know aircraft, especially military. You're not going to mistake the planet Venus for a spacecraft."

"Right now, babe, I don't know what I believe."

"Tell me about it?"

"Uh-uh. Not now. Just that I saw . . . *something*. But maybe I hallucinated everything."

Hunter's cell phone, tucked into a pocket of his shirt lying in the sand nearby, buzzed.

"Now, who the hell is calling you on your day off?"

"Don't know," he answered. "Unless they're canceling liberties . . ."

He fished the phone out of the shirt and held it to his ear. "Hunter."

"Well, well, well," a voice said on the other end of the line. "Lieutenant Commander Hunter."

"Yes . . . ?"

"Right now, Commander, you are on thin ice. *Very* thin ice. . . ."

Now, what the hell? "Who is this?"

"Never mind that. You should be more concerned about yourself. Or, if you're not worried about being court-martialed, you might at least give some thought to the safety of that pretty little girl sitting next to you."

"What the fuck!" He sat up, looking around, both nervous and angry.

And he was leaning toward "angry" more and more.

"Hey," the voice continued, "we know you like Gerri Galanis. Pretty. Smart. An amazing dancer. And we know she's fantastic in bed! We *know*. It would be *such* a shame if anything . . . unpleasant happened to her. Quite a waste."

The threat, awful in its hackneyed melodrama, like something out of the pages of some cheap detective novel, left Hunter dumbfounded. He opened his mouth to reply—he had *no* idea what he was about to say—and then he realized the line had gone dead.

He lowered the phone, then glanced up at the bluffs over the beach. A solitary figure stood up there, silhouetted against the early evening sky.

The figure raised one hand . . . and waved.

Fuck!

"Mark!" Gerri cried with concern. "What's the matter? You're white as a sheet!"

He took a deep breath. "Never mind. C'mon. Let's get out of here."

"Why? Did they recall you?"

"Yeah. Something like that."

He looked back up the bluff. The lone figure was gone.

They got dressed, gathered up the blanket, and started up the long and rugged trail back to the parking lot at the top of the bluff, the mood subdued. Behind them, in the distance, several naked people were playing volleyball while others watched, and a couple of wet-suited surfers cruised a thundering wave toward the shore.

Maybe, he thought, it would be best if he didn't see Gerri for a while.

Hell, maybe it would be best if he never saw her again.

CHAPTER THREE

Decades ago, visitors from other planets warned us about the direction we were heading and offered to help. Instead, some of us interpreted their visits as a threat, and decided to shoot first and ask questions after.... Trillions ... of dollars have been spent on black projects which both Congress and the Commander-in-Chief have been kept deliberately in the dark.

PAUL HELLYER,
FORMER CANADIAN DEFENSE MINISTER, 2010

21 February 1954

PRESIDENT DWIGHT D. *Eisenhower stood on the deck outside the control tower, looking out into the night across the endless salt flats and hard-packed sands of Muroc Air Force Base in California. He'd been on vacation at nearby Palm Springs when his aides had arrived that evening to usher him off to this godforsaken stretch of emptiness. Not that it didn't have its own austere beauty. The sky in particular was brilliantly clear, strewn with stars.*

It might have been nice if several searchlights hadn't been switched on, their beams aiming up into the sky.

"I don't see a damned thing," Eisenhower said, testily. "Did they stand us up?"

An aide checked his watch. "It's only a little past midnight, Mr. President. Let's wait a few minutes yet and see."

Other people in the select group stood in a huddle nearby: Edwin Nourse, who'd been Truman's chief economic advisor; Cardinal James Francis McIntyre, current head of the Los Angeles Catholic Church; Franklin Allen, an eighty-year-old former reporter with the Hearst Group, leaning heavily on his cane; and perhaps fifteen others. Eisenhower's aides had rounded them up that evening and driven them up to Muroc as "community leaders," asking them to witness what promised to be a spectacular event—the dawn, perhaps, of a new era for Humanity.

"We've got incoming," a voice inside the tower called over a loudspeaker. "From the north-northwest, range fifty miles." Eisenhower turned to face that direction and raised his binoculars to his eyes. He had not, he decided, been this nervous since he'd waited out D-day in his command post, code-named "Sharpener," in a Hampshire woods.

A star just above the horizon grew steadily brighter. "There it is, sir!" an aide called.

"I see it."

The star swelled rapidly to a brilliant light, like an aircraft's landing lights, and it was accompanied now by four other objects traveling behind it. Through the binoculars, Eisenhower could see that the craft was flat and circular, perhaps sixty yards across. Windows across the leading edge were the source of the light, too bright for him to see inside.

Utterly silent, the craft came to a stop, hovering two hundred yards out from the control tower, extended four landing legs, then gently settled onto the hard-packed desert floor. Light spilled onto the ground as a garage-sized hatch slid open, and a ramp extended in apparent welcome.

"Well," the President said, "I guess it's showtime."

"I still don't like this, Mr. President," Sherman Adams said. Adams was Eisenhower's chief of staff, the first man ever to hold that title. "Not one bit. We can't help you in there if they're hostile—"

"I'll be fine, Sherman."

"Sir, if this is an invasion, what's the first thing they would do? Take down the target's leadership! They could kidnap you, hold you hostage. Or—"

"Enough, Sherman! I am going to do this." Eisenhower gave Adams a hard glare. His senior advisor already had a nickname among his opponents in Washington: The Abominable No Man. He was outspoken and direct, and not afraid to tell the President exactly what he thought.

Which was why the former Army five-star general appreciated him as much as he did.

But right now, Sherman was wrong. Still, Eisenhower relaxed the glare into a wry grin. "Let Dick know what happened if things go south." Vice President Richard Nixon was back in DC, having been deliberately kept out of the loop. "But don't worry. If they wanted me dead, they wouldn't go to all of this trouble to arrange a meeting. They'd just vaporize the White House.

"It's what I'd do, at least."

Eisenhower handed Adams his binoculars, turned, and descended the metal steps from the control tower deck. A couple of Marine honor guards fell into step behind him.

It will be all right.

The meeting had been arranged by Project Sigma, a classified program signed into existence by Eisenhower when he took office. It worked under the direction of Truman's shadowy MJ-12, the committee tasked with overseeing contact with the aliens, and the recovery of their spacecraft. Just last month, Sigma had detected large alien spacecraft in orbit around Earth, and soon estab-

lished radio contact with them—in English, *which suggested that these creatures had been observing Earth for some time. The aliens had asked to talk with Earth's leadership; Sigma had suggested in return an initial meeting with the President of the United States, and specified a place for the encounter, far out in the desert away from reporters and an already anxious public. Just two years ago, large numbers of UFOs had overflown Washington DC, and while that had been hushed up, the country, already nervous about the global march of Communism and a Soviet hydrogen bomb, needed to be kept calm.*

America had tested its first thermonuclear device on November 1, 1952. Less than a year later, just six months ago, the Russians had exploded their own weapon, known to US Intelligence as Joe-4 because it was the fourth known nuclear test carried out at the behest of Joseph Stalin. The iron curtain predicted by Churchill in 1946 had just become terrifyingly deadly. The so-called Cold War, emerging from the Truman Doctrine of 1947 which called for the containment of the Soviet Union, was on the point of turning hot.

One reason Eisenhower had agreed to this meeting was the chance that the extraterrestrials might be able to provide the United States with technologies, possibly weapons, that would help America stay secure in the face of Communist aggression. That, Eisenhower was the first to admit, was the longest of long shots, but any chance at all made the risk worthwhile.

He reached the bottom of the ramp. "Stay here, fellows," he told the Marine bodyguards. "I'll be back soon."

"Sir—" one of the Marines began.

"It's okay, son. They want just me."

As if on cue, a figure was waiting for him, silhouetted against the light at the top of the ramp. Strange. The figure looked human*: six feet tall, with long hair, and a raised hand with five fingers. Eisenhower had been expecting one of the short aliens, the "Extraterrestrial*

Biological Entities," recovered from several crashed saucers. Those things gave him the creeps. So to see this new kind of being?

What the hell?

A long and anxious hour later, Eisenhower returned to the tower, looking white and shaken. "My God, Sherman," he whispered. "My God in heaven."

"What was it, Mr. President? What happened?"

"They offered . . . a trade," Eisenhower told his aide. "A negotiated exchange. They offered to begin giving us technology. No weapons, but free energy and antigravity and . . ." He stopped, then shook his head. "Jesus Christ."

"And what did they want in return, sir?"

"Nothing much. Unilateral nuclear disarmament. We get rid of our nukes, and they give us toys . . . trinkets, really. I felt like a South Seas island native being offered beads and baubles by the Europeans!"

"What did you tell them?"

"I told them 'no,' and then I told them 'hell no!' of course."

Adams seemed relieved. "That's wise, Mr. President. If we lose our nuclear deterrent. . . ."

"That's what I told them. They were ready to sign a treaty with us, but I told them no. We will be staying in contact, though. Maybe we can still work something out."

But privately, Eisenhower doubted that anything more would come out of this meeting in the desert. That disturbingly human alien had been adamant. Humans were on a deadly path which they must abandon . . . or face extinction. And while its English had been perfect, there was just the slightest hint of something foreign in the accent. Eisenhower, for his part, couldn't help but wonder if these beings were in fact Germans, a Nazi remnant escaped from the collapse of their Reich, and somehow provided with advanced technology. There'd been rumors of just that scenario ever since Operation HighJump, in the Antarctic.

There was no way to confirm any of that, though. And so he would return to the hotel. His staff would concoct a story about him needing emergency dental surgery after he lost a crown at the fried chicken dinner last night. The whole incident would be kept hush-hush.

And he would go back to the mundane world of running a country, and do his best to forget those visitors and their trinkets.

But he knew he would always wonder if he'd made the right decision.

HUNTER WASN'T sure what was in store for him now. That morning, he'd received a peremptory summons to the office of Captain Scott Mulvehill, the CO of the Coronado facility, and presumed that he would be receiving new orders.

He was still seething, though, over the phone call on the beach. How *dare* they threaten his girlfriend, a complete innocent, just to shut him up! Perhaps even worse, the timing of the call, and the call itself, strongly implied that he was under *constant* surveillance. That crack about Gerri being good in bed . . . He recognized that for what it was: a crude and blunt declaration that they were watching, or at least listening in on him, even when he was in Gerri's apartment. Was her apartment bugged? It must be. And the intrusion left him furious.

And clearly they'd been listening in on them at the beach. It hadn't been a bug, a tiny microphone planted on him at one of the interviews. He knew that much. He hadn't been wearing *anything* on the nude beach . . . and he'd been in uniform during the interviews. Or . . .

Now *there* was a thought. There were, he knew, ways to activate a cell phone from a remote location, and turn the device into a live mic even when it was switched off.

For that matter, a simple shotgun mic from the top of those bluffs might have been able to listen in on their conversation.

No matter how they'd done it, the blatant intrusion, the violation of his right to privacy had him boiling mad.

It also had him more paranoid than before, and terribly concerned for Gerri's safety. If he was about to get new orders—like back to Virginia, or even another overseas deployment—then breaking things off with her might be the very best thing for both of them.

He wondered, though, if unseen voyeur spooks were going to be dogging him and all of his girlfriends from now on. His friends. His family. Or would they just arrange for a quick, simple accident, and shut him (and them) up permanently?

Damn it all!

He checked in with Mulvehill's secretary and walked into the office. To his surprise, Mulvehill wasn't there. Instead, it was a two-striper admiral, a rear admiral, who was waiting for him.

"Commander Hunter? Have a seat."

"Sir! Thank you, sir."

"I'm Rear Admiral Kelsey. I'm with . . . let's just say I work for JSOC."

JSOC was the Joint Special Operations Command, the multiple-service umbrella under which all of the US special ops groups served. JSOC's command umbrella included DEVGRU, along with the 75th Rangers, Delta Force, and others.

"Yes, sir." More important, to Hunter's way of thinking, was the big, gaudy Budweiser pinned to the upper left of Kelsey's blue uniform jacket.

The man was a SEAL. Or, rather, he might have been an active SEAL years ago, but been promoted up to senior management. As with the Marines, however, once a SEAL, always a SEAL.

There were no *ex*-SEALs.

What the hell is this about? Did I really fuck things up even loosely talking to Gerri?

Fuck.

Because, the thing was, rear admirals did *not*, in the normal course of duty, have anything to do with mere lieutenant commanders.

"I'm authorized to offer you a new billet—a very *special* billet. And a rather extraordinary deployment."

That didn't sound like he was in trouble. In fact, that sounded interesting. He perked up—if such a thing was possible when in the ramrod straight posture any SEAL would affect in front of top brass.

"Yes, sir. Where are you sending me?"

"I can't tell you that, not yet. What I can say is that it will be a long deployment—probably in excess of two years. And it involves travel. A *lot* of travel."

Hunter considered this. One very real possibility he'd been considering was the classic Navy response to a fuckup, which was to ship him out to someplace remote. So maybe he wasn't out of the woods yet. "Counting penguins in Antarctica" was how such a duty change was phrased in a typical barracks bull session. And while that specific scenario didn't seem very likely, the Navy *did* have a facility on the island of Adak, in the Aleutians—*very* remote, and *very* cold.

No, wait a sec. NAVFAC Adak had been closed in '97. So what else was there?

Kelsey continued. "This assignment will be strictly on a voluntary basis. It will be dangerous, and it may involve combat, though we don't know that for certain at this time."

"I see, sir." Combat was no problem. And danger was already in the job description. It was the secrecy that made Hunter a little cautious—there'd been too much of that in his life recently, and he couldn't help but wonder if the events in North Korea were related to this new assignment. "And you can't tell me about it unless I volunteer, is that it?"

"That's it in a nutshell, Commander."

"Two years?"

"At least—I can't guarantee it won't be longer. I should tell you this, as well: we have already approached several of your men. Two have refused the assignment. Both of them are married, so that's completely understandable and it's no reflection on them. The others say they will volunteer, but only if you sign on as well, as their CO." Kelsey gave Hunter a wry near-grin. "It seems that you inspire considerable loyalty in your people, Commander."

Hunter was thunderstruck at that. His squad was close and tight-knit, but he hadn't realized that his men felt that strongly about it. "I . . . I'll have to think about this, Admiral."

"Of course, of course. Take all the time you want . . . just so long as I have an answer by 0900 hours tomorrow."

"Tomorrow!"

"If you say yes, you'll be shipping out for training tomorrow afternoon."

"What kind of training?"

"Again, I'm not at liberty to say, Commander. It will be extensive and it will be tough, though. Might make SEAL training seem easy in comparison." Hunter shuddered when he heard this, and Kelsey seemed to be at least a bit sympathetic—as sympathetic as a rear admiral could be with a grunt. "That's all you need to know."

"I see. And if I say yes and then wash out?"

"My recommendation? Don't." He seemed amused by the look on Hunter's face. "Don't worry. I have every confidence in you."

"Thank you, sir. Question, Admiral?"

"Shoot."

"Does this have anything to do with the spaceship my men and I saw in North Korea?"

Hunter had expected a neutral or negative answer—something like "Spaceship? What spaceship?" But that was not Kelsey's response.

Instead, he scowled, his expression darkening like a thunderstorm. "Don't you ever, *ever* ask me something like that again, Commander! You are completely out of line!"

"So you know what we saw over there?"

"I'm not at liberty to speak about it, and neither are you. I advise you to keep your thoughts on the subject to yourself. Do *not* make me regret asking you for this assignment."

But the anger inside Hunter surged up and out in a furious blast. "*Sir!* Someone phoned me yesterday and threatened the life of my girlfriend. *That* was what was out of line!" He was shouting, and it was with a bit of struggle that he caught himself and dialed it back. "I'm sorry, sir. But ever since our return from Korea, I have been the subject of rather intensive surveillance, including, evidently, in bed! If my oath isn't enough for you—"

Kelsey was mad, but it didn't seem like it was solely at Hunter's outburst. "Who made the threat? Who did you talk to?"

"Damned if I know. He didn't leave me his fucking name and number."

Kelsey seemed to consider this for a moment, then sighed. "Commander . . . let's play a game of hypotheticals."

Hunter was about to reply that he didn't play games, but stopped the words before they came out of his mouth. This was a damned good time to keep his trap shut. "I'm listening, sir."

"I'm not saying there are, but let's pretend for a moment that there *are* aliens, okay? They've known about humans, have been visiting us, watching us, maybe even interfering with us for a long, *long* time."

"I'm with you so far, sir."

"Now, just hypothetically, let's say that there are more than one group of aliens out there. Like in Star Trek. You have the Federation of good guys. You've got Vulcans, you've got humans, you've got . . . I don't know. Lots of other good guys. But you have others that aren't so good."

"Okay . . ."

"Now, just suppose for the sake of argument, that the bad guys are trying to take over Earth. It's an invasion, but they're being sneaky about it. You see, there aren't many of them, a few million, maybe, but there are seven billion of us. They might have really wizard superweapons, but they're outnumbered at least a thousand to one."

Hunter wasn't ready to admit that a mere difference in numbers would stop aliens who had the technology to cross interstellar distances. "They wouldn't need to be sneaky about it, sir. They just trot out the Death Star and obliterate the planet!"

"That's Star *Wars*, Commander, not Star Trek. Your point is taken, though. With the technology they have, just about anything is possible. But let's just assume, for the sake of argument, that they want to take over the Earth, but they want to have the planet intact. Maybe they want us as slaves. Or, hell, I don't know. For *food*."

"Sounds like your typical scenario for a 1950s sci-fi B movie, Admiral."

Kelsey nodded. "It does, doesn't it? Again, this is all conjecture. But back to our bad guy aliens. They want to invade, but they don't want to kill everyone, and they don't want to blast the entire planet into space rubble, okay? So how would they go about taking over the Earth?"

"Well, if they looked like us, I guess they could infiltrate the government. Infiltrate all the governments of the world."

"And if they didn't look like us?"

"I don't know, Admiral. Too many variables. Could they disguise themselves? Or infiltrate with a few key humans they've brainwashed or something? Use them as Manchurian candidates and slip them in to positions of power, but have them working for the aliens?"

"Bang on the money, Commander."

"But . . . this is all hypothetical, right?"

"Completely. I just want you to understand that not

everyone in the government is on our side. There are . . . elements, let's say, perfectly capable of what you described. Eavesdropping. Blackmail. Strong-arm tactics. Threats. Threats to kill you or your girl or other people close to you. Even actual murder. Make people disappear."

"And might these elements be aligned with various intelligence services?"

"CIA, FBI, DIA—you name it. A lot of our alphabet soup of current government agencies *might* have been compromised. Hypothetically speaking, of course. It wouldn't take much. A few key people at the top, giving the orders."

"Of course."

"So what do you say, Commander?"

"I still need some time to think about it, sir."

"Okay. But I do need your answer ASAP."

"Oh-nine-hundred tomorrow. Yes, sir."

He left, his mind whirling.

HE SPENT the night with Gerri.

"But where are they sending you, Mark?"

They were having dinner together at Top of the Market, a seafood and wine restaurant right on the bay with a fantastic view out over the water. Hunter's paycheck didn't normally stretch to include fine dining—not *this* fine—but he figured he owed a really special night to the girl he was about to dump.

For some reason, the food didn't taste quite as good as he'd expected.

He'd left his cell phone at home, and made a point of asking her to do so, as well. He wasn't going to spill any secrets, but, just in case, he didn't want their dinner interrupted by unpleasant threats or bombast.

He didn't think *They* could have bugged every damned table in every restaurant in San Diego.

"Can't tell you, babe. Because they haven't told *me*."

They'd finished their dinner and were talking over the last of their wine—a good '08 Merlot recommended by the waiter. Hunter had always thought you ordered *white* wine with fish, but apparently a red wine with their seared tuna was the exception to the rule.

"Isn't that kind of strange?" Gerri asked. "I mean, is it usual to send people off and not tell them where they're being sent?"

"Not really. But, well, in *my* line of work, it does happen. Look, you knew this could happen when you hooked up with me, right?"

"That doesn't make this easy, Mark," she said, irritated at his trying to turn this on her.

"I know. I'm sorry."

"And you don't know how long you'll be gone?"

"Uh-uh. But it might be a long time. Gerri . . ." He took a deep breath. "I guess what I'm trying to say . . . this evening is kind of a good-bye."

"I got that. But you make it sound like good-bye forever!"

He swallowed. "It is. I'm sorry . . . but I'm not going to string you along. I don't know when I'll come back. I don't know *if* I'll be back." He shrugged. "That's just the way it is. I'm . . . sorry."

Her lip quivered, and her eyes were luminous with tears, but she didn't cry, not yet. She dabbed at one eye with her napkin. "I thought . . ."

"What? What did you think?"

"That we had something really special together, you and me."

"We do." He'd almost said "we *did*," but he changed the tense from past to present at the last moment because he thought the same thing. "Gerr . . . you'll just have to trust me. I really do care for you and—"

"I love you."

For two months they'd been dancing around the concept of being in love like, well, like the way Gerri danced around her pole. This was the first time she'd said those words, and it hit Mark like a blow to the sternum.

"And I love you." And he meant it, staggered by both that revelation and by what he was truly giving up by saying good-bye. "But I do *not* want you waiting for me."

"Why not? You're worth waiting for!"

He smiled. "I'm glad you think so. But, well . . . you deserve the best, the *very* best. Remember, my wife dumped me because I kept getting deployed overseas. I spent Christmas of '09 sitting on top of a mountain in Afghanistan. The Christmas after that I was helping to train Kurds to kill ISIS bastards in Iraq. You deserve a hell of a lot better than that!"

"So you're afraid I'll treat you like your bitch of an ex?" The almost-tears were fading, replaced by anger.

"I'm afraid I won't be around enough to treat you the way you should be treated."

He didn't add, "And I don't want to be around if that means you might be killed."

But he also didn't tell her that he had a choice. He could tell Kelsey tomorrow that he didn't want to go. But the outcome, he knew, would be the same so far as he and Gerri were concerned. He would be shipped off to the equivalent of Adak. There was some secret stuff going on in Uzbekistan right now, and there were SEALs over there taking part in the fun and games. And even if he just went back to Virginia, he would be gone.

He could imagine her asking to come along. She would be willing to pull up stakes and move across the country to stay with him; he could sense that in her now.

But he suspected that both of them would be looking over their shoulders all the time, half expecting a sniper's bullet . . . or a mysterious brake failure . . . something that would take them both out of the way.

Hunter had been thinking about Kelsey's Star Trek analogy. The bad guys, it seemed, both human and alien, played for keeps.

There was more to it than simple self-preservation, too, *or* protecting Gerri. Kelsey hadn't been able to say much, but what he had said opened up some startling doors.

Hunter *had* seen a spaceship. His debriefing interviews, the way they'd treated him, convinced him that there was not a nice, simple, and purely terrestrial answer to the puzzle. He couldn't prove it, but he'd seen a *real* spaceship, aliens were *here*, and they meant business.

And now, Kelsey's talk about Star Trek politics suggested that the aliens were *not* friendly, did *not* come in peace, that they were interfering in human activities in a big way, and they were ruthless in how they were going about their business. This was no bunch of interstellar tourists stopping by to point and look at the funny humans. They meant to take over.

An invasion . . .

"Well . . . I don't care what you say," she told him. "When you come back Stateside, you look me up, okay? We can pick up where we left off."

He bit back his first answer, then gave a reluctant nod. "Okay. But when I look you up, I'll expect to find you with a husband and six kids, okay?"

"Stripping and cocktailing with six kids? That'll be the day!"

"Not a stripper, remember? An ecdysiast."

"Bastard. When do you ship out?"

"Tomorrow afternoon."

"Damn! So *soon*? Who the hell did you fuck over to catch this shit?"

"Only you, I think."

And *then* she cried.

CHAPTER FOUR

We should think of the craft in the New Mexico desert as more of a time machine than a spacecraft.

DR. HERMANN J. OBERTH [ATTRIBUTED], 1974

9 December 1965

SMOKE FILLED THE *tiny cabin as the vibration increased. Die Glocke was reentering Earth's atmosphere at high velocity, falling with the swollen, bottom end of The Bell facing in the direction of travel, which meant that General Kammler was being pressed back in his narrow seat by what felt like the weight of several people lying on top of him.*

Ssarsk lay strapped into its rack just above him. "What's happening?" Kammler yelled, trying to be heard above the thunder filling the cabin. "What's wrong?"

Nothing wrong. The words formed silently in his head. Slowing to atmospheric velocity.

Kammler wished that there was a window in The Bell so that he could see out. Flying blind like this, locked into a claustrophobic tin can—it was a nightmare.

They'd left der Riese, the secret complex in the Silesian woods, only moments before. At first, there'd been no sensation of movement at all, no sense of acceleration, no noise or vibration. The Bell, though, Ssarsk had told him, was already above the atmosphere and preparing to land.

Then they'd plunged into the atmosphere, and into a nightmare of heat and smoke, of raw noise and unendurable vibration. Would they break up? Burn up? He didn't know. He couldn't trust the alien pilot to tell him what was actually going on. The Eidechse were emotionally remote and inscrutable. The name was German for "lizards," and they did possess a cold, reptilian aspect that Kammler found disturbing.

Or, to be honest, quite frightening.

He tried to distract himself. Twenty years into the future! What would life be like, what would technology be like in that far-off age of 1965? Antigravity? Flying cars? The important thing was that people might have forgotten the excesses of the Third Reich. Not that wiping out the Jews was a bad *thing, but the rest of the world simply didn't understand.*

Nullifiers inoperational, *the pilot thought at him.* Brace yourself.

Brace yourself? In God's name, how?

The weight crushing him increased sharply, then fell away. It felt as though the craft had just changed its heading somewhat, slightly to the left. He wished he understood more about The Bell's technology.

He wished he could see.

He tried to remember everything he could about The Bell. Ssarsk and several of its compatriots had been helping the Nazis for almost a decade. An alien craft had come down in a wooded Bavarian valley in 1936. Of the pilots—bulb-headed, skinny, just over a meter high, with enormous black eyes with no hint of white to them at all—only one had survived, but Ssarsk's compatriots, a different species, had shown up soon thereafter. The Reich was already in the process of studying the wreckage, which was largely complete, hoping to back-engineer the craft.

The Eidechse had offered to help.

And all they'd asked in return was to become silent partners, as it were, in the world government the Reich planned to create.

The Eidechse had contributed incredible levels of knowledge to the Reich's scientists. Von Braun's rocket designs at Peenemünde, the disk-shaped craft being tested at Hauneberg, the new superbomb developed by Kurt Diebner—progress on all of them had been tremendously advanced by the Eidechse visitors. It was one of the brutal ironies of war that the Reich had collapsed mere months before the most powerful of those weapons could be deployed on the battlefield.

The machine referred to by the code name Die Glocke— "The Bell"—had started as an experiment in true antigravity, but the Eidechse had revealed a key fact of long-range space travel: traveling faster than light was *also* traveling in time. *The Jew physicist Einstein had supposedly demonstrated that space and time were the same thing, that translation in one of four dimensions could be turned into translation in another. The Bell, it seemed, was proof of this, despite the fact that Reich science had been working for years to repudiate the theories of Jewish physics.*

Ssarsk had piloted the prototype craft into space, made what it called a dimensional translation, and brought the craft back into Earth's atmosphere.

The only question now was whether they could survive the landing.

That, and what year it would be when they landed.

Another course change, *the pilot thought at him.* Acceleration surged, and again there was a sharp sensation, this time to the right.

The vibration had largely faded away now, and Kammler could hear a rushing sound that he took to be the sound of wind whipping past the hull outside. Smoke continued to fill the compartment, however, and he realized that something must be burning inside the craft.

The Bell slowed almost to a stop, then made a broad, sweeping turn. We land. Brace yourself.

They hit something hard and the vibration returned, the noise a shrill thunder as if the craft was plowing backward through dirt. And then . . .

The stillness, the silence, were eerie. The craft's internal illumination was gone, and they sat there in pitch-black darkness.

We arrive.

"*Did we make it?*" *Kammler started coughing, and finally managed to add,* "*Did we go through time?*"

Unknown. I will find out. *The hatch opened, and cold air spilled inside, clearing the smoke. There was a little light, as well; he saw that it was dark outside, but he could make out the shapes of trees against an overcast sky. It looked as though they'd come down in a wooded area. There were patches of snow on the ground.*

"*Wait!*" *he called as Ssarsk slipped through the open hatch. He struggled with his harness, but couldn't find the clip.* "*Don't leave me!*"

Remain here, *the alien thought at him.* I will be back. *And the hatch hissed shut.*

"*I don't know how to operate the hatch mechanism!*" *Kammler shouted, but there was no mental response.*

Damn!

The Bell had been reconstructed by the SS and by slave workers, but the actual design of the shell and power plant and drive had been alien, and most of the mechanisms and the secrets of how it worked were understood, if at all, by only a few humans—none of whom were Kammler. The aliens had operated it during tests, and it required an alien pilot. Kammler was only now realizing just how dependent he was on the Eidechse's goodwill. He was locked in, with no way out that he could find. Some of the craft's mechanisms, he knew, were actually controlled by thought; Ssarsk had worn a slender circlet around his head that, he presumed, let him operate the craft.

He waited there in the dark for hours.

Something thumped against the outer hull.

He jerked awake. Had he fallen asleep? More thumps and bumps sounded from outside. What was that?

"Ssarsk?" he called.

Now he could hear voices. Physical voices, not the mental transmissions of the alien.

He couldn't make them out, but he could tell from the tone and the lack of gutturals that they were not speaking German.

Was that English? He spoke a little. . . .

The hatch banged open, again admitting the dim light from outside, blinding after hours in the dark. A shape—a human *shape—blocked the entryway as someone leaned inside.*

"General Hans Kammler?" *the shape said.* "Willkommen in Pennsylvania! Und in der Zukunft! Wir haben dich erwartet!"

"Welcome to Pennsylvania and the future! We've been expecting you!"

"Mein Gott! Ich habe es gemacht!"

He'd made it.

THE NEXT afternoon they flew Hunter and five of his men out to Wright-Patt.

The so-called Hangar 18, he was told, was something of a fixture in UFO legend, the place where the Air Force stored crashed saucers and the bodies of diminutive gray aliens. In fact, that was a myth. There *was* no Hangar 18 at the sprawling US Air Force base just outside of Dayton, Ohio.

There was, however, something called "Complex-1B," a sprawling underground facility accessed through a three-story office building and layer upon layer of security checkpoints. And within the complex was "the Blue Room," where some of America's most important secrets were kept hidden from the public eye.

Air Force master sergeant Donald Gilroy was the source of this revelation. Hunter was seated next to the man in the C-17—the same aircraft that had brought him from Japan, in fact—as it droned its way east.

"So, aren't you going to get into trouble talking to us about this?" Hunter asked.

"Nah," Gilroy replied. "You people have all been cleared up to USAP, right?" Unacknowledged Special Access Programs. "You're gonna be hearing a lot of hush-hush stuff at Wright-Patt. I'm just laying the groundwork for you."

In the normal scheme of things, Hunter knew, there were just six levels of security clearance for American military personnel: Restricted, Confidential, Secret, and Top Secret, plus two special classifications—Special Compartmented Information and USAP. There wasn't supposed to be anything above Top Secret, and the UFO whistle-blowers claiming to reveal stuff at "above Top Secret" or higher didn't understand how the US government security classification system worked.

Top Secret, however, *had* been given a great many subcategories, each higher than the one before. Top Secret Crypto encompassed twenty-eight separate levels; the President of the United States, reportedly, was only at level seventeen. And there were higher classifications above TS Crypto 28.

Gilroy wouldn't tell them what his security classification level was. He did tell them that a USAP clearance did not normally allow access to information about UFOs. Special allowances were made, he said, for personnel who were being checked out for higher clearances, a process that would take time.

So during that time, however, Hunter and his five

companions would be given *some* information, with the promise of more to follow.

"What you're telling us," Hunter said slowly, "is that UFOs are *real*? Roswell and all of that?"

"Oh, absolutely," Gilroy replied. "You didn't think otherwise, did you? After what you saw in Korea?"

"No. Not really. There was still some doubt, though."

"That's right," Minkowski said. "There's always room for doubt. We could have all been on our way to a Section Eight!"

Several of the SEALs laughed. *Section Eight* meant being discharged from the service because you were crazy.

"I promise you that all of you are completely sane," Gilroy told them. "The question is whether you'll still be sane after you get a tour of Complex-1B."

"Why?" Taylor asked. "What're we going to see?"

"Ha! You'll find out." But he'd say no more about the facility.

Gilroy did tell them a story, though, about something that had supposedly happened back in the midsixties. Then Senator Barry Goldwater, who'd been the Republican nominee for president in 1964, had had a long-standing fascination for UFOs. A major general in the USAF, a senator from Arizona, and the chairman of the Senate Intelligence Committee, he'd repeatedly tried to gain access to the Blue Room.

In 1994, Goldwater appeared on *Larry King Live* to talk about UFOs. According to him, he'd asked no less a personage than the chief of staff for the US Air Force, General Curtis LeMay, for help in getting into the Blue Room. According to Goldwater, LeMay had gone ballistic. Furiously angry, madder than Goldwater had ever seen him, he'd cussed the senator out, then told him, "Don't you *ever* ask me that question again!"

Someone—quite probably someone not in the regular

chain of command—took secrecy about UFOs very seriously indeed. It seemed that not even the President was
told everything . . . and often he was told nothing.

They touched down at Wright-Patterson and were
driven to a nondescript office building somewhere in the
middle of a forest of hangars, offices, and storage sheds.
They were met in the lobby, just inside an initial security
checkpoint, by an Air Force major named Frank Benedict, who took a clipboard from Gilroy, signed something
on it, and handed it back. It was, Hunter thought, very
much like the chain-of-custody receipt required when
prisoners were transferred from one keeper to another.

Were they prisoners? It was distinctly possible. Hunter
did not imagine for a moment that he could tell Benedict
"so long!" then turn on his heel and walk away.

Benedict took his time looking through a sheaf of orders that had been transmitted to his command. "Lieutenant Commander Mark Hunter?" he asked, looking up.

"Yes, sir."

"Master Chief Arnold Minkowski."

"Present, sir!"

"Chief Roger Brunelli."

"Here, sir."

"EN1 Thomas Taylor."

"Yes, sir."

"RM1 Ralph Colby."

"Yes, sir."

". . . and TM1 Frank Nielson."

"Yessir."

"Okay. You men have received USAP clearance levels,
and I have been directed to show you what is popularly
known as 'the Blue Room.' I will remind you that all
of you have signed security paperwork in which you've
promised not to divulge *anything* that you see here . . .
right?"

A chorus of "yessirs" sounded from the Navy personnel.

"You breathe a word about any of this and you'll be

out on your ears so fast your heads will spin. You'll lose your pensions, your reputations, and even your identities, so no one will believe a thing you say. *And then* you'll spend a minimum of twenty years in Portsmouth for violating the Secrets Act. You all hear me?"

"Yes, sir!"

"Just so that's clear."

Benedict then ushered them down a series of halls, through various twists and turns, with stops at each of an additional five security checkpoints. During the journey, the six men were scanned for metal, photographed, fingerprinted, had their retinas examined, and gave voice prints. Finally, they took an elevator down; Hunter couldn't begin to guess how far down, but it was quite a way. The descent took almost a full minute.

The elevator stopped, the doors slid open, and Hunter and the other SEALs stepped into another passageway with another checkpoint. Here they had their palms scanned and their retinas checked again, before a massive steel door hissed open . . .

. . . and Hunter wondered just how far down the rabbit hole they'd gone.

"TIME TRAVEL," Dr. Lawrence Brody said with an air of utter dismissal, "is bunk."

"Physics says that, does it?" Navy captain Frederick Groton said.

"Exactly. Where would causality be if we could zip back in time and kill our own grandfathers?"

Brody and Groton were in the mess hall of a facility so secret that the government had only recently even admitted that the place existed—despite ample evidence from satellite photos and the unwinking gaze of Google Earth. Area 51 was very, very real. And actively being used.

"My understanding," Groton said slowly, "is that if we changed history somehow, we would simply move over to an alternate time line, one where we had never been born. No paradox. The universe—the multiverse, I should say—would never allow that."

"An entire universe—hundreds of billions of galaxies, quintillions of stars, worlds and civilizations without number, all of it identical to this one, down to the smallest detail *except* for my existence—created in an instant just because I shot dear old Gramps before my father was conceived? The universe is wasteful, Captain, but not *that* wasteful. It certainly doesn't create an entire universe around the absence of one man."

"That, as I understand it, is the basic theory behind the many-universe concept."

"Captain . . . do you have a degree in astrophysics? In cosmology? In quantum dynamics?"

"Of course not."

"Well, I do—all three! And I'm telling you that quantum theory does *not* support so absurd a statement about the nature of the cosmos. How do you summon an entire universe out of nothing? Where does all that matter come from in the blink of an eye? Where is the *energy*, man?"

"I believe the idea," Groton said, "is that this other universe already exists. That, in fact, every universe that could possibly exist *does* exist—including one where your grandfather was regrettably killed as a young man. Not an infinite number, certainly, but a very, very, *very* large number of them. Rather than creating a new universe, a better way to say it might be that you simply step from one reality to another."

"Yes, Captain, I *know*. You needn't lecture me on cosmology."

"That was not my intent, Doctor. But I *am* telling you that time travel is possible. We know it to be true because we've done it."

"Bullshit! Where's your proof?"

Groton melodramatically patted his white uniform jacket. "Damn. I must have left it in my other coat."

"Very funny."

A woman approached the table, holding a tray of food. "Hello, Captain," she said. "May I join you?"

"Of course!" He rose, gesturing to a chair, and Brody managed to get to his feet a moment later. The woman was, simply put, impossibly gorgeous. There was no other word for it. Brody was fifty-five years old, but his hormones were kicking in with all the force and red-faced stammer of a sixteen-year-old adolescent boy. The woman was tall and slender with large and startlingly blue eyes; long silver hair, though her face looked like she was only in her twenties; and a silver jumper or suit of some sort that Brody was prepared to swear was spray painted onto her body.

"*Please* sit, gentlemen," this vision told them.

"Elanna," Groton said, "this is Dr. Brody, our professor of astrophysics on the *Big-H*. Dr. Brody? Elanna."

"A pleasure, Doctor." She extended one slender hand.

Somehow, Brody managed to take the hand, and felt her give it a squeeze.

"We were just discussing time travel, Elanna," Groton said. "Dr. Brody was explaining to me why time travel is impossible."

She laughed. "*Really?* Do tell me!"

Brody's face burned. He had the distinct feeling that both of them were making fun of him. "Well, according to current theory . . ." he began.

"Don't even go there, Professor," Groton told Brody. "You'll lose."

"What do you mean?" He couldn't look away from the silvery beauty sitting next to him.

"Doctor . . ." Groton said, and then he hesitated. There was so much Brody still didn't know, and it was entirely possible that some of it he would never know, never *accept*, if only because his brain was too old and inflexible to wrap itself around some of this stuff. "Dr. Brody," he tried again. "You've been through indoctrination. You know the truth, or a large part of it. You've seen some things that, for most people, would be very hard to believe."

"Yes."

"You've seen the Grays—"

"Yes, yes! Horrible things! What's your point?"

"Elanna here is . . ." He paused, trying to find the right way to explain it. He settled on, "A kind of alien. Alien to us, at any rate."

"But she's human!"

"Indeed. I'm as human as you are, Doctor," the woman said. She smiled, and Brody felt the rush of hormones once more.

"Elanna," Groton continued, "*is* human, but she's from the future. She's from roughly eleven thousand years in the future, in fact."

"My God!" And the shock jolted him backward and knocked him out of his chair.

"A *SPACESHIP!*" Taylor said with an edge of sheer reverence in his voice. "A fucking alien *spaceship!*"

"Actually," Benedict said, "it's one of ours."

Hunter gave Benedict a sharp look. "So we *do* have advanced spacecraft?"

"For a good many years, Commander, yes. That is a TR-3B, and it's one reason we no longer have a space shuttle."

The craft was large—at least twenty-five yards wide, and it was shaped like an equilateral triangle with slightly rounded tips. Three landing legs held it a couple of yards above the concrete flooring of the immense room, and there were several technicians working on, around, and under the ship's body. Cables as thick as a man's leg snaked across the floor and vanished into ports on the thing's belly, while light spilled from an open hatch at the top of a long ramp. Three red lights glowed with sullen brilliance on the underside, one within each of the triangle's corners. A larger light was nestled into a recession at the underside's center, but it was not on at the moment. The hull had a matte finish, like black rubber. Hunter wondered why it wasn't polished silver, like the disk he'd seen.

Benedict led them past the looming spacecraft, though Hunter was itching to go on board. "A good many years," Benedict had said. How many years? How long had these things been flying?

"Some of you gentlemen might remember a flurry of UFO cases back in 1989, 1990, in Belgium, and out over the North Sea? Big black triangles like this one. That was us."

At least twenty-five, then. Jesus.

There were other craft stored in that subterranean hangar.

On the southern edge of Wright-Patt, Hunter knew, was the National Museum of the US Air Force. Born and raised in Dayton, Ohio, Hunter had practically lived in the place when he was growing up. This hangar was like that . . . huge and open and filled with artifacts straight out of the history of flight. The biggest difference seemed to be that this museum was not open to the public . . . and the fact that it seemed to be devoted to alien spacecraft recovered from around the world.

The craft came in all shapes and sizes, though most were saucer shaped, with silvery hulls. Many were in fragments and might have been anything. Small tags on display stands identified each. The one labeled "Roswell, New Mexico, July 1947" had had its hemispherical undercarriage shredded into fragments, many of which were spread out on several nearby tables.

"I didn't think you'd have these things on display," Hunter said.

"They're not, really. We keep them here so that our technicians and xenotech people have ready access to them. We've been collecting these things for decades, and we're still learning from them. You've heard of

Roswell, of course. . . ." He stopped, then gestured at a battered, burned, and rusty-brown-looking craft in one corner. It was an acorn shape, perhaps twelve feet wide and fifteen high.

"That's from the Roswell crash, sir?" Minkowski asked.

"No. Roswell is over there. This one is a particularly interesting craft called Die Glocke—'The Bell.' It was being constructed in Nazi Germany at the end of the war, when it mysteriously vanished, along with an SS officer named Hans Kammler, who was heading the research team. We recovered it outside of a small town in Pennsylvania twenty years later."

"Kecksburg!" Nielson exclaimed. "I read about that."

Benedict nodded.

"What's this writing around the base?" Brunelli asked. The swollen base of the craft showed a continuous line of angular markings—triangles and circles and straight lines and a wealth of other geometric figures crowded together one after another.

"Alien writing, of course. We're still trying to decipher it."

"So the Germans didn't build it?" Taylor asked.

"They reconstructed it," Benedict said. "We think it was from a crash *they* retrieved in Bavaria back in the late thirties. We also think they had some help in the reconstruction. *Alien* help."

Hunter was doing some math in his head, and it didn't add up. "You're saying," he said, "that the Nazis had *time travel*?"

"Yup. At least they managed to send this pod twenty years into the future, where it crashed a second time. We had an idea that it was coming, though, and we had a special response team ready to go in and pick it up."

"Yeah, but *time travel*?" Minkowski said. "That's wild-assed Hollywood stuff."

"Maybe so, but that doesn't mean it's not possible. You

see, gentlemen, it turns out that if you have the technology to travel between the stars, you also have the ability to travel in time. Einstein pointed that out. Space and time are part of the same thing—what Einstein called 'space-time.' Bend and twist one, and you bend and twist the other. So, apparently, the Galaxy is brimming over with life and civilizations that have spread out to fill space . . . *and time*."

"That's . . . incredible," Hunter said. He took a closer look at The Bell. A hatch in the side was open—it looked like it had been pried open with brute force. Inside there were two wire-frame seats with canvas straps, one considerably larger than the other. "Two passengers?"

Benedict nodded. "Hans Kammler . . . and another."

"What happened to them?"

"I'm not at liberty to say, Commander."

Hunter nodded understanding, but privately suspected that Benedict didn't know himself. The information would be more highly classified than USAP clearance, and might even be beyond Benedict's reach.

"Sir . . ." Hunter began, then stopped. He wasn't sure how to formulate the question.

"Go ahead. If I can tell you, I will."

"Yes, sir. Why all the secrecy? Why not just tell people that we have time travelers from space . . . and have known about them for years? I mean, people have been seeing them since God knows when. The public *knows*. Why try to keep it hidden?"

"Good question, Commander, but one with a very complicated answer. Back in January of 1953, the Intelligence Advisory Committee commissioned the Robertson Panel, which looked into the problem of UFOs. Were they really alien? More, were they a threat? There'd been a nasty scare the previous July, when hundreds of unidentified targets were tracked in the skies above Washington DC. The Robertson Panel concluded that UFOs posed no immediate threat to the US, but *did* warn that public sightings might cause military communications networks to be overwhelmed. They also warned that full disclosure might have dire consequences. Religions might collapse, once people learned that these alien visitors had had a hand in creating *Homo sapiens*. The stock market might collapse, people might riot in the streets, or succumb to mass hysteria, people would lose faith in government. Basically, civilization itself might fall."

"Orson Welles," Hunter said. "*War of the Worlds*."

"Precisely. So the panel suggested that the public not be told more, that the government push educational programs aimed at defusing the situation: discrediting people who claimed they saw them, trotting out skeptical experts to debunk sightings, that sort of thing. The whole issue was put under a very tight lid of not just secrecy, but *compartmentalized* secrecy. Even if you knew all about 'A,' if you didn't have a serious need to know about 'B,' you didn't *hear* about 'B.' Period."

"Ha!" Nielson said. "I *knew* there was something fishy about all the official denials."

"Weather balloons and swamp gas," Taylor added. "Ri-i-i-i-ight. . . ."

"I still don't see why things are still classified, though," Hunter insisted. "I mean . . . in the 1950s, sure. We didn't know if the Russians might be snooping with some sort of high-tech aircraft, or whatever. Better to keep stuff like that under wraps. But today? People are used to the idea of aliens and spaceships, and they're mostly cool with it! *Star Trek*, and all of that. . . ."

"The Robertson Panel did recommend a *slow* process toward eventual disclosure. Certain government agencies were tasked with making certain that only pieces, only *safe* pieces, were released, a little at a time. There were some movies that came out in the '80s designed to accustom the public to benevolent, odd-looking aliens, for instance. That was actually quite deliberate. More recently, you have documentary-style programs talking about ancient aliens possibly tinkering with the human genome. . . ."

"The guy with the hair," Minkowski said.

"Among others. The point was to *gradually* acclimate the public to the idea of aliens. In any case, it wasn't just the notion that there were space-traveling aliens to worry about that was being suppressed. It was something far more deadly."

"What would that be?" Hunter asked.

"The knowledge that many of those aliens—many, but not all—weren't aliens at all."

"Come again?"

"They are humans—time-traveling humans—humans from our own remote future."

CHAPTER FIVE

These babies are huge, sir . . . enormous! Oh,
God, you wouldn't believe it! I'm telling you there
are other spacecraft out there . . . lined up on the
farside of the crater edge! They're on the Moon
watching us. . . .

NEIL ARMSTRONG,
FIRST MAN ON THE MOON [ATTRIBUTED], 1969

20 July 1969

FRANK WHEATON SAT *in the lounge just off the floor of
Houston's Mission Control Center, watching the grainy
black-and-white images bearing the legend "Live from
the Moon" on the monitor in the corner. A few hours before, the* Eagle *landing module of Apollo 11 had touched
down on the lunar surface, and for the first time a human
was about to walk on the face of another world.*

*Or was it really the first time? There were hints other-
wise. And there were those strange-looking shapes and
anomalies photographed from lunar orbit. Somebody
had already been there, though the evidence was carefully being kept secret. The Russians? Aliens? An ancient
human civilization? There was no telling.*

*Perhaps those two men up there on the Sea of Tran-
quility would be able to shed some light on that.*

He turned to the other man in the lounge with him, a

pale, skinny guy in a bad-fitting suit. "So how does it feel to be a part of history in the making, Hans?"

Hans Kammler—formerly SS Obergruppenführer *Hans Kammler—shifted uncomfortably in his soft-cushioned chair. "I have not had much to do with this program," he said in heavily accented English. He'd been working hard on learning the language since his arrival.*

Wheaton waved aside the protest. "Nonsense. You've been advising us on the psychology and the attitude of the Saurians—what you call Eidechse—haven't you? And if the aliens make contact with us while we're on the Moon, you're here to serve as a liaison. Believe me, we didn't dare put our people up there without having an idea of what we could expect from our visitors."

Despite his mild, even friendly tone with Kammler, Wheaton despised the man. The son of a bitch was an unrepentant Nazi, one of the worst, personally responsible for the deaths of thousands of slave laborers, an architect of Auschwitz, a monster in human form. Other German scientists, like von Braun, claimed they'd been forced to join the SS—and for whatever that was worth, were at least outwardly repentant—but Kammler had been proud *of what he was and what he'd done.*

Wheaton was a case officer with the CIA, and as such he'd been Kammler's escort, his "keeper," since that oddly shaped craft had come down in the woods outside of Kecksburg just three and a half years ago. Kammler had been folded in with the Paperclip personnel, the German scientists brought back to the US at the end of the war to help advance America's missile program, but his role had been very different.

Thanks to Paperclip, the US had put up its first satellite in 1958, developed its first ICBM in 1959, and put Alan Shepard into space in 1961. The real star of Paperclip, of course, was Wernher von Braun, who'd run the Nazi V-2 missile program at Peenemünde. It was von

Braun, more than any other single person, who was responsible for creating the massive Saturn V rocket that had just put two men on the face of the Moon.

But when they'd pulled Hans Kammler from The Bell in 1965, MJ-12 had decided that he would be an important asset in dealing with the aliens. According to Kammler's story, Germany had made contact with them as far back as 1933 . . . and quite possibly earlier than that. They'd formed an alliance with them in 1939, after finding The Bell crashed in southern Germany and capturing its pilot. That pilot had established contact with its own people, and Hitler had signed a treaty with them not long after.

And with the aliens' technological assistance, the Nazis had damned near won the war.

THE SIX SEALs sat at their desks in a classroom, complete with blackboard and wooden floorboards. A poster on the wall had been pulled from the old television program *The X-Files*—a flying saucer above the trees, with the words *I Want to Believe* underneath in bold capitals.

It seemed odd to have such a pedestrian room buried deep within Wright-Patt's Complex-1B. But after even a few days, Hunter was coming to expect strange was the norm here.

Five other men were there with them besides Major Benedict—two from the Army's Delta Force, one Army Ranger, and two from the CIA's SAD/SOG direct action group. Hunter was surprised by the latter. Lieutenant Dorschner and Captain Arch seemed tough, professional, and no-nonsense, but Hunter definitely had been getting the idea of late that the Central Intelligence Agency was a part of the problem—the "bad guys," as Admiral Kelsey had put it.

SAD/SOG stood for Special Activities Division/Special Operations Group, with SOG being one of several groups under SAD. They were responsible for those covert military operations from which the US government wanted to distance itself. One of the most secretive of all US direct action groups, they were the action arm of the CIA's Directorate of Operations. Hunter hoped that these two guys had been well vetted.

"Gentlemen," Benedict said from the front of the room. "In the past day or two, you've learned that UFOs are real, that aliens are here, and that while some of these visitors are friendly, others decidedly are not. Today, you will learn about a program called Solar Warden, and about America's secret space fleet."

Benedict launched right in, starting with some broad strokes about what those in the room probably knew . . . or at least, thought they knew.

Those stories about the government recovering crashed flying saucers—true. Many of them, at any rate. Stories about US scientists reverse engineering alien technology—also true. Some of it. And newly emerged stories of a secret US space program, complete with antigravity starships that would make Captain Kirk envious—very true indeed.

There was also a ton of disinformation mixed in with the truth, however, not to mention so-called fake news and outright hoaxes, scams, and lies. That made understanding the situation harder than Hunter had expected.

In 2002, a British sysadmin and hacker named Gary McKinnon had carried out what US officials called "the biggest military computer hack of all time." He'd been looking, he'd claimed, for evidence of antigravity, free energy, and a UFO cover-up . . . and, evidently, he'd found all three. Among the data lifted from ninety-seven NASA and DOD computers, along with photos, had been lists of ship names, fleet transfers, and "nonterrestrial officers."

According to McKinnon, the United States had been operating a secret space fleet since 1980, and there were some wide-eyed stories of covert bases on the Moon and Mars, and even of journeys to other star systems.

Ultimately, he was caught and someone pulled the plug. Had he been extradited to the United States, he would have faced seventy years in prison, but extradition was blocked by the British government, and, ultimately, all charges were dropped.

"A lot of what McKinnon claimed is not true," Benedict told them. "The fact of the matter is that he probably didn't know what he was looking at. But the leak was serious, and the government has been scrambling to close things up again.

"But the truth is, we *do* have a secret fleet, we do have regular access to space, and we do have a base on the farside of the Moon. We also, for the record, have a secret treaty with the aliens we call the Ebens—that's EBE Grays."

"EBE" stood for "Extraterrestrial Biological Entities," and it was the cumbersome tag put on the diminutive aliens found in the wreckage of the craft at Roswell. In popular speculation, they were simply called the "Grays," but Benedict warned them that there were several similar species out there with vastly different agendas.

"There are probably tens of thousands of intelligent species scattered throughout our Galaxy," Benedict told them, pressing a hidden control that flipped the central section of the blackboard over, revealing a projection screen. "Three are regular visitors to Earth, and maintain outposts either on or near our planet. Lights!"

The room lights dimmed, and Hunter realized that there were others nearby watching them. Surveillance of the student group, he thought, was probably continuous.

He was starting to get used to the idea, and that worried him.

On the screen was the projected photograph in high-definition of a man and a woman, apparently completely human, both attractively so. They wore silvery close-fitting suits; the woman had long hair so blond it was white, the man light brown; the one distinctive feature of both were eyes that seemed to Hunter to be slightly larger than typical of humans.

"We call these the 'Nordics,'" Benedict told them. "They're not actually aliens. They're from Earth, but from about eleven thousand years in the future. They offered us a treaty in 1954, but President Eisenhower refused it. They were responsible for various contact reports from the '50s, in which they told a number of people that our atomic testing was a threat to the Galaxy and we had to give up our nukes.

"Now obviously, we could blow the shit out of our planet and it wouldn't have the least effect on Mars, to say nothing of the worlds around other stars. But it turns out they were right about the nuclear threat. They're time travelers. If we destroy ourselves, they cease to exist. *Poof!* They were—they *are*—understandably worried about that."

The Nordics were replaced by another image—the familiar shape of an alien Gray. Spindly, delicate, with an enormous head and large, black eyes, they were the creatures Hunter had always thought of as the archetypical alien visitor.

"The EBE Grays, as I said, were the pilots of the Roswell craft. They're probably the most common of our various alien visitors. They showed up at Holloman Air Force Base in 1955 and they *did* sign a treaty with Eisenhower, one in which they said they would give us technological help in exchange for permission to abduct some of our citizens. Much later we realized it was a devil's bargain. In their eyes, we're not much more than cattle. Our best information suggests they're from a star system called Zeta Reticuli, about forty light-years from Earth."

The EBE was replaced by another photo. It was much like the Gray, but in some ways was markedly different. The face was more pinched, almost insect-like, and where the Gray had had a tiny, thin-lipped mouth, this one's head seemed extended in a kind of blunt snout with a prominent mouth. The skin showed a suggestion of iridescent scales, and the creature seemed to be taller than the Gray, as well. The eyes were smaller, and they were golden, with vertically slit pupils, like a snake's.

"And these," Benedict said, "are the Saurians. Some call them 'Reptilians' or 'Dracos.' In the popular mythology they're supposed to be from the constellation Draco, in the circumpolar skies of the northern hemisphere. That much is nonsense, of course. So *very* convenient to have reptilian aliens hailing from the constellation of 'the dragon.' Cute, right?

"But constellations are simple groupings of stars as seen from Earth, and the different stars of any given group are at wildly different distances from us and for the most part have nothing to do with one another. Unfortunately, that means we don't know where these guys are from. But the stuff about Draco is almost certainly deliberate disinformation on their part.

"In any case, these are the bad guys. The Grays call them 'Malok.' They claim Earth belongs to them, and they're working behind the scenes to make that so. Both the Nordics and the EBE Grays appear to be at war with them, though some kind of convention or diplomatic understanding keeps them from actively shooting at each other near our planet. That wasn't always the case. Some descriptions of nuclear weapons in the *Mahabharata* date back several thousand years, and a famous woodcut of a UFO battle in the skies over Nuremberg from 1561 probably represents battles in that war. They've been fighting each other for a *long* time.

"Back in the early '80s, President Reagan made the decision to face the aliens on their own terms. With help from both the Nordics and the EBEs, we began construction of a space fleet. For forty years or so, we've been pushing out into space, into the solar system, in order to confront the Saurians and demonstrate to them that we are *not* primitives, *not* push-overs, that we can stand up and fight for ourselves.

"And that, gentlemen, is why we've brought you here. We want each of you for what we're calling the Interstellar Fleet Marine Force." He grinned at them. "Welcome aboard!"

20 July 1969

Wheaton and Kammler continued watching the live transmissions from the Moon.

"Ah!" Wheaton said. "He's coming down now!"

Armstrong had lowered a television camera on the outside of the lander moments before, and could be seen now descending the ladder with a curious, floating, step-by-step hopping movement in the low lunar gravity. He reached the bottom and paused for a moment. "I'm at the foot of the ladder. The LM pads are only depressed in the surface about one or two inches, although the surface appears to be very, very fine grained as you get close to it. It's almost like a powder down there. It's very fine."

Armstrong moved back off the lander.

He was on the surface.

"That's one small step for man . . . one giant leap for mankind."

Wheaton puzzled over the statement for a moment. The context sounded as though it should have been "one small step for a man . . ." but he hadn't heard the "a." There was a lot of static on the live feed, however, so maybe he'd just missed it.

For nine minutes, the two men watched Armstrong moving about on the lunar surface, watched him pick up a contingency sample of dust, then watched Colonel Edwin "Buzz" Aldrin come down the lander steps and join him.

"We've actually put people on the Moon," Wheaton said, his voice soft, even reverential.

78 IAN DOUGLAS

"Ja," *Kammler said. "But I'm not so sure we'll be allowed to stay."*

They watched for minutes more, as Armstrong and Aldrin bounced around in the eerie slow motion of one-sixth Earth's gravity. Half an hour after Armstrong had set foot on the surface, they unveiled a plaque attached to the lander's leg.

Armstrong read the words engraved on it.

"Here men from the planet Earth first set foot upon the Moon, July 1969 AD. We came in peace for all mankind."

On the monitor, both astronauts had turned, as if to look at something off-screen. "Switching to medical channel," *a voice said from Mission Control. Wheaton leaned closer. The voice transmission appeared to have been cut off. A malfunction? Or else Armstrong wanted to say something that the entire listening world couldn't, or* shouldn't *hear. . . .*

"What's there?" *the voice of Mission Control said.* "Mission Control, calling Apollo 11. . . ."

He caught a long burst of static, then heard Armstrong's voice on the secure channel.

"These babies are huge, sir . . . enormous! Oh, God, you wouldn't believe it! I'm telling you there are other spacecraft out there . . . lined up on the farside of the crater edge! They're on the Moon watching us. . . ."

"We copy," *Mission Control replied.* "Tell us exactly what you see."

"Two spacecraft, sir! They're silver, reflecting the sunlight . . . and they're big! Enormous! Forty . . . maybe fifty feet across . . ."

"So," Wheaton asked the SS officer. "Friends of yours?"

"I do not know, Mr. Wheaton. It may be. Or it could be the others. The time travelers."

"Well, it's certainly a historic moment, our first step

on the Moon. Makes sense that time travelers might be here to witness it?"

Kammler didn't reply. His eyes were wide, however, and held a sudden expression of sheer, stark terror, eyes bugging out, mouth open.

And then the German collapsed.

"SO . . . WHATCHA think, Skipper?" Brunelli asked. "Are we gonna join Battlestar Galactica?"

They were sitting together in a base cafeteria, a mess hall open to both officers and enlisted personnel. Supper was a choice of meatloaf or rather sad-looking fish. They'd been told in no uncertain terms that they would not be allowed off base; oaths and promises of prison hard-time if they broke them notwithstanding, the powers that were didn't seem inclined to trust them.

Which was fine with Hunter. He didn't trust *them*.

"At this point, Chief, I'm not sure what options we have. I think we know too much."

"Yeah," Colby said. "We get out of line . . ." He drew his finger sharply across his throat. *"Ssschk!"*

"Shit, man," Taylor said. "They gotta let us go *sometime*."

"Yeah," Nielson agreed. "At least they could let us go on liberty."

"You guys mind if I join you?" a soft voice asked.

It was John Dorschner, one of the SAD/SOG men, standing beside their table with a tray in his hands.

"Help yourself, Lieutenant," Hunter said, gesturing at an empty chair. "It's a free country. At least for the most part."

Dorschner sank into the offered seat.

Hunter studied the man closely. He was in his thirties, rugged looking, and dressed in nondescript camo battle dress, with no rank insignia and no unit patches. If he didn't trust this secret space fleet, he trusted anyone connected with the CIA less.

But Dorschner might have information they could use.

"How long have you been in this dog and pony show?" Hunter asked.

"Three weeks. They've had me on ice while they rounded up more personnel."

"Where were you stationed before that?"

Dorschner's hard, gray eyes flicked up to look at Hunter, then at Brunelli and the others.

"I was *stationed* at Bragg," he said carefully. "But I was in the field when they pulled me in."

"Yeah?" Minkowski said. "Where was that, sir?"

"Can't say."

Hunter nodded. Fort Bragg, North Carolina, was the headquarters for USSOCOM, the US Special Operations Command. Technically, there was considerable tension between USSOCOM and the CIA's Directorate of Operations, but most of the turf-war squabbles were confined to the political heads of the agencies in question. The actual operators worked smoothly together, and probably shared personnel from time to time. It had been a joint SAD/USSOCOM operation that had found and captured Osama bin Laden, for example.

If Dorschner had been at Bragg, he'd probably been teamed with USSOCOM elements for a special—and highly secret—op. And Dorschner was right not to talk about it, even with the six SEALs gathered at the table.

"Where you from, Lieutenant?" Hunter asked him.

Dorschner hesitated, as though thoroughly studying the question for possible booby traps. "Oklahoma," he said at last. "Little town just outside Tulsa."

A country boy, then. Middle America and the wide-open spaces. Probably red-state conservative politically. Probably religious.

And probably as mistrustful of big government as Hunter was right now.

"How about you?"

"Dayton," Hunter said.

"Yeah?" Dorschner said, a mumble around a forkful of meatloaf. "This is a homecoming for you, huh?"

"Not so far. Liberty ashore's been canceled."

"Liberty ashore? Oh, you mean a twenty-four-hour pass."

"That's right," Minkowski said. "And the floor is a *deck*, the wall is a *bulkhead*, and the bathroom is the *head*."

"Cut the guy some slack, Master Chief," Hunter said. "He doesn't live in *our* world."

"What world do you spooks live in?" Brunelli asked.

"The *real* one. The floor is a *floor* . . . and I do not talk shop, okay?"

"Fair enough, Lieutenant," Hunter said. "We're just looking for some common ground, okay? They're folding us together into some kind of combat team, right?" He waved a hand, taking in the SEALs to his left and right. "We're a team. We've been together for a long time, and we've been in some tight spots together. We know we can count on one another, no matter what. If you're part of our team, we need to know you a little better, is all."

Dorschner considered this. "Yes, *sir*." The emphasis on the word made it something just shy of an insult. "I imagine we'll sort all of that out in training."

"Training," Minkowski said. "Right. When is that supposed to start, anyway?"

"Tomorrow morning," Dorschner said, "bright and early, at zero-dark-thirty."

FREDERICK GROTON walked into the elevator and spoke the level he wanted. "Sub-five." Speech-recognition software both took him to his floor and provided yet another security check. Not everyone working in S4 had clearance to the deeper levels.

Like its more famous neighbor, Area 51, Section 4 was home to some closely guarded secrets. A little information had slipped out with the Bob Lazar leaks back in

1989, but the damage had been contained and Lazar had been discredited, meaning there was much less scrutiny here than on Area 51. Built into the side of the Papoose Mountains fifteen miles south of the Area 51 runways, S4 was the primary research facility for the investigation of extraterrestrials and their technology.

The door slid open, and he stepped into the room known as Deep Blue.

As at Wright-Patt's Blue Room, there were alien spacecraft here. The various alien species visiting Earth, Groton reflected, had been terribly careless with their ships, which crashed with disconcerting frequency. The earliest known crash in US history had actually taken place in Aurora, Texas, back in 1897; the first *recovery* of a downed saucer had been in 1941, at Cape Girardeau, Missouri. Witnesses had seen alien bodies and been sworn to secrecy by the military. That saucer now was spread out in pieces in Deep Blue, and technicians continued to disassemble it and glean data from the wreckage decades later. The Cape Girardeau crash had been particularly useful in studies of gravitomagnetics, one of several alien applications of antigravity.

"Hey, beautiful," Groton called as he walked up behind a young woman standing by a table covered by small technological bits and pieces. A laptop next to her was displaying complicated electrical schematics. "What's cooking?"

Dr. Ellen Michaels turned and arched an eyebrow at him. "Your balls will be cooking if you keep up with that chauvinist bullshit. And where the hell have you been? Rudy has been screaming his head off at me all morning, looking for you."

"I was checking up on Dr. Brody. He's in the base dispensary, recovering. They say he's fine, just a slight concussion. I guess he had a bit of a . . . shock."

"You and that Elanna bitch did kind of run over him with a bus. What the hell were you two thinking?"

"I thought he could take it. And the CAG wanted him brought into the fold as fast as possible."

CAG stood for Command Authority Group, and it represented the tier of officers and high-ranking officials immediately under the fabled committee known as MJ-12. Groton had to suppress an interior wince each time he heard the term. He'd served for a time on aircraft carriers, the oceangoing kind, where the CAG was something quite different. The Solar Warden carriers had CAGs—the original kind—as well.

"Brody is a fossilized old fart," Michaels said, "who couldn't wrap his brain around an internal combustion engine, much less antigravity."

"His problem was with time travel, actually."

"Worse yet. Temporal displacement is pure magic and therefore impossible, so far as he's concerned. Tell him magic is real and he'll have a conniption. Or faint."

"C'mon, it wasn't so bad, Ell. He fell out of his chair and bumped his head, is all."

"Sounds like a real asset. And why is he being 'brought into the fold,' as you put it?"

"CAG wants to put him on *Big-H* for Excalibur. He's probably the best astrophysicist we have right now."

"You do know, Fred, that the more people in the fold, the harder it will be to keep things under wraps."

"Hurray. I would *love* seeing Full Disclosure!"

"Okay, me, too," she conceded, "but speeding the process is a great way to terminate a promising career."

"Or a way to advance it. It doesn't matter," he said, staving off more arguments, "it's already done. So, anything interesting here?"

"Not really. We pretty much have gravitomagnetics down solid. Enough so that we're starting to leak it deliberately to outsiders."

He nodded. "I saw the papers out of the ESA. They've reported measuring the gravitational equivalent of a magnetic field. When was that?"

"March of 2006," she said. "They've made some new advances since."

"While we sail to the stars on fleet carriers."

She shrugged. "It's a step in the right direction." She shook her head. "But we're not going to get much more out of poking through debris. We'll need double-A sistance if we're going to take this any further."

The phrase was a humorous in-house code phrase at S4. It stood for "alien assistance."

"That," Groton said carefully, "could be difficult. Not to mention risky."

She smiled sweetly. "You knew the job was dangerous when you took it, Super Chicken!"

Groton grinned and nodded. He'd never seen the late-'60s cartoon show, but the quote was a long-running gag between him and Ellen.

He'd just never imagined that the silly line could hit so close to home.

CHAPTER SIX

They (The Disclosure Project) are some very credible, relied-upon people, all saying yes, there is UFO
technology, there's antigravity, there's free energy,
and it's extraterrestrial in origin and [they've] captured spacecraft and reverse engineered it.

GARY MCKINNON, BRITISH HACKER, 2001

20 February 1955

AIR FORCE ONE *descended from a cloudless sky to touch
down gently on the runway at Holloman Air Force Base
in New Mexico. It was almost exactly one year since his
unsettling meeting with humanoid aliens at Muroc; now,
he'd been told, a different group of aliens wanted to meet
with him . . . and this time they weren't demanding that
the United States relinquish its nuclear weaponry in exchange for technology.*

What this group wanted was worse. Far worse.

*"The pilot has ordered the tower to switch off their ra-
dar, Mr. President," his aide told him. Eisenhower nodded. That had been according to the protocol worked out
with the aliens by radio a week ago.*

*"And there they are, Mr. President," Sherman Adams
said from a window seat on the opposite side of the aisle.
"Right on time!"*

"Then I'd better get out there," Eisenhower said. Ad-

ams opened his mouth to speak, and Eisenhower put up his hand. "Can it, Sherm! I met them last time, I'll meet with them this time. Alone. Those were the stipulations."

Three disks had appeared in the skies over Holloman. One had touched down just two hundred feet from Air Force One's exit ladder. The other two hung suspended in the sky, perhaps keeping watch. These craft were different from the others he'd seen at Muroc, larger, thicker, rounder on top and bottom. Well, this was supposed to be a different race, right? Once again, the President of the United States made the long and lonely walk across the tarmac to meet with visitors from God knew where.

One of the aliens was waiting for him at the top of the disk's extended ramp, and Eisenhower suppressed the jolt of revulsion. He'd seen these aliens before; they were identical to the occupants of the craft that had come down in Roswell—large heads with enormous black eyes. He'd seen the bodies in a storage freezer at Wright Airfield a few months ago. At the entryway to the spaceship, he touched fingertips with the creature, and felt its thoughts in his head.

Welcome, President. You are welcome here. . . .

For forty-five minutes, Eisenhower spoke with the aliens . . . or, rather, he sat in a too-small seat and listened to their thoughts as they rose, unbidden, in his mind. He responded, and asked questions, speaking aloud.

He honestly wasn't certain they were understanding him. Their answers to his questions were oblique.

You will sign this instrument, *the taller, paler gray alien who Eisenhower thought must be the leader told him.* We know your people give such agreements great importance.

"And if I don't? My God, man—you are asking me for permission to abduct our citizens!"

I am not a "man," and I do not understand what you mean by your "God," *the being told him, the mental voice cold and unemotional.* We have already explained that they will be returned unharmed, and with no memory of what has happened.

"I can't—"

President, if you want access to our technology you will sign this instrument, *the being thought at him.* If not, we will deal with others of your kind who will give us what we require. We have learned that the Soyuz Sovetskikh Sotsialisticheskikh Respublik is quite interested in signing such documents with us. *Da?*

The name of America's Cold War enemies, in perfect Russian, shocked Eisenhower to the core. He'd refused the first offered treaty because it would have left America defenseless against the Soviets, who now possessed the hydrogen bomb. How much worse would it be to step aside and watch the Soviet Union win absolute domination over the planet because they had access to the super science of these enigmatic beings, and America did not?

The Soviets, he thought, would not hesitate to allow these beings to kidnap their citizens.

"The people you take . . . they will be returned?"

Yes.

"And you will tell us who you take? So we can check on their safety?"

Yes.

A document materialized, dreamlike, out of nothing, hanging in the air before Eisenhower. It laid out the details of the agreement as five concisely written and bulleted paragraphs.

- *Humans will not be involved in alien matters, and aliens will not be involved with human affairs. Aliens will not support the United States against Russia . . . at least directly.*

- *Aliens will assist US scientists and technicians with certain unspecified advanced technologies.*

- *Aliens will not make any kind of treaty with any other nation on Earth.*

- *Aliens will be permitted to abduct a few humans a year for certain genetic experiments. Aliens will return them unharmed. Aliens will provide a list of names of those taken to the MJ-12 committee.*

- *The people of Earth will not be told about the presence of extraterrestrials by either the Aliens or the American government.*

Eventually, Eisenhower signed. He could find no other solution; at all costs, the secrets of craft such as this one had to be kept from the Russians. To do otherwise meant the Soviets would dominate the Earth, perhaps as puppets of these creatures. That it meant sacrificing Americans, even only momentarily, hit him to the core.

He'd already sacrificed enough brave men in his years as general and commander in chief.

But, like then, he had no choice.

Slowly he made his way back to Air Force One, belatedly realizing that he'd left his hat on board the alien craft. He was not *going to go back for it.*

It was a humbling, an utterly humiliating, *encounter.*

HUNTER WATCHED the movie, shot in color on an eight-millimeter camera back in 1955. The President's plane was parked out on the tarmac, while the cameraman was presumably in the control tower, almost a quarter of a mile away. There was no sound, and the whir of an old-fashioned projector filled the auditorium.

Three glowing disks swept in from the northwest, hovered, and then one detached from the formation and touched down close beside Air Force One. A few moments later, a solitary man descended from the passenger plane, and walked across to the grounded disk.

"He actually gave the Grays permission to abduct humans?" Hunter asked, incredulous.

"He did," Benedict said. "Don't think badly of him, though. The aliens were quite clear that if he didn't deal with them, they would go help the Russians. This was the height of the Cold War, remember, and the Russians were already ahead of us in missile technology. In another year, Khrushchev would tell a group of Western ambassadors at a reception in Moscow 'we will bury you.' In two more years they would launch Sputnik . . . while our rockets blew up on their launch pads. The military and the CIA both were desperate to stop the Russians at any cost. Eisenhower had to go along."

"That's awful," Taylor exclaimed.

"My God . . ." Brunelli added.

"He was told the aliens would only abduct a few of our people each year," Benedict continued. "He took them at their word. Over the next few years, however, they drastically increased the pace of their operations. We estimate now that somewhere between 1 and 2 percent of all Americans have been abducted—many of them multiple times."

"Why?" Hunter demanded. "What the hell are they doing? They don't need three million–plus samples to conduct a genetic survey!"

"We agree," Benedict told them. "And actually, so did the government. By the late '70s, the treaty was breaking down. There was a firefight inside a secret base underneath Archuleta Mesa at Dulce, New Mexico. Sixty of our people—Delta Force mostly, but also some of our scientists and engineering personnel—were killed."

"I read about that," Nielson said. "I always wondered if that really happened."

"This happened," Benedict told them. "A few details leaked out. The story was pretty wildly distorted, but . . . yeah. It happened. We knew after that we couldn't trust the little bastards."

There were twenty of them now, gathered in the front seats of a small underground auditorium off the Blue Room, watching the scene unfold on a large screen at the front. A number of US recon Marines had joined them late yesterday, and there were more recruits from Delta Force, from SAD/SOG, and from USSOCOM.

Throughout that morning, the group had been shown plenty of visual proof of the aliens' existence: films of saucer recoveries at Cape Girardeau and Roswell, a film of Eisenhower's first meeting with aliens at Muroc, and one showing the dissection of a Gray alien's body after Roswell—not the famously hoaxed Santilli film, but one in which President Truman himself actually appeared at one point, a worried, watching face visible through an observation window in the green, concrete block wall.

"That's when we started seriously working hard," Benedict continued, "through various black budget projects, to build up our own defenses and find ways to strike back. Reagan's 'Star Wars'? Wait until you see what we developed—not against the Russians, but to protect ourselves against attack from space! And at the same time, we were working toward Full Disclosure."

Once more, Hunter wasn't satisfied with the pace at which this so-called Full Disclosure was going, but knew he wasn't going to get anywhere arguing about it again. He sat back as they started the next film.

This one showed a massive, cone-shaped craft on its side in the bottom of a wooded valley. Hunter suppressed a start of recognition. They'd seen that craft upstairs, in the Blue Room.

"Kecksburg, Pennsylvania," Benedict said. "December 9, 1965. This was a crude time ship operated by a German SS officer who came down twenty years after he left Germany at the end of World War II. We believe the craft to be of Saurian design but refitted by the Nazis to accommodate both a Saurian pilot and a human passenger."

A number of US Army soldiers in old-style uniforms were standing around the crash site, along with several men in civilian clothing. It was dark, with the ship illuminated by large, mobile spotlights. There were patches of snow on the ground, particularly at the bottom of the ravine. It looked like the craft had skidded down through the ravine, big-end first.

Someone was using a pry bar on the craft's side. A panel popped loose, and red interior light spilled out onto the snow. A moment later, a couple of soldiers were helping a human occupant out and into the open air.

"SS General Hans Kammler," Benedict went on. "We had a good idea that he was coming, and had positioned a recovery team not far from Kecksburg. We also picked up the alien pilot wandering around out in the woods. Kammler became a part of the Apollo mission. I have no information on the pilot. . . ."

Master Chief Minkowski caught Hunter's gaze, and rolled his eyes. Hunter smiled. This whole thing was becoming tedious. SEALs were used to physical training above all else—long runs in the sand, exhausting swims in freezing water, HALO-jumping out of airplanes at thirty-six thousand feet.

Somehow, sitting around watching ancient home movies of UFOs just didn't cut it.

DOCTOR OF engineering Ellen Michaels, Groton knew, was one of just a couple of dozen people or so who fully understood gravitomagnetics. She was razor sharp, a lifetime member of Mensa, and a research engineer with the RAND Corporation. He'd first met her at the RAND corporate headquarters in Santa Monica a couple of years ago, when he was a Navy liaison officer to the company during the final development of Operation Excalibur. They'd become close, but attempts to get her to be a close friend with benefits all had failed. "I do *not* date my coworkers," she'd told him once, in no uncertain terms.

And that was that.

"So why the delay?" she asked him. They were in the S4 cafeteria with their morning coffees. "I need to get to the Moon."

"The word is we're waiting on a load of new recruits," he told her. "Our new strike force."

She made a face. "Soldiers? Why would we need *them*?"

"This *is* a military operation," he told her. "We'll need a *few* military types around."

"Anybody we meet *out there*," she said, "is going to be so far in advance of us it's not funny. Seriously—having troops along isn't going to protect us, and it might make things worse!"

"Not my decision, Doctor. *Or* yours."

"Turning Excalibur into a military mission is inviting disaster," she said. "For the whole program."

"We've learned a few things since Dulce," he told her.

He'd been a kid in 1979, and hadn't even heard about the clandestine firefight under Archuleta Mesa until he'd been transferred from Navy aviation to join Solar Warden thirty years later. The program had hand lasers now that matched what the Grays had used at Dulce. That didn't mean American technology had caught up to theirs by any means, but it at least gave the humans a chance.

In theory.

Changing topics, he asked, "So why do you need to get to *Big-H*?"

She made a face. "It's technical."

"Try me." He hated it when people were condescending to him.

"Um. You know physicists are having trouble folding gravity in with the other three forces, right?"

"Sure. The unified field theory."

"Which we haven't managed to figure out yet. We're looking for what's called a 'theory of everything,' which would reconcile quantum physics with Einsteinian relativistic physics. Basically that means we need to understand gravity as a quantum force, and that's eluded us until now."

"But now you have a way of doing it?"

"Maybe. Toland, on the *Big-H*, has come up with a scheme for accelerating particles gravitomagnetically, and in higher dimensions than the normal three. If I can run some tests in the ship's power plant, I might be able to show how to resolve things by using string theory."

He held up his hands. "Okay, okay. You win. It's technical . . . and way beyond me. I'm just a simple flyboy."

"Let that be a lesson to you!"

"THESE," BENEDICT told them, "are Mark VII advanced Space Activity Suits, or Seven-SAS, also known as a 'BioSuit' or an EVS—that's Extra-Vehicular Suit. The Seven-SAS is not inflated like conventional space suits, but uses mechanical pressure to compress the human body. The torso shell provides radiation protection, and anchor points for hardware. . . ."

Hunter examined his arms, encased in silvered, tight-fitting sleeves with an outer surface of Kevlar. His gloves were inflated, but at low pressure, allowing considerable mobility. His helmet looked like those used by ISS astronauts on their space walks, and was attached to a heavy PLSS unit secured to his back—a personal life support system. He took an experimental step . . . then another. It was not uncomfortable, and only slightly limited his mobility.

Hunter, Arch, Minkowski, and a Marine named Grabiak, with Benedict as their guide, were inside a vacuum chamber under Wright-Patt, getting used to their military EVS, while the rest of the team waited outside for their turns. Theoretically, BioSuits were designed to be worn inside a pressurized spacecraft like jumpers or military utilities, but could be transformed to full-fledged space suits in seconds by donning the clamshell torso and backpack, and sealing on gloves and helmet.

"You say these things protect us from radiation, Major?" Captain Arch asked, flexing his gloves in front of his visor.

"To a limited degree," Benedict told him. "The suit includes built-in dosimeters that will warn you if you exceed allowable exposures. Your brain and your vital organs are pretty well protected regardless. Your legs and arms, not so much. And there are different kinds of radiation, remember. Most of the stuff coming off the sun—relatively low-energy protons and helium nuclei—your suits can handle that pretty well. Cosmic rays, though—those are high-mass nuclei traveling at close to the speed of light—are a different story.

"We don't expect that you'll be operating in hard vacuum for extended periods of time, however."

"*Perfectly* safe . . ." Hunter murmured. "Your government *says* so."

"What was that, Commander?" The voice was not Major Benedict's, but came from one of several observers outside the vacuum chamber waiting with the other recruits—Admiral Charles Carruthers. Hunter knew little about him, save that he was evaluating the recruits for their upcoming mission.

"Nothing, sir. Sorry, sir."

Briefly, Hunter considered the possibility of deliberately ticking the admiral off and getting dropped from the program . . . but he still wasn't sure what failure meant for any of them. Deployment to Kazakhstan? Or a mysterious disappearance? Admiral Kelsey's insistence that there were two sides in the secret program, good guys and bad guys, still resonated with him, a major unknown.

It had been *so* much easier going up against the North Koreans. You knew who the hell your enemies were there.

Until he had a better idea of who was who, he would call superiors "sir" and stay below their radar. "On the table over there," Benedict told them, "are your Sunbeams. They've been safed so that you people don't put a hole in the side of this very expensive vacuum facility. Go over and pick one up. See how it feels."

The hand weapons were large and heavy, designed like a pistol but clumsy to hold one-handed. They looked a lot more like something out of an old Flash Gordon serial than the sleek and lightweight phasers of *Star Trek*.

"The Sunbeam Type 1 Mod 3," Benedict said. "A 20-megawatt pulse laser operating off a grip-housed liquid-metallic suspension battery that will give you four shots. Or you can plug it into a larger battery mounted under your PLSS, and that will give you juice for twenty-five shots. The pulse, lasting one-fiftieth of a second, will deliver about four-tenths of a megajoule of energy to the target. That's the same energy, roughly, as a tenth of a kilogram of plastic explosives, or your standard blasting cap. Keep that in mind when you draw down on a target. Drop your batteries."

They'd studied the weapons earlier, under normal pressure. Hunter found the release button and pressed it, and the heavy battery slid free of the grip. His gloves interfered slightly with his freedom of motion, and he noticed that he was having trouble feeling the weapon's ridged grip through the heavy Kevlar material.

But it was doable.

"Good," Benedict told them. "Pick up the batteries and reload them."

Hunter did so. They were using dummy batteries that matched the size and mass of the real things, presumably so that some idiot didn't blast a bulkhead and explosively compress the place. Normally, he'd been told, EVA troops would carry ten to fifteen reserve magazine batteries in a case mounted on the right side of their suits.

He did wish that one unit allowed more than four shots, however. His usual sidearm, a nine-millimeter Glock G19, was a more traditional slug-throwing weapon, with a magazine capacity of seventeen rounds plus one up the spout. Four shots seemed . . . a bit on the skimpy side.

Of course, nine-millimeter rounds didn't generally run the risk of blowing holes in steel pressure bulkheads.

"This," Benedict continued, holding up a much larger weapon, "is a RAND/Starbeam 3000 variable-stream heavy laser rifle. You can adjust the timing, anything from a one-second continuous beam down to a hundredth of a second. Normally, it's set for a tenth of a second, which gives you a power output of fifty thousand joules. That's a tenth of a kilo of high explosives—about what you get in a modern hand grenade. It takes a while to recycle, though, and it requires bigger batteries. You'll get between four and fifty shots out of this before you have to reload, depending on the setting." He handed the big weapon to Gunnery Sergeant Grabiak. "How's it feel, Marine?"

Grabiak raised it to his shoulder, aiming at the far end of the chamber. Hunter noted that he seemed to have no problem aiming the weapon while wearing the BioSuit. Had he been sealed up inside a regular space suit like the ones on the ISS, he never would have made it.

"A little trouble aiming," Grabiak told Benedict. "Can't get my eye up behind the sight."

"There's a button on the side of the weapon marked 'EV-sight.' See it?"

"Yes, sir."

"Press it."

The Marine seemed startled by the result. "Son of a—"

"A small camera boresighted in the weapon relays an image that's thrown up on a helmet-mounted heads-up display. You can point the weapon blind around a corner, and still see what it's aimed at."

"Sweet!"

"Commander? Have a look."

Hunter accepted the weapon from the Marine and aimed it downrange. Sure enough, a red crosshair reticule appeared inside his helmet, centered against a small image of the far end of the chamber.

"There's a knob beside your left hand," Benedict told him. "Turn it."

Hunter did so, and the image expanded sharply. This would be a hell of a sniper rifle, he decided.

"So why don't we have these in the field *now*, Major?" Grabiak asked—a demand more than a question. In fact, he sounded angry. "A weapon like that, with that sighting system . . . they would've been damned useful at Falluja!"

"They'll be coming into general service within the next five years, Gunny," Benedict told him. "Right now, these things are being turned out in very limited numbers. We'll need a massive upscale to produce enough to issue them to a regiment."

"We could have used just five," Grabiak said, reproachful. "Fuck, we could have used *one*."

"I hear you, bro," Hunter told him.

"Damn, the corps always gets the short, messy end of the stick when it comes to the hottest new toys," Grabiak said.

"Ooh-rah," Hunter said, and the Marine smiled.

"Arch? Get a feel for the weapon. . . ."

Hunter handed the rifle over to the CIA direct action operator. The chances were good that he'd already seen the weapon, or something very like it. SAD/SOG personnel generally *did* get the latest toys.

"Major?" Hunter said.

"Yes, Commander?"

"Are we going to get some range time with these?"

"It's on the schedule, Commander. Friday."

"Major?" That was Carruthers's voice.

"Yessir!"

"Belay that. The schedule has been changed. They're shipping out day after tomorrow."

It was Monday.

CHAPTER SEVEN

Anthropological files contain many examples of
societies, sure of their place in the universe, which
have disintegrated when they have had to associ-
ate with previously unfamiliar societies espousing
different ideas and different life ways; others that
survived such an experience usually did so by paying the price of changes in values and attitudes and
behavior.

THE BROOKINGS REPORT, 1960
PAGE 183

19 April 1961

"THIS," **THE PRESIDENT** of the United States said in his familiar thick Bostonian Hah-vahd tones, "is completely
unacceptable. The people have a right to know."

Allen Dulles, the head of the CIA since 1953, and the
first civilian director of that agency, looked on disap-
provingly. "It's all spelled out there, Mr. President. It's
now a part of the Congressional Record. There's nothing
we can do about it."

"That, Mr. Dulles, does not make it legally binding."

President John F. Kennedy leafed again through the
document on the desk in front of him. It was almost three
hundred pages long; the frontispiece was headed by a
title in all caps:

PROPOSED STUDIES
ON THE IMPLICATIONS OF PEACEFUL
SPACE ACTIVITIES FOR HUMAN AFFAIRS

The paper had been prepared for the newly founded NASA by the Brookings Institution, a public policy think tank operating out of its campus near Dupont Circle. The report had been formally presented to the House Committee on Science and Astronautics just yesterday. Most of the report, already being referred to as the Brookings Report, though the think tank had created mountains of reports since 1916, concerned itself with various policy issues related to space exploration. A Brookings report had laid the foundations of the Marshall Plan, and the economic recovery of Europe after WWII.

But Kennedy was concerned about this *report and its discussion of the possibility of encountering intelligent life during the exploration of space. Specifically, he was concerned by what it* didn't *say.*

He found the page and the paragraph he was looking for. "Here," Kennedy said. "Right here. 'Questions one might wish to answer by such studies would include: How might such information, under what circumstances, be presented to or withheld from the public for what ends?'"

"It doesn't say the information must be withheld, Mr. President."

"No. But it provides the basis for such a ruling. Damn it, Mr. Dulles, three months ago you sat in that chair over there and showed me files that were, frankly, shocking. A secret group called MJ-12! Secret treaties with alien beings! And worst of all, secret agreements to allow those beings to abduct our citizens! And you showed me proof that all of this is real! I, ah, take it the Brookings people weren't in on the secret."

"No, Mr. President. Of course they weren't."

"I told you when you gave me that briefing that I was going to end this secrecy. My predecessor in this office

may have had his reasons for doing what he did, but I am not going to lie to the American people! This document, by its omissions, is a lie."

"Not really, Mr. President. Look . . . this paragraph, right here . . . just before that."

Kennedy read it aloud. " 'Anthropological files contain many examples of societies . . .' " His voice trailed off as he read the rest of the paragraph. "Okay, so you people are afraid our society is going to collapse?"

"It is a distinct possibility, Mr. President. We must not take rash or untoward actions in this area unless we are very sure of how the populace will react."

"I think you underestimate the American people." Kennedy pushed the Brookings paper back. "How much time, Mr. Dulles, will you and your people need to put together a plan by which we can, ah, gently break it to the general population?"

"Hard to say, sir. A couple of years, at least."

Kennedy gave him a hard, humorless grin. "Anything to push back the day of reckoning, eh? Well, I'll tell you what. You have six months to put a plan on my desk. We'll see where we go from there."

"Yes, sir."

"Now get the hell out of my office."

Dulles left in a thoughtful mood. He'd argued that it was a mistake to bring the President in on the secrets guarded by MJ-12. He didn't need to know.

He would have to talk to some of his associates at the Agency, to see what might be done about this brash, upstart new president. . . .

HUNTER WAS seething with anger.

They'd only just begun to get a feel for the space suits and weaponry they would be expected to use—no chance to practice with them at all—when the official word came down that they were to report to Groom Lake in just two days.

Popularly known as Area 51, Groom Lake had been the location of testing and development programs for a number of highly secret aircraft, including the U-2, the SR-71, and the F-117 Stealth Fighter. Starting in 1955, the government had been running a top secret facility there that had only been officially acknowledged in 2013.

UFO conspiracy theorists had, of course, identified Groom Lake as the center of a massive conspiracy involving crashed spaceships and recovered alien technologies. Hunter had always dismissed such tales. Now he knew those tales probably didn't tell half the truth.

A military transport touched down at Groom Lake after the long flight from Wright-Patt. The windows had been blacked out, so the passengers, now incorporated as the 1st Joint Space Strike Team, or 1-JSST, couldn't see any details of the landing field as they were on approach. They touched down smoothly, and a bus—also with blacked-out windows—met them to take them to the guest barracks.

They fell into formation in a large and empty hangar, and Hunter, as the unit's senior officer, accepted the roll-call report from Master Chief Minkowski. "All present and accounted for, sir!"

"Thank you, Master Chief." Hunter in turn passed the roster on to Colonel Grange, the man in charge of the 1-JSST project.

Grange accepted the clipboard, made a notation, and addressed them in ranks.

"Men, welcome to Dreamland. In another twenty-four hours you will be on your way into space."

Dreamland was one of several names by which Area 51 had long been known. Paradise Ranch and Homey Airport were two others, while Groom Lake was the official name, according to the CIA.

"*Almost* everything you've heard about this place is true," Grange continued. "We don't have any actual

UFOs or alien bodies stored here—most of that is in the Blue Room back at Wright-Patt—but this is where we've been building, testing, and launching some pretty amazing technology. Rest assured, gentlemen, that your security oaths are in full force. You will not discuss anything you see or hear at this facility with *anyone* else . . . including wives and sweethearts, Russian spies, or each other. Do I make myself clear?"

"Yes, sir!" the men chorused back.

"Very well. It's now 17:45. I suggest you report to the chow hall and get yourselves fed. The rest of the evening is yours. Do *not* ask for a pass into town. Las Vegas is eighty-four miles in *that* direction, and the plane has already left for the day. Rachel, Nevada, is the nearest town—population about fifty. There's not a hell of a lot to do there on Wednesday nights. Commander, you may dismiss your men."

"Aye, aye, sir. *Comp*'ny . . . dis*missed*!"

As the men relaxed, falling into small groups, Hunter approached Grange. "Question, sir?"

"Go ahead, Commander."

"Two questions, actually. First: we were yanked out of training at Wright-Patt without being able to train with our new weapons. Is there a range around here where we could do so?"

"Huh. And the second question?"

"Sir, what the hell is the mission? They've been jumping us from one end of the country to the other, telling us all about UFOs and secret space fleets, and we still don't know what it is we're supposed to be doing."

"To answer your first question, Commander: no. There is a weapons range out behind Hangar Two, but you people are not cleared to use it, and by the time we get clearance for you, you all will be on your way.

"As for the second question—that is classified above your clearance level. You'll be told the nature of your mission once you reach your first destination."

"And what destination would that be, sir? Or is that classified, as well?"

"Oh, I can tell you that, Commander. You're going to the Moon."

"I'M GOING *where*?"

Becky McClure had been called into the office of her boss's boss: Colonel Joseph Grange, a no-nonsense Army colonel in command of the Solar Warden personnel office at Groom Lake.

"It's strictly on a volunteer basis, Dr. McClure," Grange said. "But Excalibur is going to need someone with a solid grounding in biology, and you're it."

"But the Moon?" She shook her head. "There's no biology *there*!"

"There are Grays," Grange told her. "And Nordics. And possibly Saurians, as well. And the Moon isn't your final destination."

"What is?"

"You'll get a full briefing at Darkside. I can tell you that you may be away for a considerable time."

"Lovely. And just why are you asking me?"

"Because you are an excellent evolutionary biologist, with top marks from Carnegie Mellon University. Because you have been cleared to Cosmic Top Secret, and you are one of the very few research scientists to have that level of clearance. And there's your father. . . ."

McClure frowned. Her father had been Dr. Bruce McClure, also an evolutionary biologist, and also initiated into the clandestine world of aliens and government conspiracies. He'd not been supposed to do so, but her father had told her bits and pieces of what he was doing at the research lab at Wright-Patterson Air Force Base. She'd learned that Humankind was not alone in the universe when she was seven. She'd learned about her father's role at Kecksburg when she was twelve, and about the alien he'd worked with a year later.

She suspected that They had known about his indiscretion, but that the elder McClure had been too valuable to the program to punish. But she'd just been accepted by Carnegie Mellon when she'd been approached by the government guys in dark suits and sunglasses.

They'd promised her tuition-free training at CMU, and a rewarding position in research after graduation.

And of course she'd accepted.

Mostly, she'd wanted to find out what happened to her father. He'd been on a secret Majik assignment in Dulce, New Mexico, in 1979, when he'd been killed in a lab accident.

She'd always suspected that there was more to the story than that. After all, how likely was it that an evolutionary biologist would be working on something that would kill him? Oh, it was possible, she supposed, that some deadly microorganism had gotten loose in the lab . . . but it hardly seemed likely. Her dad's research had to do with decidedly *macroscopic* creatures, intelligent beings from someplace else.

She deeply mistrusted the official story, and since beginning to work for Majik and on Operation Excalibur, she'd seen nothing to reassure her.

By making mention of her father, Grange was reminding her that she was continuing a kind of family tradition . . . which meant that she was so far down the MJ-12 rabbit hole that there was really no way out.

"It's a tremendous opportunity, Doctor," Grange added. "You'll be working on Gray biology, and possibly examining their origins."

Yeah, great. But when can I publish the paper and collect my Nobel Prize?

Reluctantly, she nodded. "I'll go," she said. "When do I leave?"

"Tomorrow," he told her, "on the next shuttle."

"Then I suppose I'd better pack. . . ."

She meant it sarcastically. There would be little to pack, and no one to whom she should say good-bye.

Working for Solar Warden was damned near as restrictive as being in a literal prison.

THEY'D BEEN assigned to two-man cubicles in a large barracks behind one of the hangars. Late that evening, Hunter and Minkowski left their cube for a stroll out onto the dark desert salt flat behind their barracks. Hunter had been unable to sleep. He kept thinking about Gerri.

Minkowski was nervous. "Sir . . . I'm not sure we're supposed to be out here."

"Oh, you can be sure about that, Mink. I *know* we're not supposed to be out here. That's why I bribed the duty officer at the front desk."

"I wondered why he wasn't there."

"Call of nature, I guess. I just slipped him something to make sure it was well-timed."

"What'd you give him? Money? Booze?"

"This month's issue of *Playboy*."

"I guess they might have some problems getting them here on-base. At this base, anyway."

"That's what I was thinking."

"I'm just wondering, though. What happens if we get caught out here?"

"I imagine we'll get a *very* stiff talking-to. But I've had it up to here with the asinine regs and security. The idiots won't even let us practice with those new weapons! We get into a firefight and somebody's going to get killed. They've known about things for half a century, and now they're rushing?"

"I honestly get the feeling, sir, that they don't really care. We're just warm bodies. Numbers on a roster."

"Oh, you get that, too, do you?"

"Yes, sir."

It was chilly outside, the sky so dark that the Milky

Way stretched from horizon to horizon in soft, blue-white clouds of clotted light. The Moon, just into its first quarter, had already set, leaving the cloudless sky crystal clear, infinitely deep, and filled with stars. Hunter shivered and wished he'd worn a jacket. He'd forgotten how cold it got during the night on the desert.

"Shit! Will ya look at that!" Minkowski pointed. High overhead, among the thickly scattered stars, a single brilliant light shone brighter than the planet Venus.

And it was moving.

"I've heard that people come out here to watch the skies over this base," Minkowski said. "There are some ridges a few miles away. They say some nights you can see really strange stuff in the sky."

Hunter chuckled. "Flying saucers?"

"Beats me. Bright lights that aren't maneuvering like conventional aircraft."

"Like that one."

Together, they watched the light, which was pursuing a zigzag path across the sky, stopping at times to hover, and at others zipping from point A to point B so quickly you couldn't tell if it had traveled the intervening distance . . . or jumped across it.

"They say," Minkowski continued, "that the lights are actually ours—high-tech aircraft that we built after taking apart crashed alien ships."

"Oh, we *know* that the government has its own antigravity spacecraft. They've been telling us that much right along." Hunter considered this for a moment, then shook his head. "But reverse engineering. I don't buy it."

"You don't, sir?"

"Just imagine for a minute . . . an F-35 Lightning II crashes in the desert back in 1860."

"Okay . . ."

"And the US government decides to take it apart and see what makes it tick. You think they'd be able to do it? Think they'd be able to reverse engineer an F-35 after studying the crash, and actually build one of their own *and* figure out how to fly it?"

"Sir, in 1860 they didn't have aircraft."

Hunter shrugged. "They had balloons. And . . . just look at that thing!" Above them, the bright star had been joined by a second. They hovered side by side, unmoving and utterly silent. "The jump from a balloon to a jet fighter probably isn't as big as the jump from a jet to *that*. Antigravity? Nullifying inertia? Hell, they're using science a thousand years ahead of ours, not a century."

"So what are you saying, sir?"

The lights had been joined by a third, and now all three appeared to be descending toward Homey Airport, slowly growing brighter.

"That we had *help*. A lot of it."

A van drove up, stopping at the edge of the tarmac twenty yards away. Several men got out, wearing camouflage suits and carrying weapons. Flashlights stabbed and probed through the dark, but several of the men were wearing IR headgear.

There were plenty of stories about the "camo dudes" who appeared to provide security for the Groom Lake facility—and speculation that they weren't military, but employees of a private contractor called Wackenhut. Hunter and Minkowski eased back into the deeper shadow at the corner of the barracks. Probably, the two SEALs had shown up on infrared scanners somewhere, and the camo dudes had been dispatched to pick them up.

But they weren't about to make it easy for them.

It just wasn't how SEALs operated.

Overhead, the brightest of the three stars had resolved itself into three bright, white lights with a larger red light glowing at the center.

The security people were spreading out, obviously searching for something. Hunter tapped Minkowski's shoulder and nudged him back around the corner of the barracks. With one last glance up at the descending triangle, they slipped through the darkness to the barracks door and stepped inside.

The duty officer had his feet up on his desk, and was reading a new copy of *Playboy*. He pointedly ignored the two SEALs as they went back to their quarters.

The next morning, the twenty JSST operators stood in formation in Hangar One. The huge room was no longer empty. Sometime during the night, someone had rolled in a TR-3B and parked it under a blaze of spotlights. Armed guards—Army, this time, rather than Wackenhut rent-a-cops—stood around it, facing out.

Once again, they went through the ritual of roll call, then waited at parade rest as a gaggle of military VIPs and civilians came through and boarded the spacecraft. There were about fifty of them, including, Hunter noticed, several quite attractive women. What they might be doing headed for the Moon he had no idea. A number of men and women wore bright silver bodysuits, and Hunter wondered if they were the Nordics Benedict had told him about.

Time travelers from eleven thousand years in the future. What were they doing back here . . . slumming?

There was also, he saw, a Navy admiral, several captains, and a number of staff officers.

When the last of the VIPs were aboard, four men in pressure suits entered—presumably the TR-3B's flight crew. Only then did an Air Force crew chief named Saunders tell Hunter that he could bring his people on board.

They filed up the ramp and into the belly of the black triangle. The interior had the look and feel of a wide-body commercial passenger jet, with three blocks of seats in a two-four-two configuration: two seats to port, two starboard, and four across the center with aisles at either side. At a guess, the craft could carry around one hundred people . . . perhaps more. There were no windows along the sides, but monitors set into the backs of each seat currently showed the interior of the hangar outside, where sliding doors were slowly opening to admit a torrent of bright desert sunlight.

The civilians and high-ranking officers were not in evidence; there must be an upper deck, Hunter thought, with more seating. The TR-3B would carry a hundred and fifty, maybe even more.

The military personnel took seats on the main deck, gathering in small clusters that reflected their backgrounds and units. That, Hunter thought, was going to be a problem. If 1-JSST was going to be an effective fighting force, he was going to have to find a way to break down those barriers and get them to think and act as a single unit and *not* as SEALs and Delta Force and Rangers and CIA.

And how the hell was he supposed to do that, when he barely had time to figure out what that team was supposed to do? . . .

He knew his old men, of course. He knew them and trusted them, and they knew they could trust him. But the others . . .

The handful of civilians on the main deck appeared to be technicians, which suggested that the people on the upper deck were the high-ranking officers and the civilian elite. None of the Nordics was on the main deck, which was a pity. Hunter was hoping he could get a chance to talk with them.

"Where'd the rest of them go, Skipper?" Chief Brunelli asked.

"First class, Chief," Hunter replied. "We're in the economy seats."

"Ladies and gentlemen," a voice said over a cabin speaker. "This is your pilot speaking. We're on a short hold until Kosmos 2525 goes below the horizon. Please stay in your seats. We will be taxiing out shortly."

Kosmos 2525 was a recently launched Russian satellite, the "Kosmos" designation indicating that it was defense related, and therefore probably a spy satellite. It made sense, Hunter supposed, that the people in charge of this program wouldn't want the Russians, or anyone else, watching a TR-3B launch.

A couple of minutes later, the transport began moving forward through the hangar doors and into the dazzling Nevada sun.

Hunter found that a touch-screen pad beside his monitor could be used to shift cameras, showing the view from either side of the spacecraft, or looking directly astern.

He found one camera angle from outside the ship, and it startled him. *The landing gear was up.* The TR-3B was floating a few feet above the tarmac, moving with such precision and grace that he couldn't even feel it.

Until that moment, Hunter realized, he had not *really* believed in antigravity, even though he'd heard the term used frequently.

The ship reached a point on the main runway outside the hangar, paused for a moment, then lifted smoothly and silently straight up into the sky.

Not only antigravity, but inertial control, as well. *However we achieved it, it's damn impressive.* The desert dropped away in the aft camera to be replaced almost immediately by the blue haze of atmosphere hugging the land, then by the curve of the Earth's horizon and the empty black of space. They must have accelerated at hundreds of gravities to move so fast in so brief a time.

And he'd felt absolutely nothing.

One of the distinguishing points of UFOs over the decades had been their ability to maneuver at impossible speeds and make impossible turns, turns that would have pulped any human pilot. Evidently, humans now knew how to banish certain inconvenient physical laws.

"My *God* but we're moving!" Minkowski said at Hunter's left side. "Sir . . . what the hell have we gotten ourselves into?"

"At a guess, Mink: the future."

Earth was now a complete sphere in the rear-facing camera views, and dwindling moment by moment. From here, the planet was nearly full, with the dawn terminator visible far out over the Pacific. Hunter could see the intricate filigree of brilliant white clouds, the deep blue of ocean, the dark brown and green of continents, an impossibly beautiful jewel set in heaven.

With some reluctance, he switched to the forward view and got his first clear view of the Moon. It was in its first quarter, a slender crescent, though reflected earthlight dimly revealed the darkened part of the surface. The sunlit sliver was a brilliant, dazzling white, and he could see individual craters and maria with unparalleled detail and clarity.

The speed of their approach was nothing short of breathtaking. Lunar missions of the late '60s and early '70s had taken about three days to travel from low Earth orbit to the lunar surface. The TR-3B was making the same voyage in something less than twenty minutes. There still was no sensation of movement or acceleration . . . and there was no zero-gravity either. Hunter decided that that made sense; if you could turn gravity off, you must be able to make it to order, as well.

When the hell had they figured out how to manage that trick? There'd been rumors for years, of course . . . about antigravity, about unlimited free power pulled from empty space itself . . . all of those technological dreams from the pages of science fiction, but kept secret.

Was it possible that Big Oil was suppressing research into free energy? Hunter doubted that—"Big Oil" was a fiction, a monolithic union among cutthroat competitors who would be way better off if they found a way to offer unlimited power . . . not for free, perhaps, but at a fraction of the cost of petroleum.

But it did leave him wondering.

The lit portion of the Moon's surface was dwindling, becoming a narrower and narrower crescent. A few moments later, and the Moon's face was completely dark except for the faint, blue-gray illumination of earthlight. And then sunlight began gleaming from the opposite horizon. The transport, Hunter realized, was traveling around the Moon, coming in toward the farside.

And the Moon now was so large that he knew they were only minutes away from landing.

CHAPTER EIGHT

We cannot take the credit for our record advance-
ment in certain scientific fields alone. We have been
helped [by] the people of other worlds.

DR. HERMANN J. OBERTH [ATTRIBUTED], 1974

6 October 1970

"WHAT IS YOUR name?"

The creature sealed in the glass-walled room did not respond.

Dr. Bruce McClure sighed, leaning back in his chair. The alien had been in their custody for . . . what? Five years, now? Sometimes it was talkative enough, but lately it had become . . . sullen. Less responsive. Resentful, perhaps.

McClure couldn't blame it. Five years in captivity, prevented from communicating with its own kind.

Except no one was certain whether it really was isolated from other Saurians. They communicated among themselves—as they did with humans—telepathically. There were Saurian bases here on Earth; their ships were frequently in the skies over Southern Nevada. The Faraday cage enclosing the pseudoreptilian being was supposed to cut off its ability to communicate outside of the base, but no one knew for sure if it worked.

Suppose it was in regular communication with others of its kind?

"What is your name?"

Perhaps, he thought, it was just that it was getting tired of the same questions, asked over and over again. Who are you; where do you come from; why are you here; what do you want. It was standard interrogation practice, designed to catch a subject in lies, to wear him down, to trip him up.

But the subject this time was an alien being with an alien psychology, and God alone knew what alien motivations.

It also seemed possessed of an inhumanly deep patience—which, of course, made sense, seeing how it wasn't human.

Occasionally, he would vary the questions, attempting to catch the subject by surprise. "Were your people the ones who ordered us off the Moon?"

The thing's head turned, and its enormous golden eyes widened slightly at that, the pupils contracting to stark slits. Perhaps he'd touched something in the creature's psyche.

"Was it you?"

Not us.

The thought arose in McClure's mind, clear, but low voiced, almost a hiss.

"Who was it?"

Others.

It had been five months since Apollo 13 had safely returned to Earth after its hair-raising near-disaster en route to the Moon, and just one month since NASA had announced that the Apollo program would be shut down. Apollo 14 would still be launched in January, as planned. Three more missions would be sent after that, but there would be no Apollo 18, 19, or 20.

There were a few within the NASA hierarchy, those

few who knew about the aliens, who knew about what Armstrong and Aldrin had seen in the Sea of Tranquility fourteen months before, and McClure was one of them. NASA would tell the public that the program was being canceled because of budget cuts and dwindling public interest, but the public certainly had been enthralled by the drama of bringing the crippled Apollo 13 back to Earth. No "loss of public interest" there.

And if they knew about the real reason, he was pretty sure interest would have gone through the roof.

There were hints that the Apollo 13 disaster had not been due to faulty wiring. McClure wasn't sure, but judging from the list of questions he'd been given for the interrogation of the reptilian alien, he suspected that Apollo 13 might well have been a second, more explicit warning.

By "others," the alien probably meant the Grays. The two species—Saurians and Grays—were eerily similar in many respects, but wildly different in others. Reportedly, the Grays were behind the repeated and persistent abduction of human beings, purportedly because they were interested in the human genome, or, alternatively, because they were interested in creating human-Gray hybrids, a new species.

Bruce McClure was a biologist. Xenobiology was a bit out of his line, of course, but he understood the processes of evolution and the mechanics of DNA—at least insofar as they were understood by human science in 1970.

And there was something very, very wrong about claims that the Grays were interested simply in the biology of human reproduction—and even more wrong in the idea that they were secretly creating alien-human hybrids.

Ssarsk.

"What? Did you say something?"

You may call me Ssarsk.

"WELCOME TO Darkside Base," the pilot told them over the intercom. Gravity appeared to drain away as they cut the ship's power. "Be careful how you move. It will take you a while to adjust to one-sixth G."

Hunter unstrapped and stood, flexing his knees a bit to get a feel for the lesser gravity of the lunar surface. He felt . . . *buoyant* was the only word to describe it. Like he could kick off in a standing broad jump and touch down twenty feet away.

He'd seen very little of the base as the TR-3B had landed. Someone up in the control room had switched off several cameras during the final approach. But he'd glimpsed enough to see a barren landscape blasted with light, which put paid to the idea of a *dark* side. He knew that the Moon always kept one face to the Earth . . . and that that face right now was in darkness. That meant the farside, the side facing away from Earth, was currently in daylight. *Dark side* was an obsolete reference from the old days of lunar exploration, when absolutely nothing was known about the side of the Moon perpetually turned away from the Earth.

The monitors now showed the interior of a cavernous, underground chamber, so presumably they'd drifted in through some sort of large barn door. A pair of enclosed walkways, one above the other, were extending from one of the cavern's walls and attaching themselves to the side of the spacecraft, just like the mobile boarding tunnels used in conventional airports. These, though, had the look of pressurized docking tubes. They wouldn't need to suit up to deplane.

Darkside Base, it turned out, was entirely constructed inside a gigantic lava tube, a basaltic cave formed when the outer surface of a lava flow had hardened, eons ago, while the molten interior had continued to flow and eventually drained away. It made sense; the rock protected the base from both extremes of temperature and the harsh flux of solar and cosmic radiation outside. As he walked through the debarkation tube and glanced through the windows lining it, he saw whole cliffs gleaming in the base's lights, entire walls and hillsides covered with ice.

That made sense, too. He'd read of the discovery of ice at the Moon's south pole, buried at the bottoms of craters never touched by the sun. Comets, which were mostly frozen water, would have delivered their payloads to the Moon as clouds of hot vapor, which then would have frozen solid anywhere where the sun couldn't reach. Over billions of years, these lava tubes must have built up an ocean's worth of ice.

"Son of a bitch!" Nielson said, standing up and testing the bounce of his knees. The grin on his face made him look like a kid on his birthday. "Looks like they were right about the hollow Moon!"

"What the hell are you talking about, Niels?" Hunter demanded.

"I read about it. See, at the end of Apollo 11, before they headed back to Earth, they sent the lunar ascent stage crashing into the Moon's surface, so they could record the shock waves with the seismographs they left on the surface, right? And the scientists said the whole Moon 'rang like a bell' for an hour afterward. So the idea is . . . the Moon must actually be hollow, and that means it was artificially constructed, probably as a spaceship millions of years ago!"

"Nielson, you moron," Minkowski said, rolling his eyes. "You've been reading too many weird-ass conspiracy theories."

One of the civilians from the upper deck was filing past through an aisle between the seats, and she'd apparently heard Nielson's enthusiastic comments. She laughed. "'Ringing like a bell,' soldier, *doesn't* mean the Moon is hollow."

"Not 'soldier,' ma'am," Nielson said. He sounded a touch insulted. "I'm Navy, all the way!"

He'd not, Hunter noticed, said "Navy *SEAL*." SEALs

were careful about saying much, if anything, about their service to outsiders.

"Sorry," the woman said. "*Sailor*, then. But the fact that seismic waves kept bouncing around inside the Moon like the ringing of a bell just meant the Moon is solid all the way through. No molten core to absorb the waves."

"But this book I read—"

"Get it through your head, Niels," Hunter said gently. "Not everything you read is true."

"Aw, shit, Skipper!" Minkowski said, grinning. "Next thing you'll tell us is that what I read on the Internet isn't true either."

"Positively shocking!" the woman said, grinning, and then she turned and filed out.

Hunter wondered who she was.

A few minutes later, as Hunter stepped off the boarding tube into a bright, clean internal lounge, they were met by an alien.

Or, rather, by a time traveler. She was human, so far as Hunter could tell, and achingly beautiful. Her somewhat larger-than-life eyes gave her an exoticism that enhanced her attractiveness. Unlike the others Hunter had seen clad in tight-fitting silver, she was wearing dark blue coveralls that still did nothing to hide her figure. She was accompanied by a more ordinary-looking human, an older man in green Army fatigues and a first lieutenant's bars.

"Welcome to the Moon, gentlemen," she told the JSST after they fell into ranks. "My name is Elanna, and I will be . . . think of me as your official guide here. I understand that your departure from Earth was a bit sudden, and so I'm sure you all have a lot of questions. We'll do our best to answer them. First, however, Lieutenant Pierce, here, will take you to your new quarters and get you settled in. We operate here by Greenwich mean, so the current time is 0715 Zulu. Commander Hunter? Will you come with me, please?"

"This way, people," Pierce said.

As he walked past Hunter, though, Minkowski gave him a sly wink. "Have fun, Skipper," he said, sotto voce. "Be sure to use protection, okay?"

Hunter decided not to dignify the gibe with a reply. As the JSST filed off in the lieutenant's wake, Elanna came up to Hunter and extended a hand. "Lieutenant Commander Hunter? It is very good to meet you. I've heard a great deal about you."

Her language was a bit on the stiff and formal side, with a trace of an accent Hunter couldn't place. He shook her hand. "Elanna. You seem well versed in twenty-first century customs."

"Of course. I see you've been told about us."

"A little."

"Well, yes. I've been here for quite a while. If you'll come with me?"

She led Hunter deep into a labyrinthine tangle of passageways and compartments. The base was huge, with a large population of modern humans along with a scattering of Nordics. In a few minutes, Hunter was completely lost. He was having some difficulty walking in the low gravity, and it took him a while to get the hang of Elanna's graceful, gliding skip that carried her effortlessly along each passageway.

Eventually, she ushered him into what looked like a room. It had a long mahogany table, like one might find in the office of a corporate CEO, and one wall had a white monitor or viewscreen reaching almost deck to overhead.

She gestured toward a padded office chair. "I understand you have some questions, Commander."

"You could say that. But I'm still catching my breath. This facility is . . . fantastic. It's like some kind of dream."

"It's been here for several thousand years, Commander. Thirty years ago, we helped your people fix it up for your needs."

"Several thousand—" He blinked. "Who built it? You?"

"Not us. Others. The ones you call 'Grays.' They have

been here for a very, *very* long time, Commander, modifying our species for their own purposes."

"I see I'm going to have some catching up to do."

"All newcomers up here feel the same way," she told him. "It can be quite a shock."

"You said 'modifying our species.' Are you serious about that? Or is that some kind of joke?"

"Oh, no, Commander. I'm quite serious." She cocked her head to one side. "Why . . . are you religious?"

"Not particularly, no." He'd been raised Presbyterian, but without any particularly strong or emotional beliefs in the matter one way or the other. He shrugged. "I guess I'm in the church of 'be good, do your best, and hope everything works out.'"

"A good philosophy—and good to know. Our selection process deliberately excludes people with strong religious feelings," she said, "but a few have gotten through the screening. Let's just say some fundamentalist sects are very upset to learn that the Grays have modified humans as much as they have."

"What . . . they created us?"

"Not *created*, no. But there have been several deliberate genetic interventions through human prehistory. Your fledgling genomic sciences are only just now beginning to discover this. The rate of genetic change in humans has sped up *one hundred times* just in the past ten thousand years."

"Agriculture," Hunter suggested, frowning. "Improved nutrition."

"Some of it may be due to such factors," Elanna said, "but most has been due to deliberate genetic tinkering by outsiders."

"The Ebens—the Grays—whatever the hell you call them."

"That's right. There have been several instances, for example, where human brain size increased explosively over a relatively short period of time, and this despite the fact that the size of the human female pelvis makes it extremely difficult and even dangerous for humans to give birth to babies with larger skulls. What you may not appreciate yet is that the Ebens, the 'Extraterrestrial Biological Entities' you know as the Grays, are in fact the same as the Talis."

"Come again?"

"They are *us*, human descendants, human time travelers, but from a million years farther out into the future."

"You're saying the Grays are *human*? We're talking about the little guys with big heads and enormous eyes . . . *human*?"

"Humans, highly evolved beyond where you and I are now."

"You know, I'm not sure I buy it."

"Buy what, Commander?"

"The idea of beings from the remote future coming back and . . . uh . . . 'tinkering,' as you put it."

"Why not?"

"It's circular reasoning! Humans are smart because our human descendants went back and played around with our genome way back when, but that implies that humans are smart enough to develop time travel in the first place. If they *hadn't* gone back and changed the human genome, they wouldn't have been *able* to go back and change the genome—" Hunter shook his head. "Gives me a headache just thinking about it."

"You've heard about something called the time travel paradox, Commander?"

"The idea that we shouldn't mess around with time machines because we might wipe ourselves out?" He nodded. "Sure."

"Well, it's difficult to explain unless you have a certain amount of expertise in hyperdimensional mathematics, but suffice to say that time is *not* a single linear movement forward. It's far more complex than that. Any change to events in the past does *not* wipe out the future of that time line. It instead creates a new time line, one that incorporates that change. The end result is that there can be no such thing as a temporal paradox, because the universe—the *multi*verse, I should say—adjusts to incorporate any possible changes to the original time line."

"You make it all sound so simple."

"Simple? No, it's very much not, and only people well versed in advanced quantum theory and Poincaré polydimensional topology can appreciate it."

"Oh, *well*, then. That's different." Hunter meant it to be sarcastic, but Elanna didn't appear to notice.

"Of course it is. The important thing to remember is that while less-advanced cultures should avoid tinkering with the local time lines, truly advanced species may not have the same concerns. In many ways, they are truly god-like species with a god's understanding of space-time."

"I'll take your word for it," Hunter said. He was feeling . . . lost. He didn't like Elanna's patronizing attitude, but he liked even less the feeling of ignorance, of a deep-seated inability to understand *anything*.

Not only that, but Elanna's characterization of the Eben Grays as "gods" left him with a feeling of profound disquiet.

"Look, I don't really care if the Ebens *are* playing God. I might hope they know what the hell they're doing, but I'm not really worried about it. I'm much more worried about something else."

"And what is that?"

"What the hell are we here for, anyway? Some of the technology I've been seeing . . . damn, it's like Star Wars and then some. You people have ray guns and antigravity for Christ's sake! If there's an enemy, how are we supposed to go into combat against *that*?"

"The JSST is envisioned as a rapid-response military strike team, quite similar to your Navy SEALs or Army Delta Force. You will be assigned to one of your spacecraft carriers, the USSS *Hillenkoetter*. The '*Big-H*,' as some of your people call it, will be leaving soon on an interstellar mission."

"To another *star*?" It was very nearly a shout. The rabbit hole had just become very deep indeed.

BECKY MCCLURE was ushered into a large and windowless room furnished with sofas, low tables, and a large projection screen or monitor. At the moment, the screen showed a planet, huge and in extraordinary detail, hanging in space against the glare of . . . was that the *sun*? It seemed far too large, too close, with an odd reddish hue, and its surface was mottled by sunspots, far more than she'd ever seen in photos of Earth's sun. She thought it might be an astronomical painting of some extrasolar world, and yet the level of detail suggested that it was, in fact, an extremely high-definition photograph.

"Proxima b," another woman already in the room told her. "The nearest exoplanet out there."

"We've *been* there?"

"Oh, yes. Shortly after it was confirmed. That was just a couple of years ago." She extended a hand. "Hi, I'm Simone Carter. I'll be your boss on this expedition."

Carter was tall, black, and seemed confident and outgoing. McClure shook her hand, then sank into one of the Danish modern sofas. "And your position is, Ms. Carter?"

"Doctor, actually . . . but call me Simone. I'm head of *Hillenkoetter*'s science department, and also chief xeno-psychologist."

"*Xeno*psych?"

"The more we can understand how our, ah, visitors think, the better we'll be able to deal with them. You'll be handling the biological end of things: why they're like they are, where they came from, stuff like that."

"Does that include the time travelers?"

"If it comes up, yes. We know about the Nordics, of course. The Grays, though, are still kind of a 'gray' area."

McClure gave a polite groan, and Carter laughed.

"But the Grays *are* time travelers, as well," McClure said. "Right?"

"So far as we know. They're tough to talk to, and they aren't all that forthcoming with information about themselves, but we estimate that they come from a human civilization spread across this part of the Galaxy between 1.2 and 1.4 million years in our future. At that point, Humankind has changed. We've evolved into the Grays. In fact, we know now of several hundred distinct Gray species. Apparently, we're going to have a pretty wild evolutionary ride. There are short Grays, tall Grays, white Grays, Grays sharing a hive mind, robotic Grays, cloned Grays—"

"What about the Saurians?"

"Completely different species. They look like the Grays, but there are major differences. Digitigrade posture and forward hip articulation. Details of the skeleton and musculature." Carter shrugged. "I'm sure you know more about that than I do."

"I know some," McClure admitted. "But not enough."

One of the key points in the history of alien-human contact leading to the realization that the aliens were time travelers was the problem of parallel evolution. Humans and Nordics were *far* too much alike to have evolved on different worlds. Humans, McClure reasoned, were more closely related to maple trees than they would be to anything Out There, and the incredible diversity of life just here on Earth—from trilobites to dragonflies to octopi to frogs to platypuses to ostriches to humans—suggested that any aliens we met would be so unlike us as to be unrecognizable.

For a time, some researchers tried to explain the similarities between humans and Nordics as a case of convergent evolution. Sharks, dolphins, and ichthyosaurs all looked remarkably alike, but that was because all three—fish, mammal, and marine lizard—had been tailored by evolution to fit with superb precision into a specific niche, that of fast-swimming marine predators. Different organisms could evolve into similar shapes to fit a given environment. But the Grays, long assumed to be extraterrestrial visitors, were simply too human for them to be a truly alien species.

McClure was hoping that her extrasolar assignment would give her the chance to figure it out, though.

"Still, we do want you to learn as much about the Saurians, too," Carter said. "The Grays and the Saurians are supposed to be at war with one another. Maybe we're just being fed some disinformation."

"Yeah, but why?" McClure asked.

"I don't think the Grays know. But there are so many conspiracy theories out there about Saurians infiltrating Earth's governments. . . ."

"That English writer. What's his name . . . ?"

"And others."

The English author in question had made headlines in the '90s by claiming that the entire British royal family, plus blue bloods and the wealthy elite across Europe, plus the Bush family and forty-some other American presidents *all* were, in fact, alien lizard-people in disguise. McClure had always thought the guy had watched too much *V* back in the early '80s, a miniseries about lizard invaders from Sirius disguised as human beings. The whole idea was the cheapest sort of bargain-basement sci-fi.

"But if the Saurians *are* influencing Earth's civilization somehow," Carter told her, "we need to know."

"If we figure out that the Saurians are trying to take over Earth, what do we do about it?"

Carter sighed. "I, for one, welcome our new reptilian overlords. . . ."

McClure, however, didn't think that it was funny.

CHAPTER NINE

> I believe that alien life is quite common in the universe, although intelligent life is less so. Some say it has yet to appear on planet Earth.
>
> PHYSICIST STEPHEN HAWKING, 2010

12 January 1971

SSARSK WAS NOT *the being's name. Not really. The Surviving Few had no names, and no need of them. Within the highly organized society of the Saurians—that name would do as well as any other—each individual knew who and what it was and where it stood within a tightly structured hierarchy, and personal names would have been superfluous. "Ssarsk" translated very roughly as "Third Pilot."*

Besides, it was fully telepathic, and the touch of any other mind was distinctive, instantly recognizable. When the thought arose in its mind, it instantly identified it as the mental touch of Gajek—the "Fifth Seeker."

Where are you?

In a room deep beneath the surface . . . a prisoner.

Are you under observation?

By their security systems, simple cameras and microphones. None of them are here at present.

Be ready. We are opening a portal.

Light flared from one wall, spilling into the darkened

room. Ssarsk waited, crouching, as the vortex stabilized.
A moment later, it saw the slender, stooping shape of Ga-
jek against the light, just on the far side of the unbroken
wall.

It took you long enough.

You were difficult to find. We had to sample many
of them to determine your location. Now hurry—their
alarms have gone off!

It stepped through the portal.

"IT'S NOT as bad as you seem to think, Commander,"
Elanna told him. "No lizard men for you! We're going to
start you off hunting Nazis."

"Hunting Nazis . . ."

"I'm sure you've heard the theories of German Nazis escaping Earth at the end of World War II? In their
Haunebu flying saucers?"

"Escaping—what? Not Antarctica? Or Argentina?"

"There are many stories, Commander. It is so very difficult now to sort fact from fiction."

"Yeah, but Nazis in space? Nobody takes that seriously!" Hunter was thinking of a recent SF-comedic
movie—*Iron Sky*. There'd also been an early novel by
Robert Heinlein from the late '40s, *Rocket Ship Galileo*,
which had escaped Nazis plotting a return from their secret base on the Moon. Not a bad story, but so clunky and
unlikely today.

"For many years, your people assumed that *we* were
escaped Nazis. You even called us 'Nordics,' which in
certain contexts could be another word for 'Aryan.'"

"Yeah, but not without some justification, I'd say. You
do look the part, with that silver-blond hair and blue
eyes."

Elanna sighed. "In fact, a few of our people did help
the Germans, at least early on, but the Saurians offered
them the most help. One of the Nazi scientists, Hans
Kammler, escaped in a time ship. Others, we think, left

in a spacecraft of Saurian design. It is possible that they established a colony on the world of another star."

Hunter considered this, then shook his head. "Uh-uh. I don't believe it."

"Your skepticism is noted, but we have reason to believe that it is true."

"What reason?"

"It's difficult to explain."

He laughed. "After all this? Try me."

She produced a small hand control device from somewhere and pressed a button. The big monitor screen switched on, revealing a view of deep space. A planet hung suspended in the distance. "Is that Mars?" Hunter asked. The planet was red and ocher brown in hue, but it looked like no image of the planet Mars that Hunter had ever seen. There were clouds and . . . was that *water*?

As he watched, the angle of view changed, bringing a second world into view. This one was enormous, a red-and-yellow-banded gas giant, with other moons visible as tiny bright pearls in the distance. A thread-thin white slash, like a taut thread, bisected the giant world. Hunter's eyes widened. "Jupiter? One of Jupiter's moons is red. . . ." But was that slash a set of rings? Did Jupiter *have* rings?

"Not Mars, not Jupiter, and not Io," Elanna told him. "The gas giant is a planetary companion of the star you know as Aldebaran. The world in the foreground is a habitable, planet-sized moon we call Daarish. And there is this. . . . Watch."

Something else was drifting onto the screen now . . . an irregularly shaped piece of gray metal. It appeared as though it had been ripped from the side of something larger.

As the fragment slowly tumbled, the opposite surface came into view, and it was adorned by a black-and-white German cross—not the Teutonic iron cross, not the swastika . . . but the straight-armed version used to identify aircraft and other military equipment.

"What the fuck . . . ?"

"You recognize that emblem?"

"Sure, but it might be alien. Couldn't it? I mean, an alien symbol that just happens to look like it's German?"

"Do you really believe that's true?"

"I find it easier to believe that than Nazis fled to Aldebaran!"

"A few years ago, some of our ships came under attack as they passed through the Aldebaran system," Elanna told him. "We destroyed one of the attacking vessels, and what you're looking at *might* be a part of the wreckage. The attackers might have been Saurians, or we may be looking at some sort of automated defense system. But discovering this raises a different possibility. Why do you think the Nazis might be interested in this star system?"

The question seemed to be a sharp change of topic. Hunter struggled to keep up. "Well, the Nazis had this really sick, twisted way of seeing things, thinking that anyone who wasn't pure, one hundred percent Caucasian was subhuman. They killed millions of people who didn't measure up to their standards of racial purity."

"Of this we are aware."

"They also were off on kind of a mystic bent. Weird, metaphysical ideas . . . like that the Aryans weren't ordinary humans. The Aryans had come from someplace else, and tried to establish a civilization in northern Europe, but the subhumans kept mucking things up for them."

"Hyperborea. A mythical land in the far north first imagined by the ancient Greeks."

"Hyperborea, Thule—lots of names for it. But I read once that some of them thought that the Aryans had come from the stars."

"Correct," Elanna said quietly. "Specifically, from *this star*. There is a group located in Germany and Austria, the Tempelhofgesellschaft, or THG. They teach a rather heretical form of dualist Christianity, claiming that Jesus was an Aryan, and that the Jews and the god Jehovah are evil."

"Gnosticism?"

"An extreme and twisted version, yes, blended with certain neo-Nazi beliefs. The Aryans, they claim, came to Earth from Aldebaran thousands of years ago and formed a colony in ancient Atlantis."

"What is this thing the Nazis have for hideaways starting with the letter *A*?"

She looked puzzled. "I beg your pardon?"

"Argentina, Antarctica, Atlantis, and Aldebaran," Hunter replied.

Elanna smiled. "I see. You forget 'America.'"

"Huh?"

"The place where large numbers of former Nazis *did* settle, besides Argentina, was in the United States of America. Operation Paperclip."

"God. You're right."

"In any case," she continued, "the THG printed pamphlets claiming that the Aryans came from Aldebaran, and that this information had been revealed to them from ancient Sumerian manuscripts."

"Was it?"

"Of course not. But their religion claims that a huge space fleet is on its way to Earth from that system. When it gets here, it will join with the Nazi flying saucers secretly based in Antarctica, and together they will take over the world."

"All pure nonsense, right?"

"*Im*pure nonsense, yes. Except . . ."

Hunter felt a small thrill of fear. "Except what?"

"The THG was promulgating their religious beliefs beginning in the 1990s. An earlier version of the THG was operating in the 1980s. This image of the German emblem out at Aldebaran, and the attacks on our ships . . . those occurred in 1976."

"Coincidence?"

"Possibly. Or else time-traveling starships are involved."

The realization hit Hunter like a blow to his stomach. *"Die Glocke. . . ."*

"We know The Nazi Bell crashed in Pennsylvania in 1965," Elanna told him. "But other groups, other Nazi groups, just might have escaped to Aldebaran after the war. Or, the Saurians have an intertemporal network across many years and many star systems, and some of that information has leaked into Europe's far-right community. Or—"

"Okay! I get it! I get it!" He held up his hand. "Once you throw time travel into the equation, all bets are off—*anything* is possible!"

"That statement is truer than you realize."

"So how do we find out?" Cold realization shone through. "Ah. That's why the JSST."

"We are organizing an interstellar expedition, one built around the spaceship carrier *Hillenkoetter.* Some of us will be on board as advisors, but the expedition, codenamed Excalibur, will be entirely Earth's. You will travel to Aldebaran to find out who, or what, might be based there."

"Space Nazis."

"If you like—"

"I *don't* like. We'll still be up against some radically advanced military technology, right? I'm guessing they don't just have Focke-Wulfs and Messerschmitts up there. Jesus—something that fired at some of your ships? So why can't *you* guys go in and blow the shit out of them? It was *your* ships they shot up."

Elanna hesitated for a long moment, as though wondering how much to tell Hunter. He had the distinct impression that there were things she was not supposed to say. By now, that was an attitude with which he was quite familiar.

At last, she closed her eyes. "Mark, can you imagine

what a full-blown *time war* would be like? What it could do to Humankind?"

"A war in time?" He wrestled with the concept. "I don't know. It would definitely be different tactically. You could send an attacking force in at a time and place before the other side knew you were coming, for one thing."

"Among many other things. Imagine a struggle in which whole civilizations, whole *worlds* were—I think the word would be *edited*. Edited out of existence. Historical battles lost suddenly become battles won. Powerful leaders cease to exist. Important elections that end one way now end in another. Civilizations destined for greatness vanish before they ever get started. Asteroids smash into worlds before those civilizations ever arise. The fabric of space and time are twisted out of all recognition."

"Ouch."

"Yes, Mark. Ouch. So the reason we can't fight is because, in our war with the Saurians, we are . . . *constrained* in certain ways. We don't try to wipe *them* out of existence so that they don't try to wipe *us* out of existence. You understand?"

"MAD."

"What?"

"MAD. Mutually assured destruction. It was the reasoning that drove the Cold War, the fact that both sides knew that if they tried to annihilate the other side with nuclear weapons, the other side would wipe them out, too. So lots of pseudo-wars were fought by proxy—Korea, Vietnam, Afghanistan, Grenada—but the big powers never pushed the buttons that would have wiped out *everybody*."

"An excellent illustration. We and the Saurians fight our wars by proxies so that a major time war never occurs."

"I thought we were you? Just more primitive. If you send us back in time to do your dirty work, isn't that the

same as you doing it yourselves?" He rubbed his forehead.

"The balance between the Saurians, humans, and
Grays is more subtle, more precarious than you could possibly imagine, Commander. You are us, yes. But your culture is different, the way you think is different, even your
biology is different. And if you attack the Saurians—or
expatriate Nazis, for that matter—you will not immediately trigger a temporal apocalypse. Using you instead of
acting ourselves creates a kind of buffer behind which we
can work. You understand?"

"No. I don't. If the bad guys edit us out, you get edited
out, too. Right?"

"Which is why they won't make the attempt, knowing
that they cannot possibly destroy all of us . . . and they,
therefore, would be edited out of existence, as well." She
hesitated again. "Tell me, Commander. How much do
you know of the various treaties between humans of your
time period, and the various alien groups?"

"I've got the basics. Eisenhower with the Grays, the
Saurians with the Nazis."

"Right. Besides helping them rebuild Die Glocke, they
were also helping in other areas. There is much disinformation, fiction, and outright lies contaminating the field
today, but at the end of the Second World War the Germans were within months of destroying New York City
with a primitive nuclear device."

Hunter whistled. "Didn't know that."

Elanna nodded. "We *also* believe that some Nazis fled
Earth entirely. Whether this was on their own primitive
antigravity saucers, or whether they escaped in Saurian
craft, is unknown. But Die Glocke was not the only ship
to flee the Götterdämmerung of the Nazi Reich. The
question is: Where might they have gone?"

"Aldebaran," Hunter said, leaping to the obvious conclusion. "Looking for their Aryan homeland."

"Precisely. And part of the problem is that many in

your government in the 1950s believed that we, the ones you call 'Nordics,' were, in fact, escaped Nazis flying German saucers. That is not true, but there are still those in your government today who fear us because they assume some sort of connection with the Nazis. Old fears, like old habits, die hard."

"If the idea that the Aryans came from Aldebaran came out of the 1990s," Hunter said, following the disturbing thread of thought, "how did it get to the Nazis of 1945?"

"That," Elanna said, "is why we suspect temporal contamination. Someone from recent times is in intertemporal communication with 1945."

Hunter sighed. "This is way, way beyond me, Elanna. You're telling me that some of the worst crackpot theories in history might be real. But you don't know for sure."

"Precisely."

"And you somehow want me to fight them."

"If it comes to that. More, though, I think you and your JSST may be instrumental in helping us unravel the truth."

NAVY COMMANDER Philip Wheaton never got tired of the sight.

He was standing with Vashnu on the main hangar deck of Darkside Base, looking up . . . and up . . . and *up* at the enormous, rounded prow of the USSS *Roscoe H. Hillenkoetter* hanging against the blaze of overhead lights far above his head. As long from stem to stern as a modern nuclear aircraft carrier in the oceangoing Navy, massing nearly a hundred thousand tons, the *Big-H* was the fourth of the eight huge mother ship spacecraft carriers in the Solar Warden fleet.

Dad, Wheaton thought, *would have loved to see this.*

Majik had long made a habit of recruiting the children of their employees whenever possible. It was so much easier to break the news to them—that a parent had worked for the secretive organization, that they'd known the fact of alien contact, of the reality of Solar Warden and the secret fleet. It made acceptance easier.

Wheaton's father had been a CIA officer back in the '60s and '70s, and been sworn to secrecy about much of what he'd seen. He'd never said a word about any of it to his wife or two kids and had taken the secret to his grave when he'd died in 1982.

Phil Wheaton had been born in 1975, had joined the Navy in '98, and become a naval intelligence officer in 2011. They'd approached him about becoming part of Solar Warden five years later.

He was still getting over the shock.

But things his dad had known about back in the '60s had borne fruit in the '70s. And the first of America's top secret black space fleet had entered orbit in 1986. How MJ-12 had managed to keep a lid on the project all those years, with nothing reaching the general public but hints and rumors, was a mystery. Evidently, the government *could* keep a secret when it needed to. The Manhattan Project wasn't just an outlier.

"So what are we waiting for?" he asked the tall, pale-skinned Nordic standing next to him.

"The military contingent," Vashnu replied. He did not sound as though he entirely approved. "They are already at Darkside, going through orientation. They will arrive here in twenty-four hours."

"You don't like the military, do you, Vashnu?"

The time traveler made a face, the expression unreadable. "It's not that I don't like it," he said. "I just question the wisdom of rushing your culture into the interstellar arena."

"Oh, I think we'll be able to hold our own."

"Do you think so? The Galaxy is brimming over with life, with civilizations, with minds as far beyond yours as your minds are beyond that of an insect. With civilizations older than you can imagine, and some of those are darkly paranoid, jealous of those younger, less-developed species that might attempt to supplant them in a few million years. More, each species that has developed interstellar travel has, almost by definition, developed time travel as well, and those teeming empires and federations and communities of intellects span eons as well as light-years. I represent a human offshoot eleven thousand years beyond yours, and I can tell you that *we* do not 'hold our own.' Every new contact, every new step into the darkness, becomes an existential threat as we face challenges and conflicts which you, Philip, cannot even imagine."

Wheaton opened his mouth to reply, then shut it again. Vashnu was right. Wheaton had only the thinnest understanding of the field tentatively known as exospaciotemporal politics, or EST, and knew better than to challenge the Nordic about things that Vashnu understood, and he did not.

"Okay," Wheaton said. "It's a big scary universe and we'll have to watch our step. But we know we survive, right? Otherwise you wouldn't be here."

"I don't think you understand the niceties of intertemporal interaction," Vashnu said. "Our current time line is intact, yes. But it has also suffered innumerable changes—minor changes, to be sure, but history is constantly being rewritten."

"I'm not aware of any changes."

"Of course not. *Everything* changes, including your books, your records, and your memories. Even so, there are gaps, discontinuities. Things that don't match up perfectly. Your Charles Fort made a career of collecting reports of strange things that didn't fit. People who vanished without a trace. People who appeared, with no clue as to their origin. Have you ever wondered why you've failed to find a single solid piece of evidence for the existence of the primate you call Bigfoot?"

"Because it's not real."

"You're so sure? Thousands of credible witnesses have

encountered it all over the world. However, no body has ever been found, no skeleton, no artifact. Why? Because there are alternate versions of Earth, parallel time lines, where *Homo sapiens* never appeared, or he died out and the world was inherited by the large, hairy hominids you know as *Gigantopithecus*. But sometimes, worlds leak, one into another. They overlap for brief periods, and in such an overlap two English schoolteachers on vacation in France in the year 1901 find themselves in the gardens of the Petit Trianon at Versailles in 1789."

"That happened?"

"Their names were Moberly and Jourdain. It happened."

"I'll watch my step next time I visit France." Vashnu didn't laugh. *Okay* . . . "So why *did* your people help us? The time line must be threadbare by now."

"We are members, as you must know, of a galactic conclave. You might call it a federation, a cooperative similar to your United Nations. Such decisions are made by many species, each with their own agenda, their own reasoning. Some of my own people, government leaders, feared what would happen if you destroyed yourselves in the twentieth century. They were able to convince the others." He shook his head, a decidedly human gesture. "We do not always make wise choices."

"Well, we'll do our best not to let you down. Let's go on board, shall we?"

An elevator carried them up to a boarding tube area, and they crossed over into the *Hillenkoetter*.

Roscoe Hillenkoetter was the very first director of the CIA, and he'd been deeply involved in the secret goings-on surrounding the recovery of a crashed ship at Roswell, and the subsequent creation of MJ-12. He was also one of the first twelve members of that committee. Somehow it was fitting that one of the space-going carriers of America's secret space fleet be named for him.

They entered on the quarterdeck, a symbolic space

traditionally reserved for ceremonial receptions and formal coming-aboard rituals. Wheaton, in uniform, saluted the flag mounted on an aft bulkhead, then saluted the quarterdeck as he stepped aboard. "Permission to come aboard."

A painfully young Navy lieutenant, the officer of the deck, returned the salute. "Permission granted. Welcome aboard, sir."

"Is either the admiral or the captain aboard yet?" he asked.

"No, sir," the lieutenant replied. "But Commander Haines is the senior watch officer, and he's on the bridge. You can report to him there."

"Thank you, son." He glanced left and right, momentarily disoriented. "Which way?"

"I'll take you, Philip," Vashnu told him.

Hillenkoetter's bridge was buried deep within the vessel, and actually consisted of three interconnected areas on the O-4 level. The flag bridge was aft and highest, the place where the admiral could command the battle group. The ship's bridge was in the middle, while forward and below was the CIC, the combat information center. The compartments all were quite spacious, but the clutter of large monitors, electrical conduits, workstations, and padded swivel seats for perhaps eighty people made it feel cramped and crowded. A Navy commander in short-sleeve whites was on the bridge, leaning over a tangle of wiring with two enlisted technicians. "Yank it if you have to," he was saying. "We'll order a replacement from Supply."

"Commander Haines?"

The man straightened and turned. "What?"

Wheaton saluted. "Commander Wheaton, reporting aboard."

"As what?"

"I'm your new S2."

Haines nodded. "Bill Haines, XO. You'll be forward,

in CIC. Office below on the first deck. Quarters below and aft, third deck."

"Thank you."

"Damn it, Parker! Not *that* one! The other one!" Haines vanished back into the tangle of wires and circuit boards.

Wheaton exchanged glances with Vashnu.

Maybe the time traveler was right. Maybe twenty-first-century humans *weren't* ready for interstellar space.

CHAPTER TEN

We find ourselves faced by powers which are far stronger than we had hitherto assumed, and whose base is at present unknown to us. More I cannot say at present. We are now engaged in entering into closer contact with those powers, and in six or nine months it may be possible to speak with some precision on the matter.

DR. WERNHER VON BRAUN,
FIRST DIRECTOR OF NASA, 1959

10 February 1971

HANS KAMMLER WAS *having a bad night, one made surreal by dark and twisted dreams.*

He was no stranger to nightmares. Sometimes, and more and more often of late, his victims rose from the earth and hemmed him in, gibbering and moaning, ghosts with pallid faces and empty eyes and wearing the rags of concentration camp inmates.

And why am *I* persecuted? *he demanded of an unhearing, uncaring cosmos.* We all took part in what happened. We all followed orders. Von Braun *personally* handpicked the prisoners who would be assigned to Mittelwerk! My God, more inmates from the Mittelbau-Dora camp died building von Braun's V-2s than were killed in all of the attacks by all of those rockets in the entire war! But von Braun, the star of Paperclip, was a fucking *hero* ...

Kammler heard voices, but for once they were not the tortured, screaming and groaning voices of his victims. Voices in his head:

Is that him?

It is him. I taste his mind.

Who was that? Where were they? What did they want?

Kammler opened his eyes, awake now, but somehow unable to move. He was in his bedroom, in his suburban home on the northern outskirts of Houston. Apollo 14 had returned from the lunar Fra Mauro Highlands only yesterday, and Kammler had been out celebrating with some of the Houston engineers. Too much to drink. He must be hallucinating....

Traci, the woman he'd hired for the night, still lay beside him, nude, breathing gently, sound asleep.

Where were the voices coming from?

He was convinced now that this was no alcohol-induced hallucination. He was aware of every detail of his room, with a clarity that was frighteningly immediate and real.

Terror deepened, fear upon nightmare fear. Light spilled from the wall opposite his bed, light and a kind of open doorway within which spindly, moving, shadowy figures were visible—alien figures, like the creature that had brought him twenty years forward in time.

He screamed—or tried to. He couldn't move, couldn't cry out, couldn't blink *for God's sake—and the nightmare beings were all around him, reaching for him, lifting him, carrying him toward that Hell's gate of light.*

"Help me!" *he shrieked.*

But no sound came out, Traci slept on, oblivious, and the Eidechse creatures effortlessly carried him into the light.

HUNTER WAS furious.

There was an old, old military saying: hurry up and wait. Operation Excalibur was demonstrating the concept in spades.

Over the next four days, more military personnel arrived, joining the 1-JSST at the secret lunar base. The delay meant that his people *could* have had time to practice with their weapons. The project was even more screwed up than he'd first imagined.

Haines was no help. According to regs, the ship's executive officer was the immediate person in charge of the ship's internal operations, personnel, and personnel problems . . . and he waved aside Hunter's request for training time. "Technically, Commander," he said, "you people are not ship's crew. You're supernumeraries, which means Captain Groton is the man to talk to."

"He's not here, sir."

"I know. Find something useful for your men to do until he comes aboard. *You* are in charge of the JSST, not me."

"Can I set up a test range outside the base? Let the men practice with their suits and weapons?"

"No, Commander. I'll tell you right now that Captain Mallory will not run the risk of having people dying out there." Mallory was the commanding officer of Darkside Base.

Something *useful*, huh?

Hunter had requisitioned a large auditorium on the base and had his unit assemble there. With the new arrivals from Earth, 1-JSST now consisted of forty-one men and seven women, for a total of forty-eight.

He'd counted his people off in groups of three, had them sit together and . . . talk. Just talk. Talk about themselves, about past missions, about family, about whatever they wanted, really. After an hour, everyone switched partners.

The point was to have every person in the JSST

get to know everyone else. If they were going to be a combat team, they would have to trust one another to a degree completely beyond the comprehension of civilians. Hunter left his group—Arch and an Army Ranger named Patterson—to get to know one another while he circulated among the other groups, nudging things along, asking pertinent questions, and generally trying to keep things moving.

It wasn't easy. "Why the fucking bull session, Commander?" a grizzled Delta Force operator named Salvatore demanded. "Someone's been reading too much psychobabble!"

"Fuckin' A," another Ranger said. "You don't start trusting other people because they fuckin' told you their life story."

"If you're going into a firefight, mister," Hunter said quietly, "I would *think* that you'd want to know the guys to either side of you."

"I don't like talking about old operations," Dorschner said. "Classified stuff. *Deep* black."

Hunter knew how Dorschner felt. SEALs weren't supposed to talk about their missions or operating history either. He also knew it went deeper than that. All of them had seen and done things they didn't like to think about, and talking about it just dredged up the pain and bad memories.

"If you can't talk about your ops, talk about other stuff. Salvatore—you have a family?"

"Got a girlfriend. . . ."

"Then tell them about how an asshole like you landed a girl."

The others laughed, and Hunter nodded. Salvatore brought up a good point, and Hunter doubted that any person in that room was married. The selection process had been designed to weed out people with family responsibilities at home, because they would be gone a long time.

As much as he probably smarted at Hunter's joke, if there was one thing military people always loved to discuss—at endless length and in mind-numbing detail—it was women. Salvatore started talking about Cindy, back in Arlington, and before long Hunter seemed to be forgotten as they shared the details, some more salacious than others, of women both in and out of the sack. Hunter used the same technique to kick-start several other groups, and before long laughter and cries of "aww, *yeah*" were sounding from all over the auditorium.

The women on the team seemed more interested in hobbies, places they'd been, things they'd done. They talked about ex-lovers, and were also a lot more heavily into "yes, but how do you *feel* about that" than were the guys.

All this talk made Hunter think about Gerri.

Damn . . .

There was one crisis when a Delta master sergeant named Coulter admitted to being gay, and Chief Brunelli declared he was *not* going into combat with "a damned fag watching his ass" . . . an unfortunate choice of words. When half a dozen men—and several women—came rather heatedly to Coulter's defense and shouted Brunelli down, Hunter knew they were starting to bond (and he'd talk to Brunelli·privately to make sure that he wasn't going to be a problem).

He had them fall in and began taking them through some calisthenics, happy with the early connections being made. Emotionally, these people were getting to know each other, and that was important to create esprit de corps.

But how the hell was he supposed to forge them into a solid combat unit?

Part of his problem had to do with personnel organization. As a SEAL, Hunter was used to a basic combat unit—the sixteen-man SEAL platoon. Other services, though, had different platoon makeups. The Army tended to have infantry rifle platoons consisting of thirty-nine men. Marines had forty-three.

He was in charge, though, and that had to be for a reason, so Hunter decided to stick with what he knew and divide the unit into three sixteen-man platoons, each broken into two sections, and with two commissioned officers and a senior noncom—a master chief or a master sergeant. Two officers, Arch and Billingsly, would run his two other platoons. He brought a third lieutenant—Navy lieutenant Carl Bader—into Alfa, where he would serve as Hunter's personal staff, leaving him free to watch over the entire unit.

Why in all the hells of Hell Week had *they* not hashed this out back on Earth? Hunter felt like he was reinventing the wheel—that persons unknown higher up the totem pole had simply dropped a disparate collection of people into a box and shaken well. It didn't work that way, damn it. The whole point of boot camp—aside from the basic one of breaking raw civilians down and turning them into soldiers or sailors—was to get them to function together as a team. For Navy SEALs, boot camp was nothing compared to Basic Underwater Demolition/ SEAL training—BUD/S—which was twenty-four weeks of hell followed by a twenty-six week SEAL qualification program, all of which was designed to weed out the ones who didn't shape up, give the rest the tools they would need in combat, and *teach them to work together.*

The sad part was, Hunter thought, that in the long run, the only way to forge these forty-eight people together would be putting them into the fire of combat.

And he fully expected to lose some people along the way.

But he continued hammering at them, forcing them to get to know one another, giving them calisthenic routines that forced them to work together, making them become a team despite their best efforts. Some of his people bitched and grumbled about not doing things the *right* way—meaning the way they were used to.

But by the next day, he thought he detected a whiff of improved morale, and a bit more snap and shine when they fell into ranks.

"Commander Hunter?"

Hunter was in a base lounge going over the personnel records of some of his people when a middle-aged woman came up behind him. He stood, turning. "Yes, ma'am."

"I'm Dr. Rebecca McClure." She extended a hand. In her other hand she was carrying a small black tablet. "Remember me? From the shuttle? I'm going to be the senior xenobiologist on this expedition."

"Pleased to meet you, ma'am." He grinned at her. "Mark Hunter. I kill people and break things for a living. Or maybe it's 'kill things and break people.' I always get that part confused."

"So I've heard. Can we talk?"

He gestured at a seat. "Please."

He was glad she'd turned up. Except for some noise from Elanna about Aldebaran no one had told him a thing about this mission. If he was going to be riding shotgun, he needed to know more about what they were going to be facing.

"I need to find out what you know about the aliens we're going to be working with, Commander," she said. "The aliens . . . and the time travelers."

He frowned. "I've met one of the time travelers. She gave me a briefing on . . . well, a lot of stuff. About history, and the perils of time travel, mostly."

"That would be Four-twenty-five eight-twelve Elanna," she said.

"*That's* her full name?"

"The Talis—that's what they call themselves, by the way, not 'Nordics'—the Talis use numbers the way certain Welsh military units did, to distinguish among a very large number of soldiers in the same regiment named 'Jones' or 'Williams.'"

"Makes sense. I don't think the Welsh do that anymore, though."

"I honestly don't know if the Welsh even have a military anymore."

He smiled.

"What do you think of her?" she asked.

"She doesn't look much like the proverbial 'little green man.' She's not little, she's not green, and she most certainly is not a man."

"Come on. Be serious."

"She seems competent. For someone who came here from the year 13,000 AD, she seems to know us pretty well."

"We're actually not sure of their exact epoch," McClure told him. "Eleven thousand years is just a guess."

"They don't talk much about themselves."

McClure smiled. "No. They don't. I think they're afraid of contaminating the time line."

"We talked about how bad a time war would be," Hunter said. "And I gather we're being dragged into the middle of things with the idea of preventing a war from going . . . temporal? As opposed to 'nuclear'?"

"I've heard the same thing. I don't buy it. Bring us in and we'll just make things worse."

"That's what I thought." He spread his hands. "So . . . what can I tell you? I really don't know much about any of them."

"Do any of us? But . . . look. I'll be up-front with you, Commander. You said a moment ago . . . what was it you do for a living? 'Kill people and break stuff'?"

"An old joke. I think the Marines started it."

"But it's not a joke, Commander. We—we're going clear out of our solar system, out to exoplanets humans have never seen before. We know from the Talis that the

Galaxy is filled with alien civilizations. I want to know that you and your people aren't going to shoot first . . . and maybe not ask any questions at all."

"I'll tell you the truth, ma'am, I'm not sure what we're going to do, because I still don't know *why* we're here. They've told us damned precious little."

"Ah, the wonderful cloak of secrecy. We're not even allowed to talk to ourselves."

"And yet here we are."

"True." She looked around, but no one seemed to be paying them any attention.

Hunter went on. "The secrecy is one thing. But they also just rounded us up, threw us together, and shipped us to the Moon without even letting us practice with the new toys they showed us. Right now I'm trying to knead forty-some people into a cohesive unit. I've got Navy SEALs, US Marines, Army SpecOps people . . . for all I know there're a couple of Coast Guard guys in there. Or worse." He looked around, and then, with a dramatic whisper, said, *"Air Force!"*

She laughed at the casual demonstration of interservice rivalry. "I'm sure you'll do just fine, Commander. But seriously, can your men be trusted not to shoot something just because it looks like your worst nightmare?"

He studied her for a long moment. "Doctor, I don't have an answer for you. These men are highly trained, elite, the very best our military has to offer. They won't go off half-cocked. But I can't tell you how they'll perform in any given situation until I actually see them perform in the field. Hell, I can't tell you how I'm going to react. But we train 'em pretty good back on Earth, so I think we'll be able to handle it."

She looked at him for a moment, then took the iPad she was carrying and turned it on. Several swipes and key touches later, she turned it so that Hunter could see.

Talk about *nightmares* . . .

At first, Hunter couldn't tell what he was looking at.

Was it alive? He had the impression of a tangle of wires and small parts, all black and dripping with oil . . . or perhaps it was slime. Then the thing *moved* . . . and something eerily like a human eye opened in the middle of it, looking into the camera. "What the fuck?"

"The Talis call it an *Ecopleh*. It's highly intelligent. It's from a planet—a gas-giant moon, actually—but it's a world you've never heard of somewhere in the direction of Sagittarius. When it speaks, it sounds beautiful, like the twittering of nightingales."

"I wouldn't know a nightingale twitter if it jumped me in an alley."

"I need to know that if one of *these* jumped you or your men in an alley, you wouldn't just shoot it. The Ecopleh are highly civilized and, well, I suppose you could call them pacifists. They don't kill other beings, no matter what the provocation."

"I guess whether or not I shoot depends on whether or not it was trying to kill me. If it's as peaceful as you say, then we should be good. Are you saying we're going to be meeting these . . . things?"

"Not likely. We won't be going out that way." She shut off the iPad and set it down. "But it's one example, among many, many others of what *is* out there . . . and it's almost all new to us. The Talis will help us get oriented, I guess you would say, but they won't be with us all the time."

Hunter nodded at the iPad. "Where'd you get that video, anyway?"

"The Talis have the equivalent of our Internet. We call it 'the Encyclopedia Galactica' because it has so much information about other worlds and species and civilizations. We've only just begun to convert the data for our operating systems, and study it."

"You have any more?"

"A couple of hundred, maybe."

"It occurs to me, Dr. McClure, that some desensitization might help."

"Desensitization?"

"If my people got to look at a few hundred different aliens, they might be less likely to open fire the minute they encounter something really bizarre. Let me see a few more. . . ."

She opened another video for him. This one looked like a long, rippling ribbon floating deep within dark water, colored red-pink and translucent enough that Hunter could see internal organs. It appeared to be self-luminous, though Hunter couldn't see where the light was coming from on its body. Three black dots on the end facing the camera might be eyes; a spray of nearly transparent tendrils emerging from behind the head were for manipulation. It looked gossamer delicate, and inexpressibly beautiful.

"A Naakap," McClure told him. "One of my favorites. Purely abyssal; they live within ocean depths that would crush you or me to a pulp. They communicate by means of incredibly intricate dance—"

"Where are they from?"

"Again, you've never heard of it. A planet out near the galactic rim, I'm told. Their world is much like Pluto in our solar system: frigidly cold—minus four hundred degrees, on the surface—but radioactives deep within the core provide enough heat to keep a deep, liquid water ocean from freezing solid."

Hunter stared at the being for several moments. "I'd love to meet one someday."

"You can't. They went extinct about three hundred million years ago."

"Extinct? But someone made this video! Someone was *there*."

"Of course. Time travel, remember? But I doubt that we'll be allowed to travel so far into the past."

"But couldn't the travelers do something? Help them somehow?"

"Without changing the time line? Mark . . . the further back you travel in time, the more tiny changes can snowball. Some of the time, anyway. Some temporal changes get washed out in the background noise. A few echo through the eons, though, getting stronger and stronger. It's hard to tell which way it will go. But saving the Naakap—an entire species—might have calamitous repercussions in the remote future."

Hunter had his doubts about that. How could the survival of these beautiful ribbon-creatures possibly affect Humankind three hundred million years later?

He pointed. "Can I get one of these?" he asked her.

"A pad? Of course. They have them at the base exchange here. I'll see that you get one, and download what I have of the Encyclopedia Galactica onto it."

"Thank you. Can I get forty-seven *more* of these pads? For my people?"

"To desensitize them?"

"I suppose so. I'm thinking of it as *sensitizing* them now, though. Make them aware of how beautiful alien life-forms can be."

"Okay. Just be aware, though . . ."

"What?"

"There are . . . *things* out there. Things so horrible, so inhuman, so *nightmarish*, they make the Ecopleh look like cute, cuddly teddy bears." She was tapping at her keyboard again. "Things like . . . this."

An eye stared out of the screen at Hunter, but it was not at all human. He'd once seen a close-up photo of the eye of a toad—golden, with a horizontal hourglass shape for the pupil. This was like that. Except now it was embedded in a writhing mass of tentacles so numerous they gave the impression of thick, long, and very black squirming hair—a sea urchin with flexible and animated spines. The being filled the screen, and Hunter wasn't able even to guess how large it might be, or to tell whether or not he was seeing the whole thing. "Teddy bears, huh?" he said.

"Paka," she told him. "From a world fifty thousand years in the future."

"Not the sort of thing I'd care to run into on a dark night." He stared at the Paka for a moment more. "You know, I can't get a handle on what this critter is like. Mammal? Mollusk?"

"You'd be amazed at how little most beings in the Galaxy resemble *anything* with which we are familiar. Trust me when I say that we are *not* going to find Mr. Spock out there—completely human except for the pointy ears and a fondness for logic."

"Except the Grays."

"Exactly. And that's because they *are* human."

"Right. But what about the Saurians? They have time travel—The Bell—and they look just like the Grays. But Elanna said they're not from Earth."

"She's correct. They are . . . unusual. We know very little about them, unfortunately."

I guess we'll find out if we ever actually fight them.

She then showed him a being that was all spikes and body armor—*heavy* body armor, like a walking tank. It *did* replicate the basic humanoid body shape, but the legs were too short and the arms too long and the overall shape of the torso was all wrong. The face was not even remotely human, with the eyes in armored turrets out to either side, like a chameleon, and a vertical slit of a mouth up high, almost at the top of the head.

"Gugada," she said. "From a very cold planet, somewhat like Titan in our system. Breathes ammonia and excretes methane. But you should hear their opera."

Hunter shivered.

"It's okay—they're supposedly very sweet."

"I bet." He thought about what McClure had sat down to talk to him about, and it dawned on him that she hadn't really talked about who they *could* shoot. "What about the Saurians? Are we going to have to shoot them on sight?"

"Not on sight, no. You'll be taking tactical combat orders from Major Powell and from me. We'll be in the *Hillenkoetter*'s CIC, and we'll be in constant communication with Elanna or another Talis. It is vital that your people not fire on anyone unless you have a direct release from us. Do you understand?"

Hunter sighed. "Rules of engagement. Yes, I understand."

"Good."

Rules of engagement, Hunter thought, were a fantastic way to get you or your people killed. Some armchair admiral way up the chain of command—or worse, the President himself—decided that it was politically a bad thing to shoot them before they shot you. There were instances in recent history where US troops had been forbidden to fire *even when they were being fired upon*, and in several notorious cases, were ordered to stand sentry duty with unloaded weapons. Under Obama, troops in Afghanistan had been prohibited from shooting back if *any* civilians were present at all, and had been required to retreat if they were. Of course, the Taliban soon figured this out and always made sure that civilians were present anytime they attacked. Sheer armchair quarterbacking brilliance . . . and now they had a *biologist* calling the shots.

"There's more," she added.

He closed his eyes. "Great. Just freakin' *great*."

"We *may* be at war with the Grays, as well."

"I thought they were our kids?"

"In a way, I guess you're right. But what matters now is that we had a treaty with them, and now it's off."

"You know," Hunter said, "even if they are related to us, they are the living definition of alien. Evolved a million years beyond us, they say? I would be surprised if they thought anything at all like us. They might not even understand the concept of 'treaty.'"

"Bravo, Commander. Exactly right. But they definitely understood trade. Except they began taking more and more people. A lot of them weren't being returned.

In others, the hypnotic commands keeping the people in ignorance were breaking down. We thought just a few would be taken. I mean . . . how many specimens would they need? Turns out they were taking hundreds of thousands of people. They were fascinated by human reproduction, and took sperm and ova samples from almost everybody they captured. That was actually what put us on to the fact that they were human, you know."

"I didn't know."

"Sure. There was all of this speculation in the popular press and in books on the subject that they were busily creating some sort of alien-human hybrid race, okay? But, biologically, that's pure bullshit! You and I, Commander, are more closely related to planaria or . . . or *slime molds* than we are to anything truly alien from Out There. But if the Grays are our human descendants, well, we think they've hit some sort of genetic bottleneck up there in the remote future. Something that's threatening the species with extinction. And they're coming back to our time to pick up the genetic raw materials that might help them correct the problem."

Hunter made a face. "Okay. I guess that makes sense. I would think we could have helped them out with an account at one of our sperm banks, rather than let them kidnap us, though."

"As you said, Commander, the Grays are alien. They're human, but they are very, *very* alien in the way that they think. More alien than you could possibly imagine.

"And we are going to have to find a way to bridge that gap of mutual alienness, find a way to understand one another and communicate with one another, before we . . . and they . . . become extinct."

Maybe that's why his team hadn't gotten any training time yet.

It seemed like there was no one in the Galaxy they were going to be asked to shoot.

CHAPTER ELEVEN

The next war will be an interplanetary war. The nations of the Earth must someday make a common front against attack by people from other planets. The politics of the future will be cosmic, or interplanetary.

GENERAL DOUGLAS MACARTHUR
[ATTRIBUTED], 1955

10 February 1971

HANS KAMMLER FOUND *himself on the street in front of his house, naked, disoriented, and with a throbbing pain behind his eyes. How had he gotten here?*

He had no memories of having awoken, or of having come out here. Had he been sleepwalking?

He'd never done so before, at least, not that he knew. His restless sleep, the horrifying nightmares, those might point to some sort of sleep disorder, and possibly somnambulism was simply a new symptom.

Barefoot, he made his way back across the sidewalk, up the steps to his front porch, and reached out to open the front door.

It was locked.

Had he come outside while asleep and locked the door behind him?

He rang the front doorbell repeatedly, until Traci re-

luctantly cracked the door open, saw who it was, then let him inside. "What were you doing out there?"

Kammler couldn't answer her. He had no answers.

But he did have just the faintest shreds of memory . . . a dream.

He'd been dreaming of the alien Ssarsk.

HUNTER RENDERED a crisp salute, first to the quarterdeck, then to the man in dress whites before him. "Permission to come aboard, sir."

"Granted. Welcome on board the *Hillenkoetter*."

The ship, Hunter thought, was impressive. He and the other SEALs had taken a close look at her from outside before they'd boarded . . . or as close as they could get from their vantage point on the concrete flooring below the monster vessel.

She was twelve hundred feet long and massed sixty-eight thousand tons, a long, slender, somewhat flattened cigar shape of dark gray metal comparable in length to a modern nuclear-powered supercarrier, but with less than half a carrier's beam and a little more than half the mass. Her tubular hull was capped fore and aft by light gray geodesic domes, with four more identical domes spaced evenly around the cylinder next to and at right angles to the caps. Those ten domes, he was told, each sixty feet across at the base, housed the ship's power and flight control drives. The *Big-H* certainly looked nothing like a conventional rocket, with no venturis aft for the escape of propellant gasses, and with bow identical to stern. Instead, she ran on something called zero-point energy, which used intense magnetic fields to twist space-time, and therefore gravity, to the whim of her skipper.

That skipper was Captain Fred Groton, a tall, heavyset man with a no-nonsense attitude who met Hunter and his men on the quarterdeck. If it wasn't by the book, some members of his bridge crew had said, he wanted no part of it. He'd shuttled up from Earth with a last few dozen personnel. With their arrival, *Hillenkoetter*'s roster was complete, and the ship was cleared for launch.

Standing beside the captain was Commander Haines. "Your people will be quartered on the third deck, amidships twelve abaft Frame 40," he said. "Berthing compartments eight through twelve. I'll detail a rating to take you down."

"Thank you, sir."

"Don't thank us, son," Groton said. "Not until you know what we're going to put you through!"

"I *was* wondering about that, sir."

"Department heads briefing at 1500, Commander. Conference A. Be there."

"Aye, aye, sir!"

The *Hillenkoetter* was a small city, with miles of intricately threaded internal passageways. Where an older, oceangoing supercarrier might have a crew of five thousand, however, the *Big-H* had only about six hundred, equivalent to the crew of a guided missile cruiser with half the *Hillenkoetter*'s length and a fifth of her mass. As an enlisted man led Hunter and his team into the bowels of the ship, he reflected that it was going to take them a while to learn her layout.

On the other hand, maybe a detailed understanding wasn't expected of them. The 1-JSST was there to serve as landing team and planet security, so they'd been berthed close to the two immense hangar decks that would be used to deploy the TR-3B transports that would take them down to the surfaces of alien worlds. If they couldn't find the bridge from there, well . . . they weren't supposed to be up there in the first place, right?

"Hey . . . this is pretty fancy," a sergeant named Pomeroy said, flipping on a light.

"A real posh hotel," Nielson agreed. "I could get used to this!"

Rather than a traditional berthing space at sea where hundreds of men might be crowded together head by foot, the *Hillenkoetter* had cubes set up for two men each, with a shower head for every two compartments. Officers had individual quarters with private heads, while the women were berthed forward in their own area, two to a cube, which nicely addressed one of Hunter's biggest concerns about quartering arrangements with a mixed crew.

He wondered, though, who was paying for this opulence.

Well . . . black budgets were wonderful things. He remembered Secretary of Defense Rumsfeld going ballistic over a "missing" 2.3 trillion dollars back in 2001— money not actually *missing*, but impossible to track given the government's outdated accounting systems.

The *Hillenkoetter*, he'd heard, had cost about twenty-five billion—a supercarrier of the *Gerald R. Ford* class went for about half that, at thirteen billion per unit—and an entire space fleet battle group ran something like fifty billion—pocket change compared to a few hundred quadrillion. Back on Reagan's watch, the media had been worrying about $600 toilet seats, so this wasn't anything new. How much of the black budget came from what were euphemistically called "accounting oversights"?

He'd heard that there were eight of these huge space-craft carriers, constructed gradually over the past forty years, along with a fleet of smaller craft designed as escorts and fighters. Each spacecraft carrier was the center of a carrier battle group, and eight such groups came to four hundred billion.

Hell, where had all the rest of the money gone? One thing was certain: the Solar Warden program represented one hell of a lot of creative accounting.

But that begged another question. What was it all for? Was America gearing up for a war in space to defend Earth from aggressive aliens? It certainly looked that way.

And it wasn't just the United States either. Scuttlebutt had it that there were half a dozen different nations involved with the program, making Solar Warden a truly *global* defense force. Russians, Chinese, Brits, Japanese, Germans—they were supposedly all represented, though Hunter had yet to meet any of them.

Huh. Another thought occurred to him. What did the *Germans* think of hunting for Nazis Out There?

Hunter had his own office, which was good because his stateroom was claustrophobically tiny, with barely enough space for a desk, a rack, and a couple of chairs. *Hillenkoetter* had tons of room—room to spare, in fact, with such a small crew—but her designers apparently had been guided by the ship plans of seagoing navies. Couldn't have everything. With a couple of hours to go before the department-head briefing, he found his office, booted up the laptop he found there, and began downloading his workload off the Moon's equivalent of an Internet.

He was still going through the records of his combat team. And damn it . . . wouldn't you just know it? The last man to report in was Master Sergeant Charles N. Briggs, US Air Force.

Interservice rivalry didn't *really* drive Hunter's concerns about having an airman in the group. Briggs was a CCT—a combat control specialist, which made him a certified air traffic controller. The problem was that, together with his ATC training, he'd only completed the seven-and-a-half-week basic military training course, which—so far as Hunter could tell—was not even close to being in the same league as a SEAL's solid *year* of BUD/S, parachute training, and quals course.

Combat controllers were embedded with Army or Marine units to communicate with ground-support aircraft. Briggs was going to have to serve the same purpose, Hunter decided. He made the decision to put Briggs into Alfa Platoon, with Hunter. Master sergeant was the equivalent of "chief" in the Navy, so he held the same rank as Dixon and Brunelli. He would have to pull his weight as a senior noncom, then; Hunter was feeling damned stretched in that department.

But he thought about his conversation with McClure, and could only shake his head.

Air Force.

What *did* still worry him was integration. How was he supposed to fit forty-some men and women together into a seamless whole, despite wildly different levels of training and experience? All were elite warriors, superbly trained and disciplined, but the esprit de corps of each separate unit—Marines, Rangers, SEALs, and all the rest—made any real unit integration problematic at best.

And after that came the somewhat less immediate problem of mission. The United States military had an absolutely splendid record of service, chalking up victory after victory against enemies bigger and stronger and better supplied than they. Where things went pear-shaped, every time, was when the mission orders to those units became unworkably complicated and scattered. Beating the enemy *and* nation building. Support the local government *and* win hearts and minds *and* bomb supply routes *without* violating borders. Win a war *without* suffering major casualties *and* without causing needless *enemy* casualties because that would look bad on the evening news . . .

God save us, Hunter thought, from the political generals and the REMFs, for whom policy came before the simple need to fight and win a war.

At 1500, Hunter found his way—with several stops for guidance—up to the briefing room. *Hillenkoetter*, like Navy surface ships, had been split by her main deck, running fore and aft at about her midline. That was designated the First Deck, and the continuous decks below that were the Second Deck, Third Deck, and so on down to her keel. The continuous deck above the First Deck was the O-1 deck, with O-2, O-3, and so on above that. The flag bridge, command bridge, and CIC were located on the O-4 deck just forward of Frame 23. Unlike ocean-going vessels, *Hillenkoetter* had no need for a bridge high up on the superstructure, since all of her incoming information about where she was and who was close by was handled electronically. By burying the bridge spaces within the upper half of the ship's body, the vessel's command staff received at least some protection.

Hunter wasn't sure how much protection that actually might be; he was hearing rumors about high-energy lasers, particle beams, and nukes.

Conference Compartment A was located on the O-2 level beneath the bridge, a spacious room with a wall-sized projection screen and a podium off to the side. About forty men and women were gathering there, and Hunter wondered just how many departments there were on the *Big-H*. A lot of the people—about half—were civilians, he noticed. He spotted Dr. McClure and nodded at her. Xenobiology department, she'd said.

He noticed Admiral Kelsey on a chair up front. Captain Groton was leaning over discussing something with him. Next to him was Admiral Carruthers, who Hunter had been told would be the commanding admiral for the *Hillenkoetter*'s battle group. Hunter had met Carruthers just once before—the lone admiral boarding the TR-3B back at Groom Lake. He wished he knew more about the man. Was he a fighter? Was he any good as a war fighter? Would he back his people?

Did he know anything at all about the enemies they were about to face?

Was the *Big-H* a military vessel, for military operations? Or a civilian research vessel? Hunter was mildly surprised to find that he did not know the answer to that.

He decided that he'd damned well better find out.

The briefing officer was someone from the admiral's staff. "Gentlemen, ladies," he said, speaking from the podium up front. "I'm Commander Johnson. I imagine all of you are wondering where we're taking the *Big-H* . . . and why."

The lights dimmed, and an astronomical photograph

came up on the screen. It showed a star field in the background with two bright stars displayed at the center.

"These stars are Zeta 1 and Zeta 2 Reticuli," he continued. "It's a double star system thirty-nine light-years from Earth. Reticulum is a constellation visible in Earth's southern skies . . . not far from the Large Magellanic Cloud, so observers north of, say, Mexico City won't be familiar with it. In dark skies, it's visible as a very faint double to the naked eye. The two components are roughly 3,800 AUs apart. The two stars orbit one another once in roughly 170,000 years.

"Both Zeta 1 and Zeta 2 are quite similar to our sun. Zeta 2, a G2, is very slightly more massive and brighter than Zeta 1, a G3. Our sun is a G2.

"Those of you familiar with the lore of UFOs and alien abductions will immediately recognize the name of this star. In 1961, Betty and Barney Hill were purportedly abducted while driving through a portion of rural New Hampshire and taken aboard a spaceship. While on board, Betty was shown a three-dimensional star map. Later, under hypnosis, she was able to reproduce the map, which showed fifteen stars.

"In 1968, an Ohio Mensan and elementary schoolteacher named Marjorie Fish decided to try to use the Hill map to determine where the aliens had come from. Using beads hanging from threads in her backyard, she created a three-dimensional model of the stars nearest Earth. After a long search, she found one viewing angle that seemed to match Hill's map, one positioned at Zeta Reticuli.

"From there, Zeta Reticuli entered modern UFO lore. It's almost taken as a given nowadays that the Grays come from there.

"But . . . there are problems with that idea.

"First, we *believe* we have spotted one planet—around Zeta 2. Zeta 2 has an extensive debris field or asteroid belt which has been distorted by an unseen planetary companion. However, such a planet would be a gas giant the size of Jupiter or a bit larger, located 150 to 250 AUs from the star. This would not be a likely candidate for life, to say nothing of an interstellar civilization.

"Second, and more problematical, while we at first thought that Zeta Reticuli must be approximately six to seven billion years old—that's a couple of billion years older than our own sun—more recent data has suggested that the star can't be more than about two billion years old. Even if the star does have terrestrial planets, they would be far too young to have developed any life more complex than bacteria.

"For their part, the Grays refuse to tell us anything about their origins.

"So, Phase One of Excalibur will be to fly to Zeta Reticuli and closely investigate both stars. We will look for a putative Gray homeworld, as well as examine the entire system for *any* sign of occupation or visitation by an extraterrestrial intelligence.

"And when we're done there, Phase Two will take us here."

The screen changed to show a V-shaped pattern of stars, with a single bright orange star in the center.

"Aldebaran."

Johnson gave a brief overview of the myth of Aryans coming to Earth from the stars, and of Aldebaran identified as their home star. "UFO conspiracy literature," he told them, "has begun talking a lot about so-called breakaway civilizations, of humans who have migrated or been taken to other worlds where they have begun new civilizations of their own. In a sense, we here at Darkside could be considered such a breakaway civilization, though I'm sure all of us continue to think of ourselves as being Earthers. Unlikely as it is, if Nazi Germans fleeing the Third Reich at the end of World War II did in fact make it to another star like Aldebaran, that could certainly be construed as such a breakaway culture. And . . . our Nordic friends have found this."

The screen displayed the same video Hunter had seen, the drifting chunk of metal with that enigmatic cross painted on it.

"I assure you all, the chances of the Germans having actually made it into space after the war without help, even as far as the Moon, are essentially nil. But this video is a compelling piece of evidence. *Hillenkoetter*, therefore, will proceed from Zeta Reticuli to Aldebaran and investigate that system closely. Our Nordic friends report having been attacked at Aldebaran. For that reason, we will be going in as a military unit, cocked and loaded and ready for trouble.

"Aldebaran is sixty-five light-years from Earth, straight-line distance. It happens that it also is 68.5 light-years from Zeta Reticuli. So . . . Excalibur Phase One will be Sol to Zeta Ret, across thirty-nine light-years. That flight will be our shakedown cruise, giving us time to learn the systems and identify any potential problems with the ship or its systems. Phase Two will be Zeta Ret to Aldebaran, 68.5 light-years. We expect that Phase One will take us about two weeks, while the travel time for Phase Two will add about three and a half weeks more.

"Now, as to the aliens we expect to encounter . . ."

Johnson went on to discuss the Talis, the Grays, and the Saurians at some length. Hunter had already been through this material, and could let his mind wander somewhat.

One thing that SEALs valued above all was good intelligence. When he'd led his team into North Korea, Hunter had been fully briefed with volumes of reports, satellite photos, and HUMINT—human intelligence—to show him what he and his men could expect.

This time, though, they would be going in cold—cold, blind, deaf, and stupid. What was the nature of the defenses at Aldebaran? A powerful and well-equipped enemy fleet? Some sort of orbital fort? A few aging German saucers? Alien tech?

It was, he thought, a recipe for failure. Not only had his men not been allowed to familiarize themselves with their new weaponry and hardware, but they had no clue as to what they were going to find when they reached their objective.

Johnson was showing images on the screen now comparing and contrasting the Grays and the Saurians. He'd been talking for the past few minutes about the Grays as time-traveling humans evolved a million years beyond humans of the twenty-first century, and now was discussing the reptilian Saurians.

Huh. The Saurians, he was saying, were warm-blooded. Hunter hadn't heard that before, though it made sense. The Saurians certainly were not sluggish and as dependent on warm temperatures as cold-blooded reptiles would be.

But what Hunter really wanted were details on the Saurian technology, on their weapons. If the Saurians put up a fight out there, what would be the best tactics for 1-JSST to employ?

There were no answers to that, or to any of the other host of questions swirling around in Hunter's mind.

"And that concludes my presentation," Johnson said at last. "Any questions?"

He raised his hand, but Johnson called on someone else—an older man with grizzled hair and a neat white goatee. "Commander Johnson? Lawrence Brody, astrophysics department. I want to know: Is this a military expedition? Or a civilian one? Who's in charge?"

"I'll take that." Admiral Carruthers stood up and took the center of the stage. "Dr. Brody, I want to be absolutely clear on this. While we have a large civilian component within our crew, this *is* first and foremost a military operation."

Well, Hunter thought. *That answers that, at least.*

"Captain Groton is in command of this vessel," Carruthers went on, "while I will command the entire battle group. Where we go, what we do, will be *my* decision, and mine alone.

"However, Operation Excalibur has a number of purposes designed to fit in with one another, to work together. We will be representing Earth out there in the Galaxy. That's priority number one. We will be proving to certain civilizations out there that we are capable of reaching out beyond our own planet, and conducting extensive exploratory operations among nearby stars. For that reason, the military side of this operation will be . . . downplayed.

"As such, priority two is this: our mission has a diplomatic aspect." Carruthers gestured at two civilians in the audience, surrounded by people who were probably aides or staff. "Mr. King? Mr. Kozlov? Please stand."

The two civilians stood and turned so that the audience could see them, bowing slightly in acknowledgment.

"Paul M. King is a senior ambassador-at-large with the US State Department. Vladimir Kozlov holds a similar position with the Russian Federation's Foreign Ministry. They will be coming along to handle the diplomatic niceties, should we meet with other races or decide to enter into diplomatic agreements with them. Thank you, gentlemen."

So, Hunter thought as the two sat down again. *There were Russians coming along on this expedition. And that makes Excalibur a truly international effort.*

"Priority three," Carruthers went on, "is the military aspect. We will be exploring two distinct star systems, Zeta Reticuli and Aldebaran, in order to determine if either represents a military threat to Earth.

"And, finally, priority four, we carry a number of key scientists—exobiologists, astrophysicists, exoplanetary scientists, xenocultural experts, and others—who will be studying the worlds, the life-forms, and the civilizations that we may encounter. We find ourselves like children, suddenly aware that there is a huge, complicated, and sometimes dangerous world beyond the safety of our front door. The more we can learn about that world, the better for us, the better for our chances of long-term survival. Does that answer your question, Dr. Brody?"

"Yes . . . I think so. Thank you."

"Other questions?" Johnson said as Carruthers returned to his chair. "Time for maybe one more."

Again, Hunter raised his hand. More than anything else, he wanted someone up there to address the *tactical* aspects of a military expedition into the unknown. Dr. McClure had surprised him earlier by mentioning tactical combat orders; he'd never met a civilian who knew the difference between the words *tactical* and *strategic*.

In a military sense, *strategic* meant choices or actions aimed at achieving an overall goal or mission, while *tactics* were the specific actions used to implement those choices. For Hunter, the CO of the expedition's ground force, that meant, at least potentially, engaging in combat with a hostile alien force in order to achieve *Hillenkoetter*'s mission goals.

Which meant it was vital to know what that potential enemy's capabilities were. He wanted to ask the people up-front just what it was that he and his people were expected to do, and how they were suppoed to do it.

But Johnson picked another hand. "You. Yes . . ."

"Air Force master sergeant Bowman, sir. Supply. Uh . . . sir, you mentioned a five- or six-week trip out to wherever we're going, and I assume that means a six-week trip back. But we've taken supplies on board that will last us a year. How long are we going to be out there, anyway? Some of us have wives and kids at home. . . ."

A reasonable question, Hunter thought. The JSST personnel had been deliberately selected for a lack of family entanglements, though many had left girlfriends back on Earth. But they could not possibly have done that with *all* of the civilian scientists, engineers, and technicians on board the *Hillenkoetter*. Six hundred people—trying to find that many qualified personnel to crew the spacecraft carrier with no family entanglements, no wives, no kids, no parents, that would be a bitch and a half.

Another hand went up in the audience—a woman.

Johnson pointed at her. "Dr. Michaels? Would you care to answer the master sergeant?"

"I can't address the question as to why we have a year's worth of supplies," Michaels said. "But I *can* say that if all goes well, we will not be gone for as long as it will seem. *Hillenkoetter* has an advanced gravitomagnetic drive of alien design, which means that she will be playing some interesting games with space-time. What we hope to do is return to Earth immediately after we leave. We might be out at our objectives twelve weeks . . . or even an entire year, but to those we've left behind it will seem like we've been gone just a few days . . . maybe a week or two at most."

"Won't that screw up the time lines?" Bowman asked.

"Not unless we come back too early and *interfere* with ourselves. If *Hillenkoetter* were to set off for the stars, return a year later, but come back a year in time and stop the *Hillenkoetter* from ever setting out . . . well, that would create a temporal paradox. We're not yet certain what that might mean. So we're going to be very, *very* careful not to find out."

Gerri! He might be able to go back and see Gerri after all!

But the briefing was dismissed, and Hunter still had far more questions than he did answers.

The *Hillenkoetter* was going to be deployed to the stars, and God only knew what they would find out there.

CHAPTER TWELVE

We now have the technology to take E.T. home.

BEN RICH, CEO OF
LOCKHEED SKUNK WORKS, 1993

12 October 1979

TELL THEM, *THE voice in his head demanded.* Tell them they are not welcome here.

Hans Kammler stared at the group of soldiers in the steel-lined tunnel in front of him. Lights glared in the background, throwing most of the Delta Force troops into stark silhouette. Major Corby stood a few feet in front of him, hands on hips, a belligerent glare in his eyes. Kammler spread his hands carefully, showing the Army officer that he was unarmed. "Please, Major," he said. "Our friends here request that you leave. Please!"

"And why the hell should we?" Corby demanded. "This is our *facility! And they killed one of my men!"*

The body of Sergeant Peterson lay sprawled on the concrete floor a few feet away. Much of his head was missing, and what was left was charred black. His weapon, an M16, lay at his side, the plastic melted, the barrel twisted.

"It was a misunderstanding," Kammler said. "A tragic misunderstanding! Live ammunition is not permitted down here. Sergeant Peterson tried to enter anyway. They . . . stopped him."

"They didn't have to fucking blow his head off!"

There were twelve soldiers in Corby's group, part of the Archuleta Mesa military police. They were also Delta, meaning they were highly trained and superbly disciplined, but some of them shifted uncomfortably, obviously scared. The unit had only just been certified as mission capable a month ago. The unit had been created on 19 November 1977, and was only now, two years later, coming onto active duty. Corby, Kammler thought, was too eager, too determined to show off what the new unit could do.

"Major, I do suggest that you take your people out of here. You are all in terrible danger if you do not."

"Fuck that. I want to know what happened to Peterson! And who the fuck are you to be giving orders to us? You're nothing but a damned civilian."

If you only knew, *Kammler thought . . . but he said nothing. Corby would not appreciate the fact that Kammler was an* Obergruppenführer *of the SS—equivalent to a full general—or that he'd been one once. For years now, he'd done the aliens' bidding. While they could transmit thoughts to humans, the process seemed easier when they could use a human as an intermediary.*

Please, Ssarsk, *he thought, turning to the Saurian beside him.* They are here to do their duty. Let them through.

The aliens milled about behind him, nine Grays, together with four of the taller, bulkier Saurians with their crocodile teeth and slender, bird-jointed legs. The Saurians appeared to be the ones in command, though most of the aliens here at Dulce were the smaller, more slender, toothless Grays. And where the Grays wore simple tight-fitting coveralls of some sort, the Saurians wore armor over their torsos, and there were small decorations on their chests that might possibly be weapons.

He hadn't actually witnessed Peterson's death, but he

knew that none of the aliens carried anything like a hu-man weapon. But as a part of their clothing, that was something else.

He didn't like the way the Saurians had carefully spread out in front of the Grays, as though to establish clear fields of fire.

No, Ssarsk told him. They leave now, or we will destroy them.

Kammler faced Major Corby again. "They are . . . adamant, Major. You and your men must leave. Now."

For answer, Corby drew his sidearm. "The hell with that!"

In an instant, Kammler was dazzled by a sharp flash of light—by four flashes of light, actually. Then by four more . . . and four more—twelve pulses of laser light in less than a second.

Twelve men, including Corby, dropped to the pavement, their heads, like Peterson's, blown to burnt fragments. The last man dropped his M16 and started running for the entrance. Ssarsk put him down with a final snap of light . . . like all the others, a head shot.

Kammler sagged. "This is not good."

Bits and pieces of charred bone and tissue lay scattered everywhere around the bodies, and the air was filled with the stink of burnt hair. Slowly, Kammler reached up to wipe a bloody gobbet from his shirt.

Kill the others inside the base, *Ssarsk ordered the other three Saurians.* Hunt them down. *He reached out and grabbed Kammler's arm with surprising strength.* All save this one. It belongs to us.

Kammler shuddered, knowing the truth of those words.

THE *HILLENKOETTER* lifted off from the Moon the next day.

"Commander Hunter?" a young lieutenant said. "Captain's compliments, sir, and would you like to observe our departure from the bridge?"

Hunter laughed. "*Would* I?" He was surprised, remembering his thought from the day before about how the ground-pounders likely would not be welcome on the bridge. "Absolutely."

"If you'll follow me, sir?"

"So . . . to what do I owe this honor?" he asked as he followed the lieutenant up a metal-decked companionway.

"The skipper thought you might like to watch procedures up there, sir. I guess, well, things have been kind of abrupt for you, huh? One day you're minding your business on Earth, next thing you know you're on the Moon, and the next you're on your way to distant stars. That would disorient anybody."

"You've got that right, son."

"If you watch the liftoff from up there, maybe it'll—I don't know—seem a bit more real."

"Is it real to you, Lieutenant?"

"I've been up here for six years, Commander. Yeah, it's about as real as it gets."

He entered the bridge, and was directed to a line of seats called "the gallery" along the curving aft bulkhead. Half a dozen other personnel were already seated there, and Hunter took a chair between an attractive woman and an older, professorial type, both in civilian clothing.

"Welcome to my bridge, Commander," Captain Groton told him. "Just stay the fuck out of the way."

Hunter introduced himself, remembering that the woman was Dr. Michaels and the man was Dr. Brody. Hunter was still mildly surprised that an invitation had been extended to a grunt—him—but decided that he wasn't about to question it.

The launch process began, however, with an intensely uncomfortable period of gravity adjustment. For the better part of a week, Hunter and the others had been living on the Moon, where the pull of gravity was only one-sixth of the surface gravity of Earth. Having the ship's artificial gravity dialed up to six times more than what his body had become accustomed to was less than pleasant. The process was spread out over the course of an hour, to ease the effects, but as the weight of five men began pressing Hunter into the cushions of his seat, it left him wondering aloud why the hell they didn't use artificial gravity inside the base.

"*I* think it's because they don't want the bad-guy aliens to spot us," Brody told him.

"Yes? And how would aliens do that?"

"Stands to reason, Commander," Michaels told him. "Everybody knows that magnetogravitic generators put out a great deal of power, and the fields they create can be detected by magnetic scanners. If the base had artificial gravity switched on all the time, a Saurian ship passing overhead would pick that up easily."

"'Everybody knows,' huh?" Hunter didn't care for Michaels's condescending attitude, and she was decidedly less attractive in his eyes now. "May I ask how you know so much about it?" he asked.

She gave him a cool look. "I've been working in the field of magnetogravitic technology for fifteen years now, Commander, and I helped design this ship. I'd damned well *better* know something about it."

"Just don't get Dr. Michaels started on the subject of time travel," Brody warned.

In fact, there were portions of Darkside Base that *were* under a full Earth gravity all the time—the gymnasiums and some of the public lounge areas. During long-term stays in micro- or lower-g environments it was vital to work out daily in 1 g to prevent a loss of muscle mass. But it didn't make this shift any less unpleasant.

Hunter also didn't know why Saurian ships wouldn't pick up the generators under the floor of the gym, but he wasn't going to ask. Dr. Michaels might deign to answer him.

The bridge was a large compartment twenty yards

across, a well sunk into the deck ringed about with consoles and large-screen monitors. Above and behind Hunter's chair was the flag bridge, where Admiral Carruthers and his staff watched in nonmicromanagerial silence, as the bridge crew—about thirty naval officers and enlisted technicians—went about the tasks associated with taking *Hillenkoetter* into space.

"Gravity at 98 percent," a voice called from a console forward. "All normal."

"Inertial dampers on." That was Captain Groton, watching over his small and circular fiefdom from a complicated chair just ahead of Hunter's position in the gallery.

"Inertial dampers on, aye, sir."

"Inertial mass to 15 percent."

"Inertial mass, one-five percent, aye, sir."

"Energy feed to 5 percent."

"Energy at 5 percent, aye."

Hunter felt a growing thrum coming up through the deck.

"Where's all the energy coming from?" Hunter asked in an awed whisper, more to himself than to anyone else. "Fusion power?"

Michaels gave a short snort. "Fusion wouldn't even begin to cut it, Commander," she told him. "To accelerate a vessel this large to close to the speed of light would require the immediate annihilation of a *very* great deal of mass—roughly the entire mass of our entire solar system, including the sun. No, this is ZPE."

"ZPE?"

"Zero-point energy," Brody translated. "Turns out that so-called empty space—hard vacuum—isn't so empty after all. It's a kind of boiling, seething sea of energy coming into existence according to the rules of quantum mechanics, and almost immediately self-annihilating again. We're not aware of it because it vanishes so quickly, preserving the sacred laws of conservation of mass and energy. But our alien friends figured out a long time ago how to extract a tiny, tiny fraction of that energy—it's called virtual energy—and make it available for use."

"How much energy?"

"It is estimated, Commander, that the volume of a lightbulb—a few cubic centimeters—contains roughly one hundred times the energy required to turn all of Earth's oceans into vapor instantly. And the ship's power core is drawing on the vacuum energy of a *much* larger volume than that."

"Over two hundred cubic meters," Michaels said. She sounded smug. "The energy of a quasar at the touch of a button!"

"Quasar?" Hunter asked.

"Quasi-stellar object, Commander. Black holes very far off in the universe that we used to think were spewing so much of the gas and dust they were feeding on out into space as intense beams or jets. According to the Talis, however, it's not that these supermassive black holes are messy eaters. They actually access some of the virtual energy surrounding the volume they occupy, and release it as energy . . . a *lot* of energy. Up to several hundred times the radiation output of an entire galaxy."

"Some of it, huh?"

"A few percent."

"Give us lift, Mr. Larimer," Groton ordered. "Five meters above the gantry."

"Positive lift, taking us to five meters, Captain, aye, aye."

Hunter watched in silence. The thought of how much energy must be available to the *Hillenkoetter* was staggering. At the same time, he felt conflicted. On the one hand, they were riding a machine like an ant somehow tapping into the blast of a nuclear weapon, and that was terrifying. On the other . . . here, beneath his feet, was the final answer to all of Earth's energy problems—an end to fossil fuels and to pollution, an end to poverty and hunger

and want, an end to international energy monopolies and
high fuel costs . . .

Everything else he could maybe understand—maybe.
But how *dare* the bastards keep this secret!

The big screen forward showed a vertical face of rock
and metal slowly gliding down as the *Hillenkoetter* lifted
above the gantry support that had been cradling her.
Ahead, a circular tunnel mouth gaped open.

"Ahead slow, Ms. Briem. Take us out."

"Ahead slow, Captain."

The tunnel mouth slowly expanded.

The opening, Hunter saw, was curtained by a faint
shimmer, like the glow of an aurora.

"Force field?" he asked Brody.

"You could call it that."

"Actually it's a magnetokinetic induction screen," Michaels said.

"C'mon," he said. "Now you're just making words up!"

"She's not, Commander. The screens save us having
to spend a few hours pumping the air out of the egress
chamber."

"So . . . it's a force field," he muttered, shaking his head.

"External atmosphere now at two times ten to the fifth
particles per cubic centimeter," a bridge officer reported.

"Pressure at three times ten to the minus fifteen bar,"
said another.

Or as close to hard vacuum as made no difference
whatsoever.

Hunter could see little on the big screen now, save
darkness.

"Base, *Hillenkoetter*," Groton said. "Ready to open the
barn doors."

"Copy that, *Hillenkoetter*. Opening roof doors."

"Roof doors open, Captain. Alignment within acceptable parameters."

"Positive lift, Mr. Larimer," Groton ordered. "Slow
exit, 5 mps."

"Positive lift, aye, aye, sir. Emerging at five meters per second."

And then they were above the lunar surface. Harsh sunlight glared white from plains and mountains above an endless black sky. Hunter had expected to see stars, but there were none. The surface, he decided, was so bright that the cameras could not handle light from both the landscape and from stars.

"We are clear of the exit, Captain," Briem reported. "Altitude twenty-five meters."

"Very well. All stations report."

Hunter heard the buzz and crackle of various departments reporting in. *God* but this was a complicated process! He wondered if getting an aircraft carrier underway from a dock took as much time and effort.

Well, come to think of it . . . yes, it probably did.

"All departments report readiness for space in all respects, Captain," the XO reported.

"Very well," the Captain said. "Nav, set course to take us clear of lunar space."

"Course set, Captain. One-one-seven by minus five-two."

"One-one-seven by minus five-two, aye, aye, Captain."

"And on my mark take us out, Ms. Briem. Ahead 10 percent."

"On your mark, ahead 10 percent, aye."

"And three . . . and two . . . and one . . . *mark!*"

And the lunar surface disappeared.

It vanished away with such suddenness that for a moment Hunter thought that something had gone wrong, that the monitor was dead. Then someone switched cameras, and he saw two fast-dwindling disks—the white face of the Moon, and the smaller, blue-and-white disk beyond of Earth.

"Ten percent of the speed of light," Brody informed him. "That's thirty thousand kilometers per *second*! Pretty good, eh?"

The Earth and Moon dwindled to a close-set pair of bright stars, and Groton ordered the ship to come to a halt—one relative to the rest of the solar system, Hunter presumed. For half an hour, Groton checked with various departments and received reports on the ship's status. Finally, he looked up at the screen and said, "We've got places to go, people. Nav! Align us with Zeta Reticuli."

Hunter noticed that he could see stars now on the monitor. . . . Nothing but stars, looking clearer and brighter and sharper than he'd ever seen them on Earth. Those stars wheeled about with disconcerting speed as *Hillenkoetter* turned in space, aligning her prow with a dim and inconspicuous constellation. Two faint smears of light showed off to the left. "What're those smudges?" he asked Brody.

"The Magellanic Clouds," Brody replied. "Dwarf galaxies."

"And that's where we're going?"

"Great Einstein's ghost!" Michaels exclaimed. "Don't you knuckle-dragging military types know *anything*?"

Before Hunter could tell her exactly what he knew, Brody chuckled. "No, Commander. Those are satellite galaxies to our Milky Way Galaxy, over 160,000 light-years away. Here, look. Imagine a line connecting the two . . ."

"Okay."

"Now look for two stars, very *dim* stars, at right angles to that line, and about half that line's length up from it. See them?"

"I'm not sure." There were so *many* stars.

"Well . . . they're there. Two stars, a visual binary, very close together. Only about the fifth magnitude, which means they're right on the edge of being visible to the unaided eye. Zeta Reticuli, and they're right on our back doorstep compared to the Clouds of Magellan. Only thirty-nine light-years away."

"I think I see them. Yes!"

"Nav plots are set, Captain," the ship's navigator reported.

"Where are our chicks?"

"*Samford, Inman, Carlucci*, and *Blake* are taking up station, one thousand meters to port, starboard, zenith, and nadir."

On several of the monitors, Hunter could make other spacecraft—cylinders, like the *Hillenkoetter*, but stubbier, flattened, and with protrusions and sponsons amidships that might have been weapons housings of some sort. He wasn't sure, but something about the lights marking windows or other ports in their hulls suggested that they were quite a bit smaller than the *Hillenkoetter*.

"That's a hell of a fleet," Hunter told Brody.

"Indeed. This is a carrier battle *group* after all. Those are cruisers, heavily armed for their size, and reasonably well armored. They're named after various former directors of the NSA."

"Good heavens, why?"

"Because many of those men were members of MJ-12, and were behind the genesis of Solar Warden."

"All fleet elements report they are in position, Captain."

"Comm . . . command link with the battle group. I want everybody to stay together."

"We're linked in, Captain."

"Very well. Ms. Briem, on my mark, take us to full speed ahead."

"Full ahead, Captain, lightspeed on your mark. Aye, aye."

"And three . . . two . . . one . . . *mark*."

And the starscape vanished, replaced by a brilliant and frosty-blue circle of light.

Groton got out of his chair, ducking to clear some of the monitors hanging from the overhead. "Well, ladies and gentlemen," he said, grinning at the gallery. "How'd you like the show?"

"Fantastic, Captain," an engineer at the far end of the line of seats said. He shook his head. "To actually see those metrics transformed into reality!"

As they began moving toward the exit off the bridge, Hunter turned to the captain. "I want to thank you, sir, for letting us come up here."

"Not at all, not at all. We're bringing sci-fi to life here, and it's nice to have an audience."

"I wouldn't waste it on the *military*, Fred," Michaels said, brushing past. She said the word with the disgust normally reserved for a particularly low and loathsome creature.

"On the bridge, it's *captain*, Doctor. Please remember that."

"Sorry." She sounded anything but, though.

"She doesn't much like us military types, does she?" Hunter said, watching her as she walked off the bridge.

"Oh, don't worry about Ellen," Groton said. "I think she's a child of the sixties. Make love, not war."

"No way is she that old."

"No, but her parents were. Not that her opinon of us matters. As Admiral Carruthers so succinctly put it yesterday, this is a military expedition."

"Question, Captain?"

"Go ahead."

"My men and I came on board with very little training and less preparation. We have no idea what it is that we're supposed to do here. If we get into a firefight with slimy alien horrors, we'll be completely out of our depth. No practice with our weapons, no idea of tactics, and even less idea of the tactics and equipment in use by our enemy. Sir, to put it bluntly, this whole thing could be a clusterfuck from the get-go."

Groton stared into Hunter's eyes for a moment. "I see. And I regret the haste with which you and your people were brought on board, Commander. Here we are, able to control space and time pretty much at will, yet the bureaucracy still manages to screw it all up every single time!"

"Exactly: hurry up and wait, sir. Then everything was supposed to be done yesterday, of course."

"I sometimes wonder if our descendants—the Talis and the Grays—have managed to harness the bureaucracy. Somehow I doubt it." He shook his head. "Unfortunately, I'm not sure what to tell you, Mr. Hunter. Experience with your weapons and equipment will come. It's all pretty much idiotproof, if only because the Talis know we're idiots, okay? As for the tactics . . . well, that's why you're here, Commander."

"I beg your pardon, sir?"

"The 1-JSST is the first human deep-space tactical team ever to be put into space. Up until now, we've used Marines, but the intent here is to field a unit with the express purpose of going down to the surfaces of hostile planets and doing whatever is necessary to complete the mission. That may involve killing things. Or it may involve diplomacy. Or it might simply be to assist the scientists while they take their samples and make their readings. We expect a certain degree of *flexibility* in your deployment as well as a great deal of creativity. This means this is completely new to all of us."

"What do you mean, sir?"

"It means you're writing the book, Commander. You'll be making things up as you go along."

The words struck Hunter like a thunderbolt. "M-making things *up*?" Belatedly, he added, "Sir?"

"Exactly. You're a SEAL. Improvise, overcome, and adapt!"

"That's the US Marines, Captain."

"Good thing we brought some of those along then, too." Groton turned back to his station.

Hunter returned to the JSST's spaces aft in a very thoughtful mood.

ELANNA LOOKED up as McClure entered the Hive.

It was called "the Hive" because someone had had the idea that the Grays looked like insects, and a small, dark space where insects lived was a hive, right? In fact, there were no Grays on board the *Hillenkoetter*, and the Talis looked nothing like bugs. In particular, McClure thought, Elanna didn't look at all insectoid. Those large, azure eyes were incredible. . . .

"We're underway, Elanna," McClure said. "I wondered if you could tell me a bit about where we're going."

"We know little about Zeta Reticuli, Becky," Elanna replied. "One of our survey ships passed through the Zeta 1 system about one of your centuries ago. They reported nothing of note."

"No Gray civilization?"

"Not that we've been able to detect, no."

"Then why go there?"

"Three reasons, Becky. First, our survey was not exactly thorough or detailed. Our people could well have missed something."

"Okay . . ."

"Second, the Zeta Reticuli system has figured very large in human UFO mythology. Whether there is something there or there is not, humans should find out for themselves."

"We can't find out by simply asking you?"

"No. As I said, we have little information to give." Her large eyes blinked once, slowly. "I'm not sure you yet grasp the sheer size of the cosmos, Becky. However large you can imagine it, the reality is *far* larger and far more complex. We know only the smallest possible fraction of what there is to know, and that includes details of all of the myriad worlds and civilizations that fill this Galaxy."

"If enemy aliens were parked less than forty light-years from Earth, I'd think you'd know something about it." She sighed. "And reason three?"

"Exploration of the Zeta Reticuli system will give your

battle group and its personnel a chance to acclimate—to 'get a feel,' as you sometimes say—for extrasolar operations."

"Mark has been wanting that from the beginning. May I tell him?"

Again, a slow, catlike blink. "Of course."

"Not 'of course.' Solar Warden is one secret wrapped in a dozen others. What is it they say? A riddle wrapped in an enigma?"

"I believe the phrase you want is 'a riddle wrapped in a mystery inside an enigma.' A prime minister of Great Britain said that of Russia. Winston Churchill."

"I didn't know that. Thank you."

Elanna appeared to be thinking, as if wondering to say more.

"There is something else. A reason four."

"And that is?"

"How much do you know about extradimensional physics?"

"What, like the fourth dimension—that kind of thing?"

"Many more dimensions. You know that string theory, as you understand it now, posits either six or seven additional spatial dimensions beyond the three spatial dimensions and the one dimension of time you know, yes?"

"Eleven dimensions. Okay, yes. I've heard that. Remember that I'm a biologist, please, and not a physicist."

"I will keep that in mind. These additional dimensions are unseen, you believe, because they are rolled up very, very small—smaller than a proton. However, that actually depends on how you look at things."

"What do you mean?"

Elanna held her hand out, palm facing McClure. "A two-dimensional plane—a flat sheet, a piece of paper—and you see it easily, yes?"

"Yes."

Elanna rotated her hand so the edge faced McClure.

184   IAN DOUGLAS

"Look at it from a different angle, and it . . . goes away. Becomes unimaginably small. It's a matter of perspective."

"You're saying these other dimensions are accessible if we can orient ourselves properly?"

"Something like that. Humans are only able to see three spatial dimensions at a time. But it's possible to *rotate* in such a way that length, for example, decreases to nothing, while the sixth dimension unfolds and becomes visible."

"I think I understand."

"I doubt that, Becky. But don't feel bad—it's something that we, eleven thousand years from now, can only dimly grasp. Some may have learned how to work it, though."

"The Grays?"

"Maybe. We don't really know. But some of the stories about them—walking through walls, materializing out of empty air, ships that vanish in one place and reappear instantly somewhere else—these are all evidence that they are able to manipulate more than the normal four dimensions."

"Christ!"

"And that means that the *absence* of cities or a thriving culture on the Zeta Reticulan planets when our survey was there means absolutely nothing. *Anything* could be there. Anything at all."

"And may I tell Mark *that*?"

Elanna thought about it for a long moment. "Yes. Provided that you believe it will not negatively impact his performance. The information is generally withheld because we fear it could be demoralizing."

"I can certainly see why."

Damn. How the hell was she going to tell Mark *this*?

CHAPTER THIRTEEN

Reagan: "What would you do if the United States were suddenly attacked by someone from outer space? Would you help us?"
Gorbachev: "No doubt about it."
Reagan: "We, too."

CONVERSATION BETWEEN RONALD REAGAN AND
MIKHAIL GORBACHEV, LAKE GENEVA SUMMIT, 1985

12 October 1979

THE ALIENS STORMED *through the mesa, killing every human soldier and technician and scientist they could find. The attack had taken the humans completely by surprise, and the Saurians showed no mercy.*

The Dulce Base had been carved out of the forbidding rock of Archuleta Mesa, a plateau of sheer rugged cliffs rising above the town of Dulce, New Mexico, not far from the Colorado border. For several years, the Dulce Base had been a highly secret research facility staffed both by humans and by Gray aliens.

Kammler was dragged along by Ssarsk, unable to resist, unable to even speak. They'd done something to his mind and his will, rendering him incapable of any resistance whatsoever. All he could do was stumble along in blind obedience to Ssarsk's mental orders.

They reached one of the lower levels, surprising three

human technicians and burning them down. Mounting terror gibbered at the back of Kammler's mind. He'd only been down into this level once, months ago, and he'd had nightmares—new nightmares—ever since. The genetic experiments the aliens were carrying out here terrified him, left him weak, shaking, and ill.

During the war, at Auschwitz-Birkenau, he'd known Hauptsturmführer Josef Mengele, the infamous "Angel of Death," whose horrific medical experiments on concentration camp inmates defied all belief or reason. Much of Mengele's passion had focused on genetic studies, attempts to prove "Aryan racial purity" by torturing Jews and Gypsies in the sacred name of science.

At the time, Kammler had thought nothing of it. Mengele's victims, after all, had been Jews, Gypsies, Slavs, and other Untermenschen of no importance at all. But for the past several years, Kammler had been a virtual prisoner in this place, a prisoner of beings who thought of humans, all humans, as the SS had thought of the Jews. For Kammler, life had become a never-ending nightmare, one that placed him in the same position as some nameless Birkenau Sonderkommando. Attempts to ingratiate himself to his masters had been ignored. The worst of it was when he felt them inside his head.

And Kammler never knew when the aliens might decide he was no longer useful and order his vivisection.

To be on the receiving ends of this type of cold and dispassionate domination by implacable and merciless inhuman beings he did not understand seemed to be a bizarre reversal of the natural order.

We must abandon this place, *Ssarsk told the others.* The humans will be here soon, in greater numbers. We cannot hold them off forever.

What about . . . that? *one asked, gesturing at Kammler.*

We will take it with us. We may still have a use for it.

Kammler tried to scream . . . and could not.

"YOU KNOW," Dr. Brody said, "I miss the stars streaking past."

"What stars?" Hunter replied. "I don't see any stars."

"Exactly."

The two men were sitting in one of *Hillenkoetter*'s spacious lounges, where a long broad window looked out into space. At the ship's current velocity, however, very close to the speed of light, only an impenetrable darkness was visible. Up on the bridge, when they'd left the Earth-Moon system the week before, Hunter had seen the strange ring of frosty light ahead as they transited to lightspeed, but he'd not understood it.

The astrophysicist Lawrence Brody, however, was able to explain.

"Imagine a rainstorm," he said, "where the rain is coming down straight. No wind. Okay?"

"Okay."

"Now imagine driving through that rain very fast. What happens?"

"Well . . . the rain hits the windshield at an angle. It comes at you almost sideways if you're going fast enough."

"Precisely. And that's what happens when we move at relativistic speeds through all the light coming from all the stars around us. From our point of view, the incoming light kind of gets crowded up forward. That ring they see on the bridge is the light from all the stars around us, all the stars in the universe, but smunched together up ahead."

"So what stars did you want to see?"

"Oh . . . I was a fan of *Star Trek*, back in the sixties. I was just a kid . . . but I loved that show. I loved seeing the *Enterprise* zipping along with the stars streaming past like snowflakes in a blizzard."

"Ah. And you miss that, do you?"

"Oh, yes," Brody said, nodding. "You can't imagine how disappointed I was at MIT when I learned it wouldn't look like that."

Hunter chuckled. "Never saw the show."

"What? You benighted heathen! Not even the movies?"

"Nope. I never cared much for sci-fi." He shrugged. "Now here I am living it. Go figure."

"Well . . . just don't wear a red shirt when you go down with the landing party."

Hunter didn't understand the reference, but before he could ask, he was interrupted by a noncom.

"Commander?"

It was Sergeant Pomeroy.

"Yes, Sergeant?"

"Excuse the interruption, sir. You're needed in the gym. A fight between Master Sergeant Coulter and Chief Brunelli, sir."

"God, what now." He stood. "You'll excuse me, Dr. Brody?"

"Of course. Duty calls!"

Except that it wasn't duty . . . or it shouldn't have been. By the time Hunter got there, the two men had been separated. It looked like most of the unit was there around them, milling about and gossiping.

"Okay, what the hell is going on here?" Hunter demanded, uncomfortably aware of the audience.

Brunelli pointed. "*That queer made a pass at me!*"

"*I did not,*" was Coulter's rejoinder. "He started it!"

Both men were somewhat the worse for wear. Coulter was holding a handkerchief to a bloody nose. Brunelli had the beginnings of a shiner beneath his right eye.

What was shocking about the incident, Hunter thought, was the fact that both men were pay grade E-7. Both had been in the service for at least ten years, and both carried with their stripes and rockers considerable responsibility both as leaders and as examples to the other men. It wasn't like a couple of seamen going at one another in a drunken brawl ashore.

"You two ought to know better than this!" Hunter said, keeping his voice low and dangerous. "I have better things to do than playing nursemaid to children! *Stand at attention when I'm talking to you!*"

Both men came to attention, eyes straight ahead.

"Who threw the first punch?"

"I did, sir," Brunelli said. "I was . . . provoked."

"No amount of provocation justifies hitting a fellow member of this unit! Not to mention I *talked* to you about this. You're on report!"

"Sir, yes, sir!"

"Coulter! What did you do to set him off?"

"I . . . sir . . . we were just talking, sir."

"Uh-huh. And what did you say?"

"I just sort of mentioned that, well, we all know about *sailors*, sir. . . ."

"He *swished* when he said it, sir."

"Shut up, Brunelli! What is it we know about sailors, Coulter?"

"Nothing, sir. I didn't mean anything by it, sir."

"You're on report, too! The rest of you . . . get back to what you were doing!"

The crowd evaporated, but Hunter could hear the grumbling. Well, damn it, how was he supposed to handle this? "Minkowski! Layton! Center yourself on the hatch!"

Master Chief Minkowski was the senior NCO of Alfa Platoon, which was Coulter's unit. Master Sergeant Bruce Layton was the senior NCO of Charlie Platoon, which was Brunelli's. Both men stood side by side in front of Hunter, rigidly at attention.

"Why couldn't you two have defused this?" Hunter demanded, keeping his voice low. If he was going to give his noncoms a dressing-down, he didn't want to do it in front of the men.

"Sir, it happened so fast—" Layton said.

"Uh-huh. Mink?"

"No excuse, sir."

"The men in your platoons are your responsibilities.

You should have stopped it, and if it happened too fast you should have resolved the aftermath and not brought me into it. Now I have to take *official* notice, and that will not do morale any good at all. Do you two understand me?"

"Yes, sir."

"Yes, sir."

Hunter considered putting them on report as well but decided against it. "I expected more out of you two. Dismissed! Now get the hell out of my sight!"

The *Hillenkoetter*, Hunter thought as he walked back to his office, was a comfortable ship, a *large* ship with plenty of space . . . no pun intended. Nonetheless, when you took a large number of people and packed them in together for weeks at a time, there were going to be explosions. Enforced inaction and a lack of outlets was going to fray nerves and cause discipline problems, no matter what he or any of his noncoms could do. There'd already been problems. Two days earlier, a Ranger on night security had caught Taylor with Ann Seton, one of the members of Charlie Platoon. The two had been in flagrante delicto—meaning bare-assed naked—in a closet-sized storage locker, and he'd put them both on report. Hunter still had that little scandal to deal with, as well.

With all the talk about time travel, why the hell couldn't the people driving this thing cut the journey down to a more manageable length?

Like, say, ten minutes?

FRED GROTON wished the voyage was scheduled to take longer. Besides the usual run of paperwork and reports, he was still going through possible tactical encounters, working out battle plans to match each, and assigning them simple code names—"Plan Alfa," "Plan Bravo," and so on—so that if *Hillenkoetter* found herself in a fight, the human forces wouldn't be trying to put together an attack plan on the fly. Ordering the fleet to "execute Attack Plan Delta" was *way* simpler than trying to give explicit and detailed step-by-step battle plans for five vessels in the middle of a contested battlespace, and less prone to misunderstanding or to unexpected data dropouts.

The problem was that there were so damned many variables. How many enemy ships might there be? What kind of weapons would they carry? What if those weapons could outrange those of the human ships?

What had he and his tactical staff failed to anticipate?

He gathered up the latest stack of printouts and stood up behind his desk. He needed to clear these with Admiral Carruthers . . . and then, God help him, he had to take them to Elanna or Vashnu. The time travelers were the big unknowns. A dozen times now, he'd shown them a series of meticulously crafted battle plans, only to be told that he'd overlooked some key aspect of Gray or Saurian technology . . . or that he'd misapplied the tactics of surface naval warfare to the three-dimensional arena of space. Hardest to keep in mind—Elanna had pointed *this* one out to him several times already—was the fact that they would be facing an enemy capable of near-c travel . . . c being the symbol for the speed of light. If they spotted enemy ships five light seconds off . . . those ships could shift to near-c and be on top of him literally an instant behind the light warning that they'd moved.

This was Groton's first time in command of the *Hillenkoetter*, but he'd been in space since 2003; the last four years had been as the executive officer of the *Big-H*, so he was not exactly inexperienced.

But there was so much that was unknown.

He wished he had another year or two to work on those plans. . . .

HUNTER LOOKED up at the two men standing in front of him—Coulter and Brunelli. He'd thought long and hard about how to handle this.

Technically, as the man who'd put the two of them on report, he shouldn't have been the one to hear their case.

Technically, too, this was a captain's mast, a disciplinary hearing that traditionally would be held by the commanding officer of the ship—the captain—or at *least* by the ship's XO.

Hunter was damned, though, if he was going to bring Captain Groton into this. The 1-JSST's exact position on the ship command and control charts was still a bit vague. Lieutenant Commander Hunter answered to Major Victor Powell, but only in a *tactical* sense—taking orders from him in operations carried out on a planet's surface, not in terms of discipline or running the unit. The rank of major was the equivalent of the Navy rank of lieutenant commander, which made the TO&E for Operation Excalibur pretty damned fuzzy. So if one of his people committed murder or mutiny, then the matter would have to go up before Captain Groton. But short of that . . .

"What do you two have to say for yourselves?"

"No excuse, sir."

"No excuse, sir."

Having the two of them up before him together was another breach with tradition. Captain's mast was a kind of mini-trial, but nonjudicial, a disciplinary hearing under Article 15 of the Uniform Code of Military Justice for offenses within a military unit. However, he'd offered them the chance to come before him together, and they'd accepted that. In point of fact, the offense had to do with these two clowns' failure to work together and their failure to respect one another as fellow military noncoms. He was determined to address that problem, and not simply sweep it under the carpet.

The UCMJ laid out sharp restrictions on what he, the commanding officer, could mete out as punishment. He could reprimand them, confine them for up to thirty days, have them forfeit up to half their base pay, reduce their rank, or hand them extra duty . . . and that was about it. He thought, however, that he saw some wiggle room, here. Confinement was hardly a punishment when the two of them were confined to the ship for the duration of the mission. Same with forfeiture of pay; what did they have to spend it on? He could take their rockers—meaning break them both one pay grade—but, frankly, with so few men, Hunter needed them where they were.

But . . .

"Okay, gentlemen. You've both agreed to accept my decision in this matter. Chief Brunelli, I must say that I am surprised and unhappy with your behavior. You were clearly in the wrong. You let a stupid remark get to you, and you threw the first punch. I ought to bust you back down to first class!"

"Yes, sir. Sorry, sir."

"And you, Coulter—you were as stupid and as insensitive as Brunelli. You made a deliberately provocative statement to him. He saw you as a stereotype, yeah, but you were just as bad, seeing him as a target for your straight-baiting, making fun of him. I've seen Brunelli in a fight. You're lucky he didn't kill you! Now I don't give a fuck about your sexual orientation, okay? But I *will* have a disciplined and a smooth-running unit here."

"Yes, sir. It won't happen again, sir."

"You're damned right it won't. If it does, I'll have your ass!"

Brunelli actually smirked.

"Did you say something, Brunelli?"

"No, sir. Sorry, sir."

"Here's how we're going to do this. I can't space the two of you. I can't afford to lose the manpower. Therefore: Brunelli, I'm transferring you to Alfa Platoon, effective immediately. I will ask for a volunteer in Alfa to give up his billet and go over to Charlie.

"You and Coulter will be assigned to the same cube in the same section. For the next thirty days, you will live together, eat together, shower together, and *sleep* together, and since you'll be in my platoon I can keep an eye on both of you and make certain my orders are carried out.

I want to see the two of you together at all times. When we sound off in twos for training or calisthenics, you two will *always* be on the same team. Mutt and Jeff! Bert and Ernie! Do I make myself understood?"

"Yes, sir."

"Sir, yes, sir!"

"After thirty days, we'll reevaluate. But until then, you two are going to be shadows to each other, and each of you will damned well get to know the other one as a person. Not as a stereotype! Clear?"

"Clear, sir."

"Yes, sir."

"The two of you shake hands."

They did so. Hunter watched for some sign of reluctance, but saw none.

"Dismissed."

He wondered if he'd handled it right. A simpler, safer solution would have been to separate the two, make sure they never came in contact with one another, but that wouldn't have addressed a basic character issue—the fact that both men were dealing in stereotypes, not with each other as people.

This way, they would be forced to work together.

Assuming one didn't kill the other during the next thirty days.

After they'd left, he made some notes in their personnel records, then touched an intercom button. "Lieutenant Bader?"

"Yes, sir."

"Send in the next case."

"Aye, aye, sir."

The second mast—or set of masts, rather—were Thomas Taylor and Ann Seton. The two entered the office and came to attention.

Taylor spoke. "Engineman First Class Taylor and Staff Sergeant Seton reporting for captain's mast as ordered, sir."

"Very well. The two of you have agreed to appear before me together. Is this still the case?"

"Yes, sir."

"Sir, yes, sir!"

"What do you have to say for yourselves?"

"Sir . . . we . . . I mean . . . sir, we *love* each other, sir! We want to get married!"

Hunter leaned back in his chair, closed his eyes, and inwardly groaned. *Oh, God . . .*

"Couldn't this have waited until you got back to Earth?"

"We don't know how long we're going to be out here, sir," Seton told him.

"I . . . see."

There were various rules and regulations that could be thrown at the two of them, but Hunter wasn't eager to do so. Men and women cooped up together tended to find their own balance, and while it would have been different if Taylor had forced himself on the Marine, right now he was inclined to let them off with a warning.

Because love *would* find a way.

He couldn't even nail them for fraternizing across ranks. First class and staff sergeant were the same—pay grade E-6—and so far as he'd been able to learn they'd both been off duty when they wandered off for their rendezvous in the storage locker.

"What the hell were you two thinking?" he demanded, raising his voice to a shout. "Staff sergeant, what happens if you get yourself pregnant?"

"I . . . we plan to get married, sir."

"Uh-huh. And if something goes wrong out here, and we can't get back to Earth for nine months . . . what do you do? Run ops pregnant? Have a baby out here? Are you completely *insane*?"

"Sir," Taylor said. "It was me. And I'll take full responsibility—"

"No. You *both* had a responsibility—to your shipmates, to me, and to this mission. Now, the fact of the matter is that I can't really nail you two with anything. 'Conduct prejudicial to good order and discipline,' I suppose. Or being out of uniform . . ."

Seton burst out laughing at that.

"You have a problem with that, Marine?"

"No, sir!"

"Okay. You get off with a warning this time. Next time . . . don't get caught."

"Yes, sir!"

"No, sir!"

"Dismissed."

Again . . . had he done right? The real problem here was not their rendezvous, but the trouble intimate personal relationships in a small, active-duty military unit could cause. The Navy didn't talk about it, but it had been wrestling with this problem ever since women had first been assigned sea duty. Women and men locked up together with no way to let off steam. Things . . . happened.

But in fact, he wished both of them well.

And thought about Gerri.

CHAPTER FOURTEEN

By 1984, MJ-12 must have been in stark terror at the mistake they had made in dealing with the EBEs. They had subtly promoted *Close Encounters of the Third Kind* and *E.T.* to get the public used to "odd looking" aliens that were compassionate, benevolent, and very much our "space brothers." MJ-12 "sold" the EBEs to the public, and were now faced with the fact that quite the opposite was true.

JOHN LEAR, FORMER CIA PILOT, 1987

10 March 1981

"**THE EBE GRAY** *aliens, Mr. President, have become extremely dangerous. They have violated the terms of the treaty signed with them in 1955. They have been abducting our citizens. We fear that they may soon move against us openly. We must act!"*

President Ronald Reagan looked across his desk at the director of the National Security Agency and frowned. "Isn't this all just a little . . . overly dramatic? The public has heard almost nothing about any of this. I've heard almost nothing about any of this, and I'm the President!*"*

Vice Admiral Bobby Ray Inman shifted uncomfortably in his seat. He was a genuine patriot, a man who loved his country and the principles on which it was grounded, and he despised pulling rank on the leader of the free world. But . . .

"Nevertheless, Mr. President, the threat is real and it is extremely grave . . . a clear and present danger. MJ-12 wants to take immediate steps to contain the situation."

"That's what my advisors keep telling me about the Russians in Afghanistan."

Inman waved that off. "Two years ago, Mr. President, there was a clash, a battle, actually, between some of our soldiers and the aliens working with some of our scientists in an underground base in New Mexico. The aliens . . . withdrew. But we believe they may be preparing a response. An armed response. An open and public response.

"Believe me, Mr. President, compared to this, the Soviets are nothing. If the EBEs make themselves known openly, we have reason to believe it might well end civilization as we know it."

"Which means you and I would be out of our jobs," Reagan said, his characteristic gentle humor cutting through the tense atmosphere in the Oval Office. "Maybe I could go back into acting."

Inman opened his mouth, then shut it again. He wasn't sure of how best to reply.

"What is it you want, Bobby? Sorry—what is it MJ-12 wants?"

"A fleet, Mr. President. An independent space fleet. Something with enough muscle to send the EBEs packing if we so need."

"And you need my authorization to build this fleet?"

"Actually, Mr. President . . . no. Not exactly. The program has already been in place for several years. Research and development began in the early `70s after the Apollo encounters on the Moon. Last year, we laid the keels for the first two of a new class of spacecraft. Very large spacecraft, with radically new propulsion systems."

Reagan stared at Inman for a long moment.

"Okay," Reagan said at last. "So why are you even telling me this now? What do you need me for?"

"Sir, MJ-12 has decided that we must expand our operations, and quickly. We will be working with a large number of US corporations—and some foreign ones as well—to design and build an entirely new generation of weapons. High-energy lasers. Particle beams. EMP beam weapons that can be employed successfully against EBE craft. Black budget funding will handle much of the cost, but some is going to come from auditable sources, and the money will be going into the public sector where . . . questions might be asked. We will need your authorization to develop and produce these weapons. And we will need your help, your visible help, to sell the idea to the American public. We are suggesting this program be presented to the public as a strategic defense for use against incoming Soviet missiles."

"I see." Reagan shook his head. "Sounds more like Star Wars to me."

"The idea, Mr. President," Inman said, "will be to avoid a real Star Wars. . . ."

THE *HILLENKOETTER* and her four escorts dropped out of light drive and drifted into the star system known as Zeta 2 Reticuli. Following Insertion Plan Bravo, they pulled apart until twenty thousand kilometers separated each vessel from her sisters, the better to begin a systematic survey of the system. Hunter was in the Tactical Command Center, the "TC-squared," as it was known, with his platoon leaders and other senior personnel, along with both Major Powell and Dr. McClure. Dr. Brody was there as well to talk to them about the astrophysics of whatever they might discover in the new system.

Powell was a Marine and Hunter respected him, though they'd seen little of one another until now. The rank of major normally commanded a full battalion—

depending on the organization anywhere from three hundred to twelve hundred men. 1-JSST, with its forty-eight men and women divided into three small platoons, was about the size of a single Marine platoon, which normally would be under the command of a more junior officer, typically a second or first lieutenant.

On the other hand, 1-JSST was far too important to be put under the command of a mere lieutenant, and, in this case, the position was organizational rather than a direct combat command. Powell's official rank on the *Hillenkoetter* was that of brevet major . . . meaning it was honorary and temporary, and, in fact, Hunter outranked him. *First Lieutenant* Powell, however, had served with the Marine Raiders, the USMC's primary combat unit under USSOCOM. With two tours in Iraq and one in Afghanistan, Powell had chewed some of the same dirt as he had, and Hunter probably had as much confidence in the man's combat acumen as he did for any officer who wasn't a SEAL.

It would help, though, Hunter thought, if the Marine didn't look so damned *young*.

"What," Hunter asked, leaning forward in his chair, "am I looking at?"

The seven of them were gathered around a large-screen monitor, on which two nearby stars gleamed like gems against the darkness. One was much brighter than the other, and showed a small disk. The other was dim by comparison, but still far brighter than anything else on the screen. Together, they formed a spectacular sight.

"Zeta Reticuli," Brody said, sounding like a lecturing professor, "is a double star. Both components are very similar to Sol, a G2 and a G3, and they orbit one another at an average distance of . . ."

"We all heard Commander Johnson's presentation," Powell said, interrupting. "I don't care about the stars. What's here in the way of *planets*?"

"That's what we hope to learn from our survey, Major. So far as space telescopes in our Sol System have been able to discern, neither of these stars has any planets. But astronomers using infrared telescopes have spotted debris fields orbiting both Zeta 1 and Zeta 2, like analogues of Sol's Kuiper Belt. Its inner edge is just 4.3 astronomical units from the star—that's almost as far out as Jupiter back in our system—but it extends into space for over 100 AUs, which is three times farther out than Pluto, on average. It's enormous! It's possible that these debris fields will be a planetary system someday . . . but there's nothing here now."

"So," Hunter said, "no planets? Why are we here, then?"

"Couple of reasons," Powell said. "First of all, Zeta Reticuli has such a huge rep in the UFO community back home—the place where the Grays come from, and all of that—that I think MJ-12 wants to debunk the idea once and for all officially. And . . . it's always possible we're wrong. We need to *know*, once and for all."

"I thought the Grays were time travelers," Minkowski said. "You know, from Earth."

"Maybe it's Saurians," Hunter pointed out. "Or maybe our great-great-great-offspring built a colony out here. Kind of tough to do if there's no planet."

"There *is* still a possibility of a planet around Zeta 2," Brody said. "Those astronomers reported that the Zeta 2 debris field is . . . lopsided, I guess you would say. Asymmetrical, with a couple of odd lobes to it, rather than being spread out nice and evenly as you'd expect. There are several possible solutions for the mathematics of what they're seeing. One is a planet bigger than Jupiter, 200 AUs out. Another is an inner world, tucked in at around 3 to 4 AUs, with just 10 or 20 percent of Jupiter's mass."

"How big is that, sir?" Minkowski wanted to know.

"Ten percent of Jupiter would be . . . let's see." Brody

pursed his lips. "Almost thirty-two times the mass of Earth. That's big, more than twice as massive as Uranus. It would probably have to be an ice giant, like Uranus or Neptune . . . so not a real pleasant place to live."

"And I guess not likely as real estate for any Zeta Reticulans," Hunter said.

"No."

"So much for Operation Serpo, huh?" Sergeant Major Callahan said. He sounded disappointed.

"What," Brody asked, "is Operation Serpo?"

Callahan shrugged. "I've read a lot about UFO conspiracy stuff, y'know? There's this story about how back in the mid-1960s, we had a kind of diplomatic exchange going with the Grays. Twelve of our people—ten men and two women—were supposed to have gone to Zeta Reticuli, while one of the aliens stayed on Earth. They were said to be out here ten or twelve years. A couple of them died, a couple decided to stay here. The whole thing was supersecret, of course. Air Force.

"So anyway, the planet was called 'Serpo,' and they named the program after that."

Hunter groaned. "*Serpo?* As in 'serpent'? Don't tell me . . . it was where the Reptilians were supposed to come from, right?"

"Nah. *They're* supposed to come from a star called Alpha Draconis. Ha, get it? Draconis . . . reptilians . . . Of course, lots of people get the Grays and the Reptilians confused a lot of the time."

"I *hate* it when that happens," Hunter said, shaking his head and grinning.

"Sounds like *very* bad science fiction," McClure added.

"Well, things are awfully fuzzy sometimes for the conspiracy theorists," Callahan said. "All kinds of different stories and not too many of them agree with each other. Some think the intelligence services are spreading disinformation, to kind of, you know, discredit the *real* story . . . whatever that is."

"How about that, Captain?" Hunter said, grinning. "You people spreading lies within the UFO community?"

Captain Alan Arch chuckled. "I wouldn't know if we were, sir. They never tell us anything."

With some misgivings, Hunter had assigned Arch to be the platoon leader for Charlie. He was too senior to leave out of the command structure, so he was running the platoon. Hunter had bought some insurance, though, by putting Master Sergeant Layton in as senior platoon NCO. Layton had plenty of experience . . . though Hunter had been disappointed by his failure to safe the Brunelli-Coulter affair before it had gotten out of hand.

Still, Hunter had worked with Company men before—the term referred to the CIA. He had no reason to mistrust Arch . . . exactly. . . .

But he would keep an eye on him just the same . . . and occasionally prod him a bit just to see how he would respond.

But as for Serpo . . .

"So Serpo is a hoax?" Hunter asked.

"Probably," Callahan replied. He stressed the word to indicate that he wasn't entirely sure of this. "It's subtle if it is, and it has some unexpected sources supporting it. And the people who tell the tale give lots of corroborative detail. The stories include details like high radiation levels that killed some of our people, and no nighttime so it was hard to count the days, and 107 degree temperatures, all because of the two stars. They said the sky was so bright because of two stars, they always had to wear sunglasses."

"Nonsense!" Brody laughed. "Zeta 1 and Zeta 2 are 3,800 astronomical units apart! That's *way* too far for there to be any problems like that!"

"Yeah, but how do you *know*?" McClure asked. "I mean . . . this is the first time we've been here. Maybe conditions here are different from what we expected."

Brody looked mildly exasperated. "Look . . . Pluto is roughly 40 AUs away from the sun, okay?"

"If you say so . . ."

"And we know that from out there, our sun looks like a bright star. Maybe the brightest star in the sky, sure . . . about two hundred times brighter than the full Moon, actually, depending on where Pluto is in its year. But the two Zetas are almost a hundred times farther apart!" He pointed at the screen, where Zeta 2 showed a tiny bright disk, and Zeta 1 was a bright pinpoint off to the right. "See? That small one is Zeta 1. *Just* a bright star. You could see it in the daytime sky of a planet around Zeta 2, sure . . . but it would be, oh, say thirty times brighter than Venus is from Earth."

"So not close enough to pass any heat to the planet, or raise the radiation levels, or anything like that," Hunter said.

"Precisely! The two stars are so far apart that it takes *two weeks* for a beam of light to get from one to the other! No, if those conspiracy theorists claimed it was so bright because of two suns in the sky, they got it all totally wrong!"

"Huh," Minkowski said. "Someone heard the system was a double star and just made all that stuff up, not knowing what it really looked like!"

"Interesting," Hunter said. "I'd give a lot to know if the mistake was due to Agency disinformation."

"More likely," Callahan said, "it was because of *CE3K*."

Hunter was puzzled. "What's that?"

"The movie *Close Encounters of the Third Kind*," Callahan explained. "You know . . . where a giant alien saucer lands at Devils Tower?"

"Oh, right," McClure said. "Richard Dreyfuss! I saw that when I was seven! I *loved* that movie!"

"Right. It came out in 1977. The Serpo story first surfaced . . . I'm not sure, exactly. Early eighties, maybe? But well after *CE3K*. And in the movie, you've got ten men and two women going on board the alien mother ship, right? Dreyfuss's character goes with them. The idea is that they're part of an exchange program with the aliens' home planet."

"So . . ." McClure paused, looking puzzled. "Wait. Are you saying that Serpo is a hoax because they copied the story from the movie a little too closely? Or are you saying the movie was copied from what really happened, to kind of explain to people what was going on?"

Hunter laughed. "Jesus! Which one is easier to believe?"

"They, the conspiracy theorists, claim *CE3K* was part of a project to start gently disclosing what was really going on," Callahan said, shrugging.

"I'll go with Occam's razor," Hunter said. "The simplest explanation is probably the correct one."

Brody nodded. "Given that the details of the story provided by the conspiracy theorists don't jive with what's actually out here . . ."

"So the idea that there are Gray aliens here," Hunter said, grinning, "means it's not Zeta Reticuli. It's Zeta *Rediculi*!"

McClure laughed. "Looks that way," she said.

"There's also the age of these stars to consider," Brody added. "We used to think these stars were part of what astronomers call the Zeta Herculis Moving Group. That's a number of stars that share the same motion through the sky, which implies they were all born together, okay?"

Hunter and McClure both nodded.

"Astronomers can look at the spectrum of a star's chromosphere and make a good guess at that star's age. So it turns out that the members of the Zeta Herc group are all somewhere between six to eight billion years old."

"But then we took a closer look at Zeta Ret, and realized that both stars are dimmer than they ought to be for stars of their age and surface temperatures. The data suggests that Zeta Ret is only about two billion years old."

"So?" Minkowski asked.

"So any planets in this system aren't old enough for life to have evolved," McClure put in. "Right, Doctor?"

"Exactly right. If the planets were six billion years old—that's 1.5 billion years older than Earth, and there's been plenty of time for life to evolve."

"Right," McClure said. "When Earth was two billion years old, there was life . . . but nothing more complex than bacteria and single-celled algae. Life on Earth didn't make the transition to multicellular life until about two billion years later."

"Hence," Brody said, nodding, "no time for the evolution of advanced life-forms capable of building spaceships or hosting exchange programs with humans."

"Just who told this Serpo story, anyway?" McClure wanted to know.

Callahan smiled. "He only gave the handle 'Anonymous.'"

"Ah-*ha*!" Hunter exclaimed.

"Well, he wasn't the only source of material about Serpo. Some high-ranking people in the military are supposed to have said it was all true. But . . . well, I guess you guys are right. When you look at it like that the whole story really doesn't make much sense. I just . . . well . . . I kind of wished it would turn out to be true, y'know?"

"Good heavens, why?" Brody demanded.

Callahan sighed. "We have kind of two completely different pictures of the aliens and how we relate to them, okay? There are the fuzzy, happy, good-guy 'space brothers,' come to Earth to help us. And there's the evil, dark aliens who abduct people and do nasty things to them. The Serpo story suggests we have a really good relationship with these guys, right? But, well, I guess maybe we don't know them all that well, after all!"

Hunter watched the screen for a moment longer. *Hillenkoetter* was moving deeper into the system, moving closer to the star Zeta 2, but nothing appeared to move or change on the screen. It appeared . . . empty. Devoid of planets . . . devoid of life.

If there was a military target in there, it was not visible at the moment.

They needed to get eyes deeper inside the system if they were going to see what was there.

"CAG?" Groton said. "I'd like to get a couple of black triangles in close—just a few AUs out from that star."

"Copy that, Skipper," the voice of Captain Andrew Macmillan came back over the intercom. "We have two on ready-five."

Groton glanced up at Vashnu, who was standing impassively beside his command seat. The Nordic had appeared just as *Hillenkoetter* emerged from FTL. Vashnu gave an almost imperceptible nod, as though bestowing his blessing.

"Do it," Groton ordered. Technically, and according to regs, he commanded the *Hillenkoetter* while Macmillan commanded the fighter wing, both of them answering to Admiral Carruthers.

But in practice, Groton used the space wing as an extension of the *Big-H*, a tool for exploring their surroundings, a weapon for striking at enemies. Groton and Macmillan were both naval captains who worked together to carry out the overall mission under the admiral's direction, but Groton was the senior, and the one who called the shots.

It was *his* ship, after all, a fact of which he was painfully aware.

"What are we looking for, Skipper?" Macmillan's voice came back.

"I don't know. Planets. Intelligence. Any sign of intelligent life at all, I want to know about it."

"Aye, aye, Captain. We'll see what we can find for you."

ADMIRAL CARRUTHERS drummed his fingers on the armrest of his chair. "Nothing," he said, looking at the data relayed from *Hillenkoetter*'s bridge. *"Nothing."*

"Were you expecting the Gray homeworld?" Elanna asked. She'd entered the flag bridge moments after *Hillenkoetter* emerged from FTL, a quiet, steadying presence.

"I was expecting something. Solar Warden Command sent us here, they must have expected something."

"Not necessarily," the Talis said. Carruthers found himself lost in her large, dark blue, expressive eyes . . . slightly larger than those of most modern-day humans. "They wanted to confirm that the Grays and the Saurians do *not* have a presence here. As your government moves into Full Disclosure with your citizens, some of the myths could cause problems. Bumps in the road."

"I can see that. Okay—you're the time traveler," Carruthers said, frowning. "Is there anything here we need to be concerned about?"

"Not of which we are aware, Admiral."

"I don't see anything but gravel, and a planet that couldn't possibly harbor life." His scowl deepened. He was far more concerned about what might be lurking at Aldebaran than he was about this system . . . and assets were being wasted on exploring Zeta Retic.

"Suppose I send part of my force out to Aldebaran now?" Carruthers asked the Talis. "You see a problem with that?"

"You would be splitting your forces, of course," Elanna told him. "Is that wise?"

"In this case," Carruthers said, "yes. Commander Johnson!"

"Sir!"

"Make to the *Samford*, the *Carlucci*, and the *Blake*. They are to detach from the task force immediately and deploy to Aldebaran. I want them to begin reconnaissance of that system, so that when *Hillenkoetter* arrives, they already have a clear picture of what's there. They are not to engage with any hostile forces they may encounter, but wait for the *Hillenkoetter*'s arrival."

"Yes, sir. And the *Inman*?"

"*Inman* will stay with us, operating in support. Pass the word to all vessels, with my compliments."

"Aye, aye, sir."

Hillenkoetter's fighters should be able to handle anything they might encounter at Zeta Reticuli—not that such an engagement was seeming likely—but holding back one cruiser would be good insurance.

He also found himself wondering if he could trust the Talis standing beside him. She was beautiful, she was brilliant . . .

. . . but even if she was human, she seemed so very *alien*.

And he wasn't sure she was telling him the whole truth.

LIEUTENANT DAVID Duvall—call sign "Double-D"—strapped himself into the cockpit of the modified TR-3R. Similar in shape and overall appearance to the TR-3B shuttles, the second *R* in its designator stood for "recon" and identified the craft as one of *Hillenkoetter*'s long-range eyes and ears.

Where the 3B had room enough to transport a hundred or so people at a time, the smaller 3R was packed with high-tech sensor and communications gear. There were two cockpits, both cramped to the point of claustrophobia. His backseater, or radar intercept officer, was Lieutenant Tammy Bucknell; her job was running the electronics and performing the actual recon work, while Double-D sat up front and piloted the thing.

"TR-3R Alfa," a voice said inside Duvall's helmet. "You are free to cycle."

"Copy that, PryFly," he replied. PryFly, the primary flight control, was the equivalent of an airport tower, handling all flight deck operations. "Cycling to 10 percent."

He brought the electrogravitic effect up in order to decrease the craft's effective mass to just 10 percent of normal. They were sitting on a broad, flat, metal deck—

Hillenkoetter's primary flight deck—bathed in the harsh overhead spotlights that seemed to vanish into the recon craft's ebon surface. The deck maintained a half gravity, the better to facilitate handling, prepping, and launching spacecraft, and he could feel his craft swaying slightly, eager to move. The spacecraft had been transported over a long rail embedded in the deck, a rail running straight for the enormous, open launch port a hundred meters straight ahead.

"You ready back there, Bucky?" he asked.

"Ready to rock'n'roll, Double-D! Let's do it!"

"Anyplace, anytime, baby. PryFly, TR-3R Alfa is ready for launch."

"Copy, Alfa. Inner screen is down. You are clear to launch at your mark."

"On my mark, then, launch in three . . . two . . . one . . . and *shoot!*"

The flight bay blurred around him. Powerful electromagnetic forces hurled the craft forward down the launch rail.

The bay access port appeared to be wide-open to space, but that, of course, was an illusion. The port was blocked by not one but two magnetokinetic induction screens, force fields that kept the interior of the *Hillenkoetter* safely pressurized. With the inner screen temporarily switched off, only the outer screen stood between the spacecraft carrier and depressurization.

As the recon ship hurtled toward the port, the outer screen, under computer control, also went down. The spacecraft flashed past the threshold, and the outer screen switched on once more, the entire off-on sequence happening so quickly that there was no time for the air molecules to begin moving, no time for an explosive eruption into hard vacuum. The inner screen was there as a just-in-case. If the outer screen dropped and then failed to come on again, it would be very, *very* bad for the carrier.

Space exploded around TR-3R Alfa. Moving now at a

kilometer per second relative to the *Big-H*, Duvall hurtled clear of the carrier. As big as it was, the *Hillenkoetter* very swiftly dwindled astern to a point of light—and then into complete invisibility—and the recon craft seemed to be hanging suspended in the ultimate night, unmoving, surrounded by the utter vastness of space.

"PryFly, Alfa," he called. "We are clear of the ship."

"Copy Alfa. Transferring you to CIC."

"Roger that. CIC, Alfa. What's our heading?"

"Alfa, CIC, you are cleared to proceed sunward, bearing one-one-seven by zero-three-two, over."

"CIC, Alfa, sunward at one-one-seven by zero-three-two, roger that."

"Good luck, Alfa. Bring us back a clear skies report."

"Copy that. We'll see what we can do."

The TR-3R rotated in space until the local star was hanging directly ahead, then engaged her gravitics and accelerated. With mass nullification, the craft's passengers were immune to the relatively low accelerations employed at launch. Under gravitic acceleration—essentially *falling*, with every atom of the spacecraft and its passengers falling at the same rate—they could boost at tens of thousands of gravities and not feel a thing.

It was a bit unnerving, however, to be accelerating at 1,500 Gs and still feel like they were hovering in place, unmoving.

So vast was the cosmos.

It gave them time to think.

David Duvall had been a Navy fighter pilot, driving an F/A-18F Super Hornet off the USS *Nimitz*. In 2014, he and his RIO had spotted . . . *something* in the skies off San Diego. It had been silver, it had been round, and it had maneuvered like nothing Duvall had ever seen, playing tag with Duvall and his wingman, Lieutenant "Duff" Cotter, for ten minutes before vanishing into a hard, blue sky at what the radar data claimed was an impossible twenty thousand miles per hour.

He'd been debriefed, of course . . . and then the two suits from DC had shown up and offered him a new assignment, one that would take him into space. McCally, his RIO, was married and had simply been sworn to silence. Both Duvall and Cotter, though, had ended up first at Groom Lake, and then on the Moon.

And now . . . shit. He was thiry-nine light-years from home, accelerating straight into God knew what.

"You okay back there, Tammy?"

"Sure thing, Boss. Nothing on our ears. Not yet."

"Roger. Keep 'em peeled sharp, though. The scuttlebutt is that there could be hostiles out here."

"I don't doubt it. You could hide *anything* in all that crap out here!"

"I hear you."

"Recommend bringing us to plus four," Bucknell told him. "We're a little too close to the crap layer."

"Copy that." He adjusted his controls to bring the recon ship a little farther from the cloud of debris. Even from just a few thousand kilometers, the debris field remained invisible. He did *not* want to fly into that.

"Recon Bravo reports they're clear of the *Big-H*," Bucknell said.

"Copy," said Duff Cotter. Somehow having his old wingman out there with them made the sky just a little less empty.

"Shit!"

"Whatcha got, Buck?"

"I have no idea, Boss! But it's big—*huge!* And it's headed straight for us! Recommend changing course to—"

And then all hell broke loose.

CHAPTER FIFTEEN

Houston, this is *Discovery*. We still have the alien
spacecraft . . . uh . . . under VFR. (Visual Flight Rules.)

CDR JOHN BLAHA, COMMANDER OF
SPACE SHUTTLE *DISCOVERY*, 1989

30 March 1981

KAMMLER MOVED LIKE *an automaton—which in a very real
sense, he was. Ssarsk was riding him, riding his mind,
controlling his actions directly.*

*And there was nothing he could do to shake the
alien off.*

*Of its own accord, his right hand slipped inside the
pocket of his cheap suit jacket, touching the grip of
the .38 snub-nosed revolver there. God . . . if he could
cry out . . . if he could turn and run . . .*

But he could do neither.

*He was in Washington, DC, standing in a large crowd
outside the rear entrance to the Washington Hilton Hotel. It was 2:25 in the afternoon, and someone important,
he gathered, was coming out of the hotel within the next
few moments. A black limousine had just pulled up on
the street outside the hotel.*

It was 2:26.

I don't want to do this! *he screamed in his mind.*

You, who have killed so many? *He could hear scorn in Ssarsk's mental voice.*

Not here! Not like this! There are policemen over there! I'll be killed!

That is irrelevant. In any case, you are not the only shooter here. We will direct the one of you who has the best chance of success. Perhaps you will live.

And maybe, he thought, it would be best to die and end this bleak enslavement. The Saurians cared nothing about him save how he might be of use to them and their plans. They watched him continually. They visited him in his sleep. They filled his nightmares.

It was 2:27.

He comes.

The crowd burst into excited commotion as police officers held them back. Men in civilian suits appeared, entering the cleared portion of the sidewalk. A tall man in a dark suit stepped out of the hotel, smiling, waving . . .

My God! *Kammler thought.* It's Reagan! *His hand closed on the pistol grip, but he didn't draw it. Not yet . . . not yet. . . .*

They led Reagan to the limousine, opening the rear door. Six shots split the afternoon air, six shots in less than two seconds. Men fell to the sidewalk. Men surged at the edge of the crowd, dragging someone down. Secret Service men shoved Reagan inside the limo and slammed the door. For a moment there was indescribable consternation . . . and then the car was speeding off.

Kammler released the pistol. Who . . . who shot him?

Another of our creatures. Its mind is twisted. Its erotomania led him to do something to impress the human he thinks he loves. We guided it here, provided the mental key.

And why the President?

Because it moves against us. It signs orders that will lead to war between your people and ours. Your president will die, and its replacement will have to start over in terms of understanding us, reacting to us.

I don't want to be part of this any longer! Please . . . *please* let me die!

No. Not so long as you remain useful to us.

"HILLENKOETTER! HILLENKOETTER!" Duvall called. "We have a large alien spacecraft—*very* large—coming straight for us! We're transmitting images. We're maneuvering . . ."

Not that the mother ship could do a damned thing to help. TR-3R Alfa was currently over two light minutes sunward of the *Hillenkoetter*, which meant it would be over two minutes before Duvall's frantic warning would be heard on board the *Big-H*. While both the Grays and the Talis had devices that let them communicate instantly across light-years, the technology was so poorly understood by humans that they'd not been adopted by Solar Warden. For now, at least, human communications were limited by the speed of light, something that could be damned inconvenient in a far-ranging space battle.

Duvall had never felt so cutoff and alone.

"What's it doing, Bucky?"

"Still coming, Double-D! Range . . . sixteen thousand kilometers! Speed . . . two hundred kilometers per second in approach! We'll have intercept in 1.3 minutes. . . ."

"Let's just keep our distance, shall we?"

The recon craft flipped end-for-end, piled on the g's with a massive surge of deceleration, then began accelerating directly away from the oncoming vessel. The alien ship increased its speed, and kept coming.

"Talk to me, Bucky," Duvall said. "What the hell is it?"

"Nothing we've encountered before, Boss. It's vaguely egg shaped. Diameter of about five and a half kilometers. I'm reading a mass of . . . my God—two times ten to the twelve tons! That's a small asteroid!"

"I guess that makes sense," Duvall said. "A civilization living in an asteroid belt, they're going to use what's handy to make what they need."

"Yeah, but *spaceships*? Out of big rocks?"

"Transmit that data to the *Big-H.*"

"Already done."

Time passed. TR-3R Alfa changed course in order to avoid taking the alien all the way back to *Hillenkoetter*. The asteroid, or whatever it was, changed course to intercept. When the recon ship increased its acceleration, so did the alien. Slowly, inexorably, the huge alien ship—almost three and a half miles long and three wide—continued to close the range. After fifteen minutes, the human vessel was pushing up against the speed of light, an impenetrable barrier. The *Hillenkoetter* and her escorts could use gravity to wrap local space around them and break the light barrier, but not a TR-3R. She simply did not have the power to play that kind of trick with space-time.

The alien had the power, and some to spare. It continued to close.

"TAKE US to battle stations," Groton ordered.

"Battle stations, aye!"

An alarm sounded through the vast ship, accompanied by a canned voice intoning "Now battle stations, battle stations! All hands, man your battle stations . . ."

"TR-3R Alfa is being pursued by the alien, Captain," the senior scanner officer reported. "We estimate the bogie will intercept Alfa now in . . . five minutes."

"Can we get there in time?"

"We can, Captain. But . . ."

"Say it."

"Sir, the bogie is over three miles long! The *Big-H* would be a dinghy by comparison!"

"Talk to me, Vashnu," he said to the tall time traveler standing beside him. "Who are these people?"

"I'm sorry, Captain, but as I've explained already, the Talis have not explored this star system. From nearby stars it appears to be uninhabited. No intelligence-generated signals of any kind."

"Is it possible this alien ship is from some other system?"

"Of course."

"Who do you know who builds starships out of five-kilometer asteroids?"

"None close to here, Captain. There's a race we call the Elajid who hollow out asteroids both to create habitats and for the construction of large starships, but their realm is nearly ten thousand light-years in toward the galactic core. We have no regular contact with them."

"Could they be exploring out this way?"

"I cannot say, Captain. However, it seems unlikely. They have carved an empire for themselves roughly five hundred light-years across. They do not appear to know the secret of faster-than-light travel, however, and so they expand quite slowly."

Once more, the Talis seemed no help.

"CAG!"

"Yes, Captain."

"I need the fighter wing spaceborne ASAP. What's your status?"

"First fighters are coming online now, Captain. They'll be ready for launch in . . . two minutes."

"Ms. Briem? Execute Opplan Delta, please."

"Opplan Delta, aye, sir."

"Comm. Alert the escorts! Have them close with us."

"Belay those last orders, Captain." It was the admiral, up on the flag bridge. "Keep *Hillenkoetter* well clear of that thing. We will deploy two of the escorts to probe the object."

Groton's mouth compressed to a thin, hard line. He didn't like having his orders superseded in front of the bridge crew; more importantly, though, he didn't think

the new order was the right one, not under the circumstances. As yet, they had no reason to think the alien craft
was hostile, and only by taking the spacecraft carrier in
close would they be able to establish contact.

Contact might be successfully established by two of
the cruisers, yes . . . but if the alien was hostile, chances
were good the cruisers would not survive. In Groton's
opinion, the new order was a halfway measure, likely to
be too little, too late.

But he could not get into an argument with the commanding admiral, not in front of his people. "Aye, aye, sir."

The *Inman* was directed to close to within a thousand
kilometers of the giant alien vessel.

"Tactical officer!"

"Yes, sir." *Hillenkoetter*'s tactical officer was Commander William James, the man in CIC who directly
fought the ship under Groton's orders. He was also the
man who directed Major Powell and, through Powell,
Lieutenant Commander Hunter's JSST combat team.

"Have Commander Hunter's team prepare for tactical
deployment."

"With what in mind, sir?"

Groton actually wasn't sure he had *anything* in mind.
The situation was still both fuzzy and fluid. Hunter's
people might be useful in boarding that massive alien,
though even thinking that seemed tantamount to suicide
at the moment. Or they might need to take up positions
on the *Hillenkoetter* to repel an alien boarding operation.
Or, or, or.

"Damfino. Just have them ready to *go*!"

"Aye, aye, sir."

He heard James giving the order.

What would they do if the alien proved to be hostile?
Groton didn't have an answer to that. He had opplans, all
carefully constructed to meet any given possibility, including an encounter with a large, hostile warship.

But was this thing hostile? It was aggressive, certainly.

But its pursuit of Alfa could be anything from simple curiosity to lining up an attack.

If it was an attack, all *Hillenkoetter* and *Inman* would be able to do was run like hell.

BATTLE STATIONS! Now battle stations! All hands man your battle stations!

Hunter pounded through the ship's corridors at a dead run.

Their assigned battle stations were amidships on *Hillenkoetter*'s flight deck. The reasoning was simple enough. Should they need to be deployed off-ship, to attack an enemy asset on the surface of a planet, for instance, their TR-3B shuttles were close at hand.

On the other hand, any attacking enemy force would likely target the flight deck as the easiest way to board the giant carrier, and if they did, Hunter's team would be there waiting for them.

A hurry-up cart came up behind him—a flatbed wagon with a central handrail and six flight-suited men on board. In a vessel as large as the *Big-H*, electric people-movers like this one were a necessity. One of the riders reached out, and Hunter swung himself up and onto the cart, which never even slowed.

Hunter found the idea of boarding an alien spacecraft amusing and just a bit ironic. However, SEALs were extensively trained in what was known in the business as VBSS—visit, board, search, and seizure. There were times in modern warfare when it was necessary to board an enemy vessel—in antidrug operations, for example, or when combating piracy or terrorism at sea. SEALs also were trained in CQB, or close quarters battle, and were therefore well qualified to engage in combat within the tight confines of a ship. But the idea of forty-eight people assaulting a spacecraft, however—particularly one as large or larger than the ponderous *Hillenkoetter*—seemed both ludicrous and suicidal.

In the weeks since he'd first arrived on the Moon, Hunter had been thinking about this issue a lot, trying to make plans for any eventuality . . . even though he'd been given no clear guidelines on what those eventualities might be. Benedict had told them that they might be deployed to a planet's surface, but he'd said little about what they were supposed to do there. Forty-eight men and women would *not* be a useful force for invading a planet—especially one with a population, like Earth, of billions. If the target was something like that shield generator in *Return of the Jedi*, well . . . *maybe*. But only if the emplacement was badly undermanned and the sentries were looking the other way.

Hunter had once told Dr. Brody that he didn't care for SF, and for the most part that was true. He *had* seen that movie, though, which, quite frankly, he thought of as a comedy. The idea of Stone Age teddy bears with rocks and logs taking on a mechanized military unit armed with lasers was a real howler. In fact, movies like *Return of the Jedi* were the main reason he didn't care for the genre.

As for repelling boarders, well, the 1-JSST might serve as a security team, but the unit would be all but lost within the miles of corridors and passageways and compartments that made up the habitable portions of the carrier.

He arrived on the flight deck to find some members of the JSST filing in past a Marine gunnery sergeant who was passing out Starbeam laser weapons. Others were scrambling to get into their Seven-SAS rigs, closing up glove and helmet seals, donning heavy backpacks with the power sources for their weapons. Nielson was looking around wildly saying, "Anybody seen my gloves?"

They'd practiced getting into their suits plenty of times over the past weeks, of course, but somehow the reality of that damned alarm blaring from the overhead speakers was transforming what should have been an orderly evolution to a scene of pure chaos.

Abruptly, though, the battle stations alarm cut off. "Listen up, people!" Hunter shouted into the sudden silence. "Get yourselves squared away! *Get* your suits on, *get* your weapon, and fall in on that line over there! By platoons in an *orderly* and *military* manner!"

Nielson, he was glad to see, had found a pair of gloves and was quickly sealing them in place. "Now for the fun part, people," Hunter said, raising his voice to be heard by the entire group. "We *wait!*"

That got him a chuckle.

He accepted a suit from a quartermaster chief, squeezed into it, and took a heavy laser weapon from the gunny, who was grinning at him. "What are *you* laughing at, Gunny?"

"Just remembering my first day at Camp Lejeune, sir. Happy times . . ."

The reference to the Marines' boot camp facility in North Carolina steadied Hunter, and he grinned back. "Thanks, Gunny." He hefted the laser. *"Hoo-yah!"*

*"Ooh-*rah!" the gunnery sergeant replied, using the Marines' traditional war cry to answer the SEALs' battle call. Each military service had their own. In the Army or the US Air Force it would have been *hooah*, while Airborne troops shouted *boo-*yah. It was a simple and long-used technique designed to build morale and a sense of unity. It was said that in ancient Greece, Athenian warriors had gone into battle screaming "alala," supposedly an imitation of an owl, the bird of their patron goddess Athena.

Whatever the source, the exchange focused him.

It also inspired him.

One of the many problems of creating a combat unit out of so many disparate military forces—Navy, Marine, Army, Air Force—was the fact that they used so many different battle cries. Those war cries had been deliberately chosen to make them distinct and different from all the others—no Navy SEAL would want to be associated

with the *Army*, for God's sake—and that made forging
these men and women into a single unit that much more
difficult.

That needed to change. "Right, people. We may be
told off as boarders. We may have to defend this ship
against boarders. Let me hear you yell like pirates!"

"Arrrr!" they shouted in ragged unison.

"Together!" Hunter yelled. "Let me hear your war cry!"

"ARRRR!"

It was a small thing . . . but it was a beginning.

GROTON HAD clattered down the steel steps into the CIC
pit just below the bridge to get a better look at the tactical situation. On James's big screen, a green icon represented the recon vessel, while a red one showed the
bogie. Blocks of alphanumerics flickered and scrolled to
either side. God . . . the bogie, he saw, was as massive as
a small asteroid. Carruthers had been right to keep the
Hillenkoetter back.

But that mountain was closing on the TR-3R fast.

New data appeared on-screen. "The bogie just fired
on our recon ship," James announced, his voice madden-
ingly calm.

"What was it?"

"Unknown, Captain. Some kind of EM beam, I think.
The TR-3R shows all power down: gravitics, shields, everything. They just went off-line."

And in the next few seconds, the red blip touched the
green . . . and the green vanished from the screen.

"Jesus. Tell the *Inman* to keep her distance. They're
not going to have any effect on *that*."

"Aye, sir."

The cruiser had moved in close to the alien and was
awaiting orders.

Groton opened an intercom channel. "Admiral? Orders?"

"We wait, Captain. We wait . . ."

CAPTAIN JANICE Makilroy leaned forward in her command seat, studying the cliff face of solid rock ahead. Even at a range of one thousand kilometers, the alien vessel loomed enormous and threatening, a small mountain of nickel-iron. Under magnification, tiny installations could be seen scattered randomly across the surface, like the lights of small towns. Were those weapons emplacements? she wondered. Or did the crew of this alien leviathan ride their spacecraft on the *out*side?

The mountain floated off the cruiser's bow, a whale to *Inman*'s minnow.

"Order from the *Big-H*, Captain!" her comm officer called. "We're to pull back from the alien. Keep our distance."

"Yes, I think that would be an excellent idea," she said. "Helm! Maneuvering! Come to two-niner-five. Get us away from that monster!"

"Course two-niner-five and accelerate. Aye, aye, Captain!"

Black rock slid across her viewscreen as the ship pivoted, then accelerated.

The *Inman* was roughly comparable in size to a US Navy guided-missile cruiser of the *Ticonderoga* class—eight thousand tons and 175 meters long. Highly automated, as were all vessels within the Solar Warden program, she had a crew of just thirty-two officers and 115 enlisted personnel. The size of the crew didn't matter, though—Makilroy took her responsibilities for the men and women under her command very seriously indeed.

There was a dazzling flash from the viewscreens . . .
. . . followed by complete and absolute darkness.

DAVE DUVALL looked out into darkness.

All electrical systems on board the recon vessel were dead. He had no lights, no radar, and no way even to analyze the atmosphere outside . . . if, indeed, they weren't now in hard vacuum. All he knew with any certainty was that the alien mountain had fired some sort of beam—probably an intense electromagnetic pulse—that had rendered them completely helpless.

Then it had drawn them in, swallowed them whole, and they'd come to rest . . . *here*.

There was gravity, at least. It felt like less than 1 g, though he couldn't be sure. But with other details, like atmospheric pressure and external temperature, he remained—literally—in the dark. He couldn't even talk to Bucky. The TR-3R's intercom system was down with everything else.

Well, they could have killed us easily enough, he thought. *We're alive, so they must want to talk to us. Or at least find out what we are.*

The craft's instrumentation came on with a faint whine, and his instruments lit up. "Okay, Boss," Bucky told him over a now live intercom circuit. "I wired in some batteries. It won't last very long, but it'll give us life support for a little while."

"Well done!" The TR-3R's external sensors were online again. There *was* atmosphere outside—about 80 percent nitrogen, with lesser amounts of CO_2, hydrogen, methane . . . Damn! It looked a little like the atmosphere of Titan, the large moon of Saturn, back home. Pressure was a bit higher than the surface pressure of Earth. Definitely a reducing atmosphere, though—no oxygen, and with hydrogen likely being the principle active component.

It was chilly, too. The temperature outside was minus thirty Celsius.

He could hear . . . scrabbling noises, scratchings and probings and clatterings across the outer hull.

Then something slammed with a sharp *bang* against the left side of Duvall's cockpit.

"What was that?" Bucknell cried. "What are they doing?"

He couldn't make out what it was—but thought it

might be some kind of machine. His guess was confirmed a moment later when he heard a high-pitched whine, and the tip of what might have been a high-speed rotary drill punched into the cockpit.

"Relax, Bucky. I think they're sampling our air."

After a moment, the drill head pulled out, but it left a small gray seal over the hole. Better and better. Their captors didn't want them to asphyxiate or freeze in a hostile environment.

The cockpit lights came on full force. So did their life support, both in the cockpit and in their flight suits. And the lights came up outside, as well.

They were on a seemingly infinite flat plain, a deck stretching off into darkness on all sides. Looking up, Duvall could just barely make out the shadows of a ceiling high, high overhead.

And *something* was approaching their ship.

Duvall was having trouble processing everything he saw. So much simply didn't make sense that his brain was trying to reject it. The alien was big—at least twenty feet long. It was tubular, like a snake or a worm, but a couple of feet thick. One end—the body, as Duvall thought of it—was thicker than the rest and somewhat flattened, splayed out as though it were gripping the smooth deck through suction. The other end—he thought of it as the head—was slender and more complicated, with things that might be sensory tendrils, things that might be highly mobile mouthparts, things that might be eyes, a dozen of them, black and beady, arranged in a circle around the outside of the mouth. There was a thick pad or callus on the sinuous neck a couple of feet below the head. The being walked by resting that pad on the ground, releasing the pad at the base, and supporting the body from the head while the base oozed forward and the middle section of the body formed an upright loop. Duvall had the impression of an enormous inchworm pulling itself along a branch.

It was also clearly comfortable with technology. Though it wasn't wearing anything like clothing that Duvall could see, there were numerous devices adhering to its body, especially beneath the callus pad near the head. Things like strips of black plastic or metal zigzagged along that glistening body. Lights—most of them purple and orange, but a few white ones as well—winked and gleamed from various electronic devices. What were those for? Communication?

Communications, yeah.

Just how the hell were you supposed to communicate with something like that?

So, with no better ideas, Duvall raised a gloved hand as the creature glided closer, and said, "Hi, there!"

THE POWER came back up on board the *Inman*. Lights flickered alive, and the gentle susurration of air vents reassuringly reactivated.

"All departments, report damage status," Davis called. But Makilroy could tell from the instrumentation at her chair that weapons were back online, that the hull had not been breached, and that they had power and life support and gravity and propulsion.

"Comm! Report our status to the *Big-H*: we seem to be okay!"

"Aye, Captain."

Okay, sure—but what the hell had happened?

"Science," she said. "Tell me about these guys."

"Clearly an advanced technology, Captain," the ship's science team head told her. Dr. Albert Kellog was an older man with a beard and a know-it-all attitude that grated at times, but he seemed to know what he was talking about. "They may well be more advanced than the Talis."

"How do we talk to them?"

"I would suggest, Captain, that we remain in place and see what happens. With a technology that advanced, they may have their own means of communicating with other, unknown species. And they don't seem to be actively hostile, at least—"

"Sounds good," she said, not wanting him to go off on a lecture. "Comm, let the *Big-H* know our situation, and pass along my suggestion that they join us."

Their best hope of communicating with these people, she thought, was to put them directly in touch with the Talis. The Talis had been exploring the Galaxy for thousands of years. If anyone had the know-how or the high-tech widgets to let them talk to aliens, it would be them.

"*Hillenkoetter* acknowledges, ma'am. They're on the way."

Good.

GROTON WAS back in the CIC, looking over the shoulder of his tactical officer at cascades of data coming in from the *Inman*. Vashnu was at his side, his face giving away nothing as his fingers clacked and flicked across a keyboard.

"Are you in touch with them yet, Vashnu?"

"No, Captain. But I'm programming the computer to attempt a mass-lingual burst connection. I suspect that this civilization understands either Kudai or Chaktan, and possibly both. But I will transmit greetings in some 5,012 different galactic languages in order to see what they respond to."

"Why would they understand either if you haven't been in this system before?"

"There is, across most of the Galaxy, Captain, a network—parts of it transmitted over the neutrino channels, but most is through phase-entangled devices that can communicate instantaneously. You could think of this network as analogous to your Internet."

And that explains why we could never eavesdrop on alien civilizations, Groton thought. *SETI simply didn't have the technology. We were jungle natives listening for*

*drumbeats and looking for signal fires, totally unaware
of the flood of radio messages passing all around us.*

"Over tens of thousands of millennia," Vashnu went
on, "a number—a very *large* number—of artificial languages have been developed to enable the civilizations
across the Galaxy to communicate with one another,
despite extreme differences in sensory apparatus, in
worldview, and in Mind. We've never encountered this
particular civilization and know nothing about them, but
the chances are fair to good that they have been listening in, have decoded the nested instructions for acquiring
galactic languages they can use, and can communicate
with us if they wish. They certainly are technologically
advanced enough to do so."

He struck the enter key with a distinct air of finality.
"Transmitting."

And in the next instant, the mobile planetoid ahead
pivoted about on its minor axis, then began accelerating.

It was heading directly for the *Hillenkoetter.*

CHAPTER SIXTEEN

Many people suggest using mathematics to talk to the aliens, and Dutch computer scientist Alexander Ollongren has developed an entire language (Lincos) based on this idea. But my personal opinion is that mathematics may be a hard way to describe ideas like love or democracy.

SETH SHOSTAK, SENIOR ASTRONOMER
FOR THE SETI INSTITUTE, 2015

15 March 1983

"**WHAT AM I** *signing?*"

"*The final authorization for the Strategic Defense Initiative, Mr. President.*"

"*Okay . . . there you are. So tell me, George. Is this going to go anywhere? There's an awful lot of resistance to this in Congress.*"

"*Mr. President . . . are the tape recorders off?*"

"*Yes, they are.*"

"*Then I can tell you, Mr. President, that research into these weapons is already quite advanced. They're working on things—particle-beam weapons, X-ray lasers, plasma weapons—that are straight out of the pages of science fiction! But corporations like RAND and Boeing are going to need a bigger share of the budget, much bigger . . . and this way we can get the weapons and aircraft we need without, ah, spilling the beans, as it were."*

"You know, George . . . I've always hated the idea of MAD, of Mutually Assured Destruction. It's insanity! It's kept us and the Soviet Union standing with a knife to each other's throat for thirty years!"

"It's kept us from nuclear war, Mr. President."

"I know what it's supposed to do, George. But MAD really is insanity! And so, if we're going to do this, I want to know that, along with a lot of this Buck Rogers stuff, we're going to be able to break out of this trap here on Earth. I want a ballistic missile shield as well as a means of shooting down incoming UFOs, okay?"

"The technical problems are enormous, Mr. President. I can't promise anything. But the high-tech spin-offs will be incredible, and I would not be at all surprised to find out you had your missile shield by the end of this."

"Fine—however it works. As long as it does. At the very least, the Russians will be so pissed about this that they'll break themselves trying to play catch-up. But I would think we had a better chance to stop Soviet missiles than these alien spaceships. The reports I've seen, the advanced technologies . . ."

"They have incredible technology, yes. But we have the numbers. And the will."

"No question about the numbers. But I do wonder sometimes about the will . . ."

"SO, COMMANDER . . ." Minkowski said. "You know what some of the guys are calling the 1-JSST?"

"No, Mink. What?"

"The 'Just One.'"

Hunter looked puzzled. "What, as in we mete out justice? Or as in we're the good guy?"

"Neither, sir. As in ungodly alien monstrosities snacking on potato chips. 'Bet you can't eat just one. . . .'"

Hunter groaned. "God, Mink . . . that's *terrible!*"

"Black humor, sir. The only way to face the unface-able."

The humor did tend to corroborate the general sense of fatalism and grim expectation that seemed to permeate the unit, though. Hunter hadn't dwelt on it in his training sessions, but by now every person in the unit understood that if they went into combat, it probably would be against an enemy far better armed, far more advanced in their technology, and far more numerous than the tiny direct-action group from Earth. The mental image of a giant alien snacking on humans didn't seem to be too far off the mark.

"Excuse me . . . Commander Hunter? The captain's respects, sir . . . and would you please come see him up in CIC? I can take you there, if you want."

Hunter looked up at the earnest-faced Navy lieutenant, then at Minkowski. "Think you can ride herd on these yahoos, Mink?"

"You go ahead, Skipper. Don't worry. We're not going anywhere without you."

The JSST team was still on the flight deck, though Hunter had told them to stand down and simply remain in the area. "Hurry up and wait." They'd removed their gloves, helmets, and their bulky backpacks, but kept their laser weapons close by.

The lieutenant led Hunter up to the bridge-CIC complex, riding most of the way on one of the quick little people-movers. Captain Groton was in the CIC, watching a series of huge screens that dominated the complex. At a glance, Hunter saw the vast bulk of an asteroid peppered with lights, but what grabbed his attention was the alien face.

There was no sense of scale from the televised image. He couldn't tell how big it was. But the circle of small eyes and the writhing of the mouthparts seemed to suggest that it was large—bigger than a human, anyway. Blocks of words were scrolling down the right side of the screen, a translation, apparently, of whatever the inhuman creature was saying.

"Commander Hunter, reporting as ordered, sir."

"Ah, yes," Groton said, his voice low. "Thank you for coming up. I tried raising you on your radio . . ."

"We took our helmets off, sir. No sense in staying fully suited up when nothing was happening."

"Makes sense. But I didn't wish to make a public announcement over the shipboard intercom. Doesn't matter." He gestured at the big screen. "As you can see, we've made contact."

"Aye, sir."

A Talis male was speaking an alien language into a microphone. What sounded like a *different* language emerged from a speaker next to the big monitor, but a computer was translating everything that was said into English.

But the text seemed pretty disjointed.

". . . war . . . you invade . . . sacred . . . why . . . war . . . find base . . . war . . . you remove . . . annihilate . . ."

"He isn't making much sense, is he, sir?"

"I hate to think what he's making of what *we* have to say. But Vashnu seems to be making progress."

"Have we learned anything, sir?"

"Quite a bit, actually. These people call themselves Dreamers, which in Dhopak—that's an artificial language suited to the physiology of their speech patterns—comes across as 'Xaxki.'"

"'Dreamers'? As in Mexican nationals trying to come to the United States?"

"No, Commander. As in the Xaxki population in this star system, if I'm understanding correctly, is something like four hundred *quadrillion*. That's four *hundred million billion*. The vast, *vast* majority of that obscene number are asleep, hooked up to virtual reality machines and living in what seems to them to be a life fuller, richer, and more interesting than what you or I would call real life.

They are all but immortal, are kept alive by intricate machinery, are electronically fed whatever illusions of life they wish to experience by sophisticated computers, and in general are completely unconcerned with what's happening in the rest of the cosmos."

"Huh. Nice work if you can get it." Hunter thought a moment. "So what happens if something threatens their idyllic existence from the outside?"

Groton pointed at the image of the black mountain adrift in space. "*That* is the responsibility of our friends, here. They call themselves K'kurix, which I'm told means 'Guardians.' Turns out that the debris field surrounding Zeta 2—the inner portion of it, anyway—consists of hundreds of billions of asteroids that were hollowed out and turned into habitats for the Xaxki, okay? But a few asteroids were set aside as habitats for the Guardians, given gravity drives and weapons, that sort of thing. They're heavy naval vessels, of a sort, and they keep an eye out for anything that might threaten the Dreamer population—rogue planets, incoming alien battle fleets, whatever."

"Seems unfair that the military has to stay out in the cold and protect the peacefully dreaming population on the home front."

Groton gave Hunter an odd look. "Isn't that the way it is for us?"

"I guess. But *forever*?"

"We haven't learned the details yet, Commander, but I assume there's some sort of rotation. Maybe they figure that a few years of military service followed by an eternity of happy dreaming isn't such a bad thing."

"Well . . . *this* Guardian seems a bit grumpy," Hunter observed.

"Yes indeed. He wants to know why we attacked them."

Hunter felt a cold breath down his spine. "Did we, sir?"

"Not that I'm aware. At first we thought they were just objecting to the arrival of the *Big-H* and her escorts, but that doesn't seem to be the case. Seems the Guardians are concerned about a planet inside their inner habitat ring. They say we colonized it, and we're a threat to their Sleepers."

The computer programs that were translating between the two vessels appeared to be learning moment by moment, though it was still hard to follow the alien's thoughts.

"Remove base . . . never return . . . we annihilate . . . remove base immediate . . . break sacred place . . ."

"I called you up here, Commander, because we're going to do what they want. And your people will definitely play a part."

"But we haven't colonized one of their planets!"

"Yes, but we're beginning to think that *somebody* did, Commander. So we're going to deploy the 1-JSST to the surface, make contact with whomever is there, and find out what the hell is going on."

"Yes, sir."

"Dr. Vanover here will give you what little we know about the objective."

Vanover was a small and fussy civilian, introduced to Hunter as the expedition's chief planetologist, and a senior member of the *Hillenkoetter*'s science department. In a small briefing area off the main bridge, Vanover transmitted several pages of data from his iPad to Hunter's.

"We don't know very much at all as yet, Commander," Vanover said. "But we did detect what may very well be a settlement of some sort on the surface."

"A settlement? Just the one?"

"That's what I said, Commander. Here . . ."

He keyed a command on the iPad, and brought up the image of a planet. It was a bit grainy with a lot of magnification, and most of it was black, with a thin sliver of daylight curving around one rim. There was some light flare to one side. *Hillenkoetter* was looking toward Zeta 2 in order to image it.

"We're calling it Zeta 2c," Vanover said. "So far, we've seen three other small, rocky worlds, Zeta 2d, 2e, and 2f. Zeta 2b is farther out, *much* farther out, beyond the limits of the debris field. We guessed its existence a few years ago when we saw anomalies in the debris field."

"So what have you been able to learn?"

"It's cold. Mean surface temperature of about minus twenty, minus thirty Celsius. Reducing atmosphere— mostly nitrogen, but with gaseous carbon dioxide, chlorine, and methane as the active gasses. Air pressure at the surface . . . we're not sure, but it's probably greater than the surface pressure on Earth. Very similar in some ways to the moon Titan, though a bit warmer. Diameter is about eight thousand kilometers, making it considerably smaller than Earth. Less dense, too. Probably a lot of water ice in the crust. Surface gravity is just 0.7 G. No natural satellites. Slow rotation—we estimate fifty hours, and 2.5 AUs from the star. Period—its year—would be a bit less than four years. At that distance from the star we would expect the planet to be a lot colder, but the high concentration of CO_2 appears to be acting as a greenhouse gas. It warms things up on the surface, at least somewhat."

Hunter held up a hand. "Okay, okay. What about life?"

"*That* is not my department," Vanover said, a bit stiffly. "I can say that the surface appears rocky with extensive glaciation, but no oceans as we would know them. There are some extensive ice sheets, however."

"And what about this colony or base or whatever?"

"Again, Commander, not my department. However . . ."

He pressed a key, and a red point of light appeared on the image, on the night side, just below the equator. "We have found a significant point source of infrared. Heat, in other words. If someone *is* living down there, this would be the place to look."

"Thank you, Doctor. You've been a big help."

But he said that just to be polite. None of what Vanover had had to say seemed at all useful. The team would be going in wearing armored suits, so temperature, atmosphere, and pressure weren't considerations. They wouldn't be down there long enough to worry about planetary rotation. The only piece of data of potential use was the location of that IR source, and he imagined that they would have spotted that on the way in. In his mind, he'd already discounted most of Vanover's information.

THE ALIENS were . . . terrifying.

So far, they'd not harmed Duvall or Bucknell, hadn't even attempted to communicate. Duvall's cheerful "Hi, there" had been ignored; the looming, massive creature had simply grasped both humans with muscular tentacles that splayed out from behind the head like the petals of a flower and carried them through endless, dark compartments to a small and featureless room. There was no furniture, no toilet facilities, no food or water, nothing but featureless gray metal. Sensors on Duvall's flight suit threw an environmental report up on the tiny HUD inside his helmet—temperature minus thirty Celsius, atmosphere a poisonous mix of nitrogen, carbon dioxide, methane, hydrogen, and traces of hydrogen sulfide. Their helmets didn't have chow locks, so they wouldn't have been able to eat or drink in any case. Removing their helmets was *not* an option.

The fact that they'd not been harmed *should* have been reassuring, Duvall supposed, but the lack of communication combined with the aliens' utter lack of any emotion that Duvall could see, made them Unknowns with a capital *U*, and the Unknown is always terrifying. Besides, they commanded technologies unlike anything he'd seen before. One instant, they'd been inside the cockpit of their TR-3R; in the next, they'd been in that vast open space where they'd first seen their captors. Teleportation, then, and that suggested a command of physics, mathematics, and space-time transcending anything he could imagine.

And *that*, for Duvall, was truly terrifying.

"Double-D . . ." Bucknell said softly over their radio link. She sagged. *"David . . ."*

"What is it, Bucky?"

"I can't get them out of my head!"

IN THE CIC, the Guardian was still delivering what Groton could only think of as an extended harangue, its language gradually becoming more intelligible as computer programs slowly made sense of it. "He has a lot to say for himself, doesn't he?" he told Vashnu.

"Perhaps it simply enjoys the sound of its own ranting," Vashnu replied. "It's possible that the K'kurix are artificial life-forms created for one, specific purpose . . . that of protecting the Dreamer population."

"How? By talking us to death?" Groton shook his head. "I'm not sure I'd care to commit my survival to organisms created by my own technology. What if it turned out I'd made a mistake?"

"That would be no worse, in principle, than leaving your survival to an organism evolved over millions of years by the fits and starts of natural selection and random mutation."

"Point. Anyway, the whole idea of curling up for a billion-year nap while someone else watches over me makes my skin crawl. I . . . . Uh-oh. What's that?"

On an external view, a minute point of light was emerging from the rock face of the alien ship. "It's Alfa!" Haines said. "They've released Alfa!"

"Okay. Maybe they've decided to trust us. CAG! Take them aboard!"

"Bringing them in, Skipper."

Minutes passed. On the big screen, the K'kurix had—finally—fallen silent, and appeared to be simply waiting. Its expression was impossible to read. Was it angry? Groton wondered. Irritated? Impatient? Bored? Or were such human emotional states meaningless to a truly alien organism?

More time passed, and then Captain Macmillan over the intercom reported that both TR-3R Alfa and Bravo were safely on board, their crews shaken but unhurt.

"Take us clear of the alien, Lieutenant Briem."

"Aye, aye, Captain." And on an external viewscreen, the crinkled black surface of the asteroid ship slid to one side, replaced a moment later by the bright glare of the local sun. "We're clear to maneuver, Captain."

"Admiral? We're about to shift toward the planet. Please inform the *Inman*."

"Thank you, Captain."

"Ms. Briem? Accelerate. Take us to Zeta 2c."

Their encounter with the Xaxki had taken place some eight astronomical units from the star; the planet now identified as Zeta 2c was nearly 3 AUs from *Hillenkoetter*'s position. That translated as twenty-four light minutes—actually closer to twenty-five. At 90 percent of the speed of light, they would cover that distance in twenty-seven and a half minutes.

However, moving that swiftly, time dilation became a significant factor as well, with time slowing dramatically as the ship approached c. For the people on board the *Hillenkoetter*, only twelve minutes passed.

And so, twelve minutes subjective after maneuvering clear of the Xaxki ship, the *Hillenkoetter* and the escorting *Inman* decelerated sharply and slid into orbit around a dim and rocky planet, with clouds marking the sweep and swirl of huge storms, and sheets of ice covering large stretches of what otherwise appeared to be barren desert. Much of the surface was orange and brown, though there were ragged black patches that might be basaltic lava flows. There was no sign of life or habitation, but that lone spot of infrared radiation marked the one possible place in two hundred million square miles where technological life might be hiding.

Groton joined a small gathering of *Hillenkoetter*'s science people in the briefing lounge off the bridge. Brody was there, as well as Carter, Vanover, and McClure. The big screen on one bulkhead showed the planet below.

It didn't look very inviting.

"We've decided to name the planet 'Serpo,'" Simone Carter told him. "I suppose it's easier than 'Zeta Reticuli 2c.'"

"Rubbish," Vanover said. "The conventions established by the International Astronomical Union—"

"Are of very little importance out here," Groton said, cutting the man off. For Groton, the convention of naming new planets in the order of their discovery, with letters of the alphabet that were *also* used to identify the separate components of double stars and told you nothing about where they were in a star system, was worse than useless.

But then, he still disliked the IAU for demoting Pluto from planetary status a few years ago. Not because Pluto *should* be a planet in its own right, but for reasons—like "clearing out its own orbit"—that were completely bogus. By that reasoning, Jupiter—hell, even *Earth*—were not true planets, since there was plenty of asteroidal debris still within the orbits of both.

"So, Serpo it is," he said. "At least until it's confirmed back home. Any sign of our diplomats?"

"Not a trace," Brody said.

"So what's causing the infrared glow?"

"It appears to be a city, Captain," Carter said. "It's protected by a kinetic field. And we're reading energy pulses around the perimeter."

"Energy pulses? From power generation?"

"No, sir. From an ongoing attack."

THE JSST was descending to the planet in three TR-3B transports. Hunter had demanded it. For one thing, if one or even two transports were disabled down there, the entire team could be lifted back to the *Big-H* on the remaining ship.

Besides, there was a chance that they would be evacuating somebody—or some*thing*—from the surface. According to the Guardian, humans had tried to colonize the world, and the Guardians wanted the intruders *gone*. Hunter didn't know how many people were supposed to be down there, but each shuttle had a carrying capacity of one hundred fifty people. That would make a good start.

Hunter sat in one of the padded seats with fifteen other team members, and felt the jolt and shudder as the craft began to enter atmosphere. With gravitic control, they didn't have to worry about a traditional fiery reentry, but they were moving fast and the thickening air outside seemed like water. The cabin's forward projection screen showed dense, dark clouds illuminated by the transport's lights. They were coming down on the night side. It looked like it might be raining down there.

But raining *what*? The temperature was well below zero, so it wouldn't be water.

Alfa Platoon was fully suited up for their insertion. Hunter was just glad they were making their insertion by aircraft—not quite by helicopter, but close enough—and not parachuting into alien and possibly hostile terrain in high wind and an uncertain surface. There was little chatter on the way down. Each person in the platoon seemed isolated by their suits, and alone with their thoughts.

Minkowski, in a seat several places to Hunter's right, finally broke the silence. "What do you think we're gonna find down there, Skipper?"

"Somebody in trouble is all I know, Mink."

"Yeah . . . but *Nazis*?"

He grinned. "I don't think we'll have to worry about that."

Hunter had heard the rumors and scuttlebutt, just like everyone in the team. Nazis fleeing the collapse of the Third Reich had built flying saucers with alien assistance and gone to the Moon . . . or to the stars. There'd been no sign of Nazi bases on the Moon, he'd been told . . . and there was no evidence that they'd gone to the stars either.

Not unless you counted that floating bit of wreckage out at Aldebaran.

No, the only rumor connected with Serpo was that wild-assed one about a secret diplomatic exchange or mission back in the 1960s, and that seemed increasingly unlikely. The Xaxki controlled this system from their myriad asteroid biomes around the inner edge of the debris field disk. Wherever the Grays or the Saurians actually came from, it wasn't Zeta Reticuli.

"We have the LZ in sight, Commander." That was the voice of Marine captain Philip Merton, the transport's pilot up in the cockpit, coming in over Hunter's helmet speakers. "Three minutes!"

"Roger that. Thanks for the ride."

"Don't mention it, Commander. We're ready to drop the ramp as soon as we touch down."

Hunter stood up. "Alfa Platoon!" he called. "On your feet! Center yourselves on the hatch!"

The TR-3B had a ramp lowered from the keel, with the exit contained by a small airlock. Sixteen men in space suits and carrying weapons fit into the lock with a *lot* of crowding. It would have made sense to go out in two groups, perhaps . . . but Hunter had already decided that he wanted the maximum firepower on the ground in the minimum time. They could put up with being jammed in like sardines for a few minutes, at least.

He couldn't see the monitor from down here, and gravitics abolished the surge of deceleration, but he felt the deck shift as the ship struggled to cope with a sharp turn.

And then they were down and the hatch was descending beneath them.

The outside atmosphere blasted into the small lock, a hard gust of wind that splattered them all with some oily liquid . . . whatever it was that passed for water on this ice ball. "Go!" Hunter yelled. "Go! Go! Go!"

The platoon went.

As soon as they all were outside, the TR-3B dusted off, lifting into a rain-filled night-dark sky swirling with clouds and bits of particulate matter, its landing lights a bright smear through the thick, low clouds. The light faded, and the team was down and surrounded by night, the only light coming from the lamps on their helmets. The wind was a hard, shuddering force clawing at the team, as rain sprayed sideways out of the dark.

"Tactical Command," Hunter called. "We're on the ground."

"Copy you down, Just One. The shield should be just in front of you."

By the book, perhaps, Hunter should have been back on board the *Hillenkoetter*, in TaCom with Powell and McClure monitoring the op from the technological high ground. In fact, though, he was a tactical combat leader, and for Hunter that meant leading his people, not watching from the rear. He gestured—a silent hand signal that would register on the IR displays of the team's helmets— and moved toward the shield.

Lightning flared, or, rather, an energy burst very much like lightning. It exploded twenty meters off the ground and ahead of them, the flash illuminating the rocks in stark contrast to the surrounding night, the bang immediate and deep throated.

"TaCom, Just One," he called. "Who's doing the shooting? I thought the Xaxki wanted us to evacuate these people!"

"Just One, TaCom," Powell's voice replied. "The Guardian knows you're down there. He should have ordered a cease-fire."

"Have Vashnu talk to him again!" Another flash and bang cracked above the rocky landscape. "Somebody down here didn't get the word!"

"Hey, Skipper!" Master Sergeant Briggs called over the platoon's comm channel. He was well up ahead, reconnoitering along the base of the magnetic shield. "Eyes on!"

Meaning he'd seen someone—hostile or friendly was as yet unknown. Hunter hurried forward over rugged terrain, which was beginning to rise steeply. "Whatcha got?"

The Air Force master sergeant pointed. Just visible in the gloom at the very edge of their suit lights was a small figure. It was wearing a suit with an overlarge and completely opaque helmet, but the humanoid shape and the general details were clear enough.

It was a Gray or a Saurian. It *had* to be.

Taking an enormous chance, Hunter stood very slowly, holding up his splayed-open hand. If these critters decided to shoot first and question later . . .

But the alien repeated the gesture. Contact established.

Now all they needed was a way in . . .

"The shield's down!" Lieutenant Bader called.

"Brunelli! You and Coulter cover us! The rest of you . . . double-time!"

The platoon surged forward, scrambling up the steep slope to cross the perimeter where the screen had been established. Brunelli and Coulter crouched just outside the perimeter, weapons at the ready.

"Okay, you two!" Hunter yelled. "C'mon inside!"

But in that moment, a bolt of white fire caught Brunelli and knocked him down . . . and suddenly the night outside the perimeter was filled with alien, nightmare shapes squirming and jostling and slithering up the slope.

"Fire!" Hunter screamed. "Commence fire!"

A fusillade of laser fire snapped and hissed down the slope, catching a number of the shapes and slapping them down. Too late, Hunter remembered McClure's admonition to get permission to fire. There'd been no time for that, no time to even think as the creatures surged up out of the icy ground. Had they been there all along, unseen?

Their dark gray carapaces provided perfect camouflage for that dark, basaltic terrain.

He'd seen image captures of the Xaxki—massive and tentacled—but these creatures weren't anything like that at all. They were low to the ground and as big as Volkswagens, with rounded, humped backs and segmented armor. Jointed legs, too many of them, were visible on the things' undersides, and their heads were featureless, flattened bullets encased in high-tech masks and held inches from the ground. Hunter honestly couldn't tell if he was seeing the actual creature, or massively heavy combat armor of some kind.

It didn't really matter—they were trying to kill JSST, and that meant they had to go.

Lightning snapped from devices gripped in some of those legs; they had to rear up a bit to fire, and that gave the JSST opportunities to target the less-well-armored underbelly.

The things were slow, but they were relentless and they were *tough*. Shot after shot was necessary to take one out, and several now were inside the perimeter.

The Gray was there beside them, holding up a small box that strobed like a camera flash, and one of the armored creatures below exploded under the being's fire. The JSST was beginning to get into the rhythm of the battle as well, holding their fire until a creature reared up to shoot . . . and taking it down.

Where were Coulter and Brunelli? A dense fog was enveloping the battle area—steam, or some other vapor released by the heat of lasers. Hunter began to work his way back down the slope, looking for the two.

There! Coulter was on his feet, with Brunelli slung across his shoulders in a fireman's carry. Hunter reached Coulter's side in a bound and helped him struggle into the perimeter.

Only then did the Gray touch something on its suit, and then the attackers' fire began flashing and popping up the side of an invisible barrier. Two of them had been caught inside the defensive field; both were cut down by the JSST. Other JSST troops had found that laser beams penetrated the field without a problem, and they continued pouring concentrated fire into the seething mass of attackers.

"Magnetic screens are up again, Skipper!" Bader called.

And the attackers were already fading back into the encircling darkness.

CHAPTER SEVENTEEN

For many years I have lived with a secret, in a secrecy imposed on all specialists in astronautics. I
can now reveal that every day, in the USA, our radar
instruments capture objects of form and composi-
tion unknown to us. And there are thousands of witness reports and a quantity of documents to prove
this, but nobody wants to make them public. Why?
Because authority is afraid that people may think
of God knows what kind of horrible invaders. So
the password still is: We have to avoid panic by all
means.

MERCURY ASTRONAUT MAJOR GORDON COOPER

14 November 2004

THE OCEAN THIRTY *thousand feet below canted wildly, the
surface interrupted by stray puffs of white cloud and a
flash of sun glint. "Knight Six, Salty," sounded in his
helmet speaker. "Bogie now at angles two-five at ten
o'clock, bearing one-eight-five, range seven-five miles,
speed one-zero-five-niner."*

*"Copy that, Salty. Coming left to three-zero-seven for
intercept."*

*Lieutenant Hank "Tank" Boland felt the surge of g-
forces as he put his F/A-18F Super Hornet into a hard
left bank. "I'm still negative on AESA."*

Boland was a member of VFA-154, the Black Knights, operating off the USS Nimitz *140 miles southwest of San Diego.* Nimitz, *nicknamed by those aboard her* Old Salty—*hence the call sign—was on routine maneuvers in anticipation of a deployment to the western Pacific. For two weeks, however, there'd been a flurry of UAP sightings—unidentified aerial phenomenon—over one particular patch of ocean. Bogies would appear out of nowhere at eighty thousand feet, descend straight down at high speed to twenty thousand feet, hover there for a while, then shoot back up to eighty thousand. One aviator who'd caught a glimpse of them said they were "bouncing around like a Ping-Pong ball."*

And now, radar on both Salty *and on the cruiser* Princeton *had picked up an incoming bogie while it was still over the deserts of northern Mexico, and Boland and his wingman, flying combat air patrol, had been deployed to check it out.*

That was proving easier said than done, however. While they could see the bogie on radar back on board the Nimitz, *Boland's APG-79 AESA radar had yet to pick it up. Active electronically scanned array technology was brand-new, hot technology, and it should be reading the thing by now.*

Boland wondered if he was being selectively jammed. How would someone do that?

"Damn it, Spinner. You getting anything back there?"

Lieutenant John Mason, "Spinner" to his squadron, was Boland's rear-seater, the weapons system officer, the WSO or "whizzo."

"Not a peep, Skipper," *Mason replied.* "Maybe it's busted."

"Knight Four, this is Six," *he called.*

"Six, Four. Go ahead." *His wingman was Lieutenant Roger Drummond, call sign "Jolly." At the moment, he was two hundred feet off Boland's right wing, matching his turn perfectly.*

"You see anything, Jolly? My AESA's blank."

"Negative, Tank. I think Salty's chasing spooks again."

"Roger. Maintain three-zero-seven. We'll let Salty vector us in."

"The technology's supposed to work, damn it."

"Roger that. Going to SA." Synthetic aperture radar gave higher spatial resolution on targets, and could be used to create three-dimensional images of the target.

"Still don't see a thing, Tank."

"ATFLIR engaged." The Hornets' advanced targeting forward looking infrared gear was mounted in the aircraft's sensor and laser designator pod. On the screen on Boland's console, clouds and sky showed as shades of gray, with dark indicating cooler, light showing warmer.

At ten miles out, the targets popped up on the Super Hornets' radars, almost as if a switch had been thrown. There were six targets moving across the fighters' noses from right to left.

"There's a whole fleet of 'em!" Boland called. *"Look on the AESA!"*

"My gosh. They're all going against the wind. The wind is 120 knots to the west." His Super Hornet still in a turn, Boland's ATFLIR locked on to one target, tracking it. Green brackets embraced the object, which was hot and therefore black on the ATFLIR's black mode. He switched over to white mode, trying to get more detail, then back to black. He guessed the object was forty feet long, a lozenge or diamond shape. His radar showed the range as 4.1 nautical miles.

"Look at that thing, dude!" Drummond called.

"That's not one of ours, is it?" Mason asked.

Boland felt the surge of adrenaline, the palpable excitement. His heart was hammering. Those things were unlike anything he'd ever seen. Whatever they were, wherever they came from, they were not from Earth. *"Look at that thing!"*

They were visible now to the naked eye, bright silver glinting in the sun, streaking in between the waves and the pair of Super Hornets.

"It's rotating!" Drummond said.

Both Super Hornets continued trying to track the objects, but they were already past the Navy aircraft and inside the radius of their turn, flashing past them at a range of just half a mile.

"My God, those things are fast! I read . . . I read Mach three . . . three-five . . . and accelerating!"

"And bang!" Mason said. "They're gone!"

"What the hell were those things?"

"Damfino. Salt, Knight Six. Did you get all that?"

"We copied, Knight Six. Divert to Waypoint Charlie Echo."

The rendezvous point, a few miles from the Princeton, *already had traffic in it—another of the games-playing UAPs. As Boland and Drummond approached, it vanished from sight . . . whether at high velocity or by teleportation, Boland could not tell.*

"Copy," the Nimitz *CIC told him after he'd reported what he'd seen. "You guys come on back to the barn."*

"Roger that, Salt. CAP-one, RTB."

And Boland was damned glad to be returning to base. The UAPs—alien, ultrahigh performance, completely beyond the capabilities of the most modern fighter jet in the fleet—had weirded him out.

Still, during his debriefing later, he admitted that he would have loved to fly one of those things.

THE JSST crouched among a scattering of house-sized boulders, sheltering from the fierce wind. Their suit heaters were working well, but the icy rain carried with it a *psychological* cold that no environmental unit could hold at bay.

"I thought it was too freakin' cold to rain here!" Lieutenant Dorschner complained.

"It's not water," Hunter told him. "Dichloromethane. The stuff stays liquid down to minus ninety-six, ninety-seven Celsius. And right now the temp's only minus twenty-nine."

"Huh," Nielson said. "A balmy summer's morning . . ."

Hunter had zapped a full environmental report back to the ship for their analyses, but he wasn't sure what the results he was getting back might mean. The atmosphere here was a vicious soup of nitrogen, methane, ammonia, and hydrogen, with trace amounts of chlorine, ethane, and hydrogen cyanide. There was plenty of ice on the ground—*probably* water ice, but Hunter wasn't sure of that—and orange glops of slime that the lab back on the *Hillenkoetter* said were most likely tholins—organic molecules, the precursors of life. The lab had called the surface "prebiotic." Dichloromethane seemed to play the part of liquid water in this environment . . . though, according to the information sent down from the ship, "dichlo," as it was known within the chemical industry, was a volatile solvent that attacked many organic compounds. The stuff was used back home as a degreaser and a paint stripper, for God's sake.

"Hell of a place for life to evolve," Hunter had told them. "Any bugs in this mess might want to rethink things."

"What now, Skipper?" Colby asked.

"Did we get all three platoons inside this oversize goldfish bowl?"

"Everyone but Pennell and Crocker," Grabiak told him.

Hunter tried to remember the men behind the names. Pennell was a Marine, while Crocker had been Airborne. But he'd not had the opportunity to get to know them as *people*. . . .

Both had been Bravo Platoon. Both, according to Grabiak, had remained outside the force field dome to lay down covering fire as the rest of their unit had scrambled for cover. The field had gone up . . . and the two men, trapped outside, had been overrun by a swarm of angry, heavily armored Volkswagens.

"How's Brunelli?" he asked.

"We need to get him somewhere where we can peel him out of his suit." HM1 Vincent Marlow was Navy, but he'd been attached to the Marines—FMS—when he'd been tapped for the JSST. He was one of two "docs" attached to the unit, and Hunter was damned glad to have them both.

Brunelli was lying on the icy ground on his back, his suit ripped open at the stomach and smeared with bright red blood. Marlow had put a pressure dressing over the wound, but Hunter knew enough field medicine to realize the man was in serious trouble. The poisonous atmosphere, at a higher pressure than the pressure inside their suits, would be forcing its way into the breach in his suit.

Coulter hovered nearby, the anguish on his features not quite hidden by his helmet visor. "Is he gonna be okay, Doc?"

Marlow spread his arms, a shrug unhampered by his suit. "Depends on how quick we can evac him. I can't do much for him *here*."

"Do what you can, Marlow," Hunter said. "Where's that alien?"

Here, Lieutenant Commander.

The creature's thoughts arose unbidden in Hunter's mind. He turned to face the being, unsure whether it was worse trying to relate to that blankly opaque visor, or to the enormous dark eyes he knew were watching him from behind it.

"It's just 'Commander,'" he said. "If you're wearing a suit, there must be a sealed habitat or something here—some place where we won't be both poisoned and frozen."

Of course, Commander. The settlement is this way, at the top of this hill.

Hunter saw other Grays making their way down the slope. Some took up obviously defensive positions among the rocks. Others began leading the 1-JSST personnel up the hill.

"Mink!" Hunter called. "Grab some guys and bring *that* along."

"That" was one of the dead attackers that had made it inside the force field perimeter. Hunter wanted to have a look at one, and see just what it was they were facing.

Overhead, a portion of the invisible dome turned suddenly black as a violent flash lit the night. A laser, Hunter decided. Kinetic shields could stop solid matter—bullets, missiles, even particle beams—but they were transparent, so light passed right through. Evidently, something about the alien field detected the high-energy flux of an incoming laser beam and blocked it by turning part of the field opaque.

Pretty handy.

The "settlement" was a collection of six large, geodesic domes snuggled down into the icy terrain at the very top of the hill. The Grays requested that Hunter's men split up, with each sixteen-man platoon going to a different dome.

He initially balked at the idea of being apart, but the Gray made a convincing argument.

The airlock facilities are limited, Commander, the Gray told him. *It will be quicker this way.*

Inside the largest, central dome was a big, round room, dimly lit, and with the look of a control center, filled with screens and consoles. Once Alfa Platoon had cycled through the large airlock and removed their helmets, they were met by dozens of the diminutive, black-eyed beings. They reminded Hunter of well-behaved children as they crowded around, curious.

Hunter was startled by their eyes. He'd been used to the idea of Grays with enormous, black, and completely featureless eyes—slanted slightly and reflective—but the Grays in this room had what looked like human eyes, larger than a modern human's, to be sure, but they had whites and an iris and a pupil. Was this a different species of Gray? he wondered.

One of the entities there was a Saurian, not a Gray. It was noticeably taller than the others, taller even than Hunter, scaly, stooped, and with a decidedly reptilian look to the eyes and jaws. *Welcome to Velat*, it said within his mind, its mental voice sharper, more intense than the Gray's.

"We need a place to take care of a wounded man," Hunter said, ignoring the polite greeting.

Of course. We have medical facilities. This way.

Marlow and a couple of Marines carried Brunelli into another room, brightly lit and aseptically clean. Coulter tried to follow them in.

"We'll wait out here, Coulter," Hunter told him.

"Yes, sir." He sounded reluctant.

"That was well done, bringing him inside the perimeter like that."

Coulter gave a listless shrug. "I'm not sure it counted for anything, sir."

"He has a chance, okay? If you'd left him out there he would be dead now . . . no chance at all."

In the next several hours, Hunter learned a great deal about the Velat community. More, perhaps, than he actually wanted to hear.

We learned about this world through your own culture's imaginings, Commander, the tall Reptilian told him. *You've heard of "Serpo"? Of something called "Operation Serpo"?*

Hunter nodded. "A little."

A fascinating story, Commander. A brilliant human woman takes memories recovered from another woman through hypnosis and creates a coherent map of local space. Another story . . . emerges, citing the map's information and describing a kind of exchange program between your people and ours. We had previously visited the star system you call Zeta Reticuli, but encountered no sign of any native intelligence. The stories were . . .

a surprise. There was the possibility that there had been transtemporal leakage, from the future to the past. If that was true, it was vital that we establish a presence here, a colony, to avoid the danger of paradox.

Unfortunately, we had not counted on the presence of the Xaxki . . . or of their K'kurix instruments.

How, Hunter wondered, had that ridiculous Serpo story caused the threat of a paradox? He could not see the connection. It amused him, though, that the Saurians might be as bemused by human UFO mythology as was Hunter.

"So where did the Xaxki come from?" Hunter asked, curious. "Not from Zeta Retic. The system is too young."

We suspect that the Xaxki are . . . our name for them might translate in your language as "nomads." They move from system to system, sometimes across tens of thousands of light-years, and colonize planetoid belts and cometary halos. They prefer younger star systems still rich with protoplanetary debris.

"Okay," Hunter said. "Then where do those armored critters outside your defenses come into it? Are they working for these nomads?"

We do not recognize them. They attacked this facility without warning, twenty local days ago.

"Then it's about time we found out about them. I don't like having to kill total strangers. And I like it even less when total strangers try to kill me."

They opened another sterile room with a touch to the door's center. Hunter then stood by as Minkowski and four other guys dragged in the carcass of one of the attackers. "Okay—Mink, Daly—organize our people and do a security sweep. I don't entirely trust our big-headed little friends."

"Aye, aye, Skipper."

Hunter then had cameras set up surrounding the center of the room, and opened up a two-way visual link with McClure and several other scientists on board the *Hillenkoetter.*

"I'm not sure how this is going to work," McClure told him. "I've never done a dissection by remote control before!"

"The main thing, Doctor, is to get enough information that you can look for it on that Talis iPad-encyclopedia of yours. There's got to be a record of these critters somewhere. And maybe we can use that to figure out where they're from and why they're attacking this planet."

"You say the Grays don't know them?"

"That's what they say. Why? You don't trust their word?"

She sighed. "First off, Commander—be careful what you say. This is an unsecured channel, okay? But second, the Grays have been around for a *long* time. They have probably visited a large part of our Galaxy and explored at least a million years of galactic history. Space *and* time, you see? If they never met these beings at any point within a million years, I'd like to know why."

"Well, let's have a closer look, shall we?"

"Okay. Let's see if that carapace is artificial . . ."

Over the course of the next half hour, Hunter dissected the creature, guided by Becky McClure and one of her assistants, a young civilian tech named Cohen, both ensconced in CIC Ops and watching Hunter's every move through the cameras. Simone Carter, representing the ship's xenopsych department, had joined them, along with another civilian, Franklin Smith, a xenoculturalist. Everyone was excited about the chance to see an alien, a *new* alien, up close and personal.

The alien, McClure told him, strongly reminded her of a group of arthropods on Earth called isopods—particularly the land-dwelling forms called pill bugs or wood lice found under rocks or logs, small crustaceans that could roll themselves into an armored ball when threatened. The entire dorsal surface was covered by dark gray overlapping articulated plates. On a close inspection, these proved to be part of the organism and not, as Hunter had at first thought, some sort of defensive armored suit. There were seven pairs of jointed legs, larger and more muscular toward the rear, thinner and more dexterous toward the front. Apparently the being could choose to stand almost upright, or hunch down on all fourteens. A complicated mask fit tightly over what Hunter, for lack of a better word, decided to call the "face." Jointed mouthparts like smaller versions of the upper legs surrounded left and right mandibles, while six tiny, beady black eyes peeked out from beneath the forward lip of the dorsal armor. There was no air tank or PLSS. Instead, the mask included a complicated package of pumps, intakes, and pressurizers apparently designed for extracting or separating gasses from the surrounding atmosphere.

"What I find fascinating," McClure said over the video link, "is that this creature is already adapted to the local conditions. From what we can see of that mask from here, I'd guess that it pulls methane out of the atmosphere and pressurizes it. Its native atmosphere may be 10 or 15 percent methane, while Serpo's—sorry, Velat's—air has less than 2 percent methane. Alternatively, this being may metabolize hydrogen and excrete methane. Either way, it obviously doesn't need any protection from the cold."

"Or the dichlo rain," Hunter put in. "So what's the verdict, Doctor? Does your encyclopedia include this little gem?"

"No, Mark. I've passed the data on to Elanna and Vashnu to see what they make of it. Elanna is of the opinion that it may be an artificial life-form."

"An artificial—Huh! Like a robot?"

"No. A biological entity created by another species."

"What species?"

"We all would like to know the answer to that," Carter said.

"At a guess, I'd say that we should talk to the Xaxki,"

Hunter said. "They're already established in this star system."

"But the nomads use the insides of asteroids and comets," Cohen pointed out. "They hollow them out and manufacture made-to-order habitats. I don't think they bother with planets at all."

"Maybe they're afraid of competition in the same star system," Smith suggested. "Their use of the Guardians suggests they're somewhat nervous about other technic cultures right in their own backyard."

"With most of the Xaxki jacked into virtual reality?" Hunter said. "Yeah, I'd be nervous about any nearby neighbors, too. When you're not paying any attention to the world around you, it can sneak up and bite you."

They gave the being a thorough physical examination, photographing it from every angle, but as they worked the body began literally to crumble in dust. Chunks of carapace came off in their hands, disintegrating before their eyes.

They weren't going to be able to complete a full autopsy. "Maybe the oxygen in the atmosphere?" McClure suggested.

"Damfino," Hunter said. "It's turning into a hollow shell, and even the shell is just dissolving into dust. Maybe somebody doesn't want us looking at them up close."

It was a mystery that would have to wait for later. Hunter was needed elsewhere.

An argument had broken out in the main control room. Minkowski was squared off in front of the Saurian, who appeared to be blocking his access to a small closed door.

"What the hell is going on?" Hunter demanded.

"I went to check out that door, Commander, and lizard-face here had a conniption."

It is a storeroom, the alien said in Hunter's mind. *Nothing more.*

"What's in there?" Hunter asked.

Stores. Food, water.

"Then you don't mind if my master chief has a look, do you?"

The alien's hands moved toward a device, a small flat box, strapped on its chest. *It is not permitted.*

Time slowed to a crawl.

Hunter was aware that he and the rest of his team were in serious danger. The box was some kind of weapon, he was sure of that. The three other Saurians scattered about the room likewise appeared as taut as coiled springs, their skinny hands touching identical boxes.

The Grays in the room had stopped working, frozen in place, and were silently watching.

What was it Benedict had said during the briefing at Wright-Patt? The Grays and Nordics were engaged in a war, a very, very *old* war, with the Saurians. There were rules about shooting at each other on or near Earth, but . . .

The Grays, at least the Grays *here*, on Serpo, appeared to be working for the Saurians, taking orders from them. Hunter had wondered about that briefly when he'd entered the dome, but dismissed the niggling worry; maybe their armistice or whatever it was extended here, as well.

But Hunter was as certain as he could be that something was being concealed from the humans. The Saurian so far had been unfailingly polite, but it was also guarded, secretive. And the way they'd split the platoons up before letting them come inside. . . .

Damn it, how were you supposed to read emotions in something that wasn't even remotely human? He would *hate* to play poker with these guys.

Hunter glanced around and saw that at least two of his men were behind each of the three Saurians, weapons held—not threatening, exactly, but definitely at the ready.

Well done, Hunter thought. Slowly, he drew his Sunbeam Type 1 sidearm. "Master Chief Minkowski was performing a security check," he said quietly. "It's routine. We always want to know the lay of the land. Or building, in this case. I suggest that you let us see what's in there."

For a frozen span of seconds, human and Saurian stared at each other. The slit iris of the Saurian's golden eyes expanded sharply, turning the eye black. The nostrils flared. The scaly, gray-green skin on its head and throat reddened slightly.

And then, reluctantly, it backed down, stepping aside.

"Thank you," Hunter said, but the alien had already gathered the other three Saurians with a sharp gesture, and all four moved swiftly toward the airlock. Lieutenant Billingsly raised his weapon, but Hunter waved him down. "Let 'em go," he said. "All of you, secure the compartment! Mink, Daly, Herrera, Brown—with me."

The door, obviously designed for beings only about four feet tall, opened with a touch, revealing shallow steps leading down into darkness.

CHAPTER EIGHTEEN

There is little chance that aliens from two separate
societies anywhere in the Galaxy will be culturally
close enough to really "get along." This is something
to ponder as you watch the famous cantina scene
in *Star Wars*. Does this make sense, given the over-
whelmingly likely situation that galactic civilizations
differ in their level of evolutionary development by
thousands or millions of years? Would you share
drinks with a trilobite, an ourang-outang, or a saber-
toothed tiger? Or would you just arrange to have a
few specimens stuffed and carted off to the local
museum?

SETH SHOSTAK, SENIOR ASTRONOMER
FOR THE SETI INSTITUTE

Date Unknown

FOR HANS KAMMLER, *once an SS general of the Reich, powerful and respected, life had become an intolerable hell.*
*After the failed attempt on the US President's life, he'd
been taken by three humans to a remote spot in the woods
somewhere in northwestern Virginia. He was fully aware
of what was going on around him, but one of the Saurian
entities was riding him for the entire trip, controlling his
mind, controlling every action and movement, leaving
him a helpless spectator.*

He suspected the humans around him were in the same state. Their eyes seemed glassy and lifeless, their movements automatic . . . like men in a dream or a hypnotic trance.

They'd reached the edge of an empty field at just past midnight, a dark place encircled by tangled woods and the shadowy loom of the Shenandoah Mountains. They got out of the car and they waited in the chilly March night until a single star overhead grew bright, then descended silently to Earth. The saucer, he noted, was like the ones he'd seen at Dulce—a silver flattened disk perhaps fifteen meters across, capable of hovering silently just above the ground. A hatch had opened and, his body responding to the unspoken commands of others, he'd walked up the hatch and into the light.

They'd taken him . . . someplace else.

An alien mind no longer occupied his head. He was free to look around, to move, at least within certain narrow limits. While he'd still been under their control, they'd put him in a glass tube, then released him as the container rapidly filled with greenish liquid. The terror he'd experienced as the liquid had poured in, rising inexorably up and over his mouth, his nose, his entire face—it had been like no other terror he'd ever faced. He'd held his breath for as long as he could, and then, his lungs bursting, he'd resigned himself to drowning and had taken a breath.

And, somehow, he'd lived.

He'd read about the recent development of something called total liquid ventilation, where a perfluorocarbon liquid saturated with oxygen replaced the air normally breathed by an organism, keeping it alive even when submerged. This, it seemed, was that same medical technology, but carried to a horrific extreme. All Kammler knew was that those first breaths he'd taken were agony.

And now, they had him in storage, perhaps awaiting the next time they had use for him. He was naked, his skin was wrinkled, he was cold, so cold, and time for him dragged on seemingly forever. He didn't need food; he suspected that they were putting nutrients into the liquid around him, that he was absorbing those nutrients through his skin.

The thing was, even stark terror, he found, became boring after a time. He wanted to die. He wondered if he was lapsing into insanity, but mostly he wanted to die.

He had no idea how long he'd been here. Normally, there was no light, but occasionally one of his captors— the bird-legged Saurian Eidechse—entered the compartment, and he would glimpse with horrifying clarity the rows upon rows of other tubes around him, each filled with green liquid, each holding a naked man or woman, each captive horribly alive and aware and struggling.

A literal Hell on Earth . . . except that Kammler had the feeling that he was no longer on Earth at all.

THEY CLATTERED down narrow metal stairs, with Hunter in the lead. A light came on automatically. The basement chamber appeared to have been melted out of solid rock and was dimly lit, but Hunter felt the size of the open space beneath the alien dome. The place was *huge*.

And it was filled with six-foot cylinders of transparent glass or plastic arrayed in long, parallel rows, most filled with green liquid and a single nude human figure, a horror scene out of some cheap sci-fi movie or comic book. Row upon row of cylinders extended off into the distance, where they were lost in the gloom.

Many of the captives in those bottles appeared dead or unconscious, but a few, a horrifying few, were clearly awake and nightmarishly aware. Eyes stared, mouths gaped in silent supplication, fists pounded against transparencies in a dreamlike slow motion. Herrera gave an involuntary yelp as he took in the scene. "They're *drowning!*"

"I don't think so," Hunter said. "Look at how they're wired up. I think they're breathing that stuff."

"How?" Daly demanded.

"I've read about experiments using liquids saturated with oxygen," he said. "The SEALs were looking into it a few years ago as a way to keep breathing at extreme depths. Let's see if we can get them out. We might be able to get some hard intel from someone."

"How many of them are there?" Randolph Brown asked.

"God knows," Hunter said, peering down along the rows of tanks. "Hundreds."

A dull boom sounded from overhead. The mysterious attackers outside were again bombarding the protective shield.

"Mink," Hunter said. "Get back topside, and have them get in touch with the *Big-H*. We're gonna need some support down here. Daly, gimme a hand here."

They climbed and tugged and pulled and searched, but they could not find a way to open one of the containers, and now Hunter wasn't sure doing so would be a good idea even if they could. They could easily end up killing the prisoners instead of rescuing them.

He tried using hand motions in front of a couple of the tanks to assure the captives that they would be back, but he wasn't sure it registered. Then he led the others back up the stairs.

They would need help—from the Grays if possible, from the Saurians if necessary.

The Saurians were all gone, though, fled to one of the other domes. "Can any of you open those tanks down below?" he demanded.

A dozen Grays stood in front of him, looking back and forth at one another. He could sense their confusion, their lack of understanding. Explosions, dulled by the encircling defensive shield, sounded outside.

"Damn it, there are *people* down there!" His shout was loud enough to make several of the small beings take a step backward. "You *will* help us get them out!"

One of the Grays stepped front and center of the

others. *Commander, we cannot. Only the Malok have the codes.*

"Then we'll smash the tanks open!"

Which would result in the specimens' deaths.

"They're not *specimens*, damn it! They're our people!"

The Gray appeared unmoved. It didn't shrug physically, but Hunter could sense the gesture in its attitude. *They are not ours. They belong to the Malok.*

The name made Hunter hesitate, and then he remembered. Benedict had used that name, and said that it was the Grays' term for the reptilian entities.

"They don't belong to anyone but themselves!"

Yes? But what of the treaty? Signed by your president?

"What about returning them alive and unharmed? That was part of the deal, right? If *you* can't let them go, find me someone who can."

The Malok have the codes. Speak with them.

There was no budging the little creature. Hunter had wondered at times about the premise that the Grays were, in fact, the descendants of humans in a remote futurity, an idea he simply found too fantastic to believe without more proof than he'd seen so far. After all, an alien being *might* have evolved along a broadly human design with two arms and two legs, right? But they also possessed an unyielding stubbornness that seemed all too human in both its scope and its rigidity.

With the Grays' help, they were able to open a communications channel with the Saurians, who'd taken shelter in a dome half a kilometer away. Hunter stared into the golden reptilian eyes of the outsize Saurian leader and for the first time heard it actually *speak*, rather than transmit telepathically.

"We will not help you, human," the being said in English, its voice breathy, filled with hisses and disconcerting clicks. "The things in the capsules belong to us."

"Humans do not belong to anyone. In keeping them here, you are in violation of the Eisenhower treaty. You were supposed to let them go, remember?" It was a weak jab, Hunter knew, but it was all he had.

"What are treaties to us?" The creature seemed . . . amused. "A human concept of no interest to The Surviving Few."

Was that what they called themselves? Interesting.

"We can, however, agree to cooperate with you to some extent, *if* you drive off the nomad attackers." As if to punctuate the statement, a deep-throated boom rumbled through the dome from outside.

Hunter scowled. Treaties and negotiated agreements with alien representatives were definitely way above his pay grade, but he didn't seem to have a lot of choice right now. *Hillenkoetter* and the fleet were in orbit, not *here* and as an active part of the equation.

"I'm going to hold you to that, you son of a bitch," Hunter said. And he signaled for a Gray, seated at the console in front of him, to cut the connection.

LIEUTENANT COMMANDER Hank Boland completed his walk-around, his final visual inspection of his fighter before launch. He'd come a long way since piloting a Super Hornet off the *Nimitz*.

Light-years, in fact.

On a conventional jet aircraft, you looked at the exposed parts that might cause trouble—the fan blades of the intakes, the landing gear, the venturis, the flaps. The F/S-49 Stingray had visible landing gear while parked on the *Hillenkoetter*'s flight deck, but little else on display for inspection. The space fighter had been built by Northrop Grumman very much along the lines of their X-47B, a demonstration unmanned combat air vehicle, or UCAV—a test drone designed for carrier operations. Diamond shaped, with no vertical stabilizer and no wings, the spacecraft of course relied on alien technology to fly. The flattened craft was just forty feet long—roughly as long as the original X-47B. But the dorsal air intake had been heavily modified, and now housed the cockpit. Weapons bays along the ventral surface carried a variety of space-to-space or space-to-ground missiles.

And a hellpod.

Boland's walk-around included opening a small panel and jacking in with a handheld meter. All spacecraft systems read go—life support, drives, maneuvering, computer, weapons, all online and powered up.

He was good to go.

Around him, other members of his squadron were checking out their own craft and climbing into their cockpits. SFA-05, the Starhawks, was the United States' fifth designated space fighter squadron. He looked at the line of twelve Stingrays and wondered—not for the first time—if the UAP he'd chased southwest of San Diego back in '04 had been one of these. They certainly had the same lozenge shape, and about the same dimensions.

He remembered telling his debriefing officer after the encounter that he wanted to fly one of those things; a year later, he'd been offered the chance to participate in a highly secret program, and ended up at Area 51. There, he'd first met the F/S-49 Stingray, along with a small fleet of other unconventional craft, reverse engineered from crashed alien spaceships and, in some cases, built with direct help from the aliens. Years later, with thousands of hours in the cockpit, he was the squadron commander of SFA-05—the letters stood for "Space Fighter, Attack."

And his squadron had just been assigned to the *Hillenkoetter.*

With his crew chief's help, he climbed the narrow ladder and squeezed down into the cockpit. It was a tight fit. The old naval aviator's joke about "strapping on your airplane" was almost literally true. Once in the embrace of the formfitting seat, he began going over the preflight checklist. No red lights—everything was green.

"*Big-H*, Hawk One," he called. "Ready to taxi."

"Copy, Hawk One. Taxi runway one-alfa to cat four."

Hillenkoetter's flight deck was enormous, but it was crowded with fighters and auxiliary spacecraft. The "runways" were narrow taxiways leading to the flight bay launch area, which was divided up by hundred-foot rails set into the deck directly in front of the broad access port opening onto space. That part still freaked him a bit; the flight deck's internal atmosphere was held in by the paired magnetokinetic induction screens. Switching both fields off, even if for only an instant, seemed to him like an act of insanity.

His fighter rolled up to the catapult, where deck crew in full vac gear hooked his Stingray up to the railgun catapult. He waited there for a moment, staring through the cockpit screen into the star field of open space.

"SFA-05, you are free to cycle."

"Copy, PryFly. Cycling down to 10 percent."

"Hawk One, PryFly. You are cleared for launch."

"One copies, PryFly. Anytime you folks are ready."

"Copy, One. Launch on your mark."

"Roger, PryFly. Starhawks launch on my mark, in three . . . two . . . one . . . *shoot!*"

That sharp and sudden surge of acceleration always caught Boland by surprise, no matter how he prepared for it. A giant hand pressed down over his chest, making breathing difficult. The pressure vanished as the fighter left the rail, and the space carrier dwindled away on his aft camera screens, becoming one insignificant point of light lost among thousands within seconds. Boland checked left and right; the other eleven space fighters were strung out to either side and astern, forming an enormous chevron.

"PryFly, Hawk One," he called. "We're clear of *Big-H*."

"Copy, Hawk One. Transferring you to CIC."

"Roger that. CIC, Starhawk Flight. Where do you want us?"

"Starhawk, CIC, you are cleared to proceed toward objective Serpo, bearing zero-five-niner by one-five-two, over."

"CIC, Starhawk, bearing on Serpo, at zero-five-niner by one-five-two, rog."

"Good luck, Starhawk. Our people on the ground report heavy fire and a planet full of bad guys. See if you can help 'em out."

"Copy that. Starhawk Flight is on the way."

The sheer emptiness of space always startled him, as well. Once the *Hillenkoetter* and her escorts had disappeared, there was nothing around him but stars. The local sun gleamed up ahead, but at twice the distance of Earth from Sol it seemed wan and shrunken. Boland knew of the vast torus of asteroidal debris outward—and of the enigmatic, sleeping civilization of the Xaxki—but all of that was invisible. A few of those pinpoints of light might be comets or asteroids, but damned few, and there was no way to distinguish them from stars made dim by distance.

Moments later, Serpo expanded from one of those points of light to a slender crescent bowed away from the sun.

"Right, Chicks," Boland called over the squadron's tactical channel. "Check out the hellpods. Power up."

Hellpods were ventral weapons pods slung from the F/A-49s, each mounting five high-energy lasers, or HELs, designed to project five beams as a single powerful bolt of coherent light. The Navy had been experimenting with lasers both as shipboard defenses and mounted on testbed aircraft for several years now, but few realized the weapons were already in operational deployment. Acknowledgments came back from the other members of the flight.

"Hawk Seven, hot."

"Hawk Nine, locked and loaded."

"Hawk Three, go."

The target planet expanded rapidly in their forward screens.

"Our target zone is on the night side right now," Boland said. "We'll use Opplan Delta. CIC says our people are inside a force dome, so we don't need to worry about own goals. Get in as close as you can on each pass."

"So what's the target, Skipper?" Lieutenant Meyers asked. "They didn't tell us anything!"

"All I know is multiple EBEs on the ground outside our guys' perimeter . . . and unidentified heavy weapons sites firing at the dome. It'll be close ground support. We take out the big guns, and we shoot up the EBEs."

The flight was computer-guided in toward the objective. In seconds, the sun dipped beneath a curving black horizon, and Boland's teeth rattled inside his helmet as the Stingray jolted and buffeted through thickening atmosphere. Its screens softened the descent somewhat, but it was still one hell of a rough ride.

They broke through the dark overcast. Flashes of light appeared up ahead.

The Starhawks went over to the attack.

"HILLENKOETTER SAYS the fighters are on the way, sir," Colby said. The radioman was crouched over the transmitter they'd brought with them to the surface. The Grays were having trouble patching through to the Big-H; at least, that's what their spokesman claimed. Hunter had his doubts that the Eben beings were cooperating fully.

But it was about damned time the aerospace assets arrived, Hunter thought. The close-air support should have been over the target area the moment 1-JSST touched down.

Now he just needed to figure out how to get a Saurian over here to open up those tubes in the basement. A direct assault on one of the other domes was out of the question. The strike force would have to go through the airlock, and that meant not one but *two* sealed, airtight doors. Besides, the Saurians would know when the team entered the airlock, and be waiting with their deadly weaponry by the time the humans equalized pressures and opened the inner door.

No, there had to be another way.

"Hey . . . Mink?"

"Yeah, Skipper?"

"That tunnel underneath us. It runs that way, right?"

"Yes, sir?"

"Toward one of the other domes?"

Minkowski's eyes widened. "Yes, sir."

"How long do you think the tunnel is?"

"Dunno, Skipper, but it's long. Maybe half a mile?"

"That's what I was thinking. And the next dome over that way is maybe half that distance."

"We have a back door in."

"Something like that. Is that dome the one with our guys in it? Or with the Saurians?"

A quick consultation with the Grays established that the second dome was one of the habitats currently occupied by the Saurians. Hunter still didn't trust the little bastards, but either the habitat contained a mix of Grays and Saurians, or it held Grays, humans, and Saurians.

Either way, they had a chance to catch the Saurians in what Hunter was now thinking of as Dome Two by surprise. "Okay, people. Listen up! Minkowski, Daly, Taylor, Nielson, Dorschner, Brown, Mullaney, Herrera—you guys are with me. Marlow, Coulter, Alvarez, Colby, Briggs, Bader—you stay here with Brunelli and watch our backs. Keep a sharp eye on our hosts, too, okay? Lieutenant Bader, you're in charge."

"Yes, sir."

"And Colby, Briggs—I want you two to get in touch with those fighters. See if you can get a working circus going. Send a couple of volunteers outside if you need to, as FiSTers." The word stood for fire support team, and referred to forward observers who could coordinate with artillery or aircraft to call in close support strikes.

"Colby, while you're at it, try to raise the *Big-H* and let 'em know what's going down."

"Yes, *sir*!"

"Strike team: suit up, and check your weapons. Grab extra batteries. Everybody set? Okay—EMCON protocol, everyone. Let's go."

EMCON stood for emissions control—radio silence, in other words. Suit-to-suit transmissions might be picked up by the aliens.

Hunter led the way back down the ladder into the subsurface cavern. Again, he felt the eyes of dozens of people on him, awake and aware within those transparent cylinders. *Poor fucking bastards. We'll be back for you, I promise . . .*

They hurried down the main, central passageway heading in the direction of Dome Two. It was distinctly possible, even likely, that the Saurians were watching their approach on their equivalent of security cams, but there was simply no alternative. Hunter hadn't seen any cameras, though that was no guarantee with technology this advanced.

And then again, maybe they'd gotten lucky. The Saurians certainly hadn't been expecting them, and therefore would have had no reason to put up cameras.

He hoped.

A quarter of a mile down the passageway, Minkowski tapped Hunter's shoulder and pointed. In an alcove off to the right, a metal ladder led up a stone wall to the upper level. Hunter gestured, and the SpecOps team began filing up the stairs.

Minkowski was on point—the door kicker. Taylor and Nielson were close behind him, and Hunter was in the number four spot. They'd practiced this sort of op endlessly back on Earth, before they'd been recruited by

Solar Warden. Now they would see if close-assault tactics worked on ugly gray aliens.

At the top of the stairs, they paused. No sign that they'd been seen, or that the bad guys were waiting for them. Hunter held up his hand and gave a countdown: *three . . . two . . . one . . .*

BOLAND PULLED the nose of his F/S-49 Stingray up, the rush of dark landscape beneath his keel matching the adrenaline rush singing in his blood. At Mach 4 he would be past the bad guys before he saw them, so he began pumping hard to decelerate. The terrain ahead appeared on his IR screen in blobs of yellow, green, and blue.

And several scattered blobs of red. *Those* would be the objective, or they should be—hot spots against the frigid cold of this poisonous ice ball of a world. "I've got hot spots bearing one-niner-five!" he called. "Cut back to Mach 1 and give 'em a close flyby!"

"Copy, Hawk Leader. Right behind you."

How well could the enemy track them? The Stingrays were stealthy, and they could selectively jam hostile radar, but after entering Serpo's atmosphere they were hot, and must be showing up as fiercely burning bogies on any alien infrared gear down there.

Well, they'd know in a few more seconds.

"There're the domes, people. On a hilltop, six of 'em in a circle a mile across!"

"Roger that. I'm picking up some sort of kinetic screen over the hill."

"Hawk One, Hawk Five, I've got something that might be mobile artillery down there."

"Record everything you pick up and transmit back to the *Big-H*," Boland ordered. He eased back on the Stingray's controls, pulling into a gentle left turn that would take him around the alien base.

"Hawk One, Hawk Three! I'm being painted!"

Boland's instruments showed that he was being hit

by multiple powerful radar beams, as well. They might be targeting radars for ground-to-air weaponry. "Same here, Three. Keep alert, everyone! ECM on—see if we can jam it!"

As Boland banked hard to the left, he could see the landscape surrounding the alien force dome. The ground down there appeared to be moving, though he couldn't see details. He could also see three objects like black-and-gray toys equally spaced around the force field, definitely mechanical but of a complicated shape unlike anything with which he was familiar. Mobile batteries? Ground attack vehicles? Or static towers? They definitely mounted heavy weapons, which were playing irregularly across the dome. It didn't look so much like a coordinated, determined attack as it did harassing fire. Boland wondered how serious the attackers were about bringing down the kinetic field. Maybe they were just keeping the occupants penned in?

And what the hell would be the point of that?

"*Big-H*, Hawk One," Boland called. "I have multiple targets firing on the force field. Request permission to commence run."

"Hawk One, *Hillenkoetter*, wait one."

What the hell? They'd been deployed to provide close air support for the guys on the ground . . . and now they were supposed to *wait one*?

It made no sense whatsoever, but the rules of engagement said to fire only when you'd received permission to do so.

"Starhawk Flight, Hawk One. Hold fire."

"What's the story, Skipper?" Lieutenant Bronsky asked. "I've got the bastards dead to rights!"

"I have no idea, Bronsky. Just do as you're—"

"Hawk Five! I'm hit! Mayday!"

Hawk Five was Lieutenant Robert Selby. *"Selby!"*

"Mayday! May—"

Boland twisted around, trying to see, but visibility

in the Stingrays was sharply limited—essentially a narrow window looking straightforward. External cameras looked port, starboard, and aft, but seeing anything on the internal screen was purely a matter of luck.

"Selby, do you copy?"

He got back nothing but static.

"Hawk One, Hawk Nine. Bob just slammed into the ground outside the perimeter. I think he might've taken some of the bastards with him."

"Starhawk Flight! Engage! Repeat, engage!"

They were taking fire, and that meant they could return the favor.

And Boland intended to do just that . . . in spades.

CHAPTER NINETEEN

We have only to look at ourselves to see how intelligent life might develop into something we wouldn't want to meet.

PHYSICIST STEPHEN HAWKING, 2010

THE LIGHTS WENT on once more, and Kammler caught a glimpse of movement to his right. He turned, trying to follow a number of shapes emerging from the shadows.

Human *shapes!* Mein Gott! Menschen! *Menschen!*

Kammler tried to call out, but the liquid filling his nose and mouth and throat and lungs effectively gagged him. He tried pounding with his fists against the transparency, but the liquid slowed his movements to ineffective and slow-motion thumps.

He watched as nine men moved into the light, following the passageway from right to left. He thought they were men, though the suits they wore made it hard to tell. They were twice as tall as the Grays, taller than most Eidechse, and their legs were human legs, not the up-on-tiptoes bird legs of the reptiles.

Yes—one of the men turned and looked directly at him, and Kammler could see human features behind the space suit visor! The suits were not familiar to him—they were nothing like the bulky, Michelin Man space suits of Apollo, but formfitting black and gray. The weapons they carried were strange, as well.

But they were human!

They moved in two groups, one moving forward while the other provided overwatch, then reversing roles. Now they were climbing the stairs, the metal stairs Kammler could just glimpse from his tank that led God knew where. The way they moved—cautiously, in fireteam formation, but with a casual grace and control and above all watchfulness—*as well as the weaponry they carried convinced him that this was a human rescue party. For a long time, Kammler had been wondering about whether or not he was still on Earth, but the human combat team suggested that he was. He didn't know why they were wearing space suits; perhaps the air here was bad, or it was protection against gas or noxious chemicals.*

He didn't care.

Hans Kammler was not at all religious, but he was praying desperately now. The team was probably seeking to take out the aliens. And then . . .

And then he would be rescued.

THREE . . . TWO . . . one . . . go!

Hunter gave the hand sign, and Minkowski, at the landing on the top of the stairs, put his hand against the center of the closed door and pushed. The panel slid aside, much to Hunter's relief—there'd been the possibility that it would be locked—and the SpecOps assault force surged forward.

Following a tightly choreographed plan, Minkowski pushed forward into Dome Two's control center, Tom Taylor rolled through the open door to the right, and Frank Nielson rolled left. Hunter came in right behind Minkowski, quickly assessing the tacsit.

A Saurian, a big one, stood behind a table, raising its weapon. Hunter and Minkowski fired almost in unison, and the alien went down with two smoking charred holes at its center of mass. Hunter shifted his aim right, drawing down on another armed Saurian, and snapped off another shot. Unlike the first Saurian, this one was wearing some kind of body armor, and the invisible bolt from Hunter's weapon blackened a patch on the being's chest but didn't burn through. The alien fired, and Lieutenant Dorschner, just coming through the door at Hunter's back, flailed and collapsed, much of his head now missing. A second Saurian fired, and Mullaney fell, shrieking, most of his right arm missing, the stump gushing blood. Taylor took out one of the Saurians, and Minkowski the other. Hunter pivoted left-right-left, his laser pistol in an extended, two-hand grip as he searched for targets. He could see six Grays, none of them armed, all staring with wide-eyed confusion at this sudden surge of armed force from their rear. He didn't see any more Saurians. Damn! The whole point had been to capture one alive; had they killed all of the Reptilians?

"Clear left!" Taylor called.

"Clear right!" Nielson added.

"Room clear!" Minkowski said.

Hunter checked a readout in his helmet, making certain that his exterior speaker was on. "You! All of you!" he shouted at the Grays. "Get down! On your knees! Hands locked behind your heads!"

This dome, Hunter noted, was quite different from Dome One. There were few electronics, few consoles, and the smaller central compartment had the feel of a lounge or a recreation room, or possibly a mess hall, with diminutive seats and sofas, and several broad tables in the center. Numerous doors around the room's perimeter led to other rooms; one door slid open and a Saurian emerged, evidently drawn by Mullaney's screams.

Hunter was in front of the being in three swift steps, his laser pressed against its naked skull. "Freeze," Hunter yelled, and the being flinched. "Lose the hardware!"

The Saurian touched a point on its armor, and everything dropped to the deck, including one of the boxlike weapons attached to the chest. "Any more of your kind in there?"

The being didn't answer, and Hunter said, "Mink! Brown! Nielson! Herrera! Check these other rooms!"

"Arr!"

Nielson's raspy-voiced pirate yell startled Hunter. He'd forgotten about that little bit of team building he'd experimented with back on the *Hillenkoetter*. Nielson and the others were so jacked up by combat-generated adrenaline they probably couldn't shout anything *but* "arr."

"Daly, with me. Check Mullaney!"

They had one Navy corpsman with them on this raid, Marlow, but all SpecOps personnel received at least some training in battlefield first aid. Army staff sergeant John Daly squeezed Mullaney's upper arm, pinching hard until the flow of blood slowed. Hunter went to Dorschner's body, unsealing his space suit so that he could get at the shipboard utilities the dead man wore underneath. Hunter's suit included a survival knife, and he used that to cut through the garment's seam, then ripped off a long strip of cloth. The strip would serve as a tourniquet until Marlow could look at it. Mullaney's screams had stopped, thank God . . . but Hunter was afraid that the man was going into shock. They used one of the tiny chairs to elevate his legs.

It was all they could do for the man at the moment.

Minkowski, meanwhile, came back with a report. They'd found five more Grays in several of the surrounding rooms, plus another Reptilian. This dome, he volunteered, might be private sleeping quarters. There were slabs in those rooms that might, conceivably, be beds.

You cannot win. The voice in Hunter's mind was dark with menace. Hunter spun, looking from one Saurian to the other, trying to determine which one had transmitted that.

And at that moment, he felt the compulsion, the insane compulsion, to press his pistol against the side of his own head and pull the trigger. Several of the other men appeared dazed, and stared at their own weapons as though trying to decide what they were for.

One of the Saurians was looking at its feet; the other was watching Hunter with a deeply malevolent glare. Hunter slowly removed his helmet, then stepped up to the malevolent one and as loudly as he could screamed, *"Arrrr!"*

Startled, the being blinked, and the mental compulsion was broken. "Get out of my head and *stay* out," he bellowed, bringing his pistol up until it lodged beneath the Saurian's chin, pointed up. "If I feel even a *hint* of you messing with my head, I pull the trigger immediately, got it?"

"I . . . have it."

Hunter noted with grim satisfaction that the alien *spoke* the words, rather than use telepathy.

"You are going to open those tanks below," he continued. "You will revive the occupants, all of them, and bring them safely out here."

"And what will you do with them? Three hundred fifteen specimens, wet, naked, cold, and requiring food and water within a very few hours of decanting. At the very least, they will require environmental suits to leave these domes. Do you have what they require?"

"Do you have the code to open those tanks?" The being didn't reply, and Hunter jabbed the muzzle of his pistol harder against its neck. *"Do you?"*

"I . . . do."

"Then you will open *one* of those outsize aquariums and revive the occupant, and you will show several of us how to do it. You have a problem with that?"

"No . . . problem."

Good. One step at a time.

BOLAND GOT a solid radar lock on one of the towers and thumbed the trigger on his control stick. Invisible light lanced out from his hellpod and struck the alien device dead center, creating a dazzling spot on the tower shining brighter than a sun. He flashed past, banking left to follow the curve of the force dome. He couldn't tell if he'd damaged the alien structure or not.

His Stingray relied primarily on its gravitics for lift, control, and maneuvering, but the aerospace craft was flat with a curved upper surface—a perfect lifting body— and Boland could use that to good effect as he shed yet more speed.

He could see aliens on the ground—big dark gray humps covered with segmented armor; the ground seemed to be moving as they crawled forward in a living mass. Beams of coherent light strobed from the ground as the massive creatures fired weapons at the diamond-shaped craft that had appeared above them. The coating of his fighter's outer hull absorbed laser energy as well as radar waves, providing at least some protection. He wondered, though, what had taken Selby down. Massed lasers? Missiles? Or something unknown as yet to humans?

He skimmed low above that horribly moving surface, triggering his hellpod laser in a long strafing run. An explosion erupted into the sky ahead, momentarily lighting the dark terrain. He'd hit *something* down there. He had no idea what it might have been, though.

Continuing to hold his craft in a tight left turn, he flashed past the force dome on top of the hill. He could make out lots of the big, armored aliens down there . . . and then he saw something else, a ship grounded on the side of the slope.

In that instant, his fighter was hit, and he was tumbling toward the surface in a vicious roll.

"I'm hit!" he yelled. "This is Hawk One, and I'm hit!"

He slammed into the ground two seconds later.

THEY'D PULLED her from her tank more or less at random. The alien code was simple enough—three light taps on an inconspicuous panel at the base triggered an automated release procedure that drained the liquid from the tank, then popped open the side, at which point the captive dropped to her hands and knees, coughing violently. Someone found her a blanket—a thermal survival blanket made of a kind of light, silvery foil. "Thank God," the woman gasped, clutching the foil around her shoulders. "Thank *God*. I was in there forever!"

"Who are you?" Hunter asked, kneeling next to her. "Where are you from?"

"Judi . . . Judi Clarke. I . . . I'm from Tulsa. Tulsa, Oklahoma. I was . . . I was . . ." She saw the Saurian behind Hunter and screamed, dissolving into hysteria.

"Get her into one of the rooms!" Hunter snarled. "Nielson! Stay with her! Don't let any of the aliens come near her!"

"Aye, aye, sir."

The Saurian had been right, damn him. What the hell were they going to do with this person? Worse, what were they going to do with three hundred–some of her fellow captives?

Thoughtful, Hunter donned his helmet and called Ralph Colby. He and Briggs were outside, in contact with the fighters circling the hilltop.

"We've lost two fighters out here, Commander," Colby said over Hunter's suit radio. "The others are hammering the sons of bitches."

"Any chance of survivors?" Hunter asked.

"Not sure, sir. One of the ships exploded going in, but the other kind of skidded in on its belly. The pilot *might* be alive."

"Okay. Mark the position. We'll check it out later . . . if we can." Hunter turned to face one of the two captive Saurians, who was being firmly held by Miguelito Herrera. The man was a big and powerful Marine with the build of a football linebacker and the body mass of five or six of the skinny little Grays. Taylor stood nearby with his laser, ready to act if Herrera said the alien was inside his head.

"What *are* those bugs out there?" Hunter demanded of the being. "Why are they attacking?"

"We call them 'Dreams of Xaxki,'" the Reptilian said, its voice a soft hiss. "We believe they are projections created by the sleeping Xaxki population."

"Uh-huh. And how can dreams harm those of us who are awake?"

"You would not understand."

"Try me."

"We believe the Xaxki possess a—call it a kind of psychic technology. One that gives form to their mental imagery. They demand that we leave this system."

"Okay. And why *are* you in this system? Doesn't sound like you're wanted."

"Again, you would not understand."

"I'm getting pretty damned sick of your condescending—"

Hunter was interrupted by a burst of radio static. "This is Hunter. Go."

"Commander, this is Lieutenant Billingsly," a voice said. "We're in control of Dome Three."

"Well done! We have One and Two. What happened?"

"Those creepy lizards suddenly went berserk, Commander. They attacked us. No provocation, no warning . . ."

"They're telepathic, Lieutenant. They were probably warned by the lizards over here. Or . . . some of the lizards here fled this dome. Did you have any of them showing up over there?"

"Several, sir."

"That was it. Anybody hurt?"

"One dead—Carpenter. And Warner is pretty badly hurt. But the reptiles are all dead. We have about twenty Grays prisoner, but they haven't tried anything yet."

"The Grays—I think they're under Saurian control. Mind control. Ours are acting kind of blank. Empty."

"That's what ours are like."

"Well, keep a close eye on them. The Saurians can get inside their heads. They can get into your head, too. If you feel anything weird, a kind of compulsion to do something you don't want to do, that's what it is."

"We'll be on our toes, sir."

"Any word from Arch's platoon?"

"Negative, sir, but we know where they are. We're putting together a strike force to go give 'em a hand."

"Okay. Do you need help?"

"I think we can manage, sir. We'll give a yell if we run into anything we can't handle."

"Copy that." He hesitated. "Have you explored the basement yet?"

"Yes, sir . . . we've seen it. We were going to deploy down there to assault the other domes."

"So you've seen the prisoners?"

"What prisoners, sir? I saw something down there that might be a spaceship. And a lot of aluminum crates, it looked like."

Hunter carefully told Billingsly about the tanks holding human captives.

"Those alien bastards. . . ." Billingsly growled.

"We're looking at how we can get them back to the *Big-H*. The underground section is huge, but if you're moving around down there, you'll probably see them. Don't touch any of them until I tell you to."

"Roger that, Commander."

"Let us know if we can help."

"Copy."

Hunter was powerfully tempted to send some of his people over to help Bravo Platoon, but in tight quarters like the ladders leading up to the domes, more troops could be a liability, not an asset. Besides, if the bad guys were monitoring human communications right now, they would be on the alert. He would hold Alfa in reserve until he knew what they were up to.

Overall, things were going better than Hunter had had any reason to expect. Billingsly and Bravo Platoon had rolled with the punches and neutralized the Saurians in their dome. The JSST now controlled three of the six domes on the hilltop. Except for the minor logistical problem of getting all those people downstairs out of their tanks and back to the *Hillenkoetter*, things were freaking *great*. . . .

They were outnumbered by a technologically superior enemy, and a second, unidentified enemy was hammering at the walls of the kinetic shield outside. Forty light-years from home and not a clue as to what they were supposed to be doing here.

A typical day, he decided, for the Navy's SEALs.

Hunter confronted the Saurian again. He was beginning to think of it as a leader, the equivalent of a senior officer. Nielson took up a position just behind the alien, ready to act if it attempted another mental attack.

"We're going to have to move a large number of humans up to the *Hillenkoetter*, okay?"

"Yes."

"I know the Saurians have technology that lets them teleport. Disappear in one place, reappear someplace else. Correct?"

"Yes."

"Can we use that system to get these refugees up to the *Hillenkoetter*?"

"No."

"Why not?"

"Your ship is in orbit around this planet, traveling at nearly fifteen thousand miles per hour. The relative difference in velocities is extremely hard to compensate for."

Hunter stared at the creature for a long moment. Was it telling the truth? He found it impossible to read emotions in the face or manner of the being. It appeared that it was being cooperative now, but he didn't trust it by seven thousand light-years.

"Okay," Hunter said. "'Dreams of Xaxki.' What can you tell me?"

"Only that there are more forms of reality—what you would call 'reality'—than you can possibly imagine. Realities which we can access through the mind."

"What . . . like telepathy?"

"No. In this case, through dreams. Through various forms of altered consciousness. What we see in the world around us, or what we *think* we see, is not always what *is* . . . or all that it seems."

"So, the sleeping Xaxki are dreaming up these beasts." A puzzling thought intruded. "With breathing gear?"

"The dreams can become real beings, within a fairly broad meaning of the word *real*. Xaxki thoughts within their artificial reality can manifest, can take on substance in *this* reality. The attackers may be representations of some life-form the nomads have encountered elsewhere in the Galaxy. That life would not be able to breathe this atmosphere, hence, breathing gear."

Hunter shook his head. "It sounds too much like magic."

"Was it not one of your philosophers who stated, 'Any sufficiently advanced technology is indistinguishable from magic'?"

Hunter had heard the saying, though he didn't remember who'd said it. Nielson, standing watch behind the Saurian, nodded. "Arthur C. Clarke, sir," he said. "A writer, not a philosopher."

"So why haven't the Saurians talked with the Xaxki? Found some common ground?"

"You people seem obsessed with the idea of negotiations and treaties," the Saurian told him. It almost sounded amused. "Why would anyone allow such exchanges to dictate their actions?"

"I don't know. Maybe to foster trust and understanding between different peoples?"

"Trust," the alien said, "is a *human* concept."

Hunter thought he was beginning to get a true sense of the Saurians' alienness. They did not think like humans, were different from them on a deep and fundamental level.

"Niels," Hunter said, turning from the alien. "Lock them all up in one of the rooms. *All* of them, Grays and Saurs."

"What are you thinking, Boss?" Minkowski asked.

"First we're going to help Billingsly secure the entire complex. I don't want to have these critters in our rear."

"Aye, aye, sir."

"And after that we need to put together a combat team to go rescue those pilots outside the dome. If we can. Colby!"

"Yes, sir!"

"What's going down out there?"

"Nothing right now, Skipper. The fast movers are gone. The bad guys seem to have pulled back."

"Okay. Get hold of *Big-H* and tell them our situation. Tell them we're going to need at least three TRs down here . . . and some way of moving a lot of people without EVA suits through the airlocks without killing them."

Maybe someone up there would have an idea . . . because he was fresh out.

CAPTAIN GROTON was standing on the flag bridge with Admiral Carruthers. Seated next to the admiral were Ambassador King and Ambassador Kozlov, along with several senior staff officers. The diplomatic personnel were looking grim.

"We can *not* afford to get into a shooting war with the Xaxki," Carruthers told him. "Think of it as the equivalent of a land war in Asia. We can't win!"

"But we can't just leave our ground combat team down there on the surface!" Groton insisted. "Hunter's last message confirmed that the attackers down there are Xaxki constructs, some kind of artificial projection. I don't understand the details. Carter and McClure are working on that now. But we need to get the Xaxki to call off their dogs, and if that means parking a space carrier in their backyard, so be it!"

"*No*, Captain," King said. "We are going to respect Xaxki protocols and policies, and that includes their deployment of this imaginary army."

"It's not imaginary if our people are being killed by it, Mr. Ambassador."

"You should have your people cease their attacks immediately," Kozlov said with a scowl. "They should sit tight, and wait for us to resolve this situation peacefully."

"Order the fighter squadron to return to the carrier," Carruthers added. "Do not deploy them again, unless I give you a direct order to do so."

"We have at least two pilots on the surface," Groton said. "They may still be alive. What about them?"

"Regrettable," Carruthers said. "But we *did* attack them."

"Look, Admiral—I'm not suggesting we start a war with those creatures. But there's got to be a way to convince them to stand down. All I'm asking is that we talk to them about stopping the fighting!"

King shook his head. "We *did* suggest it, Captain, pointing out that our people were inadvertently caught in the cross fire down there. They insisted that there is no war, no fighting. Further attempts to communicate with them were ignored."

"Who were you talking to, Mr. Ambassador?" Groton asked. "The Dreamers? Or the Guardians?"

"We don't believe that matters. We communicated by radio with something that called itself the Xaxki Instrumentality. Exactly what this Instrumentality actually might be is still an open question. It may be the Guardians, or a Guardian faction in a leadership role. It may represent a kind of leading council or government within the body of Dreamers, communicating with the outside world through electronic avatars. Or, they could be an artificial intelligence running things—or possibly something so completely beyond our experience that we have no chance of ever understanding what it might be."

"I think it *does* matter, sir. Trillions of individuals are not going to be a monolithic whole. There will be factions, probably a lot of them. And some of them might not be on speaking terms with the others."

Carruthers chuckled. "My, but you *are* a cynic, Captain," he said.

Groton glanced at Kozlov. "*Earth* doesn't speak with one voice, Admiral. Why the hell should they?"

"Nevertheless, Captain," Carruthers told him, "the landing force is on its own, at least for now. They are to stand down, avoid provoking the locals, and await further orders."

Groton left the flag bridge, seething.

Somehow he was going to have to change an admiral's mind, and that was always a pretty scary evolution.

"TELL ME about the Reptilians, Judi," Hunter said. "What happened?"

"I . . . they . . ." She shook her head. "I can't think about it! I *won't* think about it!"

Hunter and Lieutenant Bader were in the dome compartment that had been reserved for Judi Clarke. Bader had been brought over from Dome One, and Hunter's team was getting ready to move out, but he'd wanted to try to find out what the abductee knew about the aliens first. He was glad he had Simone Carter looking over his shoulder via Skype. She might be the expedition's senior xenopsychologist, but she'd been a *human* psychologist first. She would be able to guide him in the questioning.

He was afraid that if he pushed too hard, the woman would go right over the edge.

"It's okay, honey," Carter said, speaking from the laptop on a nearby desk. "You don't have to tell us anything you don't want. It would help if you can answer some questions, but it's up to you whether or not you do so. You understand? *You have a choice.*"

Judi swallowed, then nodded. "I . . . I was in my bedroom . . . asleep. I woke up to find these . . . these *things* in the bedroom with me. I couldn't move. I couldn't speak. They . . . they floated me up off the bed, and I floated . . . I *floated*. . . ."

"Go ahead, Judi," Carter said softly.

"I know you won't believe it, but they floated me through the wall! They took me to this kind of big shiny room. It was round. Lots of gleaming metal. They . . . they took my nightgown, and put me onto a kind of metal examination table. I still couldn't move!"

Hunter had heard of stories like this, but never believed them. This sort of thing *couldn't* happen in real life, could it? And the US government couldn't possibly agree to let this sort of thing happen to its citizens.

Yet he was living it, wasn't he? It was very, *very* real.

"They shoved something up inside me, *hard*. It hurt. The tallest one of them put his hand on my head, and the pain went away . . ."

"When was this, Judi?" Hunter asked. "What was the date?"

"It was 2012," she said. "Sometime in July . . ."

"Twenty-twelve! My God!" Hunter was thunderstruck. Had this woman been a prisoner for all these years?

"They talked to me after the . . . the exam," she said. "I would hear their questions in my head, and they seemed to be able to read the answers as they surfaced. They found out I was living alone . . . my parents were dead . . . my boyfriend had dumped me. . . ."

"You were alone," Carter said from the laptop.

"Yeah. I didn't have *anybody*. And they said they were going to keep me for a while."

"Why?" Hunter asked. "What did they want you for?"

"I'm not sure. But once, one of them kind of explained. I was in that . . . that horrible bottle, but he was standing outside and I could hear his thoughts, y'know? According to him, they've run into a kind of genetic bottleneck, was what he called it. Way up in the future. And genetic material taken from humans today is helping them straighten things out, to fix themselves. He actually *thanked* me for my contribution. . . ."

"Hey, Skipper?" It was Minkowski at the door. "Incoming call from *Big-H*."

"On my way." He looked at Carter's image on the laptop screen. "You want to keep talking with her?"

"I would, Commander. Thank you."

He looked at Bader. "See that she's well taken care of. And do whatever Dr. Carter tells you to, got it?"

"Yes, sir."

"Good man."

The radio call was from Groton. "Hello, Commander. You're not going to like this."

Now what? "Lay it on me, Captain."

"You're to stand down. Direct orders from the admiral. He doesn't want you provoking the locals."

Hunter was stunned. "Sir, we're engaged in combat now with the Saurians in addition to the hostiles outside! We can't just break it off! I have people out there—"

"I'm . . . getting some static on the channel, Commander," Groton told him.

Hunter hesitated. The channel was clear and open, no static. Then he realized what Groton was doing.

"Sir, you're breaking up. I'm not reading you."

"Strike Force, Strike Force . . . I'm not reading you."

Hunter cut the channel.

Stand down? Now? What the hell were they playing at? Hunter turned away and went to get his gear.

CHAPTER TWENTY

Die Glocke awoke
The Great Ones in the null.

SONG: "DIE GLOCKE" *VERSVS*,
THE MONOLITH DEATHCULT, 2017

THE XAXKI DREAMER *swam through endless vistas of radiance and joy. It had no name, not as humans would understand the concept. It knew who and what it was, and its companions, by the hundreds of billions, could touch its mind directly and know it as a distinct and particular identity.*

It was also very, very old, and had already been a distinct entity for millions upon tens of millions of years. For most of that incomprehensible expanse of time, it had been here within the virtual reality of the Xaxki Harmony. And when the Instrumentality pulled it out of its deep bliss, it was furious. The feelings of absolute and total pleasure drained away, leaving a bleak emptiness impossible to describe, impossible to comprehend.

"Why do you call me out and into the shadow world?" it demanded. "You have no right."

"The Instrumentality of the Xaxki has every right," a voice replied. "We are the Gods of Dreaming."

"But why me? I was building worlds!"

"Long ago, you faced an alien presence, a primitive alien presence, within Reality," the voice told it. "Aliens

have again entered our local Reality, and we need your experience in dealing with them."

A mental shrug, the Xaxki equivalent of a casual dismissal. "Destroy them."

"That may well prove to be the best course of action. But we need to communicate with them on a deeper level than is possible for us, to ferret out their role in the Great Game. You have the necessary experience."

"I was building worlds!*"*

"And so shall you again. But we must send your mind to meet these intruders lest they pose a threat to all the Dreamers."

The Dreamer considered this. Reality—the universe within which the Xaxki had evolved billions of years ago—was no match at all for the mental and emotional paradise of the Dreaming generated by the vast array of highly intelligent AIs that ringed the system, a literal paradise within which the Dreamers wiled away through the eons. There'd always been the slender chance, however, that other beings, other intelligences might arrive unnoticed by the Dreamers and wreak untold destruction. Those who had created the Dreaming Harmony, however, had planned for that possibility, creating the Guardians . . . and the option of waking a few Dreamers when the threat was grave.

The Guardians were artificial life-forms created to monitor the Reality surrounding this system, but important decisions still had to be left to the organic Xaxki.

Grumbling at its loss of pure ecstasy, the Dreamer adjusted its intake of sensory data, in effect reconnecting with its own physical body.

The Dreamer awoke.

WHEN HUNTER and his commandos broke into Dome Four, they found a firefight already in process. They emerged through the door behind a tight knot of Saurians and cut them down, as Master Sergeant Layton shouted at his team to cease fire in order to avoid scoring an own goal. Friendly fire, as the old military saying put it, isn't.

Hunter pivoted, laser pistol in both hands, as he tracked and killed a running Saurian.

For a long couple of seconds, everything was chaos, noise, and confusion. "Down, Commander!" Staff Sergeant Ann Seton yelled as she opened up on another Saurian a few feet behind him.

He didn't turn to look as he cut down another alien. "Thanks, Staff Sergeant!"

"Anytime, Skipper!"

Both of them kept firing.

But then something yawned open to Hunter's right. He wasn't sure at first what it was. It *looked* like a pucker in space, a place where light was being sharply bent, distorting the wall and struggling shapes beyond. It flickered, swelled, then stabilized into a hole hanging in the air, a foot above the deck and stretching five feet across. A sharp wind kicked up as the atmosphere inside the dome began streaming into the opening.

"What the hell?"

Somehow, the aliens had managed to create a gateway of some sort, a portal leading into darkness. Grays and Saurians alike were scrambling for the opening. Hunter could see small shapes moving on the other side and began firing into the apparition. Oddly, when he took several steps to the side, the hole still retained its original appearance, that of a perfect circle of darkness. In fact, it appeared the same no matter what the angle of his point of view, a spherical hole, rather than a flat two-dimensional opening.

Something, he decided, was very wrong with local space.

Several Saurians and their Gray allies were cut down in the mad dash for the portal, but at least a dozen leaped through and vanished. Master Sergeant Coulter looked like he was about to follow them through. "Belay that, Coulter!"

And in the next instant, the hole in space winked out.

For a few seconds, the combat team stood there, weapons raised, gaping at the spot where the hole had been. With the wind cut off, it had suddenly become very quiet.

"What the hell just happened?" Minkowski demanded.

"Some kind of extradimensional shortcut," Hunter said. Saying the words didn't mean he understood them. Saurian technology, it seemed, still held a number of surprises for humans.

Half a dozen of the little Grays were still in the dome, huddled in small groups, their huge eyes blinking slowly. Were they slaves? he wondered. He was beginning to think of them as worker drones, biological automatons used by the Saurians to do the dirty work.

"Round those characters up," Hunter said, pointing. "Mink, take a couple of guys and search the rest of the dome. Make sure no Saurians are still here."

"Aye, aye, sir!"

Two more men had been killed in the firefight: a Delta Force sergeant named Solomonsson and Captain Alan Arch. Hunter knelt beside the SAD/SOG operator, killed by a head shot. The energy beam had left very little above the man's neck. "What happened?"

"Don't know, sir," Layton said. "Everything was copacetic, and then the damned Saurs started shooting. Captain Arch was the first one hit."

Hunter got to his feet. "Okay. Layton? You've got Charlie Platoon."

"Yes, sir. Uh . . . what are your plans, sir?"

"Get the hell off this ice-ball rock and figure out how to take a few hundred civilians with us." He looked across the room at the huddle of Grays standing under Grabiak's watchful eye. "Which of you is the leader?" he demanded.

The Grays looked back and forth at one another, as if uncertain—or maybe they just didn't understand.

"One of you is the leader!" Hunter shouted. "If not, pick someone!"

Hesitantly, one of the Grays stepped forward. It was a little taller than the others, and Hunter wondered if rank among these remote descendants of humanity was simply a matter of literal stature.

"Come with me, skinhead," Hunter ordered. "I have some questions for you." He just hoped that he would get some answers that he could use.

LIEUTENANT DUVALL was still shaken by his experience inside the alien ship or world or whatever it had been. He and Bucky had not been mistreated in any way, but the monstrous worms had kept them isolated in a small compartment for what seemed like hours, though the actual elapsed time likely had been no more than minutes.

And then, without ceremony, they'd magically found themselves back on the TR-3R being catapulted into space.

He'd come away from the encounter feeling . . . small. *Very* small. The K'kurix, the Guardians—he'd not learned their name for themselves until his return to the *Hillenkoetter*—were so completely outside the human ken that the two species might never understand one another. Their casual space-bending technology made them seem like giants; the inaccessibility of their emotions, for humans, made them seem more like forces of nature, implacable, unstoppable, and beyond the reach of merely human reason.

Perhaps his biggest problem, he decided, was his inability to shift mental gears. For years, "little green men" had been the staple of gags and cartoons about alien visitors to Earth. They were flat and two-dimensional cartoonish beings that were completely human save for size, skin color, and the occasional presence of antennae.

Then he'd found out about the Grays and the somewhat similar Saurs, as the other pilots called them. They were weird, yeah, and even the discovery that the Grays were remote descendants of humanity couldn't mask that sense that they were somehow beyond human understanding.

But they *still* looked human—or humanlike. He could relate to them as intelligent beings, even if their thought processes were somewhere out in left field.

But the Xaxki . . .

From what nightmare had *they* crawled into the real world? They didn't fit into any part of the UFO mythology with which he was familiar—poison-breathing slugs half the length of a city bus.

God in heaven!

"Bucky? How you doin'?"

He and Lieutenant Bucknell hadn't taken part in the raid on the surface facility. They'd still been in *Hillenkoetter*'s sick bay, getting checked out after their brief imprisonment on the Xaxki planetoid. Released with clean bills of health, they were in one of the ship's crew lounges. A wall screen showed the dark world they were calling Serpo hanging below, beneath the icy light of two suns.

"Hey, Double-D," she said, looking up from the sofa. Her voice sounded flat, emotionless . . .

"You okay?"

"Still . . . trying to process what we saw. Those . . . those things were *horrible*."

She shuddered, and Duvall sat down next to her. The two of them were . . . close, in a comrades-in-arms way. They'd flirted—*anyplace, anytime, baby!*—but it had never been more serious than that. There was nothing flirtatious or sexual about the way he slipped his arm around her shoulders and drew her close.

"They got to me, too," he told her. "Especially when we started *seeing* things . . ."

That had been the worst part of the encounter. Bucknell had begun seeing images in her mind, but within a
second or two Duvall was seeing them, too, myriad . . .
shapes that were incomprehensible to the human inner
eye. It was like a dream where you know you're seeing
someone or something, but you can't make out what that
person or thing is, what they look like. These were mark-
ers of a sort for something that could not be seen, and that
made them all the more frightening.

At the same time, both humans had had the inescap-
able feeling that they were being minutely and intensely
studied by minds cool and calculating, by minds utterly
lacking any recognizable emotion, minds bent on agendas unimaginably intricate and vast.

It was like, Duvall imagined, being closely examined
by gods, millions of gods, millions upon millions of god-
like minds.

Neither of them could move during that inspection,
but then, as if a light switch had been flicked off, the
mentalities around them were gone and they were back
in the cockpit of their TR-3R, accelerating into space.

Duvall didn't think he would ever be able to shake that
feeling of dread and of microbial insignificance, of being spread out helpless beneath the cold gaze of entities
utterly divorced from human emotions. None less than
Dr. Carter, *Hillenkoetter*'s senior shrink, as he thought
of her, had interviewed him after his return. He'd told her
what he imagined she would want to hear. He didn't want
to be taken off flight status.

"I don't know about you, Bucky, but I need to log some
hours. How about you?"

"Where? Doing what?"

"Schuller told me they lost two Stingrays in the strike
on the planet."

"Who?"

"Bobbo Selby . . . and the skipper."

"No! Are they . . . ?"

"Don't know. But it won't hurt to go poke around and see."

"But all aerospace craft have been restricted to the *Big-H*!"

"I know. But I think the bastards are gonna leave our people down there." Duvall tried to contain the surge of anger he felt at that. You never, *ever* left someone behind. *Never.*

And leaving people to face nightmare horrors like the inhabitants of those ring fragments made the betrayal infinitely worse.

"We're not going to get clearance," Bucknell said. "You know that, right?"

He grinned at her. "There are ways around that. You with me?"

Her jaw set in a determined scowl. "Fuckin' A. Let's go!"

GROTON SLUMPED in his command chair, glowering. That old "you're breaking up" trick would not fool anyone for long. There was an audio transcript of all radio communications, and any command authority could check and hear for themselves that there'd been no comm interference. This was the first time he'd ever heard of both parties playing the same game. Hunter had been quick on the uptake, and would do whatever he needed to do down there.

But what might happen once Carruthers checked up on them was anybody's guess.

The chances were good, though, that the incident would end in a court martial.

"Captain!" *Hillenkoetter*'s combat officer called from his console.

"What is it?"

"We have a ship leaving the *Hillenkoetter* without authorization!"

"What ship?"

"TR-3R Delta, sir. We don't know who the pilot is."

"Are you in touch with them?"

"No, sir. We're trying, but no radio contact."

Groton slumped farther. Someone else who didn't like the orders.

A military organization works, can only work, through total and complete obedience to orders. The American military was not as absolute with this as it could be. Individual soldiers, sailors, and aviators were encouraged to think for themselves, and to question any order that could be considered illegal.

But that didn't mean they were allowed to hare off on their own, refusing orders with which they disagreed. Questioning orders was definitely *not* considered to be a positive career move.

He supported Carruthers in the hope for a peaceful resolution to this.

But that hope was growing thinner by the minute, and he would *not* sit by and watch his people sacrificed out of blind desire for appeasement.

SNEAKING THE TR-3R off the flight line on *Hillenkoetter*'s flight deck and through the kinetic field had been simpler than he'd imagined. The kinetic fields were controlled by computer—they *had* to be for the precise timing required—and it had been a simple matter to shift control of the computer to his own console. Then he'd gotten things rolling by asking PryFly for permission to move the spacecraft to the number three elevator to take it down a deck for maintenance. The routine request had been granted, but he'd taken a hard turn to port en route, requested passage directly from the computer, and slipped through the field in a sudden, intense burst of escaping atmosphere. The shields slammed shut directly astern as the TR-3R cleared the deck, and Duvall turned the transport toward the looming planet below.

"TR-3R Delta!" came over the radio. "TR-3R Delta! What the hell are you doing?"

"Don't reply," he told Bucknell. "Radio silence."

"You think they'll shoot us down?"

"I doubt it." He engaged the controls and increased the transport's velocity, accelerating toward the planet. "They'll need clearance from the bridge for something that drastic, and that will take time. But no reason for them to think we're listening . . . or figure out who we are."

Besides, he hoped, there would be those aboard the *Big-H* who would hesitate, even balk, at being ordered to shoot down a friendly.

Even so, he pushed the craft as hard as he could to get them out of the *Big-H*'s particle beam range.

The night side of the planet loomed huge just below.

FOLLOWING THE instructions given to him by the Gray, Hunter dropped the perimeter defenses and led a small team out and into the icy wastes beyond. As the shield went back up behind them, he was left with a palpable feeling of isolation, of loneliness.

Thirty-nine light-years from home. . . .

Alfa Platoon picked its way down the rocky hill, spread out, alert for signs of the attacking aliens. Marlow had started calling the Volkswagen-sized creatures "pill-bugs," and the name had stuck. Hunter had assumed that they belonged to the Xaxki, but according to the people back aboard the *Big-H*, the Xaxki Guardians knew nothing about them. *Someone*, Hunter thought, wasn't talking to others in their chain of command.

At the moment, the hillside outside the alien base was empty. Where the hell had they all gone? Their dead bodies, he knew, crumbled away into nothingness. But it was unnerving to know the things could come and go so suddenly.

"Which way, Colby?"

"That way, sir," the radioman said, pointing. "I have a solid fix on the transponder."

"Range?"

"Not sure, Commander. But I think it came down right over there behind those big boulders."

The boulders were the size of a three-story building, raw, rugged, and slick with ice. The thirteen men of Alfa Platoon picked their way down through the haze-chocked darkness, their helmet lights casting bizarre shapes and movements across the faces of the rocks.

Coulter had point and was first to round the boulder. "There it is, Commander," he called. "Eighty yards."

The first of the two downed Stingray fighters lay scattered across the landscape, wings and hull shredded by the impact. There was no evidence of fire, of course, not in an atmosphere lacking oxygen, but frightfully hot metal was steaming in the night, putting up a roiling fog.

The pilot was dead.

"Okay," Hunter said. "Bring him. We're not leaving him *here*."

Hunter wasn't particularly religious, but—what was the pilot's name? Selby. Robert Selby. He deserved a proper burial back home.

Assuming they could get him there.

"Got a lock on the other transponder, Skipper," Colby told him. "*That* way."

The team continued making their way across the alien, hostile landscape.

And that was important, Hunter thought. They were a *team* now, not a disparate gaggle of military personnel from different services, different backgrounds, different traditions. SEALs, Marines, Army SOF—they all were working together, a smoothly functioning machine, and he was intensely proud of them. So much of an elite unit's élan came from their knowledge that they were simply the *best*.

And now here they were, proving it once and for all.

They struggled along across nearly three miles of rock and tholin-slimed ice before approaching the second downed fighter. This one had bellied in across a flat stretch of icy ground, the fuselage remaining more or less intact. Weapons at the ready, six men crouched in a defensive perimeter, while six more, with Hunter, moved in closer.

The attack came out of nowhere—hundreds of the massive pillbugs pushing and lumbering across the rocky ground. Where the hell had they come from? One moment the rocky ground had been bare; the next, it looked like the ground was moving in ponderous, segmented waves.

Nielson was hit, his helmet exploding in a bloody spray of plastic, metal, and bone. Then Alvarez went down, his gloved hands frantically pressing against a ragged tear in the torso of his suit. That was the terrible part of combat in a poisonous environment like this one. *Any* damage to your environmental suit could kill you in seconds, no matter how minor the wound. The human force dropped to the ground, pouring fire into the surrounding attackers, burning them down one after another after another. The aliens tried closing in, but in such numbers, and in so uncoordinated a manner, that they were bumping up against one another and blocking the rush of those behind.

And then . . .

They were gone.

Hunter stood up slowly, blinking. The field around the platoon had been filled with those lumbering horrors, and now they all had vanished. A dozen dead pillbugs were scattered about the landscape, but those would be gone as well in minutes. What the hell was going on? He was prepared to call it an illusion, some sort of hallucination, as the Saurians claimed—except for the fact that Nielson and Alvarez both were dead, their suited bodies broken, twisted, and steaming on the icy ground.

"What the fuck was *that* all about, Skipper?" Minkowski demanded.

"I don't know. Someone's playing games with us,

maybe." He gestured toward the downed fighter, now a hundred yards up ahead. "C'mon. Let's go check it out."

The fighter's cockpit hatch cycled open as they approached, and a haggard figure in a flight BioSuit stood up. "Man, am I glad to see *you* guys!"

"You okay?"

"Got dinged up a bit on the landing, but . . . yeah." He extended a gloved hand. "Lieutenant Commander Boland."

"Commander Hunter. Welcome to our world. . . ."

The downed pilot looked around. "Looks like the natives are restless, sir."

"And then some. I just wish I knew where the hell they've gone."

"*And* if they'll be back."

"Right." Hunter gestured up the hill. "Let's get back to the domes."

From everything Hunter had ever heard of the alien Grays, they had advanced technology, sure . . . but it was nothing like magic. A twenty-first century human could grasp that what they did was possible, even if humans couldn't do it yet.

But since encountering the Xaxki, Hunter was becoming convinced that there was another dimension to life in the Galaxy, that some species were inconceivably old, and possessed technologies and ways of understanding the cosmos that were completely beyond the ken of mere mortals. These were civilizations that were truly godlike, so far as humans were concerned . . . and just pray that humankind never came into conflict with them, because mere humans would not stand a chance.

Such civilizations would be powerful enough to reach out and swat the entire human species like an insect. The thought made the universe far larger, far darker, and far more dangerous than Hunter had ever imagined. The diminutive Grays and the malevolent Saurians both seemed downright homey by comparison.

Hunter shivered, as if touched by the cold outside his suit, then continued up the slope.

MOMENTS AFTER completing the fiery atmospheric entry, Duvall brought the TR-3R into level flight a thousand feet above the ground, which was lost in an icy night beneath a solid ceiling of clouds. Beside him, Bucknell had the TR's see-in-the-dark vision switched on and was scanning the ground below with the craft's ventral FLIR sensors. Information loaded on the craft's navigation computer would pinpoint the location of the surface structures seen from orbit. Finding the alien base should be as simple as following a preprogrammed guide path straight to the target.

"Got 'em, Boss. Left ten degrees."

"Left ten . . ."

He put the recon craft into a gentle bank to port. Up ahead, atop a small mountain, he could see the domes of the alien settlement. And closer, visible on Bucky's viewscreen, was a toiling line of white figures trudging up the slope. The FLIR was set to show heat sources as white and light gray, and colder surfaces as black or dark gray. Environmental suits were not particularly efficient at conserving heat, and they leaked like sieves at infrared wavelengths. He could see individual heating units like tiny, bright stars on the back of each figure.

"Hang on, Bucky. We're going down."

THUNDER ROLLED, and Hunter looked up. He saw nothing but cloud wrack at first . . . but then a barely-glimpsed black triangle passed across a slightly less dark backdrop of clouds, banking into a broad, sweeping turn. He pointed. "Colby! See if you can raise them!"

"Briggs already has them, Skipper. But I'll patch you in through him."

"This is JSST Alfa Platoon," Hunter said, "calling unidentified spacecraft over this position. Come in!"

"JSST Alfa," a voice came back. "This is unidentified flying object TR-3R Delta. You guys need a lift?"

"We're going to need a lot more than a 3R," Hunter replied. "I'll have them lower the shields. You touch down in the middle of the compound . . . and we'll talk."

CHAPTER TWENTY-ONE

I suspect that in the past sixty years or so that there has been some back-engineering (of E.T. technologies) and the creation of this type of equipment. But it's not nearly as sophisticated yet as what the visitors have.

DR. EDGAR MITCHELL, APOLLO 14 ASTRONAUT, 1996

HANS KAMMLER FELT *the alien mind as it crawled into his, icy and cold. It felt to him as though that mind had been hammering in a vain attempt to reach him, but then had surged through, a tidal wave of alien thought and purpose filling his skull. In agony, he opened his mouth, trying desperately to scream, but nothing could emerge into the green liquid around him.*

You have moved through time, *a Voice thundered inside his brain. It was like . . . like a recognition.* You have been under the control of The Surviving Few. *It was a harsh accusation.*

Please, *he thought.* Please . . . I don't know what you're saying. Please help me. . . .

Information spilled across the telepathic channel. Kammler didn't know how he knew, but he was certain that he was feeling the flame of an immensely powerful mind, something called the Xaxki Dreamer, something awakened by beings called the Guardians and sent here to . . . to . . . what?

To talk with him?

No, he corrected himself . . . to talk with humans. The Xaxki were only dimly aware of humans on this world, and sought to speak with them.

But Kammler, trapped in a bottle, naked and helpless and terrified, was in no condition to talk with anyone.

Then with a suddenness that left him broken and achingly alone, the Mind was gone.

DUVALL STEPPED off the ladder and onto the rocky surface. The hull still hot, the TR-3R rested on three landing legs, steaming in the alien night. A dozen men in combat armor faced him, weapons at the ready. "Lieutenant Duvall," he said, hands raised. These guys seemed a bit . . . hair-trigger.

"Lieutenant Commander Hunter," one of them said, lowering his weapon. "Welcome to Velat."

"I thought this was Serpo?"

"Velat is what the Saurs call it."

"Double-D!" another suited figure said. "Good to see you, bro!"

"Commander Boland?"

"The same. What the hell are you doing down here?"

"Setting myself up for a court martial, I think. You guys know they're sitting tight upstairs? No ships to come down to the planet, and you folks are to stay put!"

"We know," Hunter said with dry understatement. "I gather you two know each other?"

"Same squadron," Duvall said. "He's my CO."

"Is Bucky with you?"

"Sure is." He jerked a thumb over his shoulder. "She's on the 3R, just in case I needed fire support out here."

"Okay. How many people can a 3R carry?" Hunter wanted to know. "Maximum load, really packed in."

"I dunno, sir. Things are pretty tight. There's a cargo hold aft . . . might hold fifteen, maybe eighteen people if they didn't mind being real friendly."

"Damn."

"Why? How many you got, sir?"

"Three platoons . . . forty-eight people, with several casualties. Problem is, we have a shitload of civilians, human civilians, in the basement. We're not going to leave them here!"

"How many?"

"Three hundred or so."

Duvall whistled. "No way in hell I could carry *that* kind of load. That's three trips for a TR-3B, at least."

"Or three TR-3Bs in one flight." Hunter appeared to be thinking furiously. "Okay, tell you what. I'm going to send you back to the *Big-H* with one platoon, including all of the casualties and Commander Boland, here, okay? Meanwhile, I'll get on the horn to see if we can get an evac going."

"And how are you going to strong-arm an admiral into doing what you want? Sir."

"I'll get him to see reason," Hunter said, "if I have to crawl through the radio link and dope-slap the bastard."

ON THE flag bridge of the USSS *Hillenkoetter*, Admiral Charles Carruthers scowled at Paul King. "What do you mean they refuse to talk with us?"

"I do not believe humans matter to them in any way whatsoever, Admiral," King replied.

"Da," Kozlov added. "In fact, I feel we may have here the solution to the so-called Fermi paradox."

"I thought the Fermi paradox was null and void," Captain Groton said. "'Where are they?' Turns out they're right here. . . ."

"That's not the point," King replied, a little brusquely. "We know alien civilizations are everywhere, even right on our cosmic doorstep, and yet all are silent. The paradox remains."

Carruthers considered this. In the mid-twentieth century, physicist Enrico Fermi, over lunch with his colleagues, had famously put forward the question, "Where is everybody?" The question centered on the likelihood of intelligent alien life, and the mathematics that declared that *even without faster-than-light*, a star-faring civilization would fill the entire Galaxy in just a few million years. Some civilizations, perhaps, would be uninterested in colonizing the stars, some would exterminate themselves before getting that far, but all it would take was *one.* . . .

Of course, at that time, in 1950, Fermi had no way of knowing that space-traveling aliens *had* been discovered, and their recovered technologies were already being studied. But the question remained; planets were now known to be ridiculously commonplace; the chemistry of life dictated that it would arise almost spontaneously on any planet with even remotely favorable parameters; the sky *should* be filled with the noise of alien civilizations.

But it wasn't. Even with proof of alien civilizations out there, the skies remained dark and silent.

Or, at the very least, humans were technologically deaf to their communications networks, and no one was building megaconstructions out there big enough to be visible from Earth.

So even among those cognoscenti aware of the alien presence, the Fermi paradox remained . . . troubling. Humans now knew of some eighty alien species, either directly or by way of the Grays, but for the most part they remained silent and unseen.

Kozlov was suggesting that if there *were* many more civilizations out there far more advanced than humankind, few, if any, had any interest in something as primitive as humans.

"Maybe so," Carruthers said. "But these Xaxki had damned well *better* talk to us. We have people down there on the surface!"

People . . . and a rogue recon transport. TR-3R Delta had been tracked down to the alien mountaintop compound. Carruthers had the nightmare feeling that the entire mission was going right down the tubes.

"And it is for that reason that we must be particularly careful," King told him. "We appear to have landed in the middle of a full-blown war. One side is so powerful we don't dare anger them. The other, the Grays and the Saurians, are powerful as well . . . and they're currently on Earth and must be placated."

"We cannot afford to anger either group," Kozlov added.

"With respect, sir," Groton said, "we can't leave our people down there on Serpo."

"I *heard* you, Captain." Carruthers was annoyed with the man. Groton had been hammering out that same complaint for hours, now. He more than half suspected that Groton had sent that TR-3R down to the planet against his orders.

"Sir, from the sound of it, they've already been in combat with the Saurians. We also have reports of a number—a very large number—of civilian prisoners. Human prisoners. I respectfully submit that the Saurians aren't going to get any madder than they are already, and that the Xaxki want us out of there anyway. The faster we move on this, the better. Sir."

Carruthers felt trapped, and he didn't like it one bit. He'd ordered a halt to hostilities on the planet's surface at the urging of the two ambassadors in order to appease the Xaxki, only to learn that the human forces down there were battling it out with the Saurians. And that, apparently, the Xaxki didn't really care about humans one way or the other.

An old declaration had it that "the enemy of my enemy is my friend." Evidently, the Xaxki didn't think like that. They seemed to want nothing to do with any outsiders entering their system—true xenophobes.

And Carruthers wasn't sure he could blame them. They lived a precarious existence, hidden away within their artificially generated dream worlds, but vulnerable to any psychopathically inclined aliens who might come along. Their Guardians were the equivalent of crotchety old men, standing on their porch and shouting, "Hey, you kids! Get off my lawn!"

And the conflict between humans and Saurians on their planetary doorstep could only reinforce their opinion of outsiders. No wonder the Xaxki didn't want to talk with them.

"Admiral?" Colbert, a senior aide, said from a nearby console.

"What is it?"

"Sir, message from the planet. Commander Hunter reports that he has 315 civilian nudists down there who require immediate transport back to the *Hillenkoetter*. He says . . . uh . . ."

"Out with it, Lieutenant. He says what?"

"Sir . . . that if you don't send down two TR-3Bs and a team of medical technicians to help with the transfer stat, then he will *personally* come up here and, ah, *explain* things to you."

"Those weren't his exact words, were they?"

"No, sir."

Carruthers chuckled. "Okay. We'll deal with the issue of insubordination later. Right now, Captain Groton, please send two TR-3Bs down as . . . *requested*."

King shook his head. "Admiral, I still feel that—"

"We tried giving peace a chance," Carruthers said. "Now let's let the military have a go."

"YOU THINK Carruthers will cave?" Briggs asked Hunter. Alfa Platoon had returned to Dome Two, where he stood in a puddle of water as the stuff condensed out of the air and onto the frigid surface of his environmental suit.

"I don't know, Master Sergeant," Hunter replied. "If I need to hitch a ride upstairs on the recon ship and have words with the guy face-to-face, I will. Mink? How are things going with the decanting?"

"We've got a good start, sir," Minkowski replied. "Last time I checked they had about thirty people pulled out of those cylinders and recovering." He shook his head, his eyes showing horror. "My God, sir! Those people were just being *stored* in those tubes. Like spare parts! Awake and everything!"

"Any . . . problems?" Hunter tapped the side of his head with a forefinger.

"You mean psychological problems? Not really, sir. Most of them seem to be feeling relieved more than anything else. A few had hysterics when we pulled them out. Doc Marlow is giving them sedatives."

"Okay. Keep them warm and dry, and we'll see about getting them up to the *Big-H*."

"Absolutely, Skipper."

"Staff Sergeant Daly!"

"Sir!"

"Pick three men and suit up. You're going to go up to the ship with Duvall on that TR-3R outside."

For just an instant, Hunter thought the Army SpecOps operator was going to give him an argument, but the man shuttered his expression. "Yes, sir!"

"You will take all of the wounded with you, Miss Clarke, and as many of the other civilians as you can pack on board that ship. And when you board the *Hillenkoetter*, you make a *big* noise about getting a couple of 3Bs down here stat. Go all the way to the admiral's office and sit on his desk if you have to. Understand?"

The expressionless mask broke with the slightest of grins. "Yes, sir. *That* I can do, sir!"

"Good." He thought for a moment. "Take Marine staff sergeant Seton with you."

"Commander!" Seton said. She'd been standing close enough to hear. "Are you saying that because I'm *female*?"

"Yes, Staff Sergeant. I'm saying it because Miss Clarke and some of the other women from downstairs might appreciate having a *woman* with them."

"Yes, sir."

Hunter was torn between sending as many of the refugees up to orbit as he could, or as many of his own men as possible. The cold truth remained, though, that only a tiny fraction of the humans on this planet could reach the *Hillenkoetter* on the recon transport; they needed at least two of the far larger TR-3Bs down here to get everyone off.

In the meantime, if the vanishing pillbugs launched another attack on the compound, he needed enough men down here to hold them off. Ultimately he'd decided to send the absolute minimum of his personnel—just enough to maintain order on the transport . . . and to make that "big noise" back on the *Hillenkoetter* he wanted.

"Mink?"

"Sir!"

"Get that lizard in here. The leader."

A moment later, Minkowski returned with the Saurian. He looked down at the alien. "Do you have a name?" he demanded.

"No."

The answer surprised Hunter, but so little about these beings made any sense at all.

"As of right now, your name is Joe. Okay?"

"Joe. But I do not require a—"

"No, but *I* damn well do!"

"Yes, sir."

The honorific startled Hunter more than the alien's lack of a name. Evidently, it had been listening . . . and learning.

Or perhaps it assumed that "Sir" was Hunter's name.

"You told me a while ago that we can't teleport from the planet onto the *Hillenkoetter* because of the difference in relative velocities. Right?"

"Yes."

"The way I see it, we have two options. We have the *Hillenkoetter* match velocities with this spot on the planet . . . or we have them send down transport space-craft to pick us up."

"Yes."

"Okay. Are you willing to show us how to work this system, so we can get off this planet?"

This was the worrisome part. Would the Saurian leader help them? Or would it refuse, or, worse, pretend to help them but pull some kind of sneaky, high-tech trick that would teleport them all into hard vacuum or the interior of a sun? Just missing the target and dropping an unprotected man on the surface of Serpo would be more than enough to kill him.

Hunter had no idea how he could even begin to trust the alien.

"Joe" seemed to be reading Hunter's thoughts. Perhaps it was.

"Sir . . . I assure you that we want you and your kind off of this planet just as much as you wish to be gone. Further, *we* wish to be gone, as well. Our one ship on this world was destroyed in your last attack."

"Your ship? When was that?"

The Saurian passed a skinny hand over a nearby console. On a screen, a building, low and squat like a bunker, could be seen embedded in the side of the mountain. Human fighters flashed overhead, one after another, and then the bunker erupted in a violent flash.

Hunter studied the image. "That building . . . it connects with this base?"

"Through a tunnel to the lower floor, yes."

"Could we get out that way?"

"No. Not any longer. The tunnel has collapsed completely."

Damn. For a moment, there, Hunter had thought he'd seen a way out.

"So how do we get out?"

"We do have a dimensional transport system operational . . . what you call teleportation. If one of your ships were to land outside this base, we could use the system to . . . to open a kind of tunnel *past* space. Your people— and we—could use that tunnel to get on board your ship and make our escape."

"What about that kinetic field outside?"

"That would have to be lowered, of course, for your ship to land within the compound."

Hunter nodded. They'd lowered the shield to let Duvall in with his TR-3R, and to permit the recon team to enter. The shields were up once more. "What if they land outside?"

"They would be attacked by the Dreamers, of course. When we drop the shield, the Dreamers will be able to enter the compound and attack us here."

Hunter nodded, picturing the tactical problems. If Carruthers got off his ass and sent down a couple of TR-3Bs, they could escape, along with all of the human prisoners in the basement downstairs. The discovery of all those civilians changed things, made things far more urgent.

Hillenkoetter couldn't help, not directly, not blocked by that damned shield.

No, it was up to him.

Could he trust the Saurians?

Of course not! But what other choice did he have?

"Where are you guys from, anyway?" he asked the being. "What is your homeworld?"

"Earth," it replied.

"You mean you plan on taking over Earth? Earth will be yours in the future?"

"Earth was ours in the past," it told him. "From one point of view, it still is."

It seemed open and forthcoming with its answers, but Hunter didn't understand. No matter. He had a plan of action now, a way to get out of this trap.

"You or your people will show us how to operate the dimensional transporter?"

"Of course."

"And you will help us free the people you've been holding downstairs?"

The being hesitated at that. "There is no reason to bring them along. They are useless to us now."

"They are human beings!" he shouted, and some of the people in the control room jumped at the yell. The Saurian flinched. Hunter took a deep breath and added, somewhat more calmly, "They are our people, they are under my protection, and they are going back with us. Period."

"As you say."

But the Saurian did not sound convinced.

TWENTY MINUTES later, Duvall stared at a *spherical* something shimmering above the control center's deck. "That leads to my ship?" he asked.

"That's what the lizard says," Hunter told him. Their pet Saurian had manipulated some controls, and a kind of hole had opened up inside the control room, a hole with edges blurred by sharp distortions of space, a *spherical* hole which suggested a twist through higher dimensions— like the one they had seen in Dome Four. Hunter raised his voice and addressed the room at large. "Listen up, people! I need a volunteer to check this out. . . ."

"Never mind," Duvall said. "I'll do it. It's my ship. Besides, I'm already suited up." He snapped down the visor of his helmet, sealing it.

"Lieutenant, I don't—"

"Bucky here can fly the ship if . . . well, if things go bad."

"Stay in radio contact, then."

"Yes, sir." Steeling himself, he stepped into the sphere, crouching a bit to make his lanky frame fit . . .

. . . and immediately stepped onto the narrow cargo deck of the TR-3R.

"I'm through," he said over his radio link.

"Copy that," Hunter's voice came back. "Lieutenant Bucknell's coming through behind you."

A spherical blur opened nearby, appearing to be unfolding from the bulkhead, and then Bucky materialized within the blur and walked out. "Permission to come aboard," she said, grinning through her visor.

"Granted," Duvall said. "Jesus, that is the *weirdest* way to travel I've ever seen!"

"Just like *Star Trek*."

"Well, not exactly. No sparkly lights. C'mon, let's get topside."

The two of them had climbed the ship's ladder forward and entered the flight deck. Strapping into their seats, they began running down the launch checklist and warming up the ship's systems.

"Main power," he said, his gloved hand dancing over the main touch screen.

"Green," Bucky told him.

"Drive."

"Hot."

"Nav."

"Green."

"Com."

"Go . . ."

As they went down the checklist, the ship rocked ever so slightly. People were filing through that damned weird hole in space and entering the cargo bay, their accumulating weight causing the craft to shift slightly as they moved. A few moments later, Staff Sergeant Ann Seton's voice came over the TR-3R's intercom. "We're all on board, Lieutenant," she told him. "As many as we could squeeze in, anyway."

"How many is that?" he asked.

"Twelve refugees, four wounded, and the four of us."

Duvall tried to imagine twenty people packed into that cargo deck. The word *sardines* came to mind.

"Brace yourselves as well as you can back there," he said. "There won't be any high accelerations, so you should be okay braced against one another on the deck, but if I have to maneuver you might get thrown back and forth a bit." He opened a radio channel. "Velat Base, TR-3R Delta ready for liftoff."

"Copy, Delta. We'll drop the compound shield in five . . . four . . . three . . . two . . . one . . . *now!*"

The triangular ship rose from the ground on humming gravitics, rising straight up until it was well clear of the base. "Velat Base, Delta, we are at five hundred feet. We're clear of the shield."

"Thank you, Delta. Shield is up. Have a safe trip!"

"I'll be back with a couple of 3Bs in tow, Velat, just as quick as I can manage it!"

And he swung the ship's nose toward heaven and accelerated.

"THEY'RE AWAY," Hunter said. "Okay, people. Everyone into your BioSuits. Check your weapons. I want everyone ready to move as soon as those transports arrive. Bravo Platoon? Are you ready?"

"Will be in a moment, Skipper," Billingsly replied. "We're still down here hauling civilians out of these damned vats."

"Any problems?"

"Yessir. Not enough towels."

Hunter chuckled. Unlikely as it had seemed, they *had* turned up a supply of towels and blankets in a kind of alien linen closet. Evidently, even highly evolved Grays from the remote future needed to dry off occasionally, though the shower facilities appeared to use jets of warm air for the purpose, rather than cloth.

But there weren't enough, not by far, for over three hundred people.

"Do the best you can. Charlie Platoon. What's your status?"

"Outside on the perimeter, sir," Layton told him. "No sign of activity."

"Okay. When the transports touch down, I want you guys to hold that perimeter, just in case the Dreamers get frisky. When I give you the word, you will fall back on the transports and board one through the airlock."

"Roger that, Commander."

Was there anything he was missing? Hunter was racking his brain, trying to spot any holes in the opplan. There were only two major problems he could see. If Admiral Carruthers refused to send the transports down was one. The other was the danger of trusting the aliens. The Grays seemed meek, even docile, but those Saurians were downright sneaky, and they could be nasty. A number of Saurians had escaped at the end of that last firefight. Where they might be and what they were up to were the great unknowns here.

"So what are we going to do with you, Joe?" he asked in a conversational tone. The Saurian looked at him through emotionless, vertically slit pupils, the eyes golden and unblinking.

"I imagine your superiors will determine that," the being told him. It didn't sound concerned. "We have a large colony on Earth at this time. I imagine we will be released to them."

"A large colony? Where?"

The slitted eyes remained fixed on his. "I can't imagine that you expect me to answer that, Commander. We have a number of bases there, however, in large caverns and under the oceans. We've been there for a *very* long time."

Hunter had known that, though he still didn't know how they managed to stay so completely hidden from humans. Scuttlebutt said they were everywhere, manipulating human politics, abducting humans, possibly even working toward the overthrow of humankind. Hunter wasn't sure how much of the scuttlebutt to believe, but they say there's no smoke without fire.

"Commander!" Colby called out. "Message from the *Hillenkoetter*: two TR-3Bs are now en route to Velat!"

Hunter's eyes remained locked with the Saurian's unblinking gaze. "Excellent," he said. "Pass the word to Bravo to step up the decanting."

The sooner they were off this nightmare world, the better.

CHAPTER TWENTY-TWO

> Would we, if we could, educate and sophisticate
> pigs, geese, cattle? Would it be wise to establish
> diplomatic relation with the hen that now functions,
> satisfied with mere sense of achievement by way of
> compensation? I think we're property.

CHARLES FORT, *THE BOOK OF THE DAMNED*, 1919

HELPLESS, KAMMLER WATCHED *as a pair of space-suited men unsealed the narrow tube within which he'd been floating in green liquid for God alone knew how long. A third man tapped away at a small touch screen nearby, and with a shock of renewed terror, Kammler felt the tubes in his throat and in more private parts of his anatomy being withdrawn, and needles embedded in his throat and at his groin retracting. He tried telling himself that these people were trying to rescue him, to get him out of the tank, but his mind gibbered and thrashed, certain that any change would be bad.*

The memory of that intrusive, invading Mind still haunted him. Full-blown paranoia stirred nightmare horror, chilling his brain and throat and belly.

The green liquid drained suddenly away and he began gasping and retching, a terrible pain clawing at his lungs as the oxygenated liquid was violently forced from them. He drew his first ragged, agonizing breath in . . . how long?

How long?

Abruptly, the tube tilted forward, bringing him horizontal and face down. Several hands reached in to haul him bodily out into the air and light.

"Take it easy there, mister," a not-unfriendly voice told him. "Go ahead and cough as hard as you can to get that green shit out of your chest."

After one desperate, gurgling breath, he couldn't inhale again. He retched . . . and retched again, as green liquid gushed and then dribbled from both nose and mouth. His heart hammered in his chest as though it was going to burst. He was strangling, drowning in air . . .

. . . and then, at last, air flooded his tortured lungs. He lay on the cold deck for a moment, gasping, panting, coughing, trying to catch his breath.

Fingers pressed at the angle of his jaw, seeking his pulse, then patted him on his back. "Okay," a voice said. "This one's good to go."

Elsewhere in that dark room, other tubes were being upended, their pitiful human contents spilled coughing and gagging onto the floor. Someone handed him a towel. It was sopping wet, having been used by God knew how many other rescued prisoners.

"I need my clothes," he managed to say, though the effort seared his burning throat.

"Sorry, fella," the voice said. "We don't have 'em and you don't have the time if we did. I need you to sit up as soon as you think you can manage it. Here, let me have the towel. . . ."

The room, he saw, was filled with naked people being ushered along by a handful of space-suited figures. The room was freezing cold, a sharp and abrupt shift from the temperature-neutral environment of the tank.

"Please," he said. "What is happening?"

"No time! Think you can stand? Good. Go with that group over there. Quick, quick!"

Kammler stumbled forward on cold bare feet.

The terror grew worse. He'd seen scenes like this, exactly like this, decades before—before his escape through time. At Auschwitz . . . crowds of terrified, naked people in a shambling press, herded through cold, dark passageways toward a room behind a massive steel door, toward a room with a sign above the door reading Duschen.

Showers.

"Raus, Juden! Bewegt euch! Schnell! Schnell!" *The memories, the screaming memories came flooding in, filling his brain.*

Kammler shrieked as his knees buckled under him, and he collapsed.

TWO HOURS had passed since the two TR-3Bs had departed from *Hillenkoetter*'s flight deck. Carruthers looked at his senior aide, who was seated at a nearby console monitoring the ship's communications channels. "Colbert!"

"Sir?"

"Status update."

"TR-3B Alfa and Charlie are now on the ground, Admiral. They report that 1-JSST is loading the refugees as we speak. Estimated liftoff . . . they say another ten minutes. TR-3R Delta has recovered on the flight deck. Medical personnel are seeing to the refugees and the wounded, sir."

"Any problem from the aliens?"

"Not that anyone's mentioned, sir."

Carruthers allowed himself to relax ever so slightly. Perhaps they were going to get away with this after all. Like Hunter, he had deep reservations about trusting the aliens, *especially* the Saurians. Vashnu had told them repeatedly not to trust the ugly little creatures, but he didn't need the reminder.

What he still needed to give some careful thought to was what disciplinary actions he was going to take. Duvall and Hunter both had been operating out of the very best of motives, but that did not excuse rank insubordination and direct violations of orders. Damn it, the chain of command needed to be respected.

In a far corner of the flag bridge, Vashnu was in quiet conference with King and Kozlov, and Carruthers watched them narrowly. He didn't trust *them* either. Not the beings that called themselves humans from the future, and not the so-called ambassadors. Carruthers had heard endless stories back on Earth and at Darkside about aliens infiltrating the highest levels of every government on Earth, of alien influence behind the scenes as they brazenly manipulated everything from stock prices to oil futures to international politics to government social policy. World leaders were puppets controlled by aliens . . . or by beings who might as well *be* aliens despite their claims to the contrary. According to some, Earth was already owned by alien powers, and they'd quietly invaded the planet and taken it over without firing a single shot or landing a single spaceship on the White House lawn.

He'd dismissed those stories, or most of them, as sheer moonshine . . . but lately he'd begun to wonder. That aliens were present on Earth was undeniable. So was the fact of wholesale cover-ups and disinformation from the government. The question soon became . . . *why?* Why the secrecy? Why the transparent lies?

Why a policy of deception that had dominated human politics for the past seventy-some years?

As one of the cognoscenti, Carruthers knew the official line. If humanity knew the truth, people wouldn't be able to handle it. There would be panic . . . riots . . . revolution . . . the collapse of every human institution from the stock market to the Vatican.

But sometimes the official line just wasn't enough. What were the visitors *really* after?

"Admiral!" Colbert called. "Sensor department reports an unknown spacecraft has just come up alongside!"

"What?"

"It's *pacing* us, sir! Matching course and speed!"

"Show me."

On a big monitor above Colbert's console, a view of space came into focus: myriad stars across a jet-black sky. The twin suns of this system were not visible.

In the center, a silver disk gently moved from left to right.

"What is it? Xaxki?"

"Don't know, Admiral. It looks like a Gray Sports Model."

"Sports Model" was the slang term for one of several extraterrestrial spacecraft recovered by human operations over the years, and one supposedly had been given to humans as part of an exchange program of some sort.

Carruthers doubted that the saucer alongside was one of the human ships, though.

"Captain Groton has ordered our weapons systems to track the unknown, sir."

"Good. I—*What the hell?*"

On the flag bridge, just in front of Carruthers's command chair, a point of light had winked on, then expanded into a fuzzy silver sphere some five feet across. And within the depths of that sphere . . .

"Sound the alarm!" Carruthers yelled, but it was already too late as small figures poured out of the sphere and onto the flag bridge deck. At first he thought they were children, children in black armored suits and carrying—

Energy bolts snapped, the air stung with ozone, and Admiral Carruthers pitched back against his command chair . . . and died.

CAPTAIN GROTON whirled at the admiral's shout, turning in time to see the first armored figure emerge from the blurred sphere and shoot Carruthers in the chest. A second figure emerged close behind the first, turning its weapon on Colbert and several other aides on the flag bridge.

The flag bridge was aft of the main bridge and elevated like a stage perhaps six feet high. Vashnu and the two ambassadors turned and dived for the edge; Kozlov was cut down from behind, but King and Vashnu leaped off the stage as Groton yelled, *"Vac doors!"*

Massive panels slid from deck and overhead at the edge of the stage to meet as a single airtight door, sealing the two bridge compartments off from one another. The system was designed to allow crucial compartments on board the *Hillenkoetter* to be sealed in the event of a hull breach, but it worked now to isolate the invaders boarding the ship. Groton could hear yells and screams from the far side of the partition. He'd just sealed eight or ten men off from any possible escape, but there were no weapons on the bridge, no way to fight off the intruders.

"Where the hell did they come from?" he demanded.

"Quickly!" Vashnu said, rising from the deck. He appeared to have injured his arm in the fall. "Maneuver the ship!"

"Why?"

"So that they . . . *look there!*"

A bright white point of light appeared above the main bridge deck, swiftly expanding into a sphere of blurred space. "Helm!" Groton yelled. "Acceleration *now!*"

The *Hillenkoetter* lurched forward and the sphere vanished.

"That is a Saurian ship alongside," Vashnu told him. "By matching course and speed they can use their dimensional transport system to open a pathway between their ship and this one."

"So if we're each on different vectors, they can't link up?"

"It is extremely difficult to do so," Vashnu told him. "Not impossible, but . . ."

"You're hurt."

"A broken arm." The Talis gave a dismissive shrug. "I've switched off the pain."

"We'll get someone to look at it. Helm!"

"Sir!"

"Stay focused on that alien ship and don't let them match course and speed with us!"

"Yes, sir. They're a lot more maneuverable than we are, though."

"Random movements, then. Change course and velocity randomly."

"Yes, sir."

"Fire control!"

"Fire control, aye!"

"Target that ship out there and burn it out of my sky!"

"Aye, aye, sir."

"Captain!"

"What is it, Commander Haines?"

"We're getting in reports from all over the ship, sir. We've been boarded."

"What, *more* of those pint-sized freaks?"

"Saurians, sir. In battle armor and with advanced weaponry."

"How bad is it?"

"I don't know, sir. But bad. They're in Engineering . . ."

Shit! That meant the *Big-H* might not be able to keep maneuvering for much longer. *Or* firing her weapons. And when that happened . . .

"McKelvey!"

"Yessir!" the fire control officer snapped back.

"Talk to me."

"Target is too damned maneuverable, sir. It's jumping all over the damned sky!"

"Keep after it." So long as the alien saucer was maneuvering like that, it couldn't board the *Big-H*. And maybe the humans would get lucky.

Groton touched an intercom switch. "S-2."

"Here, Captain," Philip Wheaton's voice replied.

"What the fuck is going on aboard my ship, Commander?"

"S-2" referred to the intelligence section of a given military unit. Besides providing information on the enemy—where they were and what they were doing—the S-2 section on board ship managed security clearances, intelligence oversight, and physical security for the vessel.

And *Hillenkoetter*'s physical security had just been compromised big-time.

"We're getting reports of unknown alien incursions on board, Captain," Wheaton replied. "Seven so far. Two in Engineering, one at the power plant, two in PryFly, two on the main flight deck . . ."

"They're on the flag bridge, too."

"Eight, then."

"Can you stop them?"

"Working on it, sir. Spain and Milhouse are on the flight deck. Hot firefight, sir."

Lieutenant Commander Milhouse was the security officer; Chief Ed Spain was the master-at-arms.

But . . . shit *again*. Aliens on the flight deck suggested the nightmare possibility that they planned to switch off the kinetic fields maintaining the atmospheric pressure on the ship. If they accomplished that, the entire ship would depressurize in minutes, save for isolated pockets that managed to get the vac walls closed in time.

Briefly, Groton considered ordering all vac doors closed and sealed throughout the ship just in case, but that would seriously hamper efforts to get from one compartment to another, and thoroughly screw their chances of organizing against the invaders.

"We've got the weapons locker secured, sir," Wheaton continued. "We're trying to link up with the JSST guys who just came back aboard."

"Okay," he said, keeping the stress out of his voice. "Keep me informed."

"Yes, sir."

A hot firefight on the flight deck. That was *not* good.

"STAY DOWN!"

Duvall took his own shrill-shouted advice and crouched behind the landing gear of the TR-3R, parked on the flight line in Bay Twelve. Alien energy bolts slammed into the spacecraft's hull a few feet above his head, splattering him with droplets of molten titanium. Carefully, he peered past the strut, took two-handed aim, and squeezed off a laser pulse. He saw movement across the broad open deck space—a small figure in black moving in the shadows—but he couldn't tell if he'd hit anything or not.

He'd been in the middle of an argument with Ann Seton. She and the other three JSST people were insisting that they go back with him to rejoin their unit, now that the first batch of refugees had been turned over to *Hillenkoetter*'s medical section. He'd been explaining for the third time that as far as he knew, the rest of 1-JSST was already on the way back to the carrier and there was no *point* . . . when a blurred sphere of emptiness had opened in empty air a dozen yards away and space-suited kids had started pouring out. Marine sergeant Randolph Brown, standing just a few feet away, had gone down as a high-energy bolt flashed against the shoulder and upper torso of his suit.

The personnel gathered around the lowered ramp of the TR-3R had dropped immediately, unshipping their weapons and trying to return fire. Seton and Gunny Grabiak both had their Starbeam 3000 laser rifles in action, and Duvall saw at least one of the aliens pitch backward as a section of its body armor exploded.

"Duvall!" a voice crackled in his helmet. "Lieutenant Duvall, this is Spain!"

The ship's MAA. Duvall had yelled for help as soon as the shooting started. "Go ahead, Chief!"

"Sir . . . we're in Bay Five. What's your position?"

"Bay Twelve!"

"Can you see the Kinetic Field Control Center from your position?"

"I don't know, Chief. Where is it?"

"Forward end of the flight deck. You see a bulkhead with a big number 8 on it?"

"I see it, Chief."

"And windows up high, just above the eight?"

"Yes, Chief. There's a ship's ladder. . . ."

"That's it! Can you reach it?"

"Negative, Chief!" He ducked back behind the shelter of the landing strut as three more alien lightning bolts snapped past his head or flared blue-white against the transport's hull. "We've got six . . . maybe seven hostiles right below it—some in the recess beyond the ladder, some behind some equipment crates stacked up in front of it."

"Can you take them out, Lieutenant?"

Another bolt struck the TR-3R, splattering him with hot metal droplets. He was very glad he was wearing the protective BioSuit, though with much more of this kind of treatment it would have some serious holes in it pretty soon. "I'm working on it!"

"Okay, sir. Try to keep the little bastards busy, will you? I'm going to try to reach the hostiles from behind."

"Right, Chief."

"And if you see them going up the ladder, for God's sake take them down! If they reach the kinetic shield control room, they could drop the field and open the ship to space!"

"Copy that!" He took aim again and fired . . . a clean miss.

Damn it.

HUNTER WAS in the cockpit of the TR-3B, a narrow space with just enough room for two seats side by side. He didn't have room enough to turn around . . . but from here he did have one hell of a view.

The big transport was rising in her gravitics smoothly into the upper atmosphere, on the point of transiting into space. The planet was below the atmosphere showing two distinct layers. Above was a thin band of blue consisting mostly of nitrogen, but beneath that was an orange cloud deck—a witch's brew of methane, ammonia, and organics. The cloud layer was patchy and tended to open up quite a bit in sunlight; Hunter didn't understand the chemistry involved, and was glad he didn't have to.

Ahead, the two suns of Zeta Reticuli gleamed in darkness, a bright white disk a little smaller than the sun as seen from Earth shining brightly a little ways off from its companion, a brilliant star perhaps as bright as the planet Venus.

"How long to the *Big-H*?" he asked.

Lieutenant Manuel Ortega was the craft's pilot. "Normally, sir, we'd take our time and pull a couple of orbits to catch up. Maybe three hours." He jerked his thumb over his shoulder, indicating aft. "With the current passenger manifest, though . . ."

"Pedal to the metal, Lieutenant," Hunter told him. "The sooner we're back aboard the *Big-H*, the better."

"Aye, aye, sir." He made some light-fingered adjustments on the touch screen in front of him. "How's twenty minutes sound?"

"Better. I'd settle for ten."

"Right now, Commander, the *Big-H* is on the other side of the frickin' planet! We have to catch her. We can push *c* in this thing, but that's going in a straight line. Turning corners around a planet, that's something else."

"Right."

"Uh-oh . . ."

"What is it?"

"Trouble on board the *Hillenkoetter*. I can't quite . . ."

"Put it on speaker."

Ortega touched a screen.

". . . boarded us and we are under attack! Repeat, hostiles have boarded us and we are under attack! TR-3B Alfa and Charlie, do you copy?"

"Let me have that," Hunter said, pointing at a microphone. Ortega handed it to him and opened a channel. "*Hillenkoetter, Hillenkoetter*, this is Hunter on TR-3B Alfa. We copy! Where do you want us?"

"TR-3B Alfa, we suggest you stay clear." The voice sounded like Groton's.

"Captain Groton? Is that you?"

"It's me, Commander. Saurian boarders came in. Not sure how they did it. Vashnu is talking about some sort of dimensional transporter. Admiral Carruthers is dead, and the flag bridge is under their control. We have reports that Saurians are in Engineering, on the flight deck, and in other key areas, as well. I repeat . . . stay clear!"

Hunter thought furiously. He had two TR-3Bs loaded with over forty combat personnel, plus three hundred–some rescued civilians. He didn't know how many Saurians were on the *Big-H*, or how many shipboard personnel were fighting back, but he also knew that if the aliens took over the *Hillenkoetter* the humans were royally screwed. The TR-3Bs couldn't make it back to Earth—they didn't have the time-bending gravitic stardrive. They would be stuck at Zeta Reticuli and Hunter didn't think the Xaxki would be interested in helping them.

If the two transports could get back onto *Hillenkoetter*'s flight deck, they might have a chance. The refugees could stay safely aboard the TR-3Bs, while the JSST attacked the Saurians from an unexpected direction.

But there was a problem with that. Also with the group were thirty Grays and eight Saurians—though whether they qualified now as prisoners or as refugees was anyone's guess. They were *telepathic*, though, meaning they could easily be in touch with their kin on board the *Big-H*.

What was their range? How far apart could two Saurians be and still be able to think at one another? How far away did a Saurian have to be from a human to read his mind? Hunter had no idea.

He was afraid they were about to find out.

"How far behind us is TR-3B Charlie?" he asked the pilot.

"About three hundred miles, sir."

All of the Saurians and Grays brought along from Velat were on board the other shuttle, Charlie. Hunter had not wanted to mix them with the rescued humans, many of which were in near-psychotic states after their ordeal. There were too many of the former prisoners to put all of them on one TR-3B, so Hunter and Layton had worked out a half-assed solution. Two hundred and three refugees were on board Alfa, along with Hunter's Alfa Platoon. One hundred refugees were on TR-3B Charlie, plus Bravo and Charlie Platoons and all thirty-eight aliens. Before lifting off, Hunter had ordered Master Sergeant Bruce Layton to keep the aliens under heavy guard, and to keep them sequestered from the refugees in the shuttle's upper passenger deck. He wanted to get them back to the ship alive.

Things would have been so much simpler if he could have just killed them all. But there were rules about stuff like that.

"Give me a channel to TR-3B Charlie," he said.

"Here you are, sir."

Hunter took the mic again. "TR-3B Charlie, this is Hunter. Let me talk to Master Sergeant Layton."

"Layton here, sir. What's up?"

"You heard the alert from the *Big-H*?"

"Yessir. What are we going to do about it?"

"I'm concerned about our *special* passengers. About them listening in."

"I was wondering about that, too, sir."

"Okay. Listen close. I'm not too concerned about the Grays, but those Saurians are a real menace. Put some armed men behind them, and give them orders: if they feel *anything* crawling into their minds, they're to kill the prisoners. Got that?"

"Yes, sir."

"We're going to dock with the *Hillenkoetter* at its forward lock. Pass the word to your pilot."

"Sir? Why not go into the flight deck?"

"Because we may have hostiles there. Right?"

"Copy that, sir."

"Hunter out."

He hated lying to his own people, but there was no other way. With any luck, the Saurians would read Layton's mind without him even knowing, and pass the word to their buddies on board the *Big-H*. If they were sincere about their desire to surrender, well, no harm done.

And now he just hoped the bastards weren't reading his mind from three hundred miles away.

CHAPTER TWENTY-THREE

Meeting an advanced civilization could be like Native Americans encountering Columbus. That didn't turn out so well.

STEPHEN HAWKING,
STEPHEN HAWKING'S FAVORITE PLACES, 2016

HANS KAMMLER, HEAVILY sedated, was adrift in a world of dream . . .

He'd been distantly aware of the stab of a needle in his wrist, of people placing him on a stretcher and carrying him out of that basement, but the noise and jolting had all swiftly faded, and he was now . . . someplace else.

He floated within a universe of extraordinary color, of sensation, of movement, of joy . . . a joy so alien in texture he could only register its touch as terror. Some part of his tortured mind knew that all of this was a hallucination. Odd how he could feel such a flood of free and happy—even orgasmic—emotions, and have those unfamiliar emotions fire such terror in his thoughts.

There were alien beings here as well, myriads of them, beings of every conceivable shape and size and form, and quite a few that were inconceivable, as well. Kammler floated among them, feeling himself, his mind being sucked down into a vortex of madness. There were six-meter worms, sinuous and writhing, with twelve black eyes encircling what might be a mouth. There were things *like gray pillbugs with segmented backs and complicated underparts. There were faces, horrible faces drawn from sheerest nightmare, gaping lamprey mouths filled with rasping teeth and surrounded by Medusa-like tendrils. There were blobs of jelly unfolding in the light, alive with inner, rippling patterns of light visible through transparent flesh. There were things like geometric shapes constantly turning themselves inside out as they somehow shifted through multiple dimensions. There were—*

Why are you here?

The words thundered within his brain.

What are you? Why are you here?

Kammler wanted to reply, wanted to beg for help, but he couldn't stop screaming.

DUVALL LEANED around the landing strut and snapped off two shots from his laser pistol in rapid succession. A pull on the trigger a third time set off a single warning chirp over his helmet radio; the weapon's battery had been completely drained.

He thumbed the battery release and fished in his hip pouch for another. *Damn!* Only one left. He snapped it into the pistol grip and looked for another target. Why the hell did they make these things only good for four shots? Or why didn't his flight BioSuit come with a full backpack PLSS with a longer lasting battery? He had to make every shot count, but the targets were small, fast, and maneuverable. He didn't think he'd hit anything yet.

Across the flight deck, a small, black figure made a sudden dash up the ship's ladder toward the elevated control booth for the magnetokinetic induction screens that kept the ship's air from spilling out through the open flight deck. The bastards seemed determined to get up there.

Grabiak and Seton were behind Duvall, facing the other way. Several more of the Saurian commandos had appeared on the other side of the ship, threatening to catch the three humans from behind.

It was up to him. . . .

Duvall gripped the laser pistol in two hands, sighting carefully. He'd just realized that he'd been leading his targets slightly. If his pistol had fired lead slugs at eleven hundred feet per second, they would take a fraction of a second to travel all the way to the target—not very long, certainly, but just enough to miss against a target that was moving quickly and erratically. A trained shooter, Duvall had been automatically allowing for the targets' speed and distance.

But a laser pulse across a hundred feet was, for all practical purposes, instantaneous.

He aimed dead center as the armored figure reached the door to the control booth and squeezed the trigger.

Hit! The Saurian's armor flared in a burst of white light, and it staggered, hitting the ladder railing, then pitching over and falling eight or ten feet to the deck.

"Good shot, Lieutenant!" Seton called over her shoulder.

Duvall measured the long distance between his position and that ladder.

If he could make it across that open deck. . . .

HUNTER LEANED forward in the TR-3B's cockpit, peering through the windscreen at the long, cigar-shaped bulk of the *Hillenkoetter* which had just come into view. The carrier was moving erratically, using its gravitics to shift and dodge and change course every few seconds. The *Inman* was farther off, staying clear of the *Hillenkoetter*'s drunken walk. Closer to the carrier, a point of light dodged in an apparent effort to match course with the behemoth. "Look at that thing move!" Hunter said. "What the hell is it?"

"Saurian ship," the pilot replied. "Sports Model. Fifty-two, fifty-three feet across, sixteen feet high."

"Is it armed?"

"Don't know, sir. It'll at least have energy weapons for vaporizing meteors and space junk that get too close. Whether it can hurt the *Big-H*, or us . . . can't tell you."

The TR-3B was unarmed, and there was nothing they could do about the alien ship, save keep a close eye on it. If it decided to attack them, it was game over.

But it appeared to be totally fixated on the *Hillenkoetter*.

"What about the other ships? Can they help out?"

"Don't think so, sir." The pilot shook his head. "That hostile is sticking so close . . . I don't think *Inman* or the others can get a clear shot without hitting the *Big-H*."

"Okay," Hunter said. "Get us in close."

"You want to go in by the bow?"

"No. The flight deck."

"But you just told Charlie—"

"So that the Saurians would pick that thought from Layton's mind, and tell their friends on board the *Big-H*."

"Ahh . . ." Hunter could see the light dawning in the ship's pilot. "We're not going to be able to board with them jittering around like that."

"I know," Hunter replied. "Open a channel to the *Big-H*."

"Here you go, sir."

"*Hillenkoetter, Hillenkoetter*, this is Hunter. We're going to try to board. Please stop maneuvering so we can do so."

"Alfa . . . we copy and will comply. But for God's sake make it quick! If we don't maneuver, we might get more bad guys jumping in from the fourth dimension!"

"Roger."

The TR-3B began accelerating. Ahead, the *Hillenkoetter* stopped her random movements across the sky.

And the Saurian ship, detecting an opportunity, moved in for the kill.

IT WAS a long, long way across that open deck to the ship's ladder leading up to the kinetic field control room. But the black figures had vanished—called away, perhaps, on some other mission. There was not going to be a better chance.

"I'm gonna try to get to the control booth!" Duvall said.

"Go for it, sir!" Grabiak replied. "We'll cover you!"

Crouching low, expecting an energy bolt out of the shadows at any moment, Duvall ran for the access ladder. Several small, armored bodies lay scattered about on the deck, but there were also human forms as well, broken and motionless.

To his left, a point of white light winked on . . . and then swelled into one of those blurred spheres.

"Keep going, sir!" Seton yelled. "Go! Go! Go!"

Grabiak and Seton opened fire on this new threat, loosing bolt after bolt into the unfolding alien vortex.

Duvall kept going.

Just before he reached the foot of the ladder, a Saurian stepped out of the shadows to his right, leveling some kind of weapon at him. He snapped off an instinctive shot without slowing his pace, and was rewarded by a shrill, gurgling cry as the being fell backward. A second being appeared from the same shadows, and Duvall shot that one, too.

Then he collided with the metal ladder . . . hard, grabbed the rung, and spun around. A hundred feet behind him, Saurian commandos were spilling from the light-distorting impossibility of the sphere, firing their weapons at Grabiak and Seton as they emerged behind the two JSST soldiers.

One of the humans was hit—Duvall couldn't tell which one. The BioSuited figure twisted away and dropped in the half-g gravity, smoke and hot ceramic armor everywhere. The surviving human kept firing at the attackers, taking shelter behind the TR-3R's landing strut.

Duvall snapped off another shot from his laser, but there was nothing more he could do to help from here. He pounded up the ladder and palmed the door.

Two human bodies lay sprawled on the deck, the

control booth watch officer, presumably, and another. A Saurian stood above the control panel, its helmeted head turning as Duvall burst in. He raised his laser pistol . . .

. . . and heard the despairing whine over his helmet speakers warning of a dead battery.

Damn! Four shots per battery was next to freaking *useless*! He shifted his grip and hurled the weapon straight at the alien as hard as he could, then leaped, arms spread. The pistol bounced off the Saurian's helmet in pieces—cheap junk—but Duvall collided with the being with a crash, driving it backward into the control panel. Duvall outmassed the creature three to one, but he felt its twisting, wiry strength as it tried to wriggle away from him. Grabbing the strangely elongated helmet in both hands, he slammed its head hard against the deck . . . and again . . . and again . . .

When it stopped moving, Duvall stood up, slowly and panting. He was now in command of the control booth, for whatever that was worth. Now, how was he supposed to hang on to it?

The alien's weapon lay on the deck nearby. It looked weird, black and silver and all smooth curves, no angles at all, and he couldn't even guess what it used as a trigger.

Hell, he was having trouble deciding which was the business end.

"THAT'S IT!" Hunter said, watching as *Hillenkoetter* dropped onto a steady course and speed. *"Punch it!"*

The long, slender cigar shape of the *Hillenkoetter* swelled rapidly in size. Hunter could see the central flight deck port brightly lit from within, a long, flat slit in the vessel's hull a hundred yards wide. Instinctively, Hunter braced himself for an impact, but the TR-3B's pilot was a true artist in balancing the ship's gravitic field. He slowed at the last moment. "Shit!"

"What is it?" Hunter asked. The shuttle had come to a near-halt outside the landing bay.

"The force field . . . it's locked!" the pilot said. "It won't open if we try to go through!"

"I thought it was automatic—the field cutting out then coming back up!"

"Depends on how the thing's set, sir." The pilot pointed at a screen. "That queries the control booth and reports whether it's locked or not, see?"

And the screen said "fields locked."

For a moment, Hunter wrestled with the incongruous vision of David Bowman outside the recovery lock of the *Discovery* in Kubrick's *2001*. Even he knew that image. *Open the pod bay doors, HAL.*

DUVALL DROPPED the alien weapon. A slightly more pressing issue was visible on a large wall-mounted monitor. An external camera had focused on an oncoming TR-3B as it accelerated toward the landing bay. A warning light flashed, and he read the legend "containment field locked" on the instrument panel. That shuttle was coming in for a landing, but the force field would *not* be coming down for it. He scanned the booth's controls desperately, looking for . . . *anything.* A button, a knob, a touch screen. . . .

HUNTER'S HEART was hammering in his chest. They could not hang around out here for long. That alien saucer was on the far side of the *Hillenkoetter*, but it would swing around to this side at any moment, and when it did . . .

"Can you connect me with the control booth?"

"I think so. Try that. . . ."

"Kinetic field control booth, this is TR-3B Alfa! What the hell is going on? Open the damned doors!"

"I'm working on it, Commander," a familiar voice came back.

"Duvall? Is that you?"

"Double-D at your service, Commander. I'm just trying to figure out what to push."

"Look for 'manual override,'" the pilot said. He glanced up at Hunter. "I've stood watch in that little box," he explained.

"Got it!" Duvall said. "You should be clear now."

"Thank you, Double-D," Hunter replied.

"Watch your ass coming into the flight deck, Commander," Duvall said. "Hostiles are on board. There's a firefight in the landing bays!"

"Affirmative."

The TR-3B surged forward, accelerating hard, slipping through the containment shields easily, then flaring suddenly to a hovering halt, then setting down gently in the deck. Damn, that pilot was *good*! Hunter felt his weight fluctuate, then drop to about half normal as the pilot switched off the shuttle's gravitics. Hunter hurried back to the main passenger compartment. "Listen up, people!" he shouted into the crowded room. "Civilians . . . stay put! All of you! Just One, check your weapons and gear, and form up at the ramp. And watch yourselves—it's a hot LZ!"

He heard the multiple snicks of weapons being checked and safeties going off.

An absurd thought clammered at the back of his mind for attention, and he grinned. "Just like Blackbeard's pirates," he called. "Are you with me?"

The chorused response came back, a thunderous *"Arrr!"*

"Hoo-yah!" He led the platoon to the ramp access. At least the atmospheres matched, inside and out, and they wouldn't have to cycle through the airlock a few at a time. With a shrill whine, the ramp dropped, the ventral doors swung wide, and two platoons of the 1-JSST banged and clattered down the ramp.

A bolt took down Lieutenant Carl Bader halfway down the ramp, searing in from a stack of crates and gas bottles off to the left. Hunter and several others returned fire, but most importantly they kept moving, rushing to get clear of the shuttle. If combat taught you anything, it was that when you got hit with an ambush in the open, you didn't just stand around with your thumb up your ass, or even stand and return fire. You *moved*, fast as you could, clearing the ship to let the others get out behind you, and rushing the enemy position before the bad guys took you all down.

So Hunter sprinted across the *Hillenkoetter*'s flight deck toward the far bulkhead, seeking cover. There were a number of ships here—fighters, TR-3Bs and Rs, auxiliary craft of various kinds—but the only shelter was the forest of landing struts and the spacecraft themselves. He did *not* want to get pinned out here, exposed.

"Alfa Platoon, to the left!" he called. "Bravo, to the right!"

Energy bolts snapped out of the shadows. The bulkheads were broken into numerous recesses, with doors and ship's ladders leading to viewing alcoves overhead and plenty of dark corners for shooters to hide. Hunter slammed into a bulkhead, looking to his right, trying to penetrate the darkness as something moved . . .

Mike Kelly screamed and flailed, his BioSuit engulfed in flame, just yards away. Hunter, holding his weapon in a tight, two-handed grip, returned fire, but couldn't tell if he'd hit anything.

His weapon chimed empty.

Rather than snap in a fresh battery, he dropped to his belly and crawled out to the smoking remains of the ranger, picking up the RAND/Starbeam 3000 Kelly had dropped on the deck. The laser rifle—and why the hell did they call the thing a *rifle* when it shot pulses of laser light?—was far better in combat than those crappy little pistols. If he kept the weapon dialed down to tenth-second pulses, he should get twenty shots or more.

Just to be on the safe side, he fished several spare battery packs out of Kelly's smoldering suit and placed them in his own reserve pouches. He was not, he told himself, looting a corpse. Kelly was giving him that extra edge that might keep him alive through the next few minutes.

GROTON LEANED closer to examine the fire control officer's screen. "He's coming closer! Try for a lock!"

"Yessir!" McKelvey replied, obviously nervous at the thought of his commanding officer literally looking over his shoulder.

Too bad, Groton thought. *Things are tough all over* . . .

The thumps and bangs from behind the sealed partition in front of the flag bridge had stopped some minutes ago. Groton had ordered a couple of ship's Marines from the MAA department to stand guard on the flight bridge and watch for the appearance of any more of those dimensional spheres. The enemy hadn't tried that tactic here, but that didn't mean they wouldn't try soon. Everything hinged on factors that Groton had no way of guessing. How many Saurian commandos were packed onto that little ship? Had they all been sent across to the *Hillenkoetter*, or were there still a few left who might pop through onto the bridge at any moment?

Groton thought it likely that there was no one left on that saucer except the pilot and crew, however many that might be. But might they decide to transport some commandos back, then send them here?

Was the bridge even important enough to capture? *That* depended on how the Saurians thought, and Groton was the first to admit that he was anything but expert on Saurian psychology.

"Target is coming alongside!" McKelvey said suddenly. "Locked on with four heavy DEWs!"

"Fire," Groton said.

The result was anticlimactic. Four particle-beam cannons—the ship's heaviest direct-energy weapons—loosed silent and invisible hellfire at the target.

And nothing happened.

"HIT 'EM!" Hunter yelled, his voice shrill inside his helmet. He hoped he didn't sound that unsettled to his troops.

Alfa Platoon had encountered several Saurian commandos sheltering behind a line of supply crates at the forward end of the flight deck, and were hammering them with laser fire. The enemy returned fire, but in scattered, disorganized fashion, and the human troops were picking them off every time they showed themselves.

It helped not having to brace yourself and take careful aim. Using the in-helmet display, Hunter could stick his rifle around a corner, watch the crosshairs moving against his visor, line them up, and trigger a burst strong enough to burn the target down.

Sometimes, the target exploded in a noisy, messy display of pyrotechnics.

It was more satisfying than he would have thought.

A couple of Saurians ducked through a door into a passageway leading forward. A third followed, and Hunter nailed him, a clean shot that burned away the creature's helmet and the head inside.

A fourth and a fifth emerged from the shadows and sheltering supply crates, their arms raised in a very human gesture of surrender. "Pollack!" Hunter called. "Take charge of the prisoners!"

Alfa Platoon had taken heavy casualties so far. How many were left . . . eight? Nine? Fifty percent casualties was no joke in a tight-knit and tightly bonded unit like this one, but it felt like the momentum of the battle was shifting, the tide turning.

They had the bastards on the run.

"FIELD CONTROL center, this is TR-3B Charlie. What the hell's going on in there? We were told to board at the forward lock!"

"I don't know where they're sending you, Lieutenant," Duvall replied. "Alfa has already trapped on the flight deck."

"We're coming in."

"Careful when you do," Duvall told him. "You've got a hot LZ."

"Copy."

The second TR-3B slipped in through the double kinetic screen. Duvall immediately relocked the screen mechanism so that no one else could come through. The transport set down on a bare stretch of deck next to his TR-3R. Moments later, the access ramp lowered, and a platoon of JSST troopers charged down onto the flight deck.

Duvall met them at the foot of the ladder below the control booth. "Welcome back aboard," he told them.

"Thank you, sir," Master Sergeant Bruce Layton said. He looked around, puzzled. "I thought you said it was a hot LZ?"

"It was, Master Sergeant. But I think the little gray monsters are on the run now. But I suggest not taking any chances until we have them all accounted for."

"Good." He gestured over his shoulder. "I have a shuttle full of them here—thirty-eight. They're under guard, but I don't know for how long. Tricky little bastards. . . ."

"I'd say leave them on the transport under heavy guard," Duvall told him. "They shouldn't get into too much trouble there. When the *Big-H* is secured, we can move 'em all to the ship's brig."

"So why the hell did the skipper tell me we were boarding the ship up forward?"

"Because," Hunter said coming up on Layton from behind, "I didn't want the aliens to read your mind and find out we were coming in *here*. I figured if they *did* read you and they *were* helping their friends in here, they'd tell them we were going in at the forward lock and maybe divert some forces up that way."

"Didn't think of that, sir," Layton said.

"I think it worked, too," Duvall put in. "A lot of them started hightailing it out of here and moving forward just before you trapped."

"That's what I was hoping," Hunter said. He slapped the rifle he was carrying. "Let's go see if we can round them up."

A man's scream sounded over the tactical channel, followed by a string of foul imprecations. It didn't sound like he'd been hit—not *physically*, anyway.

"Taylor!" Hunter said, recognizing the voice. "What's wrong?"

"It . . . it's Ann! They *killed* her!"

Safing his weapon, Hunter walked back to the tableau beside the 3R's nose strut. Taylor was kneeling beside Ann's body, as Grabiak held his shoulder.

"Easy, Thomas," he said. "Hold it together . . ."

But Hunter knew that it had been his orders that had put her there.

Damn, damn, *damn*.

"HIT 'EM again!" Groton snapped.

Hillenkoetter fired her main weapons once more, targeting the alien saucer. The lack of return fire either meant the alien was unarmed, or that they didn't want to wipe out the human carrier when they still had their own commandos on board.

The lack of any appreciable effect when the *Big-H* scored direct hits on the little craft suggested that it was well shielded. Human technology included protective shields around starships; they *had* to be well shielded, given that if they hit a dust mote while traveling at near-c they would end their journey very quickly.

But the protective fields around Saurian craft appeared to incorporate a whole other level of high technology. The xenotechnologists claimed the Saurians were using gravitics to twist both space and time around their craft, which explained why they tended to look a bit fuzzy when they were in flight. Gigaton energies from *Hillenkoetter*'s DEWs simply vanished into those fields. No effect.

Groton remembered someone telling him that if you

saw a crystal-sharp image of a UFO in a photograph, that was almost proof positive that it was a hoax, a model on a string or, more recently, CGI manipulation. *Real* alien spacecraft always looked fuzzy, their outlines blurred by the space- and time-bending gravitic shields surrounding them.

He heard a clatter at his back and turned. Several humans, anonymous in their combat BioSuits and carrying bulky Starbeam rifles, came through the aft hatch to the bridge. A Marine guard beside the door raised his weapon, then snapped to attention.

"Permission to enter the bridge," the lead figure said.

"Commander Hunter!" Groton said. "Permission granted. It's damned good to see you!"

Hunter removed his helmet. He looked . . . haggard. Very tired, a bit pale and drawn. "Thank you, sir."

"What's the situation?"

"I think we've got them on the ropes, Captain. Charlie Platoon is down in Engineering and the power plant, and report they've cleared the place out. And we've been chasing the bad guys forward, all the way from the flight deck. They've broken, sir. They can't wait to surrender."

"Thank God!" Groton said. He gestured toward the sealed pressure door leading to the flag bridge. "We may have some locked up there. Care to check it out?"

Hunter hefted his weapon. "Yes, sir. Okay, people. Spread out, and be ready . . ."

The pressure doors slid open.

There was nothing inside. No Saurians. No bodies, human or alien. "Looks like they got out of Dodge, Captain."

"Captain—" McKelvey said. "I think they're making a break for it!"

Groton and Hunter looked over the fire control officer's shoulder at his screen. The saucer was dwindling . . .

. . . and then with a suddenness that made all three men jump, it was replaced by a wall of rugged, dust-clotted rock.

"What the hell?" Groton said.

"The Xaxki," Hunter said. "Looks like they finally decided to put in an appearance."

"They *ate* the Saurian ship?"

"Looks like. I guess they're dealing with the bad guys in their own way."

The Game ends, a voice said inside Groton's mind, and from the expressions of the others, they were hearing it, too. *Take your people . . . and leave.*

"Son of a bitch!" Hunter said softly.

There was nothing more to say.

CHAPTER TWENTY-FOUR

The most merciful thing in the world, I think, is the inability of the human mind to correlate all its contents. We live on a placid island of ignorance in the midst of black seas of infinity, and it was not meant that we should voyage far. The sciences, each straining in its own direction, have hitherto harmed us little; but some day the piecing together of dissociated knowledge will open up such terrifying vistas of reality, and of our frightful position therein, that we shall either go mad from the revelation or flee from the deadly light into the peace and safety of a new dark age.

H. P. LOVECRAFT
"THE CALL OF CTHULHU," 1926

COMMANDER PHILIP WHEATON *leaned over the old, wrinkled figure strapped down on the gurney. "You know him?" Simone Carter asked.*

"I know . . . of him," the intelligence officer replied. "It's been a long time. My dad used to talk about him."

"Who is he?"

"The name is Hans Kammler," Wheaton replied. "He was Nazi SS, one of the worst. He helped design Auschwitz. And he was in on Hitler's treaty with the Saurians, back in the late '30s. He escaped the fall of the Third Reich in an alien time ship, jumped twenty years and

crash-landed in a little town in Pennsylvania in 1965. The Agency knew he was coming, of course. The Talis were feeding us information ahead of time . . . literally. We had a recovery team pretty close by. They went in, cordoned off the area, and started C and C."

"C and C?"

"Containment and control. Shut down anyone spreading eyewitness accounts. Stop the story from leaking."

"I knew you guys did that!"

"That was my dad, not me. I wasn't even born in 1965. But I did the same thing later on. I'm not proud of it."

"Okay . . . so it was your dad that rescued this guy?"

"Yeah. He was Kammler's handler for a bunch of years. Then Kammler disappeared."

"When was that?"

"I dunno. Early '80s."

"You think he's been their prisoner this whole time?"

"Seems that way. So what's wrong with the poor bastard?"

"We're not sure," Carter replied. "He had a psychotic break of some sort down on the planet, while they were packing him out. They sedated him, but we haven't been able to bring him back. It's like he's lost in his own tight little world. EEG traces show brain wave activity consistent with dreaming . . . dreaming with violent emotions."

"Nightmares."

"Probably."

Kammler twitched in his stupor. . . .

And then gave a small, despairing whimper.

"THE XAXKI," Elanna said carefully, "don't think of it as *war*. They think of it as a game."

"A game," Hunter said, feeling like the bottom had just dropped out of his world. "A *game*?"

It was a meeting of all department heads, with the senior members of *Hillenkoetter*'s officers and scientists gathered around an enormous boardroom table in Conference Compartment A. Elanna was present as a representative of the Talis.

She spread her hands. "I'm sorry, Commander, but that's the best interpretation we can put on it. Maybe it's the only interpretation possible."

"So I guess," Hunter said, "that the things we were calling 'pillbugs' were kind of like . . . I don't know. Game pieces?"

"That seems to be the simplest, the most direct explanation," Elanna said, nodding. "And Dreamers apparently inhabit those bodies, running them by remote control."

"Kozlov and King kept trying to establish contact with the Xaxki," Groton pointed out. "Shouldn't that have stopped this 'game'?"

"Maybe the Xaxki are so far ahead of us they just didn't notice us," Dr. Steven Vanover said. "The way we might not notice ants, or cockroaches."

"If a cockroach is in my kitchen, I notice it," Hunter said. Others around the table chuckled at that.

"Not when they're in the walls," McClure said.

"So what you're saying," Groton said, "is that to them we're vermin?"

"Something like that," McClure agreed. "That, or they just came to the conclusion after our brief chat that we had nothing to say that would be of interest to them. Or . . ." She shrugged. "Maybe they just didn't understand us. And with quadrillions of individual Dreamers—a number that we, as humans, really can't come close to comprehending, but know that it's massive—they couldn't sort out who within their population was attacking the Saurian base. In other words, who was playing the game. The pillbugs numbered . . . what? A few thousand, maybe? Controlled by that many Dreamers, but out of a population exponential magnitudes larger? For the Xaxki leadership, that's like finding one specific pinch of sand out of all the beaches and all the oceans in the world. We don't even know if they have something that we might recognize as leadership. In any case, we think those Dreamers *were* playing a kind of game, one with the goal of driving the intruders, the Saurians, out of the system without forcing them to simply annihilate them."

"Nice of them," Brody said. "So very *civilized* . . ."

"So a few Dreamers got together and were having a games night," Hunter said. "When we came along, we were nuisances . . . vermin. Some of them, the Guardians, were talking with us, but they weren't taking us seriously, and maybe didn't talk to the leadership, if there *is* a leadership. Is that it?"

"We *think* so," McClure told him. "But remember: this is all guesswork on our part. We don't know how these beings think or what they feel, any more than we understand what's going through a cockroach's brain."

"We came in, and we almost didn't come out," Hunter muttered.

"What made them call Dreamers out of retirement?" Captain Groton asked. "What was the big decision that needed to be made?"

"Whether or not we must be destroyed."

There was a long silence around the table. Finally, Simone Carter said quietly, "I gather they've decided not to wipe us out?"

"If we agree to leave right away, yes," Elanna said. "The one thing they've been very clear about is that they don't want us here. Having outsiders, aliens in-system in proximity to so many vulnerable members of their civilization, makes them . . . nervous."

"It would make *me* nervous," Groton said. "I don't blame them. The question is whether or not we can leave the system knowing our mission here is complete."

"I'd say it is, Captain," Hunter told him. "Operation Excalibur was tasked with finding out if the Saurians had a homeworld here at Zeta Retic. We found they had a base, but not a homeworld."

"There's also Zeta 2 Retic to consider," McClure

pointed out, "but we have the Guardians' assurances that there are no Saurians there."

"The Xaxki *claim* to be building planets at Zeta 2," Vanover said.

"You think that's true?" Hunter asked.

Vanover shrugged. "Who knows? They possess technologies we can't even begin to understand, but—"

"We should jump over there and take a look," Brody said, "just to see for ourselves."

"Sounds good," Groton said. "Assuming the Xaxki permit it. Then we shape a course for Aldebaran."

Hunter slowly shook his head. "Ah, with respect, sir . . . I think we need to rethink that." By which, of course, he meant that *Groton* should rethink things. "We need to get back to Earth, and the quicker the better."

"Negative," Groton said. "The mission orders for Operation Excalibur clearly—"

"Sir," Hunter said firmly, "we have three hundred–plus civilians on board now. I don't think the *Hillenkoetter* is equipped to take care of that many evacuees. There's also the JSST wounded to consider. We've got them in sick bay, but they need a full hospital to give them the proper treatment."

"Commander Hunter is right, Captain," Carter pointed out. "Three hundred civilians, *all* of them badly traumatized. Some of them comatose. They need treatment we can't offer them on this ship."

"We sent the rest of the task force to Aldebaran," Groton said. "They expect us to follow. I am *not* going to abandon them!"

Hunter thought about that. The cruisers *Samford, Carlucci*, and *Blake* all were almost seventy light-years away by now, awaiting the arrival of the *Big-H*.

"If I might suggest, sir," Hunter said carefully, "you would still have the temporal option."

"'Temporal option'? What do you mean?"

"Yes, brilliant!" Brody put in. "The commander is

saying you could take these people home, back to Earth, but then, since you'll be traveling backward in time anyway . . ."

"We get to Aldebaran with no delay," Groton said, completing the thought. He looked thoughtful. "We'll need to do a detailed paradox assessment, of course, but it *might* work . . ."

"I don't see what the problem would be," Brody said. "So long as the *Hillenkoetter* doesn't get to Aldebaran *before* those cruisers, what's the problem?"

"Time travel," Groton said, rubbing his eyes with both hands, "makes my head hurt."

"Okay," Commander Haines said, "what I want to know is why the Saurians had that base here."

"We've asked them," Wheaton said. "For hours now, my people have been questioning the ones Commander Hunter brought up from the planet. All they'll say is that *we* led them there. But we don't know what that means."

"I wonder," Hunter said, "if they're referring to our UFO mythologies?"

"What do you mean?" Groton asked.

"There's a sizable fraction in the UFO community claiming Zeta Reticuli is the Gray home sun, right?"

"Right," Haines said. "But they were wrong. Disinformation."

"Maybe. Or maybe the Grays and Saurians do more than use higher dimensions to jump from point to point. Maybe they actually visit other dimensions . . . other universes. Maybe in a universe next door, Serpo *is* their homeworld."

"That's kind of a reach, Commander," Groton said.

"Is it? Isn't this whole damn thing a reach? But isn't that the point? And maybe that's not it. Maybe, since they're from the future, in that future Serpo is more like home. Not their homeworld, necessarily, but a place where they can live. A place where they have a colony and we *do* have an exchange program with aliens."

"You're making my headache worse, Commander."

"All I'm trying to say, Captain, is that the universe isn't nearly as neat and rational as we like to think it is. Stuff happens that seems to make no sense at all, coincidences convince us that the cosmos is completely screwy, but if we could look at things from outside, from a different perspective, it all might make sense."

"Commander Hunter is right," Brody said. He shook his head slowly. "The Copenhagen interpretation of quantum physics suggests that there are myriad different universes overlapping in a gigantic multiverse, where anything that can happen *does* happen . . . in one universe or another."

"I don't think I buy that," Vanover said.

"Doctor, the multiverse doesn't care whether you buy it or not," Brody said. "Between time travel and quantum physics, the universe is one vast, black, twisty infinity so strange, so irrational in some ways, that we may never be able to fully understand it. But we know aliens are real. We know time travel is real. So, as more of our science fiction becomes proven, isn't it worth considering that our other 'outlandish' theories can be true, too?"

For a moment the room was silent. Then, "We should ask the Grays if *they* understand it," McClure said. "Betcha they say 'no, and *hell*, no!'"

"I just want to know why the Saurians have been abducting humans," the ship's senior tactical officer, Commander Bill James, said.

"Dr. McClure and one of the people we rescued both told me on different occasions that the Grays have run into a genetic bottleneck a million years off in the future," Hunter said. "They're abducting humans to repair the gene lines, I guess." He shrugged. "That's as good an explanation as we're going to get, I think. At least for right now."

"Right," McClure said. "And I don't want to hear any

more nonsense about human-alien hybrids! The idea is pure hokum."

"That's the Grays," Groton said. "What about the damned Saurians? *They're* not related to humans."

"Actually," McClure said, "they are. At least distantly."

"What the hell?" Hunter exclaimed.

She laughed. "You know . . . some people in the conspiracy community insist that humans are the descendents of aliens who crash-landed on Earth a long time ago, right?"

"I've heard that."

"And it's patent nonsense, because we are related genetically, *closely* related, to every other life-form on Earth. We share something like 60 percent of our DNA makeup with *starfish*, for God's sake. Fifty percent with *bananas*! Humans very definitely evolved on planet Earth."

"Ah. So you're saying . . ."

"We're related to them, yes. Very distantly." McClure had her laptop open, tapping away at the keys. "Back in 1982," she said, "a paleontologist at the National Museum of Canada named Dale Russell speculated about what dinosaurs might have become if an asteroid hadn't smashed into the Yucatán sixty-five million years ago. He pointed out that one dinosaur in particular, the troodon, had quite a large brain compared to its body size, three partially opposable fingers, and binocular vision. He had a model made of this animal and of a creature that he called a 'dinosauroid.' He imagined it as having evolved from the troodon over the course of several million years. Here it is."

On her computer screen, two life-size resin or acrylic models strode forward on flat bases. One was obviously a dinosaur, walking on its hind legs, its forelegs reaching forward as if to grab something. The other, however, looked far more human. *Too* human. Both models were dark green on their backs, pale and reddish on their fronts, and shared details of yellow, slit-pupiled eyes and three-fingered hands. Hunter guessed that the dinosauroid was about the same height as a human, or maybe a bit shorter.

"It looks awfully human," James said.

"That was one of the main criticisms of the idea," McClure said. "Somehow, the troodon loses its tail, adopts an upright stance, and goes from a plantigrade to an upright posture. Russell was pretty viciously castigated for his efforts.

"However, the point of the exercise was simply to get people *thinking*. Evolution is a continuous process, okay? Life-forms continue to evolve until they go extinct. *We're* continuing to evolve. The Grays are proof of that."

"Wait a minute," Hunter said, seeing where this was going. "You're saying that the *Saurians*—?"

"Are dinosaurs evolved to intelligence, yes."

"So when they claim to be from Earth . . ."

"They're telling what for them is the simple truth. Yes."

"Hold on a sec," James demanded. "Where the hell have they been for sixty-five million years? That's sixty-some times longer than the evolutionary gulf between us and the Grays! They would have changed a *lot* more in that time. And their technology would be—I don't know. Beyond imagining!"

"Actually, we think they developed an industrial civilization a few thousand years before the asteroid hit Earth," McClure told them. "Modern cities, all ground to dust by time. Spaceflight, *star* flight. We've found some artifacts on the Moon that might be theirs. Ultimately, though, Earth became uninhabitable. So they moved someplace else."

"We call them Malok," Elanna said, "but their name for themselves translates as 'The Surviving Few.' You can guess what it was they survived."

"An Earth devastated by the asteroid impact," Vanover said softly. "Enough dust in the air to block the sun's light for centuries. Every forest consumed by fire. The oceans turned acidic . . ."

"Exactly," Elanna said.

"And because faster-than-light drives are, of necessity, also time machines," McClure added, "they began exploring time. Specifically the future."

"So the Grays are time travelers from the far future," Hunter said, thoughtful. "And the Saurians are time travelers from the remote past? Wow! That kind of puts a different spin on things, doesn't it?"

Groton scowled. "Elanna? Why weren't we told any of this?"

Her large, startlingly blue eyes blinked slowly. "It was not deemed important, Captain. Besides, certain aspects of time travel are restricted and not shared with humans from your period. Attempts to go back in time and attack the Saurians would result in truly inconceivable paradoxes. You might do terrible damage to the time lines in a hundred different interrelated universes."

"Do we know any alien species that *aren't* from Earth?" Brody wanted to know.

"Quite a few, actually," McClure said.

"There are currently some eighty distinct species secretly in contact with various of Earth's governments," Elanna said, completely missing Brody's sarcasm. "Of these, only the Talis, the future humans you call the Grays, and the Malok are originally from Earth. The rest are from all over the Galaxy, and from across time. Some are from what you think of as alternate universes or dimensions. Life, as we currently understand it, is staggeringly complex and diverse."

"Still begs the question," Groton said. "Why are our dinosaurian friends kidnapping modern-day humans and keeping them in giant test tubes?"

"The Malok have their own agenda, remember," Elanna said. "The Saurians have been modifying the human genome for thousands of years . . . tens of thousands of years. They may have been responsible for creating humans in the first place, by modifying the DNA of *Homo erectus* half a million years ago. They hope to remake Earth as their home, but, as their name for themselves suggests, they are still few in number. Besides, they prefer to remain in the shadows, ambush predators, if you will. Opportunists. Their plan may be to redirect human evolution in a direction that will make our species more . . . docile."

"The Grays," Hunter said. "I'd call *them* docile. And down on the planet, a lot of them seem to be working for the Saurians. Almost like slaves. Or biological robots."

"We don't believe they succeed in changing humankind," Elanna said. "In our time, the Malok are not in evidence, and the Talis, along with all of the other human species we know of, are free. But . . ." She gave a shrug. "They are *very* good at hiding in the shadows."

"I'd say we still have a lot to learn," Groton said. "Okay—I think you're right, Commander. We'll shape a course for Earth. For home. But we'll have to turn right around and come back out to Aldebaran, once the ship is refitted and supplied. Anyone have a problem with that?"

No one did.

"We'll depart as soon as Damage Control reports on all of the compartments the Saurians got at, make sure everything is in working order. Current guess, Jeff?"

Jeff Markusky was the senior Damage Control officer. "Give us twenty-four hours," he said.

"Twenty-four hours, then," Groton said. "I just hope the Xaxki go along with that."

THE *HILLENKOETTER* and the *Inman* jumped, transiting the nearly 354 billion miles between Zeta 1 and Zeta 2 in an instant. Dropping to a more reasonable velocity, they floated above a vast disk of dust and gas side by side. And within that disk were . . . infant worlds.

"Dr. McClure . . ."

"Please, Mark," she said. "Call me Becky. We're way past formalities—at least off duty and in private."

They sat next to one another on a couch in the ship's main lounge. An entire wall had been converted to a viewscreen displaying the ultimate night outside. The scientists were still studying the newborn worlds, and speculating as to whether the Xaxki claims of creating them could be true.

Hunter didn't know about that . . . but he knew an inner quiver of awe and wonder at the thought that giants walked among the stars.

"*Becky*, then. I was just wondering: What are you going to do when we get back to Earth?"

She laughed. "I haven't had the time to think about that. I'll stay with Solar Warden, of course. And write some papers on the Talis and The Surviving Few and evolutionary studies using time travel. They'll all be kept top secret, of course, and just for scientists within the program. *Someday*, though, they'll be more widely read, and I can graciously thank the committee for my Nobel Prize! How about you?"

"I don't think I have any choice but to stay with the program. They aren't going to let me and my people just walk out and go back to Earth, are they?"

"Depends. You've already been sworn to secrecy numerous times. And if you break your oath, you'll find yourself counting boulders on Mars."

"We have a base on *Mars*?" He thought about it. "I guess we would, wouldn't we?"

"We have *something* there. I don't know what. I did see a classified paper a few months ago about areologists confirming the discovery of fossils on Mars. Turns out there used to be life there, back when life was just getting started on Earth. Apparently life pops up *everywhere* where there's liquid water and available energy."

"So what's NASA do, anyway?" Hunter asked.

"Nowadays? Serve as a front for America's public-facing space program, mostly." Her brow furrowed. "I think they're also in business building a solidly *human* space program. Remember, the *Hillenkoetter* and most of what we have on the Moon and elsewhere is alien technology. Stuff we don't really understand."

"C'mon! How can we run it, then?" Hunter said.

"Can you turn on a TV? Change the channels?"

"Sure . . ."

"Do you understand how it works? I mean *really* understand about cathode-ray tubes? LED technology? How to convert radio signals to a scanned image? How a composite video signal works?"

"Well . . ." He shrugged. "I don't need a degree in electronics to push a button on the control unit. But could I build one myself? No."

"That's okay. None of us can. We can still enjoy watching it without the physics and the engineering. But as long as humans are flying alien spacecraft, we'll be completely dependent on them for *everything*."

"You know," Hunter told her, "there are stories about how the Apollo astronauts, during the Moon landings, actually saw alien spacecraft watching them. I wonder if they'd been waiting for us to get there on our own."

"Almost certainly. That was when they began taking us seriously. By actually crossing the gulf of space to land humans on our nearest neighbor, we proved . . ."

"Proved what?"

"That we were worthy, I guess."

"Okay, so NASA does have a reason to exist. That's comforting. But it's criminal the way they keep all of this hidden from the general public."

"The general public wouldn't know what to do with most of this stuff. Forget panic—I'm talking about actually being able to comprehend. Think about how long you've been here, and how much you still question. But remember, the powers that be *are* working toward full disclosure. Slowly."

"Too slowly, if you ask me. I get it—it's a lot to take in. But zero-point energy *alone* could solve all Earth's energy problems, not to mention climate change, pollution, and by extension end poverty, end hunger—"

"Sure. And releasing knowledge of ZPE would bring down the oil industry, crash the stock market, and throw tens of millions out of work. Politicians losing their jobs, mobs rioting in the streets, governments collapsing . . ."

"Shit," Hunter said, dismissive. "It would be worth it, wouldn't it? If we could save the oil for what it *should* be used for . . . plastics? Stop the Earth from turning into Venus? But I'm sure the oil companies have a plan in reserve if any of that happens!"

She laughed. "If Earth becomes another Venus—a possibility—then the oil barons will have other things to worry about than staying in business."

Hunter wondered if anyone within the so-called seven supermajors, the major Big Oil companies, had been let in on the Alien Secret. He tried to picture a conference of Big Oil magnates, all of them sweating bullets at the possibility that the internal combustion engine was about to be declared obsolete.

On the other hand, what if all those Big Oil CEOs were actually controlled by the Saurians, slowly consolidating their grip on Earth through filthy politics and a shaky, fear-lashed economy?

Something about the whole UFO package lent itself to wild conspiracy theories. But Hunter now knew that the conspiracy theories themselves were but the palest shadows of reality—a reality hinting at the true insignificance, the utter *irrelevance* of humankind. The Grays and even the Saurians were far, *far* too much like human caricatures, nothing at all like the real aliens. Humans, it turned out, were mites scurrying about in the shadow of godlike beings of Mind and technologies inconceivably vast and forever beyond the human ken.

Maybe that was the real truth behind the tangled web of

UFO secrets, he thought. Maybe the Brookings Report had been right. The human psyche might well be crippled by the sudden release of the knowledge that aliens surrounded them . . . not the "little green men" of popular culture, the pathetic Grays and the sinister Saurians, but the *truly* alien, nightmare god-beings like the Xaxki, and worse.

Perhaps *much* worse.

Hunter shivered at the dark thought.

"How about you?" McClure asked. "Would you go home if you could? Or stay with the JSST?"

"Beats me. You know, we might have just started a shooting war. *I* might have started a shooting war . . . a war that humans can't possibly win."

"You rescued three hundred human civilians from a literal fate-worse-than-death. You proved that the Saurians aren't our friends. You proved to our friends out here that we can handle ourselves, that we can be a presence in galactic politics. You proved that *we take care of our own*! Solar Warden does need the JSST." She grinned. *"Space Marines."*

"I'm Navy," Hunter said glumly. "Not Marines."

"You transformed a ragtag mob of different special forces personnel into a single, well-integrated and well-disciplined elite force. The JSST *works* . . . and you're the reason for that."

"Arr . . ." Hunter said, utterly without enthusiasm.

Together, they watched the vista—bright-burning worlds embedded in a vast disk of dust, worlds forming out of emptiness. Somehow, Hunter thought, that creation was being handled by the Xaxki, a staggering, awe-inspiring, and utterly terrifying thought.

"Mark?"

"Mm?"

"Do you have anybody waiting for you, back home?"

"I'm not *supposed* to. But . . . yeah. There's someone."

"I hope you can get back together with her." She sounded . . . disappointed.

Her question, however, raised a new worry for Hunter, something even more immediate than . . . *that*.

Nearby, against bright stars, a dark gray rock floated in the Void. It had showed up shortly after *Hillenkoetter* arrived at Zeta 1, a lone sentinel twenty miles across, keeping watch.

A Xaxki Guardian.

"I'll be happier," Hunter said, "after we shake that thing. I wouldn't want them to be *nervous* about us."

As if in reply, an overhead speaker announced, "All hands, all hands, prepare for immediate departure."

And, moments later, the *Hillenkoetter* and her escort cruiser folded local space-time around themselves and departed for Earth.

EPILOGUE

GERRI'S APARTMENT WAS occupied by someone else, an older man who grumbled at Hunter's intrusion. She'd left no forwarding address, and no one seemed to know where she'd gone. Hunter even flashed his Navy ID at a desk sergeant with the San Diego Police Department, told him he was with Navy Intelligence, and asked for police help in tracking her down.

All of the SDPD's computer resources, all of the California State Police records, everything came up empty. There was not even a record of her vehicle registration or driver's license.

What the hell?

It was as if she'd disappeared right off the face of the Earth . . . and Hunter began to wonder if that was *exactly* what had happened to Gerri Galanis. Someone had been following him ever since a TR-3B had silently and gently delivered him to the Groom Lake airbase. Had *They*—the invisible but ever-present and sinister *They*—done something to her?

If they had, there was going to be an accounting.

"I think, sir," Hunter had told Rear Admiral Kelsey, "that the MIBs have abducted my girlfriend. I mean, we got back to Earth just two days after we left, thanks to a bit of time traveling, right? And she's gone without a trace. I want to know what happened."

He knew as he said it how paranoid he sounded. But, damn it, there was no other reasonable explanation! A person doesn't just vanish in two days, right down to her driver's license and her credit history.

To his surprise, Kelsey actually took him seriously . . . but then the older SEAL had to explain things to him. "You did sign papers promising not to seek . . . entanglements with people outside of Solar Warden," Kelsey said.

"First off, we were already 'entangled.' Regardless, that has nothing to do with it. Go ahead and court martial me, sir . . . but in the meantime a young woman has been abducted or scared into hiding and I want her found! Who did it?"

"I don't know, son," Kelsey said. "And I do wish I could help you. But you must realize by now that there's a kind of low-level war going on."

"Between the Nordics and the Saurians. Yes, sir, I know all about that!"

"Not just them. Some of the wilder conspiracy theorists are right. Saurian influence has penetrated quite deeply into the halls of government. And not just in DC either. London. Moscow. Beijing . . ."

"You're saying dinosaurs are running the planet now?" The idea, crazy as it sounded, somehow almost made sense.

"Not entirely—the Saurians can only pull their strings with human help. But there are agencies within the government, especially among the intelligence agencies, that have been deeply compromised. And, as always, it never seems like the right hand knows what the left hand is doing."

Like the Xaxki, Hunter thought. *No one knows what the hell is going on.*

"If it's any consolation, Mark, I doubt very much that this young lady—Gerri is her name?—that Gerri was killed."

"She'd better not have been. Damn it, she doesn't know anything!"

"Most abductees are kept alive, cared for, used for genetic research."

"That doesn't relieve me, sir. I've seen a few of them, Admiral. Those bastards had 315 humans crammed into bottles breathing green goop. Some of them had been kept alive inside those things for *years*, awake and aware! Fifty-nine of them had breakdowns of one sort or another after we rescued them. Eighteen are so deeply comatose we may never get them back. What they went through out at Zeta Retic—that's not *living*, sir. It's more like hell!"

He considered, too, that even those rescued civilians were now at Darkside on the Moon, their legal status the subject of considerable debate. Would they ever be allowed back into the general population?

"Like I said, I wish I could help you," Kelsey said. He frowned for a moment. "There is *one* thing you might do . . ."

"Name it, sir."

"This won't help Gerri directly, but it *will* put you in a better position to track her down. We're now taking part in a planetwide secret operation called Divine Guidance."

"Okay . . ."

"Divine Guidance is a Navy, Marine, and Talis project helping to defuse tensions between nations all around the world, and to reduce the risk of a nuclear calamity. The Talis, remember, are terrified that we're going to annihilate ourselves, which would kind of wreck the time line for them, y'know? Come with me on the next op. You'll get a higher security classification out of it, and you'll meet some people who are in the fight against the shadow government. The Saurians."

"Okay," Hunter said, not hesitating. "I'm in."

Four days later, Hunter filed off a bus inside a hangar at S4, along with seven Grays, two Talis, Kelsey, and a couple of other humans.

He didn't get to see the spacecraft from the outside, as he was hustled up a ramp in the ship's belly. He'd assumed it would be a TR-3R, but the control deck, he saw, was larger, empty of furnishings, and circular. Shortly after boarding, the ship drifted out of the hangar, then accelerated into the crisp, blue desert skies of Southern Nevada.

And moments later, the ship descended out of the clouds over a dark and viciously rugged landscape— sheer mountains and twisting valleys. Hunter stood by one of the flat, oval ports, watching the unforgiving terrain drift by.

It looked . . . familiar. Hauntingly so.

And then he saw why.

Hunkered down on a barren, boulder-strewn slope, was a handful of men, heavily armed, sheltering beneath ghillie suit camouflage, monitoring various high-tech gadgets, including the bulk of an AN/PED-1. The ship was close to them—less than a hundred feet. Even so, they would have been invisible if not for the fact that the saucer's technology was letting him see past the camo ghillie suits, and let him see what was down there.

And with a jolting shock of recognition, Hunter realized exactly what he was seeing.

One of the people down there was staring back up at Hunter with his mouth hanging comically open, binoculars pressed to his eyes. Grinning to himself— literally—Hunter raised a hand, a silent greeting and acknowledgment.

And then the ship had passed, leaving eight heavily camouflaged Navy SEALs behind.

He'd not been aware that they'd slipped back in time while crossing the distance between Nevada and North Korea.

In position, a Gray thought to the others.

"Very well," Kelsey said. "Engage the device."

Hunter couldn't see what was going on, but he heard a deep thrum coming up from somewhere belowdecks. Ahead, Mantapsan loomed above a secret North Korean weapons testing base. Unimaginable energies beamed from the saucer to Earth to a cavern deep beneath the earth where North Korean weapons of titanic destructive power had been tested, gouging out a vast submountain chamber.

Manipulated from the saucer, the cavern collapsed, bringing down much of the mountain with it.

As awed as he was by just seeing himself, he was also livid.

"What the fuck did you send us in there for?" Hunter demanded of Kelsey. "There was no need for our mission! You knew this ship would show up to take care of it!"

"Actually, there *was* a need," Kelsey said quietly. "We needed you and your team to go in and watch us destroy the mountain, then exfiltrate and tell us that we'd been successful. Our Gray allies knew the operation would be a success because you and your team told us it was. That's the only way they would agree to it."

"With respect, sir, that makes no sense at all!"

Kelsey shrugged. "It worked. Not long after this, North Korea did a complete about-face and offered to give up its nukes. Turns out they saw this ship, a few of them, and they were terrified. An exceptional outcome, and a *necessary* one."

"How many of them were killed, sir? How many of those slave laborers were killed inside that mountain?"

"That was regrettable, of course. It was also necessary in order to shut down Kim's nuclear playground. There was no other way." Kelsey hesitated, then looked Hunter in the eyes. "Carrying out military operations across time can be . . . challenging. But it offers advantages you simply can't win any other way."

Hunter wondered if Kelsey might not be giving him an unspoken hint, just a shred of hope, that he would be able to find Gerri after all. With time travel *anything* was possible.

Including, he thought, rescuing her from Saurian-influenced agents of the US government.

"Hillenkoetter is refitting on the Moon," Kelsey told

him. "The review board gave its okay for the *Big-H* time-traveling to Aldebaran to meet up with those three cruisers out there. You still want to come along?"

"I didn't know I had a choice, sir. But . . . yes, I would."

"Outstanding."

One of the Grays gave a command, and the saucer accelerated into space and time. Hunter would return to his command, the battle-tested 1-JSST. Next stop . . . another star. Aldebaran.

But when he returned he would find Gerri.

Somehow, some*when*, he would find Gerri.